A LILLY SINGH "LILLY'S LIBRARY"
BOOK CLUB PICK

LONGLISTED FOR THE 2021
**CENTER FOR FICTION
FIRST NOVEL PRIZE**

"A page-turner with humor, heart, and lots of pop music."
—JENNIFER KEISHIN ARMSTRONG,
NEW YORK TIMES BESTSELLING AUTHOR OF *SEINFELDIA*

"A sweeping saga . . . Cinematic and intimate."
—DEVI S. LASKAR, AUTHOR OF
THE ATLAS OF REDS AND BLUES

"Introspective and entertaining."
—*KIRKUS REVIEWS*

"A story about ambition and greatness, wealth and family, full
of secrets, love, and music, and those eternal pop song complements: heartbreak and hope." —KATE RACCULIA,
AUTHOR OF *TUESDAY MOONEY TALKS TO GHOSTS*

**"A THOUGHT-PROVOKING
FAMILY DRAMA."**—*BOOKLIST*

"Ramisetti takes us on a journey that terrifies, exhilarates, and
plunges us into a place of freedom and truth that can only be
achieved when life meets death." —*BOOKTRIB*

"A RICH PORTRAIT...FULL OF MUSIC [AND] MAGNETISM." —EMMA STRAUB

Praise for
DAVA SHASTRI'S LAST DAY

"A rich portrait of a family facing their powerful matriarch's death, *Dava Shastri's Last Day* is full of music, magnetism, and familial obligation. If *Succession* were about a multicultural family who actually loved each other, it might look like this."

—Emma Straub, author of *All Adults Here*

"Kirthana Ramisetti has written a sweeping saga and also a poignant story about sacrifice and the exacting price of secrecy. Cinematic and intimate, *Dava Shastri's Last Day* is an intricate story about family and love."

—Devi S. Laskar, author of *The Atlas of Reds and Blues*

"*Dava Shastri's Last Day* is a story about ambition and greatness, wealth and family, full of secrets, love, and music, and those eternal pop song complements: heartbreak and hope. It's a gripping, deeply satisfying story about one woman's tremendous life—and the infinitely complicated ways we create our own legacies."

—Kate Racculia, author of *Tuesday Mooney Talks to Ghosts* and *Bellweather Rhapsody*

"Ramisetti beautifully weaves keen analysis of celebrity culture and a deep love of music into this perceptive, intergenerational story of resentment, trauma, love, and redemption. A page-turner with humor, heart, and lots of pop music."

—Jennifer Keishin Armstrong, *New York Times* bestselling author of *Seinfeldia*

DAVA SHASTRI'S LAST DAY

DAVA SHASTRI'S LAST DAY

A novel

KIRTHANA RAMISETTI

GRAND CENTRAL
PUBLISHING

New York Boston

Copyright © 2021 by Kirthana Ramisetti
Reading group guide © 2021 by Kirthana Ramisetti and Hachette Book Group, Inc.
Excerpt from *Advika and the Hollywood Wives* copyright © 2022 by Kirthana Ramisetti

Cover art and design by Sarah Congdon. Cover copyright © 2022 by Hachette Book Group, Inc.

Hachette Book Group supports the right to free expression and the value of copyright. The purpose of copyright is to encourage writers and artists to produce the creative works that enrich our culture.

The scanning, uploading, and distribution of this book without permission is a theft of the author's intellectual property. If you would like permission to use material from the book (other than for review purposes), please contact permissions@hbgusa.com. Thank you for your support of the author's rights.

Grand Central Publishing
Hachette Book Group
1290 Avenue of the Americas, New York, NY 10104
grandcentralpublishing.com
twitter.com/grandcentralpub

Originally published in hardcover and ebook by Grand Central Publishing in November 2021

First trade paperback edition: September 2022

Grand Central Publishing is a division of Hachette Book Group, Inc. The Grand Central Publishing name and logo is a trademark of Hachette Book Group, Inc.

The publisher is not responsible for websites (or their content) that are not owned by the publisher.

The Hachette Speakers Bureau provides a wide range of authors for speaking events. To find out more, go to www.hachettespeakersbureau.com or call (866) 376-6591.

Library of Congress Cataloging-in-Publication Data

Names: Ramisetti, Kirthana, author.
Title: Dava Shastri's last day : a novel / Kirthana Ramisetti.
Description: First edition. | New York : Grand Central Publishing, 2021.
Identifiers: LCCN 2021026605 | ISBN 9781538703861 (hardcover) | ISBN
  9781538703854 (ebook)
Subjects: LCSH: Women philanthropists--Fiction. | Philanthropists--Fiction.
  | Secrecy--Fiction. | LCGFT: Domestic fiction. | Novels.
Classification: LCC PS3618.A4656 D39 2021 | DDC 813/.6--dc23
LC record available at https://lccn.loc.gov/2021026605

ISBNs: 9781538703847 (trade paperback), 9781538703854 (ebook)

Printed in the United States of America

LSC-C

Printing 1, 2022

For my parents,
and their parents

Shastri-Persson Family Tree

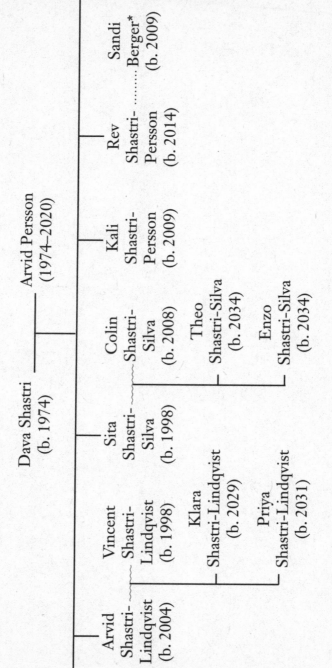

*engaged to Sandi

DAVA SHASTRI'S LAST DAY

CHAPTER ONE

Dava Shastri, Dead at Seventy

**DAVA SHASTRI, RENOWNED PHILANTHROPIST,
DEAD AT 70**

Dec. 26, 2044, 8:24 a.m.

NEW YORK—Dava Shastri, founder of the Dava Shastri
Foundation, has died at age 70.

Shastri's lawyer, Allen J. Ellingsworth, confirmed she died
Friday from an undisclosed illness.

The philanthropist created the influential music platform
Medici Artists before founding the women empowerment–
oriented Dava Shastri Foundation in 2007.

Shastri's husband, Arvid Persson, passed away at age 46
in 2020. She is survived by four children and four grandchildren.

*This story will be updated as more information becomes
available.*

DAVA DID NOT EXPECT to howl with laughter after reading her obituary. But she had been lying awake in bed since dawn, alternating between giddiness and anxiety as she speculated how the story would break. So to see her death announced with a breaking news bulletin—the kind usually reserved for politicians and pop stars—overwhelmed her with delight.

She wanted the view from her master suite to reflect her victory: a smiling sun over the water, or the rare sight of a humpback whale breaking the waves in a magnificent splash. But the outside world remained a white shell, with Beatrix Island blanketed in ice as if enclosed in a snow globe. Even so, her joy could not be contained, and she clapped a hand over her mouth to stifle her laughter. The sudden movement worsened her ever-present headache, and to distract from the pain, she returned to the article and focused on the word "influential." Dava enlarged the obituary until "influential" was the only word left on the screen, and marveled at how smoothly she had been able to turn her plan into reality. "Easy peasy," as her late husband, Arvid, would say.

The harder part would be explaining this to her family. She needed to tell them what was going on but wanted to savor her accomplishment a little longer. Their interweaving voices rose up from the first floor, mostly lamenting the weather. *The whole East Coast is a shitshow. God, I need coffee. Next Christmas we're going to Hawaii.* Dava could pick out her children's voices most clearly, having spent a lifetime listening to Arvie, Sita, Kali, and Rev tease and argue with each other.

Dava didn't mind their noise. The chatter reminded her of a time before she was an empty nester, and provided a welcome contrast to her bedroom's stillness. Designed to be an "oasis of no-tech tranquility," the room was several shades of lavender, from the silk damask wallpaper to the limestone fireplace. The one exception was the king-size bed, one of only two hundred that existed in the entire world, a stupidly expensive cream puff of cashmere, silk, and cotton with real gold and silver threads stitched into the headboard. Dava felt tiny and adrift whenever she slept in it, since the bed rippled across half the room like an infinity pool. She had wanted her bedroom to feel like a refuge, but within its walls she instead felt like a queen whose subjects were planning to overthrow her.

The soft knock on the base of her skull persisted, so Dava put on her noise-canceling headphones. Though she enjoyed the Shastri-Persson clatter, she feared aggravating her headache. Wearing them reminded Dava of a vastly different climate, hot, sticky Arizona, lying on her twin mattress with her head happily stuck between headphones, the rest of the world silenced by music.

In an instant, her family's cacophony dispersed into whiteout silence. Yet as much as she needed to guard against a migraine, the lack of noise instilled in her a low, humming anxiety threatening to explode into a panic attack. She hoped the sight of the obituary would help her calm down. But the tablet had disappeared somewhere in the layers of her plush bedding, so Dava snatched her BlackBerry off the nightstand instead. She pulled the covers over her head until every inch of daylight was obscured, then rolled the device's trackball up and down with her thumb, which for her was akin to putting a damp towel on a feverish forehead. The ancient smartphone, with a crack in the left-hand corner and the letters on the keyboard faded from overuse, dated back to her Medici Artists years. Now, it only served one purpose: as a time machine.

A few months earlier, Dava had paid an exorbitant amount to have the device restored so she could access all of her and Arvid's text messages. She had always thought of her life in cinematic terms, and the BlackBerry period, spanning a near decade at the start of the twenty-first century, was the sunny montage with a feel-good pop song that came right before the inevitable complication in the second act.

As her distress lessened with every thumb roll of the trackball, Dava gave herself permission to read her old text messages. Her brand as a philanthropist was built on progressivism, which she often summed up in interviews as "look forward and live forward." Yet in her personal life, she was embarrassed by her bouts of sentimentality and likened them to hoarding: a shameful habit she strove to keep hidden from the rest of the world, especially her children.

As she had done with increasing frequency in the past month since her terminal diagnosis, Dava closed her eyes and scrolled through her texts, and then looked to see which part of her life she had landed on.

When will you be home? This was a common text to receive from her husband and no doubt the one he sent the most often during their marriage. So Dava scrolled again, as if she were playing her second-favorite childhood game show, *Wheel of Fortune*, hoping to land on a fabulous prize. Her second time out, she landed on the following message: I swear I saw Bono in line at Zabar's. This is totally him, right? She couldn't load the attached photo, but from what she could remember, he had photographed a man with flaming red hair, wraparound shades, and a leather jacket. Dava snorted when she saw her reply: No way. If Bono is a redhead, then I'm Julia Roberts. Arvid was always thinking he had spotted stars in their Upper West Side neighborhood, surreptitiously snapping their photos and sending them to Dava for confirmation. He had stopped his hunt when they started actually meeting celebrities as part of her work, first with Medici Artists and later with her foundation, and Dava had been a little sad her success deprived

Arvid of his hobby and made encountering them a little less magical.

But it had never lost its magic for her. Because she had been able to work her way up from nothing into a rarefied circle, in which she was not gawking at the elite, but one of them. And the fruits of all that effort would mean her life, and her death, would have a genuine impact on the world.

She needed to see the obituary again. Dava stripped the bed of its covers, then took off her headphones so she would have all five senses to help her locate her tablet, which had ended up at the foot of the mattress. She climbed back into bed, switched on the device, and gazed at the word "influential" with fascination until the screen went dim. Is that how my life will end, she wondered, fading brightness and then a sudden cut to black? But she didn't want to think about endings yet, the totality of it all. There were still words to read, words of praise about all she had achieved. The darkness on the other side of living could wait a little longer.

She had almost fallen asleep when she was startled by her bedroom door sharply swinging open. Arvie stood in her doorway.

"What the fuck, Mom? Why is the news saying you're dead?"

CHAPTER TWO

A Strongly Marked Personality

I hold that a strongly marked personality can influence descendants for generations.

—*Beatrix Potter*

TUESDAY, DECEMBER 23
(THREE DAYS EARLIER)

SANDI SAW BEATRIX ISLAND rise out of the mists like some sort of fairyland, the kind discovered by sweet, red-cheeked children in old-timey novels. When her fiancé, Rev, had invited her to spend Christmas with his family, he had joked the Shastri-Persson compound looked like a ski chalet dropped into the middle of the ocean. He wasn't wrong. As their motor yacht moved through the choppy currents, she was able to discern more details piece by piece: it was two stories, made of some kind of timber almost golden in hue, and it featured a grand, sloping roof and a balcony that extended the entire length of the second floor. The island itself seemed to be the size of several football fields, the perimeter dotted with wintry pines wrapped in Christmas lights as if they were candles on a birthday cake. She let out an awestruck laugh, her cheeks flushing when Rev's arms encircled her waist.

"It's pretty amazing, isn't it?" he said into her ear, his stubbled chin on her shoulder. "Sometimes I forget."

"How could you ever?" Sandi breathed, and wondered how her stomach still fluttered with excitement nearly one year into their relationship. "It's...tremendous." Even as she nestled deeper into Rev's embrace and took scandalized pleasure that his tight hug revealed his excitement for her, she could feel Kali's eyes on them.

As if she heard Sandi's thoughts, Rev's sister joined the pair at the ship's bow, her patchouli-ish scent irritating Sandi's nose. After standing beside them silently for a few moments, Kali said, "Home sweet home."

In response, Rev let out a guffaw signaling this was an inside joke between the two youngest Shastri-Persson siblings. Sandi dug herself closer into Rev as she listened to the two of them reminisce about Christmases past, none of which had taken place at their current destination. After several minutes of their banter, she had the distinct feeling she was intruding upon them, even though Kali was the one who had entered into their cozy moment.

"I'll be right back," Sandi murmured as she disentangled herself from his grasp. Neither seemed to notice she had slipped away, only moving closer to each other and speaking in a conspiratorial tone that likely meant the two were gossiping about their older brother and sister. Sandi walked to the back of the cabin and sat down at the table in a huff, watching them together. Rev beamed at his older sister and teasingly pulled at her waist-length braid, intricately colored to resemble a peacock feather. In the presence of Kali, he was even more ferociously handsome than usual, a sun that became hotter and brighter, which she scarcely thought possible. She counted to 403 before allowing herself to rejoin them.

"They were going to war over a brownie!" Rev said, doubling over in laughter.

"I know!" Kali giggled. "But it was one of Anita's chocolate-mint brownies, so I kind of get it." Sandi was relieved she at least knew Anita had been their childhood nanny.

"Did Amma resolve it by having them write an essay about who deserved it more?"

"No, that was when Arvie and Sita both wanted her extra ticket to a Beyoncé concert. I can't remember what happened with the brownie, but it was our last Christmas with Dad, so . . ."

The siblings dissolved into silence as the yacht continued to slice through the gray waters of Gardiners Bay, speeding to the island like a magnet unable to resist the pull of metal. After the cramped, bumpy train ride from New York City to East Hampton ("I wish she would have let us take the helicopter!" Kali had groaned), Sandi was pleasantly surprised by the smoothness of the boat journey. She had been worried about seasickness prior to boarding, even after the yacht's captain, a stout man with friendly eyebrows, reassured her "not a single passenger has ever tossed his cookies on my boat, and none ever will." Sandi wished the captain's garrulousness would draw Kali into conversation so she and Rev could have more time together, but even he was quiet now, the only noise coming from the motor powering the gleaming white ship eastward through the bay.

Out of the corner of her eye, Sandi noticed Kali open her mouth as if she was about to speak.

"So are we the first ones to arrive, or the last?" Sandi cut in brightly, hoping to bring Kali and Rev back into the present with her.

"We are the last," Kali said, turning to face the island, which was now close enough that a Christmas tree could be seen sparkling in a massive window on the first floor.

"The gang's all here," Rev said with a snort, and the two were off laughing again, down their rabbit hole of private amusement. Sandi could not wait to get off the boat.

⌒

After she had accepted Rev's invitation to spend Christmas at Beatrix Island, hugging him so swiftly she nearly nicked him with the knife she had been using to butter her toast, he forwarded her a message that had been sent by his mother to her four children.

"Amma's very particular, especially when it comes to family time on the island," he told her. "Just so you know what to expect."

In the three weeks leading up to the holiday, Sandi reread it so often she nearly had it memorized, in particular, Dava's admonition about technology:

> As this is the first time in several years we'll all be together for Christmas, I don't want anyone to be distracted and off in separate corners. So you should know if you don't leave your devices and gadgets at home, you must check them into a lockbox upon your arrival. You will, of course, have access to communication with the outside world, but at my discretion.
>
> This is family time. If you fear getting bored, bring some books, playing cards, and whatever else you need to amuse you that doesn't require an outlet, solar power, or a charging station. I trust you can also find enjoyment in each other's company.

As they disembarked from the yacht and walked along the dock to the house, Sandi began to sweat underneath her heavy coat. She had been so cowed she had left her devices at home and instead packed two books—a memoir by a former First Lady turned human rights crusader, and a novel by a prize-winning female Indian author—purchased specifically for the trip. But as Sandi gazed up at the stately timber-framed mansion, she wished she could have brought a camera of some kind. How else would she prove she had been there?

They entered the house through a side entrance, which opened into a mudroom, where a long row of mahogany lockboxes indeed waited for them, as well as an enormous closet where they were meant to leave their coats and boots. Rev and Kali exchanged an eye roll as they deposited several devices into the wooden squares that had their names written on them. To her delight, Sandi saw she had her own lockbox under her fiancé's. But she had nothing to place inside, and her face turned red from embarrassment.

"Wow, you listened!" Kali said as she unzipped her parka, revealing an emerald-green tunic with gold embellishments along the V-neck collar. Sandi sensed an undercurrent of mockery in her tone but was relieved when Kali added, "Amma will be impressed."

After the trio shed their outer garments, boots, and what Rev had jokingly called their "hi-tech doodads," Sandi followed them through the kitchen to the foyer and had to stifle a gasp. Before her was a massive, ornately carved staircase, a waterfall of deep oak hardwood that flowed stiffly from the second floor. She had never seen such a stairway before, which took up nearly the entire length of the foyer, the architectural version of a statement necklace drawing all attention to itself, and rightly so.

"Amma?" Kali called out.

At the top of the stairs stood a petite woman with sleek black hair that just touched her shoulders, save for the white streak framing her face. Dressed in a cashmere turtleneck and impeccably tailored trousers, Rev's mother was even more elegant and intimidating in person than what Sandi had seen of her in photos. She reminded Sandi of a Disney villainess, the kind of character who makes the heroine seem dull in comparison. Sandi could not quite look at Dava as she made her way downstairs. Instead, she tilted her face toward the foyer's magnificently arched ceiling, where a chandelier resembling silver fireworks watched her from up high.

"You're here," Dava said warmly, her gaze focused solely on her children. "Welcome." Then, noticing Kali's top, she added, "Someone's raided my closet again."

"Yes, but isn't it festive?" Kali did a small twirl before engulfing her mother in a hug.

"My kurta looks lovely on you." At first, Dava seemed to endure her daughter's embrace, her expression strained before relaxing into a tentative smile. When she then turned toward Rev, she softened even more. "Hi, R—"

He picked her up off the floor, and Sandi laughed to see Rev give his mother the same "hug and lift" treatment he gave her when they had not seen each other in a few days. Only by seeing Dava and Kali in relation to her fiancé did she realize how tiny all the Shastri-Persson women were. He was only six feet tall but, compared to his mother and sister, seemed like a near giant.

"Oh, Rev, stop," Dava gasped as she was returned to the floor. She put her hand to her forehead and closed her eyes for a brief second, then laughed and swatted her son's arm. As the three reunited, Sandi snuck a quick glimpse of herself in a nearby mirror and was dismayed to see her brown ponytail mussed from the wind, and her pink sweater covered in lint.

"Amma, this is Sandi," Rev said with a grin. After a beat, he added, "My fiancée."

"Mrs. Shastri. Mrs. Shastri-Persson. So nice to meet you," Sandi stuttered, nearly slipping in her socked feet as she went to shake Dava's hand.

"Welcome, Sandi. How are you? You must be exhausted from all that travel." She clasped Sandi's icy hand in her warm ones and pressed it briefly before letting go. "And you can call me Dava."

Before Sandi could respond—to say, *Thank you for having me; I was so touched when Rev said you wanted me to join you for the holidays*—Dava began to engage in a brisk back-and-forth with her children, asking them if they had eaten breakfast ("Yes, Amma") and if they had checked their devices into the lockboxes already ("Of course, Amma"), before informing them which rooms they would be staying in (Kali swore under her breath when told she had the "cozy room," while Rev did a quick fist pump upon hearing he had one of the downstairs guest rooms).

The rat-a-tat nature of their conversation was interrupted by others emerging into the foyer, a blur of color and voices that bounced across the high ceilings.

"I thought you were getting here ahead of us," Rev said in the direction of the group, their morass of luggage squeaking noisily on the hardwood.

"We were supposed to, but then Sita—"

"Let's not start, Arvie. I'm exhausted. Hi, Amma," said Sita, giving her mother a wary hug. Dava's oldest daughter seemed to be a near-perfect replica of her mother, except an inch taller. "We didn't have anyone waiting at the dock to help us with our things."

"No household help this time." Dava gave her a wan smile.

"Ha, so we're roughing it," said Rev, putting an arm around Sandi. "Guys, this is—"

"Wait, what about Mario? I thought you gave him my list of dietary restrictions for the twins," Sita said, while her boys yelled out, "Hi, Gamma!" as they ran past, her husband, Colin, waving hello as he chased after them.

"No chef either," Dava replied. "But I brought some meals Mario whipped up for us. He promised to incorporate your requests."

Sita let out a loud sigh and muttered, "Fine."

"Surely we can cook for ourselves? I'm pretty sure one of you married a chef."

"Vincent's on vacation, Mom. He doesn't want to cook for us," Arvie, Dava's eldest, groaned on his husband's behalf.

"Yes he does," Vincent said, bending down to kiss his mother-in-law's cheek. Both men were pale and balding, and the only way Sandi could distinguish between them was Arvie wore glasses and Vincent had the height and beard of a Viking.

"Vincent, do you know anything about preparing gluten-free, protein-enriched meals?"

"Sita, give him a moment," Arvie said. "We just got here five seconds ago."

Sandi saw Rev and Kali lock eyes and repress laughter while their mother shook her head with a bemused smile.

"Where did your girls go?" Dava said, trying to look past Arvie and Vincent as if peering between two giant redwoods.

"They have a lot of things to check into their lockboxes," Vincent said with a laugh. "They're having a hard time letting go."

"Boys, come back here, we need to take our bags upstairs," Sita called out as she walked into the interior of the house.

"Why do you assume you have the upstairs guest room?" Kali asked.

"We always do, Kal," her sister said, brushing past her.

"We always do, Kal," Arvie mimicked under his breath as both he and Vincent followed Sita into the house, with Dava following after them.

"Here we go," Rev and Kali said in unison, and the younger Shastri-Perssons laughed as they headed out of the foyer with the rest of their family. Sandi watched them leave, waiting for someone to remember she existed. Just when she was about to give in to self-pity, wondering how she could have believed she would be welcomed with open arms, Rev poked his head out from behind the stairway and called out, "Coming?"

⁓

Sandi would only have two real conversations with Dava during the length of their stay. The first one occurred as Dava showed her around the house with Rev tagging along. Sandi had hoped to quickly bond with her future mother-in-law, but Dava had the officiousness of a museum docent, pleasant yet distant.

She walked them around the first floor, with the downstairs guest rooms next to the great room on one side of the staircase, and the kitchen, dining room, and cozy room on the other side. As they toured the home, Dava explained that the inspiration for the house was a nineteenth-century chalet she had once stayed at in Switzerland.

"Amma loved it so much she brought it here," Rev said once they returned to the foyer, as if he was explaining something slightly embarrassing.

"Not brought—duplicated. The exact same layout, in fact, with a few modifications. You'll see a photograph of the original hanging in your room." She raised an eyebrow at her son, and he ducked his head meekly, though he could not hide his grin. "And so when I decided to build a family home, my own Kykuit, if you will, I knew that chalet is where I wanted us to have memories together, spend holidays, celebrate birthdays."

"Couldn't we have had a Kykuit in Hawaii instead?" Rev teased. "I swear we'd all come more often."

"It's an amazing home," Sandi gushed, leaning forward so she could see past her fiancé and make eye contact with his mother. "I am just so honored to be here with you all." Then her hands began to tremor as if she were standing on a fault line. As she furtively hid them in the back pocket of her jeans, she berated herself for succumbing to a "blush attack," a phrase coined by her smug college boyfriend to describe how she became red-faced and jittery when meeting one of her favorite authors.

But Sandi had never met someone as famous as Dava Shastri before. Before Rev, she knew of her future mother-in-law as the woman who appeared on cable news shows speaking about feminism or charity initiatives, occasionally going viral when she steamrollered the windbag pundits who attempted to interrupt her. After meeting Rev, Sandi learned that Dava was so much more than those appearances, and felt ashamed that she had been ignorant of how much she had accomplished—starting a business that disrupted the music industry, then selling it for tens of millions—by the time she was Sandi's age.

She needed to ask Dava something, anything. Sandi was about to inquire what a Kykuit was but decided against it, thinking she only wanted to ask something that would earn Dava's respect. She bit her lip and then rushed forward with a question she hoped would present her as a thoughtful, literary person.

"Where does the name Beatrix Island come from? Did you name it—"

"I loved the Beatrix Potter books. My mother read *Peter Rabbit* to me when I was a child." Dava sighed, as if this was a question she had answered many times before. "Very sentimental of me, I know."

Sandi kept beaming, even as she inwardly deflated. She had a feeling that the estate had been named after the beloved children's author. If only she had been given an opportunity to say so. She decided to take one last chance at impressing Dava.

"And Rev told me this island was built with the same technology as—"

Dava stopped and pressed two fingers to her right temple, and all at once her energy seemed to flag. "You know, why don't you take a moment to unpack? You've had a long trip. And I should go check on how the others are doing." Without waiting for their response, she went upstairs.

"See you later," Sandi called up to her. "Take care. Lovely to meet you." And those were the last words she would say to Dava until after Christmas.

⁓

Sandi had two goals in mind for her stay at Beatrix Island: develop a relationship with Dava and enjoy the perks of vacationing at the private residence of one of the world's wealthiest women. Neither seemed close to coming true.

Prior to moving in with Rev, she had lived in seven different apartments in Queens, none bigger than a one-bedroom, including the basement unit she and her mother had lived in for most of her childhood. So she was initially awed by Beatrix Island, especially the dramatic ocean views greeting her from every window. But the thrill soon wore off because Sandi couldn't help viewing the house through the eyes of her profession as a real estate agent.

Dava's "modifications" seemed arbitrary and downright odd. A subterranean-level den had been added to the property but not extra bedrooms, which meant Arvie's and Sita's kids had to sleep in their parents' rooms. And while Dava's house shared the same layout and architecture as the original, she had tripled its square footage. So despite featuring all the hallmarks of a Swiss chalet—vaulted timber ceilings, stone walls, wood beams—her manor was vast yet hollow, akin to a museum costumed as a vacation home. A home that didn't see a lot of visitors, or even a housekeeper, judging by the faint seaweed odor and furnishings coated with dust.

The main reason Sandi had been excited to visit Beatrix Island was because it had been built by the same eco-architecture company that famously saved Grenacia—an island nation in the South Pacific consumed by rising sea levels—by constructing new archipelagos for its displaced citizens. Like the new Grenacia, Beatrix was a floating estate built to withstand storm surges and extreme flooding. Every item and fixture inside, and tree and stone outside, had been chosen by Dava, the entire estate custom-made to her exact specifications. Sandi had arrived expecting a wonderland of technological marvels only billionaires could afford. The lack of them was a real letdown, and something Dava's eldest could not help pointing out. Over and over again.

"This place could power a small African nation, but it's not equipped to play a movie that came out in the past five years," said Arvie as his daughters, Priya and Klara, grumbled in front of a television that took up nearly the entire length and width of the wall of the great room, the two sighing dramatically as they scrolled through brightly colored squares that flashed and then evaporated from the screen.

"Omigod, I forgot you have to open the door to check whether it's cooked through. You'd find better appliances at a backwoods diner," Arvie groaned to Vincent as his husband stuck a fork in the pot roast he was preparing for dinner.

"I must have asked the shower to turn on five times before I remembered where I was," he laughed, looking to his siblings to nod in recognition about the difficulties of having to press a button to activate the shower.

All of these complaints took place on the Shastri-Perssons' first day on the island, the latter occurring as the adults had dinner in the dining room. It featured tree branches gathered in twine serving as the lighting fixture, and an oval dining table designed to look like the cross section of a tree trunk, with its rings echoing outward in gold-flecked concentric circles. The room was trying its best to pretend it was located in a wintry cabin in the mountains rather than the edge of the Atlantic.

She had only been half listening to Arvie's anecdote, which he told as if it were part of a sweaty stand-up routine, heightening the comic absurdity in a bid for laughs. Instead, Sandi's attention was on Dava. She watched her as if sneaking glimpses of an Oscar-winning actress on the subway, someone so familiar yet alien at the same time. In anticipation of their meeting, Sandi had read as many profiles and watched as many interviews as she could, so she would be ready with her own anecdotes to impress her. And yet the words were just sitting there, dull and useless on her tongue, while Arvie went on and on about the dumb shower.

"It's intrusive," Dava said, and the sound of her voice seemed to freeze time. Cutlery clanged to plates, even sneezes seemed to stop midexhalation. "I never understood voice-activation technology. To me, it was the beginning of the end. People just gave up, and it was okay to be lazy, and okay to have your privacy devalued and stolen. It disturbs me. I see it enough out there. I don't want it here." She gave her eldest a pointed look. "And you know that, *Arvind*."

Arvie shrugged, his face hardening into embarrassment as Dava excused herself to use the powder room. After she left, he shredded his pot roast into dozens of pink-brown slivers with a meticulous zeal.

"She can spend, like, fifty million to build an island, but I'm an asshole for mentioning how old-fashioned it is here." Arvie paused dissecting his roast and glared at Rev. "I know I'm not alone. I've heard you complain about the lack of a screening room. And sauna. And a pool."

Rev seemed stricken. "I said that during our first visit," he replied, his eyes on the mess of meat his brother was creating. "I don't care anymore. If it makes Amma happy, that's all that matters."

Sandi looked from older brother to younger brother and couldn't help but wonder how they were siblings. Her Rev was a Michelangelo statue come to life. Arvie was the famous painting of the man in an unyielding scream. Perhaps Arvie could be attractive if he did not always seem on the precipice of rage, but he could not come close to her fiancé's unearthly beauty, the kind that often led strangers to mistake him for a movie star.

"So did you see on the news—" Vincent began.

"The earth is rotting," Arvie interrupted, tossing pieces of pot roast into his mouth as if they were peanuts. "Humans have been terrible tenants, and our landlord is getting ready to evict us." His lips twitched into an odd smile, as if he was proud of his metaphor. "And what does Mom do? Build herself a floating bunker. Who cares if the world is burning or drowning or whatever as long as she and her rich friends have a way to take cover?"

"I can't get a handle on what you're mad about." Rev kept his tone even, though Sandi could see him clenching his fists in his lap. "Is it that this house isn't fancy enough for you, or that Amma has the means to build this place?"

"Why can't it be both?" he snickered. "If she was going to waste money on a floating mansion, do it right, or it's just a waste of cash."

Sita and Colin traded exasperated glances, their plates of organic greens and wild rice mostly untouched. Sandi liked how close they were sitting, their chairs practically glued together. She scooted her seat a few inches to the left until she felt her leg brush up against Rev's.

"Beatrix Island isn't for her. It's for us," Sita said calmly, crossing her arms. "Not just us, but our children, our children's children. How is that a bad thing?"

"Dontcha think it's ironic Mom is obsessed with her name

being passed on to the next generation without considering the planet might not survive past them?"

Sita's cheeks turned bright pink. "Don't *you* think it's ironic that Amma is paying an allowance to a grown man who only works at her nonprofit, like, three days a month?" Her brother's lips twisted into a sneer, and she gave him a smug smile. "Oh, sorry—I meant 'salary,'" she added, making quotation marks with her fingers.

"Can we not?" Kali waved her arms in the air as if trying to land a plane.

Arvie rapped his knife against his plate several times, making a tinny noise that hurt Sandi's ears. "I know you think you're doing holy work at Mom's foundation, but billionaires are not some benevolent gods sharing their wealth with the pathetic downtrodden. They take advantage of loopholes and tax havens—"

"Not this again!" Rev groaned.

The room erupted into a tangle of conversations: Arvie spoke loudest, raining statistics to make his case as the other three rebutted with examples of their mother's various good works, while Colin and Vincent murmured to each other as they stayed out of the fray. Sandi, having studied Dava's charitable endeavors as if they were her college major, largely agreed with Rev and his sisters. Yet watching them debate philanthropy's role in society as if reciting lines in a well-rehearsed play unsettled her. They weren't being hypocritical, exactly, not in the way that Arvie could decry billionaire philanthropists as unethical while accepting his mother' money. But their sentiments rang hollow. What did they actually know about making a living on minimum wage, or choosing between buying groceries and paying the electric bill?

The Shastri-Persson children acted as if their wealth didn't exist, even as their every sentence and gesture shone with it.

Their clothes were so expensive they didn't have labels, as Rev had once confessed to her that their wardrobes were designed for them personally, even items as simple as T-shirts and jeans. All of their foreheads were smooth, never dinged with the creases of those who worried about student debt or living paycheck to paycheck, as if they walked around the world in Bubble Wrap, fully able to see class and income disparities but completely untouched by them.

Kali's anxious voice startled Sandi out of her thoughts.

"Stop it. Right now." Kali stood up from the table and cocked her head. "She's coming back." On the word "back," Dava re-entered the room and sat down, her hand resting briefly on her forehead, as if she were shielding her eyes from the bright sun. After a few moments of uneasy quiet, Kali broke the silence by pointing out how heavily the snow was falling and, with a chuckle of forced merriment, noted how it meant they would definitely have a white Christmas.

"I didn't realize Winter Storm Imogen would be hitting us so soon," Dava remarked, mostly to herself, as she gazed outside, where snowdrifts were piling up in huge clusters, partially obscuring the dining room's windows. "I thought it wasn't coming until tomorrow."

"Will we be okay out here?" Sandi whispered to Rev. She was thinking of a seismic squall that had devastated several coastal communities in Long Island two Christmases ago.

"Amma, are we prepared for it?" Sita asked loudly, nodding her head at Sandi to acknowledge she had heard her concerns.

That question prompted Dava to give a mini-lecture only Sandi seemed to find fascinating. Using terms such as "triple-glazed panels," "drilled-down concrete," and "rainwater-harvesting tanks," Dava explained how she had worked closely with engineers and architects to ensure the island and the house itself were specifically mettle tested for the North Atlantic's extreme weather conditions. She also noted that with three backup generators, she wasn't concerned about a power outage. "The worst that could happen is we might be snowed in until New Year's, if you kids can handle it," Dava added with a quiet chuckle.

"Oh, really? Isn't Imogen only a Category One?" Kali said between mouthfuls of pizza. She had opted to eat the remaining slices of Mario's vegan pizza the kids had wolfed down earlier that evening.

"What?" Dava squeaked. Her kids looked at her with surprise. "I thought we were getting over six feet of snow."

"We are," said Colin, wiping a smudge of salad dressing from his silver beard. "I bet you're thinking of the storm hitting the Midwest, Kal."

"Oh, that's right," Kali said. She fixed her mother with a quizzical look. "What does it matter, Amma?"

"No reason," Dava replied, letting out a deep breath. "No reason." She quickly changed the subject and asked Colin about his parents' renovation of their home in San Paolo. But her bearing was unsteady, as if she had just spun around in circles and was now trying to regain her equilibrium. Her hand fluttered constantly to her forehead as she conversed with her son-in-law, until she forcefully yanked it down to her lap. Sita and Kali looked at each other, then their mother, and then back at each other, so many words seeming to be communicated without actually speaking. Watching them made Sandi wish she had a sister, rather than an ex-stepbrother who only seemed to appear in her life to ask her for a loan.

Sita's son Theo ran into the room and squeezed into the space between his parents' chairs. "I'm boooored," he said. "Can we go play on your— I mean watch TV?"

"Uh, okay. Just do so in our room." Sita shifted nervously in her seat, and he gave a whoop as he ran out of the room. "Enzo, told you she'd say yes!" the adults heard him call out, followed by two sets of footsteps pounding up the stairs.

"There's no TV in your room," Dava said abruptly, pointing her fork at Sita. "How will they watch?"

Sita opened her mouth, then closed it, then opened it again. With her mother's penetrating gaze still on her, she brushed her bangs out of her eyes and screwed up her mouth in a pout.

"Amma, I brought just one thing, okay? Linh and I are working on a big project for the GlobalWorks initiative, and I need to be able to touch base with her twenty-four-seven."

Dava narrowed her eyes, and her daughter shrank down in her seat. Colin placed a supportive hand on his wife's shoulder. If Sandi had any regrets about leaving her devices at home, she was thankful she had followed the rules. She reached under the table for Rev's hand, and feeling his large palm warm against hers made her sigh with relief.

"I told you I'd have a laptop available to you if you needed to work," Dava said.

"But if there's a work emergency at two a.m., I can't knock on your door to get it from you, can I?"

"Oh boy," Kali whispered under her breath.

"You know the rules, Sita. I made myself very clear." Dava tapped her red fingernails impatiently on the table.

"It's ridiculous, Mom," Arvie said. "And you know I'd rather eat dirt than agree with Sita on something, but c'mon."

"I don't ask a lot of you, do I?" his mother said, her voice low, the rumble of anger unmistakable. She turned back to Sita. "Please go put it in the lockbox. Now."

"What's a Kykuit?" Sandi asked Rev later that night in bed, the darkness only pierced by a single candle glinting on the windowsill.

"Just some rich house owned by some rich family," Rev murmured against her neck.

"Do you mean like a vacation home, or a family compound? And which family?"

"The Rockefellers," he said, yawning. "What does it matter?"

"I'm just curious—that's all." She took his arm and wrapped it around her waist like a seat belt. "Do you think your mother likes me?"

"Of course she does."

"Really?"

"You're very easy to like." Rev kissed her bare shoulder.

"But how do you know?" She tried her best to sound even-keeled, hoping she didn't seem too needy. "You know, I think if I sat down with her—"

"She actually does ask a lot of us."

Sandi turned around to face him. "What, sweetie?"

"It's funny she says she doesn't. Because she does. All the time. It's weird how she can't see that." She waited for Rev to elaborate, but he did not. And in the days to follow, Sandi would remember her fiancé's words, the exasperation and resentment he let slip out when he said them, and understand what he meant.

CHAPTER THREE

Philanthropist and Rumored Inspiration

DAVA SHASTRI, PHILANTHROPIST AND RUMORED INSPIRATION FOR OSCAR-WINNING SONG, DIES AT 70

By Rachel Tsai, *The New York Times*
Dec. 26, 2044, 9:25 a.m.

Dava Shastri, founder and president of the Dava Shastri Foundation, an organization dedicated to supporting artists and women's empowerment, died Friday at her estate on Beatrix Island in East Hampton, Long Island. She was 70.

Her death was confirmed by her lawyer, Allen J. Ellingsworth.

Ms. Shastri was a self-described "committed New Yorker" whose spirited personality served as a bridge between two different worlds she traversed with ease: the independent music scene and the high-bred world of New York philanthropy.

According to *Forbes,* her net worth was $3.8 billion, ranking her in the top 20 of the publication's list of the world's richest self-made women.

Ms. Shastri was 26 when she created Medici Artists in 2000, a company that challenged the traditional record business by connecting musicians with patrons who funded their work. She sold Medici Artists to Sony for $45 million in 2006, a controversial move that divided the music industry.

Soon after acquiring the company, Sony shut down Medici and voided the patronage deals, which was viewed as a move to protect the industry from nontraditional avenues for artists to disseminate their music. The sale was viewed as a betrayal of the artists Ms. Shastri's organization had once championed.

Ms. Shastri rebutted those complaints during a Q&A at the Davos Women's Business Forum in 2011. "I poured my life and sweat into building Medici Artists so it could be a force of good in the world. I had hoped Sony would continue my vision, not dismantle it. But I can't look back with any regrets."

Not long after selling Medici Artists, she established the Dava Shastri Foundation to align with the ethos of her first company, in the form of grants awarded annually to musicians, which were termed "Medici grants" in a nod to her first company. Currently, five $10,000 grants are allotted to applicants from all walks of life; seven $25,000 grants are earmarked for people from diverse and disadvantaged backgrounds.

Ms. Shastri's business savvy also led her to become an early investor in MobileSong, an MP3 player that was perceived as a quirky upstart and chief rival to Apple's iPod. When Apple purchased MobileSong for $3 billion in 2009, she netted $540 million, and her net worth increased twelvefold overnight.

A turning point in her philanthropic career occurred ten months later, when she donated $5 million to Independent Woman, a nonprofit founded by Vash Myers that assisted low-income women and victims of domestic violence in finding jobs and housing. A lawsuit filed by Ms. Myers's ex-husband had left the organization on the brink of bankruptcy.

"I just didn't want it to close," Ms. Shastri explained in an interview with the *Times* in 2010 about why she had made the donation, which she described as "impulsive." "Someone had sent me an article about IW's plight, and it seemed barbaric such an amazing organization could be brought down by a man's arrogance. Then I remembered I could actually do something about it. And that feeling was so satisfying."

Taking this action led Ms. Shastri to expand the foundation's mission to focus on international giving to organizations supporting women's empowerment, and she brought on Ms. Myers as vice president of development. By the time Ms. Myers was promoted to chief operating officer nearly two decades later, her previous position had been taken over by Ms. Shastri's daughter Sita, 38.

"I always thought charity should be a family business," Ms. Shastri said in a speech after being named Philanthropist of the Year by New York Cares in 2032. "My ultimate goal is that the name Shastri become synonymous with giving and generosity."

Dava Anoushka Shastri was born on March 8, 1974, in Calliston, Ariz., to Rajesh Shastri, a mechanical engineer, and Aditi Shastri, a homemaker.

She attended New York University, and after her graduation in 1996, she spent two years volunteering for the Peace Corps in Ruiz, Argentina, where she met her husband, Arvid Persson.

They married in a civil ceremony at Manhattan City Hall in 2002.

As Ms. Shastri pursued entrepreneurship and philanthropy, Mr. Persson established a career in private school education, first as an English teacher and later as a vice principal. He passed away from stomach cancer in 2020 at age 46.

Two years after his death, Ms. Shastri created the nonprofit Helping Perssons in honor of her husband. Their son Arvind, 40, oversees the organization, which awards one $2,000 grant per week to an eclectic array of applicants.

In addition to Arvind and Sita, Ms. Shastri is survived by daughter Kali, 35, a visual artist, and son Revanta, 30, a former model (both of whom also serve on the Helping Perssons board), as well as four grandchildren.

Ms. Shastri expressed a desire that her surname would always be linked to charitable giving, but it is her first name that lingers in the popular consciousness. Tom Buck's Oscar-winning song, "Dava," sparked rumors he and Ms. Shastri, who met at a 2012 MusiCares benefit, had been romantically involved. Both she and Mr. Buck, who died in 2035, had always denied the rumors.

"If I knew the song would be so popular, I would have named it 'Mary' or 'Lisa' instead," laughed Mr. Buck in a 2019 interview with *Rolling Stone*, the same year he won the Oscar for best original song. "It was a throwaway love song I gave to my pal (*The Skylight* director) Jinna Azure when she asked me for something to use in her movie. The tune needed a name, and I thought hers was pretty unique."

Despite their denials, "Dava" retains a hint of scandal. Several internet sleuths have posted detailed theories arguing that the song, which spent 6 weeks at No. 2 on the Billboard charts, was indeed about Ms. Shastri.

When asked about her namesake song, Ms. Shastri was always known to turn the conversation back to her namesake foundation instead.

"The song—as beautiful as it is—has nothing to do with me," she said in an interview with *Feminist First* last year. "But my foundation, the people I've helped, I hope that will be my legacy."

Correction: Dec. 26, 2044

Because of an editing error, an earlier version of this obituary misstated where Ms. Shastri and Mr. Buck had first met. It was at a MusiCares benefit, not a Grammy Awards party.

"WHY DO THEY THINK you're dead?"

Despite all her careful planning, Dava never anticipated her family learning of her news without telling them herself. So Arvie's arrival left her dumbstruck, and she had not yet answered his question when Sita appeared in the doorway, her soapy hair soaking the shoulders of her pink robe.

"Amma, are you okay? Colin said—"

"She's still breathing." Arvie paced back and forth with the cold, manic energy of a tornado. "She won't tell me what's going on. Maybe she'll tell you." He cocked his head. "Unless you're in on this too. Is this some weird publicity stunt?"

"What? No!"

The words "publicity stunt" returned Dava to her body. "Kids, I'm fine. Go downstairs. I'll be right there."

"She's okay, right?" Kali raced in with a mug dangling from her fingers and a coffee stain blooming on her shirt. "I knew it. Someone's playing a prank."

Rev followed, wearing nothing but boxer briefs, his chest heavy with sweat. "Oh, thank God."

His siblings did a double take. Then all four began speaking at once, and to escape their cacophony, Dava looked past them toward a portrait hanging over the fireplace. She felt unstuck in time as her gaze traveled from the painting of her children—toothy smiles, kid-size suits and velvet dresses—to the adults grousing at the foot of her bed.

"What happened to your clothes, dude?" Kali said.

"Sandi and I... and then I heard Arvie yelling..." He trailed off when Kali burst out laughing. "Seriously, Kal? You're laughing at me?"

"Not at you." She gently touched his arm. "The situation. They're saying Amma's dead, you're here in your underwear, and Sita still has shampoo in her hair. It's all so bizarre, you know?"

"No." He jerked away from her. "I don't."

Kali stumbled back a step. "Oh my God, relax."

"Can you two stop?" Sita said, nodding toward Dava. "You're upsetting her."

"Always her watchdog," Arvie snorted. "Always on the clock."

Dava ground her palm against her throbbing forehead and longed to put on her noise-canceling headphones. Instead, she looked to the painting again, a gift from Arvid on her forty-first birthday. The older three encircled their baby brother with an almost defiant pride, their little hands on each other's shoulders. "Our gang of four," her husband had referred to them fondly.

"When are you ever on the clock?" Sita turned to face Arvie as if she were challenging him to a duel.

"We can't all be work robots like you."

"Better than being a loser and a mooch. Helping Perssons deserves better."

"Enough," Dava said in her boardroom voice, the one she used to indicate her decision was final. "Go to the great room. I'll be there shortly."

◠

The estate's great room more than lived up to its name. The size of a basketball court, its vastness was only heightened by the vaulted ceiling, exposed beams, and two floor-to-ceiling windows. One faced east to capture uninterrupted ocean views, and the other looked west toward the dock and boathouse and, farther afield, the bay and the mainland several miles away. Both views were also meant to show off the swath of woods populating the ten-acre island, made up of Swiss stone pines and firs bioengineered to thrive in the synthetic soil. But at the moment, none of the greenery could be seen from the great room, with the island weighed down by several feet of snow.

On one end, three velvet sofas encircled an enormous stone fireplace, and on the other, an L-shaped gray sectional, slightly faded from being directly in the sun's path, faced the television. A vintage pool table was situated in between them as an attempt at dividing the space into two cozy nooks. But the room was so comically oversize the Shastri-Persson clan had taken to calling it the gigantic room.

All twelve of them were gathered there now for the first time since Christmas morning. As she sat in the rocking chair in front of the fireplace, Dava felt her family's eyes on her as they waited for her to speak. But she was staring across the room at the enormous flat-screen. She had no idea the ancient device included a "live TV" connection, which Arvie discovered earlier that morning, desperate for an update on Winter Storm Imogen. And even though she was irritated at not being able to control how her family learned of her "death," Dava still longed to know how it was being reported by the twenty-four-hour TV news networks. But of course she couldn't ask them. At least not yet.

Pockets of hushed conversation erupted in the wake of her continued silence. Rev spoke softly into Sandi's ear, his hand resting on her knee. Arvie whispered to Vincent in Swedish, while Colin and Sita murmured comfortingly to their boys, their heads bowed like scolded puppies. Theo and Enzo looked small for their age, although in truth Dava couldn't remember if they were nine or ten. In contrast, Arvie's girls seemed too grown-up. They shone with lip gloss and surly attitudes, reminding Dava of herself during her own teen years.

Only Kali remained quiet, her arms and legs tightly crossed as she sat by herself on the sofa closest to the window. Her younger daughter no doubt still smarted over not getting permission to invite her partners to this family holiday, especially since Rev was allowed to bring Sandi. She hoped to make peace with Kali on this issue eventually, after she finished the speech she had rehearsed at least once a day since her visit to Dr. Barrett's office.

Then Dava was hit by a dizzy spell. She cradled her head in her hands.

"What's wrong?" Sita said, jumping up.

"Give me one moment." Dava slowly raised her head. "Okay, I'm fine."

"Colin, can you get her some water?"

"I said I'm fine, Sita."

"Well, the news says otherwise," Arvie muttered.

"I know I have a lot of explaining to do." Now that the moment she had scrupulously planned for had arrived, her emotions choked her words. Dava steeled herself with the idea that always brought her back to focus during times of crisis: she had to think of the bigger picture.

"So," she began, disliking how tremulous her voice sounded. "I have cancer. It's terminal."

Dava paused to let everyone adjust to the terrible information she had just dropped on them, echoes of a conversation she had with her children concerning their father decades earlier.

"I've been having headaches over the past few months. And dizzy spells, vertigo, some issues with blurriness. I just thought it had to do with getting older, or working too hard. But then just before Thanksgiving, I realized something was seriously wrong." Dava avoided Sita's horrified expression as she tightened her grip on the rocking chair, the diamonds on her wedding band digging into her skin. As her only child who saw her with any regularity, Sita had been urging her for almost a year to slow down at work. And Sita had been telling her this despite having no idea about her mother's episodes.

Nobody in Dava's life knew. She kept these incidents hidden from everyone, also choosing not to mention them during her annual physical in September. At first, she could stave off the headaches with aspirin. But then the dizzy spells started, and the headaches became more unrelenting and impervious to pain medication. Dava knew something was amiss but kept making excuses to herself, petrified about what a doctor's visit would reveal to her. Whenever she considered calling her physician, she remembered Arvid's doctor saying "cancer." Specifically, she could vividly recall the doctor's mouth, his mustache glistening with sweat and a piece of lettuce stuck between his yellowed teeth. Dava would get nauseous each time the memory arrived like a malevolent ghost, haunting her until the dizzy spell faded or migraine retreated.

And then on the day before Thanksgiving, a headache over-whelmed Dava so intensely that she stumbled to her knees after crossing the threshold of her Upper East Side apartment building. After shooing away the doorman's fumbling assistance, she ordered him to summon her driver so he could take her to a medical clinic twenty blocks north.

Dava paid a seven-figure sum annually so she could have immediate and private access to the best doctors in the city. As she explained her symptoms to her primary care physician, she told herself that having enough money to afford gold-plated medical care would somehow equal a clean bill of health. Yet after her initial consultation with her doctor, she was subject to a whirlwind of tests that resulted in her worst fears. Her spate of worsening migraines and dizzy spells was linked to adenocarcinoma in her left lung: stage 4 lung cancer. And the cancer had spread far and deep, resulting in two metastatic brain tumors, a lesion on her liver, and another on her adrenal gland.

"But I've only been having headaches for a few months," Dava pleaded with her oncologist, Dr. Barrett, upon receiving the news. "And I've never smoked in my life," she added as she stared at the scan of her brain, which showed a silver dollar–size lesion on her occipital lobe and a smaller one near her brain stem. After her doctor gently explained that even nonsmokers could develop lung cancer, Dava asked if it would have made a difference if she had sought treatment as soon as she started experiencing headaches.

"The X-ray shows that your primary tumor is already quite advanced," Dr. Barrett said sadly, shaking her head.

Dava's heart dropped to her feet. "Of course it has to be an overachiever," she murmured.

"You needn't be hard on yourself, Dava. Lung cancer is often diagnosed in later stages because it can go undetected for years. One-third of patients with adenocarcinoma present symptoms as a result of distant metastasis—in your case, the brain. Usually patients don't even realize they have the primary kind of cancer until they present with symptoms where it metastasized to." The doctor paused, then put on a reassuring smile. "But we have made promising advances in treating your condition, with the potential to achieve remission."

"Remission doesn't always last," Dava spat out more sharply than she intended, remembering her husband's painfully brief remission period before his cancer returned. She tapped her fingers against her chest. "Just be straight with me. Can this be cured?"

As Dr. Barrett detailed the treatment options, Dava understood her ending was clear: the cancer was terminal. The treatments could extend her life from a few months to possibly another year. But the medical regimens would eventually lead to a diminished quality of life even as they extended it, making her susceptible to memory loss, seizures, and diminished vision with the possibility of blindness.

"So the answer to my question is no," Dava said, sighing deeply. "Okay. If I pursue any of these treatments, how long will I be able to continue on in my day-to-day?" She brought her fist down hard on her thigh. "How long can I remain active at the foundation?"

Dr. Barrett opened her palms skyward, as if waiting for a blessing. "It's hard for me to say," she responded carefully, her forehead creasing in sympathy. "But your day-to-day will not be the same as it is now. It will be a new normal."

"I see." Dava's fist unfurled like a dying flower. "I'm not interested in a new normal," she said quietly, reaching for her purse to call her driver.

～

"Due to how advanced my cancer is, I've opted against treatment," she told her family after sharing the dire extent of her prognosis. "According to my doctor, this means I only have several weeks left to live," Dava continued, as she pushed aside the memory of Dr. Barrett's green eyes widening as she urged her to reconsider her decision. "So you can—" And then she stopped talking, because Rev began weeping, and the twins responded by erupting into tears too.

"Oh dear," she stammered. "Maybe the grandchildren should step out for a moment."

The room was quiet except for the crying, which had now been caught on by Sita and Kali. The teens looked stunned, but their faces also gleamed with curiosity. Sandi's mouth hung open in a thick, pink O. Arvie seemed to be shaking as Vincent swallowed him up in a bear hug. Dava found the silence to be excruciating, to know she was the cause of their shock and pain. That was until Klara spoke up.

"I want to stay," she said, chewing her gum thoughtfully. "Because there's more you're going to tell us, right? Like why the news says you already died?"

"Klara!" Vincent scolded. By this time, Arvie had disentangled himself from his husband's embrace and sat stiffly beside him, his expression inscrutable.

"Well, it's true."

"Can someone get Rev a tissue?" Dava said to no one in particular.

"I'm okay, Amma," Rev mumbled, his sobs subsiding. Sandi tentatively patted his leg, and when Dava glanced in her direction, she shrank down in her seat.

"If everyone needs a moment before I continue—"

"No. Just finish it," Arvie barked, looking her squarely in the eye.

"Okay," she said, returning his gaze until he looked away. "The day I learned about my terminal diagnosis...well, I had a thought." Dava twisted her wedding ring on her finger as she spoke. "Your father's cancer was devastating, but we had six years together to prepare ourselves for the...worst eventuality. And I decided to look at my condition as a gift, in which I could say goodbye to the world—and all of you—on my own terms."

Behind her, the roaring fire started to oppress her with its warmth. She tried to ignore the heat, and the stirrings of a new migraine, and press on.

⌐

"As you now know, I only have a limited amount of time left," she said, resisting the impulse to press her hand against the back of her head. "And since all of us would be gathered here for Christmas this year, I arranged to have"—Dava caught sight of Theo's wobbly chin and was again walloped by regret to be saying this so plainly in front of her grandchildren— "to have a doctor help me take my life." She sat up higher in her chair, waving her hand in front of her face in a futile effort to cool down. "Again, I want to go out on my terms."

Dava never meant to announce it this way, so clumsy and rushed, and she couldn't bear to look at their faces as they absorbed her news. So she stared instead at the Christmas tree, its twinkling lights and cheery ornaments seeming cruel as a backdrop to her family's pain. Just twenty-four hours earlier, they had been gathered around the tree drinking champagne and exchanging lavish gifts. As she had experienced her final Christmas with them, Dava also recalled her last one as a regular person. It had been a simple affair with Arvid and baby Arvie: a plastic tree the size of a desk lamp, three stockings hung over the television, and several toys for their little boy to unwrap. But later that night, Dava had burst into tears, lamenting to Arvid that they had given their son an "ordinary, almost Dickensian" Christmas, which had made her husband laugh, until he realized she wasn't joking.

When she became a millionaire by selling Medici Artists nearly a year later, she vowed to herself that there would be no more ordinary Christmases for the Shastri-Perssons. Four decades later, as she glimpsed their stricken faces, Dava understood she had fulfilled that vow all too well.

Despite their distress, she pushed forward and explained how she had arranged for one of the doctors in New York State licensed to perform assisted suicide to come to the island. The doctor and her wife had been secretly ensconced in the guesthouse for the past four days—"So that's why Mom wouldn't let us stay there," Arvie murmured to Vincent—ready to administer the medication on Dava's word.

"And the news report?" Sita asked.

"Ah, well, yes," Dava answered, her nerves fluttering. "I told my lawyer my appointment with the doctor was scheduled for this morning. And so he dutifully made the announcement before I could let him know I wanted to wait another day—"

"This is such a major breach of ethics!" Arvie thundered. "No doctor or lawyer in good conscience would announce you're dead before you're actually dead!"

"Well, what does it matter? I will be soon enough," Dava said, wincing at the loudness of her son's voice. "And I get to see what the world thinks of me before I go. Isn't that kind of . . . nice?"

"You planned it," Kali said. Dava saw her younger daughter staring at her with fascination.

"Kali, dear," she started.

"That's why we weren't allowed to bring our devices," Kali continued. "I think you wanted to be able to control the situation. No one can contact us, and we can't contact them. And now with this storm, we're basically cut off from the world, so no one will know you're still alive."

Dava watched everyone absorb these words, the sting of their eyes on her, trying to comprehend all they had learned so far.

"Holy shit, Gamma," Klara said, sounding impressed.

CHAPTER FOUR

Our Condolences to the Shastri-Persson Family

Our condolences to the Shastri-Persson family on the loss of their beautiful, inspiring mother, @DavaShastri. Our thoughts & prayers are with them during this difficult time.

> —*The Dava Shastri Foundation social media account, December 26, 2044, 10:00 a.m.*

DAVA RUBBED HER TEMPLES in frustration. She wondered if she should try to persuade them this was truly a last-minute decision, rather than one in a series of calculations she made in the aftermath of her visit to Dr. Barrett.

The first thing she did when she came home from the clinic was to trade her stiff skirt and blazer for Arvid's black Beatles T-shirt and sweatpants with a hole in the crotch, which was one of the last things he wore before he passed away. Arvid had owned the shirt since he was a teenager, and the sweatpants had been an artifact from their Peace Corps days. The clothes were thick with him, not of his cologne, but the purity of his scent and his sweat, as if his essence had been sewn into their very fabric. She only turned to these clothes in her darkest moments, her own "in case of emergency" fail-safe. To wear them was almost like having him by her side, and Arvid's scent helped her calm down. And think.

When Dr. Barrett had described her life following a cancer diagnosis as a "new normal," Dava immediately understood what that meant: constantly in and out of hospitals, enduring a gauntlet of debilitating procedures that would necessitate stepping down from the foundation, leading a purposeless life as her children argued over "what to do about Amma." Dava at least had been able to be by her husband's side throughout his final years, but she couldn't ask them to do the same for her. And she didn't want to watch her children shrink from her life more than they already had, as the burden of taking care of her—or watching her wither away—became too great.

The last thing Dava Shastri wanted to be was helpless; that would be her waking nightmare. She could accept death more easily than a slow decline, and in some ways, she could even convince herself to see it as a blessing. Dava remembered the abrupt, heart-ripped-from-her-chest pain of losing both of her parents to heart attacks. With her husband's death, as drawn out and gut-wrenching as it had been, the two of them at least had time to plan his final days, as well as make preparations for their family's life without him. And now, to know the end was coming, she could do the same for herself.

In the early hours of Thanksgiving Day, nursing a cup of coffee in her kitchen as she looked out at the dark expanse of the East River, she officially decided she did not want to seek treatment and would instead pursue an end-of-life plan. In doing so, she felt better, because she could stop wallowing in self-pity and channel her energy into strategy, which gave her the same kind of endorphins as a runner's high. She had originally planned to spend Thanksgiving weekend at a spa wellness retreat, largely because all of her children had made their own plans for the holiday knowing they would be together for Christmas. So Dava's schedule was already cleared of all commitments until the following Monday, and she planned to take advantage of the rare, and now welcome, solitude.

She spent the day on her living room sofa wrapped in blankets, nibbling on cheese and crackers with the television on mute, researching end-of-life options, and then analyzing her calendar. Should it take place after the next board meeting or the upcoming Helping Perssons benefit? Dava took perverse pleasure in trying to schedule her death as if it were just another important appointment. Which, in a way, it was.

Even with her computer in 3D mode, the screen's contents projected in front of her, by evening her sight began to blur. Dava let herself take a break, closing her eyes and unmuting the television for company. A year-in-review program was airing, and she was just about to nod off when an "in memoriam" segment began to play. Dava sleepily watched the faces of actors, pop stars, tech geniuses, and politicians parade by. She recognized most of their names and had been acquainted with quite a few. She had even attended two of their funerals. Then Dava sat up with a start, the blanket falling off her shoulders. *My face will be included next year.*

She tried to envision how coverage of her death would play out in the media. Unlike others who had inherited their fortunes, married into money, or received it in a divorce, Dava was a self-made billionaire—and a woman. A brown woman at that. So of course she would be eulogized in "in memoriam" segments and business publications and philanthropic circles, and that was fine. It was, well, expected.

But unlike the fusty gray hairs whose net worth also topped ten figures, Dava was one of the quiet stitches that made up the fabric of American culture. The infernal Tom Buck song was a part of it, yes, but she was so much more than that too. She was name-checked in books and documentaries as a key figure in the early-aughts music scene. Praised in interviews by former Medici Artists and grant winners, some of whom flowered into critically acclaimed musicians. Sought after for keynote speeches and news programs to discuss feminism and philanthropy. Befriended by artists and filmmakers, actors and writers—in fact, if there was a photo taken of a party thrown by a New York City celebrity in the first two decades of the twenty-first century, odds were high she could be glimpsed, *Where's Waldo* style, in the glittering crowd. Dava had even ranked twelfth on a list of the most popular names in crossword puzzles alongside perennials like Etta and Ali. (Having a unique, four-letter name helped, but still.)

She was a different breed of philanthropist. She had lived a life of service, yes, but she had also lived a *life*. The kind that earned words like "visionary" and "icon" from those who knew her and those who wished they had. But did that mean she would be lauded? And by whom?

Dava's curiosity quickly mutated into hunger, gripping her thoughts so painfully she was driven to crack open a bottle of red, taking deep swigs that burned her throat. But the wine's numbing effect would only be temporary. Because she knew her desire to know how the world perceived her would only grow stronger as her health worsened.

Then she had a series of thoughts in quick succession, one idea leading to another and then to another like an electrical current: For the first time in years, she had wrangled the entire family into spending Christmas together on Beatrix Island. And just as fortuitously, her research had shown New York was one of the few states to legalize assisted suicide for patients with terminal illnesses. Not since the launch of her foundation nearly forty years ago had Dava faced such an immense challenge. She only had a month to figure out the logistics, but she knew she could pull it off.

But when Dava came up with her plan, she had not factored

in that her family would so easily surmise that the timing of the announcement of her death was not accidental. And now, as she sat with her family, her embarrassment deepened when her stomach grumbled loud enough to be heard over the wind gusts outside. But no one else seemed to notice, and Dava again saw the words "bigger picture" flash in her mind. *Take charge of this*, she told herself. *You're in control.*

"Yes, I did plan it," she said, invoking her boardroom voice. "I wanted to know what was said about me, and what people really thought of me. I don't think that idea is so strange." Dava looked at the adults in the room, most of whom seemed bewildered and slightly nauseous, like they had just stepped off a roller coaster after riding it several times. "One day, when you're my age or older, maybe you'll understand why I chose to do this."

Dava paused for a few beats for dramatic effect. She wanted her next words to settle on her family carefully, and she wanted to help them empathize with her actions.

"I am choosing not to fade away as a shadow of myself, but as someone still in command of her faculties. I don't—"

"What about our choices?" Arvie asked. Dava ignored his question and pressed on. For the first time that day, the blizzard-like conditions had eased up, and there were thin streams of sunlight cascading through the windows, casting slim shadows throughout the room. Late morning was easing into afternoon. Time was passing. Since her diagnosis, Dava had become all too aware of how easily hours and minutes slipped away.

"In the meantime, there are several things we have to do, and do quickly. And so, yes, I did restrict you from bringing your devices for this reason. I know I'm asking a lot putting all of you—and my four precious grandchildren—in a position where you have to be untruthful about what is transpiring here."

"Five," Rev said.

"Five what?" Sita said woozily, as if shaken from a deep sleep.

Rev and Sandi exchanged glances, and then she gave him a small nod. "We're pregnant," he said, smiling shyly. "I know this isn't the best timing to announce this, and we wanted to wait until Sandi was safely out of her first trimester, but . . . there you go."

A loud but hollow round of congratulations echoed around the room, with Kali running over to hug Rev and Sandi, followed by his older siblings and brothers-in-law. Dava watched them impassively, then beamed a strained smile in her youngest son and his fiancée's direction. So this was the reason for the rushed engagement after only a few months of dating. And then a wave of sadness enveloped her. She would never meet Rev's child, her new Shastri grandchild.

"Sorry to interrupt, Amma," Rev said, once the congratulations were over. "I just wanted you to have all the facts."

"My love to both of you," she said, this time mustering genuine warmth in her voice. She reached out her arms and they both gave her quick, awkward hugs. "I'm so glad you told me. Your good news actually leads me to explain some arrangements I've made." She took another deep breath. "I think I need a drink. Does anyone else need a drink?" She had meant this humorously, but when she saw Colin walking toward the wet bar, she waved him back. "We don't have a lot of time. Let me speak quickly."

Dava explained she had changed her will in one significant way. Initially when she had drafted her will, she hadn't allotted any financial inheritance for her children or grandchildren, due to the fact she felt her children were already taken care of, in the form of $10 million trusts she and Arvid had created for them. The trusts were designed so a third of the amount was accessible on their thirtieth birthdays, but the rest would permanently stay in the trust, with the children receiving monthly checks derived from the interest. (So far, everyone but Sita had withdrawn the $3.3 million sum within forty-eight hours of turning thirty.) Besides the income from the trust, the Shastri-Perssons had the opportunity to earn additional monies from "family bonuses," an idea Dava came up with after her husband's death: she gave $100,000 to those who kept Shastri as part of his or her surname after getting married, and $500,000 to anyone who bore her a grandchild, as long as he or she was also bestowed with the Shastri surname. Dava had also created trusts for her grandchildren, which had the exact same terms as the ones created for her kids.

In her revised will, she had instructed her lawyer to award everyone in the family what she told them was a very significant sum. "And I mean each of you," Dava emphasized, "not just my children." She noted that while the funds would be available immediately to the adults upon her death, the money would be added to the grandchildren's existing trusts.

"This isn't appropriate," Arvie said. "You're buying our silence—my kids' silence."

"I'm simply compensating each of you for putting you out in this way. But in return, you're absolutely forbidden to talk about the circumstances of my death."

"My God!" Arvie was shouting now. "Your corrupt lawyer is going to yank our inheritance away if we breathe a word about this farce?"

"You're forbidden," Dava said, glowering at him, "because to do so would diminish the family and the foundation." She turned to look at each of her children. "I'm trusting you all to do the right thing. Because if this comes out, it would wreck the legacy I've worked so hard to build for all of us, and you and your own families would have to live with the consequences." She took another deep breath, as she was feeling fatigued and intensely hungry.

"Look," she rushed on, "the outside world is waiting for a statement, and I honestly lucked into this storm, which gives credible cover for the lack of immediate response."

"And the need to start funeral arrangements," Kali pointed out. "I mean, if you were actually, you know, we would have to start thinking about transporting your..." She trailed off as she comprehended her mother's previous fixation on the weather. "Anyway, that too."

"Right, that too." Dava had originally only planned to stay alive for about twenty-four hours after her death was announced. But once she became aware of Winter Storm Imogen, she was excited because it meant she could live another day longer, which gave her a chance to read even more of the news coverage. "Okay, kids, here's what I've decided: Sita, I'm granting only you phone and email access."

"You mean I can access my lockbox?" Sita asked, for the first time sounding like her usual self.

Her mother shook her head. "I have a special device prepared for you so you can monitor all foundation-related business and act as the family spokesperson." When she saw her daughter opening her mouth to respond, Dava added, "You don't have to lie or talk about my illness. Just issue a statement; it can be as vague as you like. Put out any immediate fires, and the rest can wait until after this weekend is over."

Sita nodded, and she sat up straighter, as if she was already making a mental to-do list. Dava stifled a smile. Sita was such a diligent worker bee, no matter the circumstances.

"Everyone else, I'm sorry, but I would like to keep this as contained as possible, so I'm going to keep access away from you for now." As everyone started to grumble and ask questions, Dava shushed them. "Please, let's just get through this. I have assignments for each of you."

CHAPTER FIVE

Force of Nature

Our mother was a force of nature, and our family is still in the midst of grappling with the idea of her loss. We will have more to say in the days to come, because we fully intend to celebrate our mother's tremendous life and legacy. Please respect our privacy at this difficult time.

—*Sita Shastri-Silva's statement to the media on behalf of the Shastri-Persson family*

ARVIE AND KALI WATCHED Vincent inspect the cabinets, methodically examining each sauce, spice, and nonperishable before jotting down notes in a notepad. After leaving the great room, the siblings had made a beeline to the liquor cabinet to fix themselves vodka sodas, and then they sat side by side on the black marble island as Vincent took account of how much food they had and how long it would last them in case the snowstorm continued past the weekend.

"You married a good one," Kali whispered to her brother.

"I sure did." Arvie beamed despite the sick feeling in his stomach. He was proud of his husband's good-natured industriousness, which had been forged from years of managing his family's restaurant. "Vincent, take a breath. You haven't stopped moving since we got here."

"But we need to be able to feed twelve people for who knows how long, and we've already used up most of the groceries.

At least we have a few prepared meals left," Vincent said with a shrug.

"I can't believe she thought we could subsist on Mario's frozen pizzas," Arvie scoffed. "She knew a snowstorm was coming and she still didn't think to have a stocked kitchen. Too focused on her headlines."

"Must everything out of your mouth be so angry?" Kali said, wrinkling her nose. "We're dealing with a lot, and your negativity isn't helping."

"My kids are caught up in this craziness, so I can be as pissed off as I want."

"Or is it fourteen people?" Vincent asked, ignoring their squabble. "I can't remember if we're going to feed the doctor and her wife too. What did your mother say? Do you remember?"

"She didn't say anything," Arvie grumbled. "Because even when she's dying, she can't stop treating us like heirs to her throne."

"Don't exaggerate," said Kali.

"I'm serious. She acts like the Shastri name is a sacred birthright that gives her the right to dictate our lives, just because she got lucky and made a lot of money." He jumped off the counter. "I'm going to break out the Glenlivet this time. The XXV. Any takers?"

Both Kali and Vincent raised their hands. Arvie poured out Scotch into three tumblers over two cubes of ice, then added a dollop more into his own glass before handing them out.

Ever since their first night on the island, when his mother had scolded him at dinner for daring to criticize her outdated vacation home, Arvie began allowing himself more "dollops" of drink than usual. What angered him was not just that she had scolded him in front of everyone, but that she had invoked his birth name: Arvind. The name was supposed to be a synthesis of his parents—a tribute to his father, Arvid, while also a reflection of his mother's Indian heritage—but everyone, including his late father, referred to him as Arvie. Only Dava ever called him Arvind. And when she called him Arvind at dinner that night, she said it as if placing it in quotation marks. As if he wasn't worthy of it.

As Arvie took a sip of the Glenlivet, he watched his sister sniff hers and then put it aside. His first instinct was to hope she wouldn't waste excellent Scotch. But when he saw her wipe away tears, her cheeks dotted with mascara stains, he softened.

"How are you holding up, Sis?" Arvie asked, rejoining her on the counter, his gray-socked feet inadvertently knocking into her rainbow-print ones.

Kali's eyes widened. "You're asking me about . . . me?"

"That can't really be so hard to believe." Arvie tried not to feel offended by her surprised reaction and gave her a reassuring smile. She looked away from him, tracing the faded coffee stain on her shirt.

"Well . . . I feel so alone."

Vincent turned away from the fridge, where he had been inspecting the produce, to envelop her in a hug. Arvie, for his part, patted her awkwardly on the back.

"It's like being hugged by a lumberjack," Kali laughed as Vincent returned to the fridge. "He even smells like pine trees." She turned to her brother and raised her tumbler. They clinked glasses, and then after they both took nips, she continued.

"What we just experienced in there with Amma was so big," she said. "I thought I would never be more devastated than when we learned Dad's cancer had come back." Vincent walked over again and pulled out a handkerchief from his breast pocket. She thanked him and dabbed at her eyes. "And now, here we are again, but it's fast-tracked. We're not going to lose her in a few months; we're going to lose her in a day or two.

To know it's coming—and she planned it—is weird. And that doesn't even include the surrealness of her pretending to the world she's dead."

Arvie snorted. "As usual, all she cares about—"

"I agree she didn't think this through," Kali said. "And she's put us in a weird position." He nodded and tipped an ice cube into his mouth, as if sucking on it would temper his anger. Kali lifted her legs up onto the counter and hugged them to her chest. "But this was the most unreal moment of my life. And as Amma's telling us everything, I see you with V and the girls, and Sita with her family, and Rev has—ugh—Sandi..." Her voice faltered, and she hugged her legs tighter. "Can you believe they're having a baby? How come he didn't tell me before now?" She drummed her fingers over her lips, as if she had said too much. "Anyway, I didn't have anyone in my corner."

Arvie was sure Vincent would have given Kali a second hug if he hadn't been out of earshot in the walk-in pantry. So Arvie put his arm around her narrow shoulders, something he had not done since they were kids. He wasn't used to being tactile with his siblings or having them pour out their feelings to him. But Sandi disrupting Rev and Kali's twin-like bond was nearly as unthinkable as his mother's recent shenanigans. He could not help taking a sour delight in their estrangement.

"Now that we know Amma's plans," Kali continued bitterly, "I guess that's why she wouldn't let me bring Mattius and Lucy."

"You're still, um, with them?"

"Yes, Arvie," she said, shifting her weight so his arm fell from her shoulders. "We've been together longer than Rev and Sandi. Over a year. They're *my* family."

Arvie inwardly rolled his eyes. Kali's dating history was like her artwork: colorful and baffling. He had never met her artsy couple, with whom she lived part-time in a log cabin in

Poughkeepsie with their toddler, Jicama, and hoped he never would.

"They should have been here," Kali said, banging her glass on the marble counter. "Amma just launched an emotional torpedo at us and I had to take that hit all by myself. She didn't even consider I might need their support." She was crying again, this time wiping tears away with a balled fist. Arvie sympathized with his sister, but he could not imagine being stuck on Beatrix Island with Mattius and Lucy, and he was thankful his mother had made at least one good decision regarding this train wreck of a weekend.

"Welcome to the Rage Club," Arvie cracked. "We've been in need of a treasurer." Kali gave him a sad smile, and they clinked glasses again before downing the remaining Scotch. By the time Vincent returned from the pantry, the two Shastri-Perssons were lost in their own thoughts but connected by a dark mood that hovered over them like a storm cloud.

⌒

Sandi jumped up off the sofa when the bookshelf swung open and Rev entered the den brushing dust from his jacket. Dava had asked him to check on Dr. and Mrs. Windsor in the guesthouse. They had arrived a day before the Shastri-Persson clan and were tucked away in the cottage on the north end of the island. The guesthouse and main home were connected by an underground, insulated tunnel, with an entrance hidden behind one of the den's bookshelves.

"I can't believe Amma has been going back and forth to see them without telling us," he said, shivering, as he gave her a hug. "It's not a long walk, but it's pretty cold down there."

Rev collapsed on the couch, and Sandi curled up in a tight

ball next to him. "You okay?" He laced his fingers through hers. "Do you need something to eat? Or—"

"I'm fine," she said with a tremulous smile. "Just glad you're back. I didn't know how long you'd be gone."

"Where's Kal?" Rev took off his shoes, and then took Sandi's legs onto his lap and massaged her feet.

"Still in the kitchen with Arvie and Victor."

"Vincent," he corrected. "You could have hung out with them instead of waiting by yourself."

Sandi shook her head, willing back her tears. "You're back, and we finally get time to ourselves. Because…wow, I don't know about you, but I'm still in shock."

Rev nodded his head and pressed his fingers into her left arch. After several moments passed, she moved her feet off his lap and rested her head there instead. He reached for her hand, and they both sat quietly for a moment, stirring in their own thoughts.

Located on the basement level, the den was the only room that seemed to belong in a regular person's house and marked the biggest deviation from the Swiss chalet the mansion was modeled upon. The room contained furnishings from the old Shastri-Persson brownstone where Dava and Arvid had first raised their kids, including a royal-blue sofa flattened from years of use and a walnut coffee table with a big crack in the middle. Three of the four walls were lined with bookshelves filled with paperbacks and vinyl records, with the fourth occupied by an upright piano.

Rev told her he often visited the den when he came to Beatrix Island. His parents had sold the brownstone and upgraded to a three-story penthouse by the time he had been born, and the furniture had been languishing in a storage unit until Dava had unloaded it here. Spending time in the den was like time traveling to an era he had heard so much about—the brief period when his mother had become wealthy overnight after selling Medici Artists, but not yet a billionaire—a time when his parents slow danced in the kitchen and folded laundry together while watching television.

"How old were you?" Sandi asked, pointing at a silver-framed photograph on the piano. "You seem so much younger than your brother and sisters. You have chubby cheeks, and they're like teenagers."

"I think I was six."

"You were so adorable!" Sandi gushed. "I mean, you were definitely destined to be a model."

"If you say so," Rev said, laughing, even though he seemed pleased by her words.

The two had met nine months earlier, when Sandi was Rev's real estate agent. She had helped him close on a one-bedroom condo in the most desirable high-rise in Brooklyn, purchased a week after his thirtieth birthday with the funds available from his trust. When they went out for drinks after closing, Rev charmingly confided that when he listed "model" as his occupation on his application, he was referring to a post-collegiate stint. "I was doing print and runway for B-list Italian designers—and now my life's work is erasing the evidence from the internet," he had said. Sandi, four credits shy of a bachelor's degree, a quarter of a way through paying off her student loans, and the recipient of fifty rejection letters from literary journals, tried not to fall for Rev after realizing he was an unemployed trust funder who was also five years her junior. But then he invited her over for one more drink, and four months later his condo became hers as well. And now they were engaged, and she was expecting. The Sandi of nine months ago could scarcely have imagined how wonderfully her life could change in so little time.

"How old were all of you then?"

"Arvie was sixteen, Sita fourteen, I think, and Kali...eleven or twelve."

"I knew they were older than you, but not that much older."

"It feels like a bigger age gap when you're six," Rev said. He added wistfully, "My dad died a few months after it was taken." He paused. "Now that I think about it, we probably took that photo because Amma and Dad knew it might be our last one."

"Oh, babe." Sandi reached up and gently placed her hand against his cold cheek. He smiled down at her, but his eyes were melancholy.

"I'm okay, honestly," he said. "After all my crying earlier, I'm actually feeling numb. But like a warm, fuzzy numb. The Windsors gave me an Irish coffee, heavy on the Irish."

Rev explained the reason he had taken so long was that he quizzed the doctor extensively about his mother's condition, as well as how the assisted suicide process worked. He also learned that she was taking medications to manage her symptoms, which is why she still seemed mostly herself, except more tired and withdrawn. As for his mother's end-of-life plan, Rev didn't go into details—"Basically the doctor said Amma will feel like she's drifting off to sleep"—but he left the cottage feeling his mother was in capable hands. And Dr. Windsor seemed to have an inkling his mother had already declared herself dead.

"Wow. Did she come out and say so?"

"No, but she just seems so unfazed by all this." Rev firmly pressed his hand against the sofa's velvet upholstery, then released it to see the ghost of his handprint on the cushion, which she remembered him mentioning his older siblings used to do when they were kids. "I wonder what Amma is giving her in exchange for her...services. A hospital wing? Or an entire hospital?" As Rev continued to speculate on what his mother had promised the doctor, Sandi fixed her gaze on a large family portrait that hung above the piano on the wall opposite them.

The portrait was taken on a sloping rock on the eastern edge of the island, offering an unfettered view of the ocean. The entire family was wearing white button-down shirts and were arranged so the four men stood at the top of a rock, followed by the three Shastri women with Dava in the middle, and then the four children making up the final row. The children caught Sandi's eye first, since the twins were making goofy faces, while Klara and Priya posed as if getting their photos taken on the red carpet.

Seeing Sita and Kali standing next to their mother, Sandi was surprised by how similar they looked to each other in the portrait compared to real life, with their finely arched eyebrows and shoulder-length wavy hair. Dava was shorter than her daughters, but Sita had her mother's curvy, hourglass shape, while Kali was slimmer and taller than both of them. Since the photo was taken, all three had changed their hairstyles: Sita's was long and straight; Kali's was even longer and always worn in a braid; while Dava wore her hair slightly shorter and sleeker.

Above them, Vincent and Arvie looked nearly like twins because of their balding heads and light-brown goatees, with Vincent's height the quickest way to tell the two apart. Rev was the most handsome by far, with his square jawline and finely etched cheekbones, although Colin, diminutive compared to the other men, was also cute in a vaguely exotic way.

"What are you thinking about?" he asked tenderly.

Sandi broke out of her reverie, and her face turned bright pink. "What is Colin's . . . heritage?"

"He's half-Brazilian, half-Japanese."

"And Vict— Vincent is Swedish, like your dad."

"That's right. Why?"

Sandi slowly sat up and inched closer to him on the sofa, tucking her legs beneath her, avoiding his gaze as she swept her long, brown hair into a ponytail.

"It's okay—you can ask me," Rev murmured, taking her hand again.

She nodded toward the portrait. "That photo was taken recently?"

"Yeah, Amma had it done the last time we were all here. I think two years ago."

"I was just wondering... I'm looking at Sita's kids, and Arvie's kids... They look the same. I mean, like, skin color." She blushed even harder. "Like, I can't tell the twins are of Japanese descent at all. And the girls don't look very Indian, especially Klara. I think they look more like me." Sandi gave Rev a worried look. "I sound so white, don't I?"

He chuckled. "I get what you're driving at. Yeah, they all look pretty wheatish."

"Wheatish?"

"In matrimonial ads, when Indian people want to describe their skin color but don't want to admit they're dark, they call themselves 'wheatish.' It's like the skin color that's the happy medium between fair and brown. We're in the middle." They both sat up hungrily as the aroma of garlic and fried onions wafted down from the kitchen. "Vincent is working his magic— thank goodness."

Sandi's stomach rumbled, and she rubbed her belly. "Me and baby are so appreciative. No more pizza, hopefully." When she saw her fiancé looking at her expectantly, she finally gave in and let her potentially un-PC thoughts trickle out.

"I was just trying to figure out what our baby would look like—that's all," Sandi said carefully. "I've been trying to imagine our baby based on your nieces and nephews, but that's only making me more confused."

Rev let out a big laugh and unzipped his parka and tossed it on the floor. He drew Sandi close, and she nuzzled into his chest, comforted by the soft flannel against her cheek. He then gave her the full lowdown on what he called his "rainbow family, heavy on the beige." He explained that Klara, his brother's fifteen-year-old, was Vincent's child with an egg donor, and Priya, the thirteen-year-old with the same egg donor, was Arvie's. So Klara was full-on Scandinavian, while her younger sister was one-quarter Indian. The boys, Theo and Enzo, were a quarter Indian, a quarter Swedish, a quarter Japanese, and a quarter Brazilian.

"They're so many different things they don't look like anything in particular," Rev said, then added with a chuckle, "Sita would kill me if she heard me say that."

"I guess that means our baby will be the same," Sandi mused. "My mom is Irish, and my dad's German but likes to claim he's a quarter Cherokee. That means Baby Shastri-Persson-Berger will be…"

"Incredibly loved and cared for," Rev said. "Don't get hung up on the color thing so much, Sandi. All I hope is the baby has your smile and your brain."

She sat up to look at him. "But what about…" Sandi hesitated to ask the question weighing on her since Dava had made her announcement in the great room.

"About what?"

Sandi let it all out in a burst before she lost her nerve. "When your mom was talking about the will and about how she had already set up trusts for her grandkids, now that she knows about us, will she set up a trust for our baby even though she technically can't since she's already dead?"

"Huh," Rev said, scratching his head. "Well, there's just been a lot going on, San."

"I know." Sandi cradled her nonexistent bump. "But after we

told her we were pregnant, it seemed like she was going to bring it up, but she didn't."

In one of her most recent interviews, Dava had called herself a pragmatist when it came to her relationship with wealth: "To me, it is a responsibility and a promise. A responsibility to leave this world better than I left it, and a promise that generations of Shastris will always be taken care of, so they can focus on helping others who are less fortunate."

When Sandi had read this while on the train to East Hampton, she began to fully comprehend what joining this family would mean for her child. Baby Shastri-Persson-Berger would never struggle to make rent or worry about paying for college, spared society's worst anxieties and indignities for an entire lifetime. But now, with Dava's announcement throwing everything into chaos, Sandi needed assurance that her and Rev's child would truly be treated as a member of the next generation of Shastris.

"I imagine your mom would want to make sure her new grandchild was looked after in the same way Sita's and Arvie's children are." Sandi nestled deeper into Rev's chest, only to feel his body tense underneath her. "I know it won't be easy. But I think you should talk to her."

Rev bit his thumbnail, and Sandi knew he was irritated. Eventually, he patted her hand and promised he would try to speak with Dava. The two sat together in silence until they heard Kali calling their names, telling them lunch was ready. As they got up to exit the den, Sandi paused in front of the photograph on the piano.

"I wonder if she ever feels alone," she said.

"Who?"

"Your mother," she said sadly. "She's the only one who has brown skin. Your dad and you guys are so much lighter than her. I . . . I wonder how that makes her feel."

Sandi left the den without waiting for his response, leaving Rev staring at the portrait for a few moments longer. She waited on the top step until he picked up his jacket and followed her upstairs.

⌒

Sita could not sit still. She paced the length of the library, walking in a hexagon as she followed the room's perimeter, and then zigzagged from the leather sofa to the globe in the corner, back to the mahogany desk, and then finally halted at the large bay window, contemplating the whiteout conditions that had turned the view into a void of nothingness. Sita hugged her sweater tighter around her and shivered.

Behind her, the door opened and she turned around to see Colin carrying a tray with a bowl of chili, a glass of water, and a glass of wine. Even with her world flipped upside down and sideways, she couldn't help but feel proud that this impossibly handsome man with the silver hair, hazel eyes, and muscled shoulders was her husband. That with so much in flux, she had him in her corner.

"I said I'd be downstairs in a minute," she said with a smile.

"That was forty minutes ago," Colin said, setting the tray down on the desk. "If I didn't bring this to you now, there wouldn't be any left. The boys had thirds." He added that Vincent had tried his best to make the chili while still following Sita's dietary guidelines.

"He's the best," Sita said, sitting down at the desk. "And so are you. Thanks, honey." She took a long sip of wine before tucking hungrily into the chili. "How are the boys? What are they up to?"

"They're, um, reading," he said. "With Klara and Priya. They're fine right now."

"Amma? And everyone else?"

"They're conducting a thorough investigation of the wet bar. I think your mother's napping. She's not going to have any Scotch left by the end of the night."

"So they're just down there getting drunk."

"Except Sandi." Colin came over and gave her a kiss on the head and then sat down in the chair opposite her.

"Sandi," Sita muttered, swirling the chili with her spoon. "Oh right, she's pregnant. That's a shitstorm waiting to happen. But let me deal with the shit hurricane first."

"Sita, you don't have to handle this all by yourself," Colin said. "You can have others help you."

"You mean the drunk brigade in the gigantic room? Or my mother, who's probably reading her obituaries in bed with a glass of champagne?"

"Speaking of obit—" Colin began.

"You know why I haven't been able to come downstairs?" Sita heard herself become high-pitched, just shy of hysterical. "What's been keeping me pacing and going out of my head?" She leaned back in the chair, clutching her glass of wine. "Was."

"Was? Was what?"

"I mean the word 'was.' In that statement I issued, I said, 'Our mother *was* a force of nature.' I had to lie."

Colin began to stand up, but Sita waved him away. "I racked my brain trying to find a way to issue a statement without using the past tense, but it was impossible. And now I feel like a liar. And you know I hate lying."

"I do, honey, I do." He reached for the glass of water and drank most of it in one noisy gulp.

"Amma orchestrates this massive lie without telling us and then drops it in our laps—my lap, really. She really didn't think through how this would affect us at all."

"You sound like your brother," Colin observed, kicking his legs up and perching his navy loafers on the desk.

"Bite your tongue, baby." Sita laughed, despite herself. "And the thing is, I do get it on some level. I mean, at least more than the others would. But I wish she had at least told me beforehand, because then I could have tried to have a strategy in place for how to go forward—how to deal with donors, board members, the press." She picked up her notepad and showed him her to-do list with fifty-seven items on it and only three checked off as completed. "Right now, I'm just frozen."

Colin nodded sympathetically. "Were you able to get in touch with Emilia and Linh?"

"Yes, thank goodness. They've been great so far. I told them all our services are intermittent—which is sort of true, at least—and it would be hard for me to be in touch until the storm dies down. They said just take care of myself, and they'll handle any foundation business and press requests for the next few days. Emilia's on vacation in Cabo and Linh is hosting fifteen people at her house! And still they both stepped in and have my back. Unlike my brothers and sister."

"And then I should have noticed something was off with her," Sita continued. "I mean, she seemed tired during meetings and more easily distracted than usual. But I'm the only one who sees her on a regular basis, and yet I had no idea." When Colin consoled her by saying she couldn't let herself be overrun with guilt, she said sadly, "I can't turn it off like a light switch. Especially not when it comes to Amma." She choked back tears. "She's dying, about to be dead...and I don't even feel I have time to mourn. Or get drunk," she said, passing the wineglass to her husband. "I just have to handle everything. Now it's all on me."

"I'm sorry, hon." He reached over and squeezed her hand and then took a sip of wine and returned it to her. "I can't imagine what you're going through. To know you'll lose your mom soon, and in these circumstances, and to have to think about the foundation on top of that…" He then cocked his head as if a new idea had dawned on him. "But maybe, in time, you'll also find it liberating."

"What do you mean?"

"Haven't you said sometimes when you make decisions, asking for your mom's approval is like having her check your homework?" Sita shrugged, then nodded. "Well, going forward, you'll get to be in charge. One hundred percent." He gave her a big smile, showing off his perfect white teeth. "A little 'silva' lining, if you will."

"What a silly pun, Mr. Shastri-Silva." Sita laughed.

"Why, thank you, Mrs. Shastri-Silva," Colin replied in a gentlemanly drawl.

"Thanks for the 'silva' lining," she said. She took a beat and then had another spoonful of chili. "This is amazing."

Colin encouraged her to finish it before it cooled, and she did, feeling an ounce of stress melt off with every bite. They discussed turning the foundation's spring auction into a tribute to her mother, which would mean inviting some of Dava's colleagues and famous friends to speak at the event. The conversation then turned to whether the couple should post-pone their planned February trip to India and Nepal. For Sita, it was easier to focus on work-related duties far in the future, rather than the million and one things needing her immediate attention.

As the afternoon stretched into evening, shadows loomed large and long throughout the room. Sita switched on the light and then crossed over and sat in her husband's lap.

"It's all going to be okay, right?" she asked him softly.

"Yes, honey, it is," he said, giving her a peck on the cheek. "Let's just take one thing at a time." He gave her a nervous look. "So, your mom had an assignment just for Enzo. I'm not sure how you'll feel about it."

⌒

Enzo was stumped. Should he show his grandmother what he found? He looked over at Theo, flipping through a Batman comic book they unearthed from the den's bookshelf. His brother wouldn't be any help. So he turned around to see his cousins, sprawled on the bed behind him, whispering to each other in Swedish.

After lunch, the twins had gone upstairs to the guest room they were sharing with their parents, when Priya and Klara burst in and declared they needed a break from "all our parents' drama." Not long afterward, Dava had beckoned Enzo into the hallway to give him a specially wired tablet along with a request: to keep a running list of articles and social media messages related to her "passing," which she would review after her nap.

"I would do it myself," she had told Enzo, speaking rapidly as they heard footsteps ascending the stairs, "but I'm not feeling the best. You're so smart I think you can handle this, yes?" Enzo could only nod, awed by the immensity of the task given him. "And maybe you'll learn something about your grandmother."

But what Enzo had learned gave him the queasiness of a stomachache. He knew not to tell his parents, even though they were just across the hall. When his dad had checked in on them before taking lunch to his mother in the library, he seemed skeptical in the face of Enzo's pride about his grandmother's assignment. Priya and Klara were the best option, although they were in a foul mood after their futile attempts to contact their friends with his tablet. ("You can only read stuff? Ugh!") But two hours had passed, and his grandmother would likely be waking soon. So he wiped his sweaty hands on his jeans, swallowed his nerves, and approached his cousins.

"Can you watch this video? I'm trying to figure out if I should show it to Gamma." Klara looked up from examining her nails and nodded with an exaggerated yawn.

She grabbed the device from his hands, and he hovered over Klara's shoulder as they watched "Dava Shastri: Tom Buck's Sexy Secret Muse?" A narrator breathlessly explained the theory that Dava and Tom had an affair, which inspired him to write the song with her name. The video included individual photographs of Tom and Dava and a group photo of Dava, Arvid, Tom, and another woman, with the latter two holding Grammys.

"With Dava's passing," the narrator concluded, "perhaps these star-crossed soul mates finally found each other...in heaven." The video ended with a snippet of Tom's performance of "Dava" at the Oscars.

"Whoa!" Priya said. "That dude is sexy as fuck." She said the last word fumblingly, as if trying it out to see if it sounded cool coming out of her mouth.

"Gamma would *hate* this," Klara squealed. "Omigod, he's so hot though. Go, Gamma!"

"What should I do?" Enzo asked, taking back the tablet. "She said she wanted to see everything said about her."

"I don't know if she'd want to see this." Klara ran her long, sparkly blue fingernails through her dark-blond hair. "I've heard Dad say how much Gamma hates that song."

"But it's all anyone's talking about," Enzo said, hopping from one foot to another. "All the articles mention it. Some mention it a lot."

"Do you really think Gamma and this guy, like, did it?" Priya asked, copying her older sister by running her short, pink fingernails through her light-brown curls.

"Um, I hope so," Klara said, dramatically licking her lips. "He's yummy."

"What about Grandpa Arvid? That would mean she—" Priya

stopped when she saw Enzo's confused expression. "Never mind."

"What are you guys talking about?" Theo said, glancing up from his comic book. "Who's yummy?"

The girls exchanged glances. "Don't show her," Klara told Enzo.

"Show her what?" Dava asked.

Their grandmother stood in the doorway, her red-framed glasses precariously perched on her head and her black silk robe giving her the look of an off-duty witch.

"Enzo will tell you," Priya said, bugging her eyes out at her cousin.

He gulped, then picked up the tablet and showed it to her. Theo took a few steps forward to see, but Enzo waved him away. The girls exchanged glances again, and Klara sucked in her breath, a small smile pricking her lips.

"There's this video about you and a man named Tom Buck. I wasn't sure if you wanted me to include it in my list."

"Fuck," he heard his grandmother whisper, her chin dropping to her chest. "You can exclude anything that mentions him," Dava told him, spitting out each word. As she turned to exit, Enzo heard himself sputter the question he'd been dying to ask since embarking on the project.

"Did he write that song about you?" She halted midstep. "It's just that...so many of the articles mention him. A lot of them are speculating he did, so I...I dunno."

"No," she said, facing the door, but her voice was as thick as ice. "I gave him permission to use my name and have deeply regretted it ever since." She took another step, then stopped again. "Have my friends or my colleagues said anything?"

He desperately scrolled through his list, but he had no idea who Gamma's friends were. "Um, maybe? There's a lot I still have to read through." Dava reached for the door frame with trembling fingers. Enzo swallowed. He couldn't let her down. "I'll find it, Gamma. I just need a second."

She stood there for a few moments and then turned around. "I'm quite dizzy," she rasped. "Help me sit."

The girls clambered off the bed and led her to a high-backed chair next to the armoire. As his cousins fretted over whether they should alert their parents, Enzo received a new "Dava Shastri" news alert, one that had a significant traffic spike and zero mention of Tom Buck.

"Gamma? A new article was just published about you. It's getting a lot of attention." With apparent difficulty, Dava fixed her attention on her grandson. "And," he added with a relieved smile, "it doesn't mention that guy at all."

"What is it about?"

He showed her the story. "Do you know Chaitanya Rao?"

When Enzo was seven, he had nightmares for weeks after finding a raccoon in his bathtub. He had caught a glimpse of his reflection at the sight of the animal and remembered the shock and terror in his eyes, similar to the expression on his grandmother's face now as she slumped down in her seat.

CHAPTER SIX

My Friend, My Mentor

The last time I spoke with Dava was a week ago. She was her usual warm, chatty self, but there was a tinge of sadness too. I felt like she wanted to say something to me but was holding back. For the over ten years I've known her, she's been an open book—amazing stories and pure loveliness. So it was rare when she held herself back, and easy to recognize when she did.

Now, of course, it seems obvious she knew she was dying. I wished she had confided in me. Maybe she didn't want me to see her in a weakened condition. But still. My heart aches we didn't have more time together. She was my friend and my mentor . . . and, I think, maybe my mother.

—*Excerpt of a post written by Chaitanya Rao in the private chat group Oakland Reading Club, published on* The Takeover *(December 26, 2044, at 3:15 p.m.)*

THE SKY WAS BLUISH BLACK, resembling a deepening bruise, yet no one had bothered to switch on any lights in the great room except for the strands of gold twinkling ones on the Christmas tree. Sita noticed the pool table was sparkling, too, but with liquor bottles and half-empty glasses. Just as Arvie angled his pool cue in an attempt to hit an eight ball through the maze of glass, she illuminated the chandelier.

"Let there be light!" Arvie cackled, pointing his cue at the ceiling.

Vincent was snoring loudly on the TV side of the great room, his body so long that his feet hung off the edge of the sectional. Nearby, Kali and Rev were cross-legged on the floor as Sandi sat far across the room in the rocking chair with her hand on her flat stomach, watching them with a pained expression. Sita shook her head at the scene and yanked the cue out of her older brother's hand.

"You're being a moron, Arvie." Sita handed it to Colin and began collecting the glasses from the pool table and stacking them on the wet bar.

"Can you turn off bitch mode for a second? We're trying to blow off steam." Arvie looked for support from his husband, and then remembered he was asleep.

"The only one blowing off steam like a frat boy is you," Sita said, still shuffling back and forth between the pool table and wet bar. "Can you get up and help?" she said to the other siblings.

Kali ignored her. She instead whispered animatedly to Rev, who barely nodded back, his eyes focused skyward. The tension that had first cracked between them in their mother's bedroom earlier that morning was ongoing, as were Kali's desperate attempts to make amends.

"Honey, where does this go?" Colin said, holding the cue like it was a sword. Arvie lurched toward it but tripped over his own feet, landing with a crash on the floor.

"Are you okay?" Colin asked, standing over him.

"He's fine," Sita said. "I don't know how Vincent puts up with his crap."

"Keep my husband's name out of your mouth." Arvie shakily stood up, waving away Colin's outstretched hand. "He's exhausted after making something your twins could eat with their millions of dietary restrictions, and you couldn't give a shit."

"Don't speak to her like that," Colin warned. He was several inches shorter than Arvie but still muscled and fit from his years as an Olympic gymnast and was therefore a more imposing presence than his gangly brother-in-law. Arvie muttered an apology, then sulked by himself near the fireplace.

Sita smiled gratefully at her husband and pointed out where to put back the cue. She then picked up an empty bottle of Johnnie Walker Black from the pool table and set it down with a crash on the bar.

"What's going on?" Vincent said sleepily, lifting up his head.

"Nothing important," Kali said, patting his back. "Go back to sleep."

"For the love of God, can you get your asses up and help?" Sita called out to them.

"Just leave it and sit with us," Rev replied. "We're still recovering from this long, crazy-ass day."

With encouragement from Colin, Sita let go of the mess and joined them. As she sat down on the Vincent-free part of the couch, she looked over at Sandi, who seemed to be trying to make herself invisible. Sita could have waved her over to join them on the sectional but decided that was Rev's job to make her feel comfortable, not hers. After a few minutes, Arvie also came over and perched awkwardly near his husband's feet. Just as he did, Enzo raced into the room, his face shining with tears.

"Amma, Amma!" he said, running into Sita's arms. "I think Gamma's having a heart attack."

It wasn't until two in the morning that the Shastri-Persson siblings were able to assemble in the den, accompanied by a bottle of tequila and Enzo's tablet. After his outburst, Dr. Windsor had been summoned to look in on her patient and diagnosed a panic attack. Dava had claimed it was brought on by a sudden realization about her imminent mortality, then insisted she felt better and still wanted to proceed with the end-of-life treatment on Sunday. The doctor advised Dava to get bed rest and said she would return in the morning to discuss next steps.

After the doctor left, Dava commanded to be left alone, and so her family let her be. It was only once she retreated to her bedroom that her children learned about what Chaitanya had written, and how it had been published by a gossipy news site. As they went through the rituals of dinner and bedtime, Sita took each of her siblings aside and suggested the four of them meet privately after everyone had gone to bed. By the time they had settled in the den, the shock had mostly worn off, and anxiety and exhaustion had set in. They passed the tablet back and forth, reading the article and scrutinizing the photographs of Dava's mother and Chaitanya.

"They totally look alike," Kali marveled, passing the tablet to Sita, then picking up the bottle to refill her shot glass. "It's almost like this woman is Avva's clone. It's eerie."

Sita looked at her sister with a mixture of awe and disdain. "How are you still drinking?"

"Practice," she said, before downing the shot. Seeing her sister's concerned expression, Kali looked ashamed. "That was the last for me tonight—don't worry." She took a beat. "Why aren't you drinking more?"

"I'm a mom," Sita snapped. But she came off harsher than intended and decided to tell the truth. "Honestly, if I start drinking now, I'll never stop. I don't know how to deal with Amma faking her death *and* a secret daughter."

"Alleged secret daughter," Arvie said with a snort.

"I have, like, seventeen messages from Emilia and Linh asking how to handle this. Apparently it's been picked up by the gossip pages and become this major story. Like, the leading entertainment story. It's insane." Sita explained that their mother's "death" led many celebrity publications to rehash the Tom Buck rumors, so when the long-lost-daughter angle emerged during a slow, post-Christmas news cycle, the story exploded. "I don't know what to say. I haven't gotten back to them yet, letting them think we're cut off because of the blizzard."

"Well, I guess the storm is one small thing to be thankful for," Rev said. He now had the tablet and enlarged the photo so Chaitanya's and his grandmother's faces took up the entire screen. He let out a low whistle. "I don't even think they have to do a DNA test. It's uncanny."

"They or we?" Arvie asked, followed by a loud belch. The foursome traded uneasy glances. Besides the unwanted attention on themselves and the foundation, a new sibling would mean Chaitanya could be entitled to a portion of their mother's estate.

"Let's think this through one thing at a time," Sita advised in a soothing way, the same voice she used on the twins when they were upset over being unable to eat a friend's birthday cake because of their egg allergy. "Let's start with the fact Chaitanya never seemed to want this story to become public. She posted her thoughts in a private chat group, and someone sent it to this website."

"Actually, let's start with the fact that Amma had befriended Chaitanya knowing who she was but never once told her she was her daughter," Kali said, pulling her oversize pink sweatshirt over her knees. "That means Amma didn't want her to know the truth, which means she didn't make an allowance for her in the will, at least as a Shastri-Pers— I mean as a Shastri heir."

An online search by Rev brought up a career site in which Chaitanya had uploaded her résumé. "Going by when she graduated from college, she's close to fifty years old. Which means Amma gave birth to her—"

"In college," Sita said irritably. She issued three booming claps. "Let's focus on two things: how to talk to Amma about her, and how to deal with this in terms of the outside world, including if we should contact this woman."

Arvie, who now had the tablet, let out a gasp of recognition. "She's a Helping Perssons person." He explained he had been staring at her name, trying to remember why it seemed so familiar to him, and then, while reading the article, came across Chaitanya's explanation about how she had met their mother.

"Dava reached out to me after I received a Helping Perssons grant, a charity she founded as part of her foundation," Arvie read out loud, slurring slightly. "I was shocked when I received a call from her office requesting to meet me while she was in the Bay Area for work. At the time, I just thought she was a really hands-on person. And when we hit it off so well the first time she came to my home, I never again wondered why Dava wanted to meet me. Until after she died, and I saw a photo of her mother."

"Do you think Amma had been looking for her?" Rev asked. "Or was it just pure chance Chaitanya applied and they were able to find each other?"

"Why are you just assuming she's Mom's daughter?" Arvie blew his nose into a used Kleenex he found in his sweatpants pocket. "We have no evidence they're related."

"Why else would Amma seek her out?" Kali retorted. "She hates the West Coast yet makes a habit of visiting her once a month—and at her house too. Chaitanya would have to either be a billionaire or her long-lost daughter to get that kind of special treatment." Kali sounded hurt as she said this and looked away from her siblings to the family portrait hanging above the piano.

"Maybe she thought this woman might be her daughter because of her resemblance to her own amma," Rev mused, tracing the large crack on the coffee table with his finger.

Annoyed her siblings couldn't stay focused on the pressing issues at hand, Sita messily filled her shot glass and downed the tequila in two half-choked gulps.

"Whoa, there," Kali said with a shocked smile. "Good on you."

Sita set down the shot glass with a smack on the coffee table. "Yeah, well," she said, shrugging, and took out her notepad. As her siblings speculated about when their mother could have secretly given birth and if she had kept it a secret from their father, Sita rapidly paged through her notes. Each time she tried to ask their opinion on a myriad of issues that needed addressing—such as their mother's funeral arrangements ("I'm sure she's already planned a Viking funeral with a thousand crying doves") or if they should reach out to her attorney ("That seems like your department, Sis")—they all but ignored her, fixating only on the mystery at hand. Finally, she gave up on involving them and stared at her notes until her vision blurred.

Most urgent was determining the family's public response to Chaitanya. How could they possibly address it without courting more speculation? And surely Amma would want to have a say. But did that mean she should? The words "'silva' lining" flashed in her mind, providing a sudden but welcome clarity. Even though Dava was still alive, Sita was in charge of the family now. And there was a dizzying kind of freedom to be the final say on these matters. On *all* matters. She didn't need her siblings' help. What she needed was for them to shut up.

"I think," she said, shoehorning her voice through their chatter, "in the morning, I'll tell Emilia we're still processing Amma's passing and not ready to comment at this time but that, no matter what is being reported, we hope people will remember her for her work helping—no, championing—women around the world."

"That sounds good, Sita." Kali squeezed her arm reassuringly. "Amma would approve of the last part especially."

"I'm going to sit down with her and Dr. Windsor about the logistics for Amma's last day," she continued, speeding through the last few words as if they were hot on her tongue. Sita added she'd keep an eye on the weather reports to see when the storm was expected to end and they'd be able to leave the island.

"What about the secret daughter?" Arvie asked, tiny bits of Kleenex clinging to his nose. "Mom has to explain herself. We at least deserve to know the truth. Who votes we ask her about that?" Rev and Kali exchanged glances and then raised their hands, and Arvie raised his too.

"Okay, fine," Sita said, sighing. "But let me please talk to her first and get some important details squared away, because we don't have a lot of time." She reminded them Dava wanted her treatment to take place before the end of the weekend. "If she gets defensive and shuts down, that will make everything ten times harder."

"And Chaitanya?" Rev asked anxiously. "Should we contact her?"

"Let's leave her be for now. We have enough happening right now with Amma and getting through these next few days. After we're able to leave Beatrix, I'll contact Allen and my own lawyer on how best to proceed in terms of a potential sister, and what that means for us and the estate's assets." Sita looked at each of her siblings, and when she saw each of them nod, the weight on her shoulders lessened exponentially.

"Pour her another," Kali said to Rev, handing him the shot glass. "She deserves it. In fact, pour one for each of us. Even you, Arvie. Take just a half a shot at least. I want to make a toast."

Rev poured shots for each of them and then passed them around, giving himself and Kali more than their older siblings.

"To us, for surviving this crazy day," Kali said as she held up the shot glass with her hand pressed to her heart, as if she were about to recite the Pledge of Allegiance. "To Rev, on his new baby with Sandi. You're going to be a wonderful papa, just like our papa." Rev blushed, and Arvie clapped his brother on the back with a stilted whoop.

"To Sita, for being our fearless leader. The foundation will be lucky to have you as its new head bitch." Sita smiled with uncertainty, restraining herself from informing her sister the board would vote for a new CEO, and it would likely not be her.

"To Arvie, for having a kick-ass husband who is going to help us survive this blizzard without having to eat any more pizza." Arvie looked at his younger sister expectantly, and when he realized she was done speaking about him, a tipsy smile faded from his thin lips.

"And to Kali," Rev began, then stopped as he tried to think of something to say. "For just being you," he finally added with a sheepish grin. Just as Sita was about to speak, Rev came up with a new toast. "To being the heart of our family." Kali clobbered him with a hug, and Sita laughed with relief that their discord had dissipated.

"Cheers," Arvie said softly. Soon after their toast, they wished each other good night and headed to their rooms to sleep. But none of the Shastri-Perssons were able to get much rest, with their respective tributes haunting each of them in ways that spoke to their innermost fears.

CHAPTER SEVEN

A Cliffside Conversation Leads to a Lifelong Commitment

**A CLIFFSIDE CONVERSATION LEADS TO A LIFELONG
COMMITMENT**

By Therese Samuels
Excerpt from *The New York Times* Vows column
Sept. 22, 2002

They had spent a fateful night together in Ruiz camped out on a cliff overlooking a vibrant sunset and the Paraná River. As the sky faded from twilight into darkness, Ms. Shastri and Mr. Persson had to decide whether they had a future together, as their two-year stint with the Peace Corps was ending the next day. Mr. Persson was due to return to Stockholm and resume working at his aunt and uncle's bar while he figured out his postcollege plans. And Ms. Shastri was set to return to New York City and decide whether to attend business school or take a chance at starting her own company.

"We talked all night," Mr. Persson recalled. "And when I say all night, I mean we filled up every second with our voices. We talked so much we were both hoarse the following morning."

By the time the sun rose behind them, they had made several choices: Mr. Persson would apply to several graduate schools in the United States to get his master's in education (he would be accepted to Teachers College at Columbia University); Ms. Shastri would pursue her start-up dreams and create the online musicians platform Medici Artists; Mr. Persson and Ms. Shastri would move in together as soon as he came stateside; they would make their home wherever he attended school; and they would get married after he graduated.

"Luckily, he went to Columbia," Ms. Shastri noted. "If he chose a school in California or Texas, we might not have gotten married after all," she added with a throaty laugh.

Six years after they met in Ruiz, and four years after that cliffside camping excursion, the couple wed on Sept. 6 at Manhattan City Hall. Only a handful of friends had been invited, and all of them brought musical instruments, ranging from guitars to violins (plus triangles for the non-musically-inclined). The groom wore a tan suit and blue tie for the occasion, while the bride wore a midnight-blue silk dress with cap sleeves and gold accents.

"They are a stunning couple," gushed Juliet Maribel, Ms. Shastri's college friend, who designed her wedding dress. "Dava likes to say Arvid's doppelganger is the front man for Blur, because he's so slim and boyish. And then she'll joke she looks like a C-list Bollywood movie star. But my goal was to make her look glamorous, like Elizabeth Taylor in her prime. I think I pulled it off."

After Mr. Persson and Ms. Shastri exchanged vows and

emerged outside, their friends performed an instrumental cover of The Flaming Lips' "Do You Realize?" The couple slow danced at the courthouse steps before adjourning to a French restaurant in the West Village for their reception.

But even with the charming, quirky nature of their wedding, both Ms. Shastri and Mr. Persson agree their night together in Ruiz was the true moment when they committed to each other, and the city hall ceremony was a mere formality of paperwork and rings.

"It was the most glorious, intense night of our lives," Ms. Shastri said fondly. "A perfect memory. Arvid likes to describe it as a snow globe: perfectly preserved, separate from the world. We're so happy we'll be able to look back on that time and think of it as the foundation for what's to come."

DAVA'S LEFT LEG WAS asleep, a consequence of huddling in her closet as if playing hide-and-seek. After retreating from her family, she had grabbed her BlackBerry and took refuge in the windowless room, scrolling through Arvid's messages until the battery died, cursing Tom Buck in her head. Of course she figured he would appear in her coverage. But she never thought he would consume it, because no one had mentioned the song to Dava in over ten years. For the first few months of their friendship, she waited for Chaitanya to bring it up, but she never did. So Dava had lulled herself into thinking that the drama had been reduced to a footnote, left behind in the 2010s like Segways and Candy Crush. But Tom Buck and his infernal song trailed her the entire time, a phantomlike presence that became corporeal the moment she officially stopped living.

But it was Chaitanya's betrayal that left her feeling like a fish flopping on land, gasping for air that would never come. She hadn't read the *Takeover* article, but the headline made clear Chaitanya had gone public with her belief Dava was her mother. And this revelation, coupled with the Tom Buck rumors, was coloring the world's response to her death. No longer was she being memorialized by *International Business Times* and *Feminist First*; instead, her personal life was fodder for *E! News* and *LeGossip*.

When Dava finally rose from the closet floor, her body audibly creaked from the effort, her joints screaming in harmony. She limped into her master bathroom to relieve herself and, as she washed her hands, was stopped short by her reflection in the mirror.

She did not expect to look so haggard. Dava turned away from the mirror, then looked back, hoping her reflection would somehow transform into someone "exotic and alluring." A perk of becoming a well-known figure was that she could see herself described in the words of journalists sent to profile her. *A Marilyn Monroe–esque figure with a Kewpie doll face. A quiet beauty hiding a spine of steel.* They were not that creative and often reductive, but they had been written about *her*. Dava had memorized their descriptions, imprinted them on her mind like a talisman she could return to when her spirits were low or, more recently, when she was feeling her age.

When she officially became a senior citizen, Dava despaired her face was becoming too full and loathed the extra chin that had attached itself like a growth. But in recent months, her cheekbones lost their softness and her face thinned out like a deflated balloon. She believed Arvid would not recognize this crone-like woman at all, save for the white streak glinting on her forehead. It had crept into her hairline after his cancer diagnosis, a lightning bolt left behind long after the shock had worn off. She had wanted to dye it along with the rest of her grays, but Arvid teased that it made her look distinguished, like a bank president or judge. And because her ailing husband seemed to find an inordinate amount of joy in coming up with a list of staid professionals to compare her to, she had kept the lick of white hair sweeping down her forehead. After he died, to see herself in the mirror with it gave her solace, as if Arvid were returning her gaze, an impish smile on his lips. But in this particular moment the white streak only magnified her distress.

This is how I'm going to look before I die? This is how my children will remember me? Dava slapped her hand over her face in the mirror's reflection with a hard thwack, followed by a pang of guilt. Because at least she could recognize herself. Whereas Arvid became ghoulish in his last days, almost skeletal, his already pale skin even whiter, save for the dark bags under his eyes and discolored patches of skin all over his body. All the boyish beauty had been drained out of him by surgeries and chemotherapy, with only his light-green eyes a vivid reminder of the beautiful, sunny man he had once been.

The abrupt slap aggravated an intense headache behind her right eye. With her head spinning and leg still asleep, she hobbled back to the bedroom, praying she would not trip and fall over. For the first time since her diagnosis, Dava was acutely attuned to her body's deterioration. Dying was a nasty, humbling business, and she was awash in relief that she had arranged for her own end rather than let her tumors conspire to claim her at their leisure. *You will not defeat me*, she fumed as she staggered toward her bed.

Once there, her thoughts returned to Arvid. The past twenty-four hours had been so overwhelming, and Chaitanya's betrayal still so fresh, she doubted even his presence would comfort her.

In her Medici Artists years, when she hadn't yet mastered dealing with wealthy patrons' bloviating narcissism or musicians' artistic temperaments, she could count on him to make her feel better after a frustrating day placating egos. First he would listen, nodding sympathetically while she recited her woes, pacing their bedroom as she punched the air. After Dava had finished and collapsed beside him, he would wrap his long arms around her. "Good thing there's a brand-new day around the corner, right?" he would whisper into her ear, melting her heart. When Dava was in a particularly foul mood and even his patented hugs couldn't quell her fury, he would try to make his wife laugh by breaking into his favorite Van Morrison song. "Brand-new dayyyyy," he would sing, and she would giggle and plead with him to stop, but his off-key singing helped her move past her anger.

Of all the times in her life when she needed to hear his song, this was truly the moment she needed it most. But Dava let out a strangled gasp as she realized Arvid's mantra about a "brand-new day" no longer applied, because she only had one day left. The realization mirrored the sensation of slamming a door on her thumb when she was nine: numbness, followed by a bolt of pain that dropped her to her knees, then numbness again. She had always thought of herself as a "steadfast atheist" (and, in fact, used those exact words in multiple interviews), but with death's arrival only hours away, here was one of the rare times she hoped she would be proven wrong, and that on the other side awaited a heaven that included only her husband, a record player, and a view of the Paraná River.

Dava turned on her bedside lamp, casting an Africa-shaped glow on the left corner of her bed. She slipped off her robe and silk pajamas before crawling under the covers in a faded yellow sports bra and cotton underwear. Curled into a fetal position, she finally let herself cry. Dava was consumed by regret for the thousands of big and small choices that had landed her in this absurd predicament, leaving herself alive long enough to see her stature in the world diminished without the ability to defend herself.

She soaked her pillow with an ugly spewing of tears. With the wind unfurling at peak strength, the house creaked too, as though weeping in solidarity, an unnerving noise akin to ten million zippers being simultaneously undone. How ironic, Dava contemplated bitterly, if the whole Shastri clan was wiped out in a snowstorm. All her efforts would have been for naught.

The idea was silly, irrational. But there was a hard nut of truth at its center. Because if she let the current perception of herself stand, then her whole lineage might as well be wiped out. The Shastri-Perssons as a family dynasty on par with the Rockefellers only worked if Dava Shastri herself was taken seriously. A lifetime of work would not be undermined by wagging tongues hungry for scandal. There must be a way to counter the narrative. And to do so, she needed to know exactly what was being said about her.

She wiped her tears away with the back of her hand and opened her tablet, entering "Dava Shastri + Chaitanya Rao" into the search bar. Earlier, she had been too wounded to even attempt skimming the article when Enzo informed her of it, even after her panic attack had abated. So her heart stuttered as she clicked on the *Takeover* story, ready to speed through the words as if ripping off a bandage. But her eyes caught on two images positioned side by side: a picture of twentysomething Chaitanya and a slightly blurred 1980s-era photo of Dava's mother, Aditi.

"My God," Dava said, her chin trembling. Never once during their time together did she think Chaitanya resembled her mother. But when seen together, with their ski-slope noses and angular jawlines, they could have passed for twins. The longer she gazed at them, the calmer Dava felt, especially since her headache had receded too. With a deep breath, she dove in and read the article.

She learned several important things: Chaitanya's thoughts,

expressed in a private chat group, had been leaked to the
Takeover; Aditi's image was sourced from a Shastri family
portrait posted to her foundation's website; and Chaitanya had
first seen Aditi on social media, as part of a video series
called *90 Seconds* that summarized major news stories in bite-
size, consumable chunks. For the first time in weeks, Dava's
face lit up with a genuine smile. Chaitanya hadn't betrayed
her. Far from it. But what had she seen about her in that
video?

Dava clicked Play, and her face—moon-shaped and girlish,
with rosy cheeks and bright-red lips—filled the screen. "Dava
Shastri: Her Life in 90 Seconds" was superimposed over the
image. The video comprised several still images with text on
the screen explaining the details of her life. When the photo of
her and her parents appeared on the screen, Dava hit Pause and
read the accompanying text: *Dava was the only child of Rajesh
and Aditi Shastri, and raised in Calliston, Arizona. She described
her childhood as "pleasant and dull."* Had she really said this in an
interview? She didn't recall. And while those were apt words to
describe the Sears portrait, showing eight-year-old Dava wearing a frilly dress, her mom in a yellow sari, and her father in
square-framed glasses and a brown suit, they weren't adequate
enough to communicate the truth. She had only expressed her
feelings about her childhood one time. Not in any interview,
but in the form of a mixtape she gave to Arvid before they
started dating.

While they had met at the Peace Corps orientation, their
flirtation began several weeks later during an organized hike
for the volunteers. Feeling disoriented and sleep deprived, they
had lagged behind the others, and to keep each other's spirits
up, Arvid and Dava had discussed their favorite albums. Upon
realizing they had similar tastes, they started joking about forming their own band. As they bantered, their Converses kicking

up red dust and pebbles as they traversed the rocky trail, they came up with a band name (The Nonsense), their style of music (a mix of '80s college rock and power pop), and the instruments they would play (guitar for Dava, bass for Arvid, and after a lengthy debate, they decided on Dave Grohl as their drummer).

The next day, Arvid charmed her by giving her a mixtape of songs he imagined their band would have recorded. An entire album, in fact: ten sequenced tracks that included a title and liner notes. "Charmed" was not even the word. He had floored her. For the first time, someone was on her exact same wavelength, sharing her particular brand of weirdness. And just like that, she was in love with him.

Throughout her life up to that moment, she had ached for someone to understand her, to know everything about someone and to be known in return. So before she could lose her nerve, Dava created a mixtape for Arvid titled *Favorite Thing (A Biography of Sorts)*, with an accompanying letter explaining why she chose the songs.

"Academy Fight Song," Mission of Burma. My mission statement in Me versus That Fucking Suburb, aka Calliston, Arizona. It reminded me not to take shit from anyone in that stupid town.

Especially people in high school. They called me Apu for as long as I can remember. During my freshman year, they said it to my face. By senior year, they wouldn't dare. By then, I had established a reputation of taking no shit. They had learned to stay far from me.

"Once in a Lifetime," Talking Heads. You called it the lightning flash. When music was no longer background noise but a sudden magical resonance, and nothing was ever the same. This was mine. (12th birthday, new Walkman, $20 gift certificate to Sam Goody, bicycling at sunset. And then boom.)

"We Got the Beat," The Go-Go's. The Go-Go's changed *everything* for me.

Post–lightning flash, when I started listening to music, like really listening, it seemed bands who write their own songs and play their own instruments = dudes. And while I liked Madonna and Whitney, I *respected* bands. And if any women were in a band, they had to play "feminine" instruments (e.g., tambourine or piano). Like The Archies—yes, I know they're a cartoon—or Fleetwood Mac.

And then I saw the music video for "We Got the Beat" late at night on some sort of MTV rip-off channel. To see all women on stage, playing guitar and drums and bass, and NO ONE BANISHED TO THE KEYBOARDS, was a revelation. They weren't trying to be pretty. They were dancing, sweating, and having a glorious time.

To know women were making music like this made me feel less alone. They shifted the world for me, opening a door I keep walking through.

"Cannonball," The Breeders. My birth name is actually Deva. It's a unisex name because my mom had a lot of trouble getting pregnant, and when she finally did, my parents wanted my gender to be a surprise. And then it was misspelled "Dava" on my birth certificate, and I like it so much better. It's unique—no one in the world has my name, because it's not supposed to exist.

Did you know Oprah's name was supposed to be Orpah, and it was misspelled on her birth certificate, and so she kept it? And then created an empire with a name that's wholly her own. It's going to be the same for me. And I'm going to hit the world like a cannonball.

"Happy House," Siouxsie and the Banshees. Here's a family portrait. Let's title it *Shastris in Still Life: 1986–1992*. A father and daughter arguing, and the mother watching with sad, pleading eyes. When I discovered this song, I felt vindicated. My sense of alienation was valid, and I would not pretend otherwise. I'd turn this up full blast in my room, my version of a primal scream.

"You Are the Everything," R.E.M. The rare times I felt connected to my parents were during long car trips, especially at dusk. To look out the window and listen to them murmur to each other in a language I never learned but that was as familiar to me as breathing made me feel so safe. This song captures that experience so well it takes my breath away.

"Thirteen," Big Star. It's just the most perfect song in the world.

"Norwegian Wood," The Beatles. My dad didn't understand why I spent all my time and waitressing money at record stores. So I thought if I played him this song, which has a sitar in it, then he would start to get it. I made a mixtape of songs to play when he was teaching me to drive, and when "Norwegian Wood" came on, he smiled. After the song ended, he rewound the tape. I was so excited I told him endless facts about George Harrison and Ravi Shankar and how it was the first time an Indian instrument had been featured on a pop song—and he interrupted me with, "You think I haven't heard of the Beatles?" And then we both laughed, so loud and so long. I wonder if he ever thinks back to that time as much as I do.

"A Design For Life," Manic Street Preachers. Did your family suffer at all from the 1987 crash, or was that just an American thing? My dad had a lot invested in stocks, so we were hurt when the market crashed. I was a freshman in high school when this happened, and I think at one point my parents were afraid we'd lose the house. Somehow, my dad was able to get it together financially. But he seemed haunted afterward, like he was forever afraid the floor would give out underneath him. Seeing my parents stress so much changed me in a big way: I decided I'd pay my own way for college so I could take the burden off of them.

Which also meant I would be under no obligation to fulfill their dreams for me. They would have no say over where I went or what I studied and, ultimately, who I dated and what I did for a living. All my choices and mistakes would fully be my own.

This song's soaring chorus reminds me of that light bulb moment and the strength of my resolve. My personal Declaration of Independence.

"Favorite Thing," The Replacements. The inspiration for this mixtape's title, and how I felt about The Mats from 1991 to 1993. (I still love them a lot, but for those two years I was saturated infatuated.)

"Sheela-Na-Gig," PJ Harvey. Another perfect song.

"Sunken Treasure," Wilco. Brings back how I felt living in Fake Suburb: yearning and lonely. Not just among the white people either. Even within the small group of Indian families that made up our community, the only people my parents socialized with.

We all lived in the same neighborhood called Paradise Valley. It's ten blocks made up of tract homes (beige walls, pink stucco roofs) next to a golf course.

The Shastris were decidedly middle class—not poor, but not wealthy enough to take overseas vacations. We did the American classics: Disneyland, Grand Canyon, Mount Rushmore, Yellowstone. The Jaga-shits, the Raja-blahs, the Pra-poops, and the Shahs—they were actually not so bad, so I have no bitchy nickname for them—traveled to India (I've never been! But I will one day) and Hawaii and went on safaris in Africa. The dads in the family were all doctors, which is why I think my dad wanted me to be one, so I'd be able to afford the things he could not.

And so every Friday or Saturday night, we'd rotate going to each other's houses, and the dads would smoke cigarettes on the patio and talk about cricket, the moms would cook and gossip in the kitchen, and the kids would go upstairs and watch TV. They purposely cracked jokes in Hindi because they knew I wouldn't understand. My parents spoke Telegu, but I never learned that language either. I was also the youngest, so they either treated me as invisible or as their servant. ("Can you get us some more Coke? Thaaanks!")

It was one thing to feel isolated from the white kids. But to feel iced out by kids who looked like me was devastating. And it fueled my desire to escape.

The last lines of "Sunken Treasure" mean the world to me. I'm too embarrassed to write them here, because they are so earnest and speak to some essential truth about me I can't say out loud. I wish this song existed when I lived in Calliston. But I'm glad I found it after.

As Dava remembered the mixtape, she winced as she recalled struggling with whether to include the PJ Harvey song. Dava thought she had been ready to pour herself completely to Arvid but stopped when describing "Sheela-Na-Gig," because the song had been connected to Panit, and she hated he was a part of her story. It was still too raw, even though it had been a full two years since their breakup. But in the end, she decided she had to be true to her concept of mixtape as biography, promising herself if things did become serious with him, she would tell him why the song truly mattered to her. (Arvid, for his part, had responded to her mixtape by presenting her with another one titled *I'd Like to Take You on a Date*.)

"Panit," she said out loud, the first time she had uttered the name of her only college boyfriend in close to fifty years. Doing so conjured up a sickening feeling in her stomach, though only briefly. Because as Dava reflected on him now, reclining in her cream puff bed in her custom-built mansion designed as an exact replica of a beautiful home she had stayed at in Switzerland, constructed on a private island off the coast of East Hampton that she had purchased for eight figures, she didn't regret him in the slightest. Because the aftermath of their relationship had spun her in a completely different direction: toward Arvid and their children and, ultimately, her foundation. And, of course, Chaitanya.

She drifted off to sleep and dreamed she was having a picnic with the versions of Chaitanya and her mother from the *Takeover* story, watching them laugh together with identical smiles and kind eyes. Dava was just about to touch her mother's face when she was awoken by a knock at the door. It was Sita.

"What's wrong?" Dava said hoarsely, only half-awake.

"I couldn't sleep," Sita said, entering her mother's bedroom. "Actually, none of us could." Following after her were Rev, Kali, and Arvie. "We have to know about Chaitanya, Amma. We need to know the truth."

CHAPTER EIGHT

A True Warrior, A Mighty Defender

I have been dogged for requests for comment so here it is for all to read: Dava Shastri was a true warrior, a mighty defender of women around the world. She especially prided herself on amplifying the voices of women who were suppressed or ignored. As for the other stories, it reflects poorly on the media for choosing to focus on gossip over an incredible legacy that changed so many lives, including mine.

—*A statement from Vash Myers, chief operating officer of the Dava Shastri Foundation*

SATURDAY, DECEMBER 27

BEFORE DAVA WOULD TALK about Chaitanya, she made her sons wait in the library while her daughters helped her shower. She was afraid of falling because upon waking up, her vision had temporarily blurred. After she changed into a set of white silk pajamas with a matching robe, Sita and Kali guided her across the hall. Dava chose to hold the conversation in the library because its refined interior, a tasteful symphony of dark wood paneling and arched bookshelves, helped her feel more commanding. To that end, she insisted on being seated at the desk while her children gathered opposite her on the leather sofa.

"So what do you want to know?" she said, clasping her hands in front of her.

"The truth," Arvie said. "Is she our sister?"

"Yes." Dava was amused to see four pairs of eyebrows shoot up in surprise. "What else?"

"The hows and whys would be nice," Rev said. "If you're up to sharing it."

"Not really—"

"We already have to fend off gossip about that stupid song, and now we have this," Arvie broke in. "So sorry—you gotta tell us."

"Have a little respect," Sita huffed. She was at the very edge of the sofa, as far from her siblings as possible, her body language all but shouting how upset she was with them. Dava guessed Sita had a plan about how they would approach her, but the others had been insubordinate as usual.

"Any other skeletons in your closet we should know about?" Arvie continued, jabbing a finger in her direction. "We're the ones who are going to have to live with it, you know."

"Calm down," Kali said, tapping him on the knee. Sita glared at Arvie and shook her head.

"If you had let me finish, Arvie, I was going to say, 'Not really, but I owe you the truth,'" Dava said, her voice catching as her vision blurred and their faces looked slightly melted. "So here it is. I had a boyfriend in college. His name was Panit, and he got me pregnant."

Dava surveyed her children and was relieved she could see their features distinctly again. She dug her fingernails into her palms and pressed forward.

"Your grandparents were very strict with me. So, when I went to NYU, I felt like I had to make up for lost time." Dava explained she treated her freshman year in an almost anthropological manner, which she described as American Teenager 101.

"I won't embarrass you by telling you what I did. Let's just say I did it all," she recalled with a faraway expression. "Honestly, it was one of the happiest times of my life. I didn't have a care in the world and only had to worry about myself.

"But my grades were suffering, and I was on a scholarship, so I had to buckle down and study so I could keep my spot. I majored in English lit with a minor in film—did you know that?" Dava peered at them curiously over her glasses, which had slipped down her nose. Two of them shrugged, and the other two nodded. "Well, I did. And I started feeling guilty about being so nontraditional. My parents couldn't brag about me to their friends. I think I fell for Panit because I thought my parents would like him, and it was the one way I knew I could make them proud of me."

Thinking of Panit now, she remembered he wasn't handsome, with his bulbous nose and teacup-shaped ears, but he was six feet tall, which made him attractive to five-foot-one Dava, who at the time considered herself squat like a pumpkin. They had met at a rooftop party at the beginning of her sophomore year, when they both went to grab a Heineken out of a cooler and quickly recognized they were the only two Indian people there. They had talked for hours and bonded over their shared experiences of being Indian-Americans at NYU and navigating their parental relationships and quirks.

"It was all typical caught-between-two-worlds kind of stuff, very clichéd." Dava waved her hand dismissively. "But at the time, it felt revelatory. By the end of the night, I thought I was in love. We both did. He never asked me out; we just were a couple from then on."

Every minute of Dava's fall semester had been devoted to only two things: her classes and Panit. "My friends got the message and dropped out of my life, so everything I did revolved around him. He was just so perfect. And I felt anything but perfect at the time: awkward, short, too loud, too angry. It was like a miracle he actually loved me despite my flaws." Kali and Sita nodded knowingly at their mother's words. "He was the dream Indian boyfriend"—an economics major who planned to go to Harvard Business School, was fluent in Hindi and Marathi, and knew enough about Bollywood to mock it while also introducing her to movies she came to love—"almost like he had been created in a lab."

She noticed a glint of recognition from Sita as she talked about Panit's perfection and knew she was likely thinking of her first husband, Bhaskar. Dava sucked in a breath, then released her fingers from her fists. When she saw her hands were shaking, she tightened them again and hid them on her lap.

"Of course, once your grandparents learned about him, they approved. No doubt they believed we would get married one day. Maybe Panit did too. And maybe so did I. He was my first experience with romance—or what I thought was romance."

"Oh no," Kali said softly, leaning forward.

"He had a lot of expectations about how I should act, what I should wear, and eventually demanded I get his permission before going anywhere without him. It was slow and insidious, this controlling side of him, but being new to dating, I just thought that's what it meant to be in a relationship. And when I finally began questioning him and pushing back, it would get...ugly." The worst kind of movie montage played in Dava's head: Panit's eyebrows furrowed together in one thick, jagged line; screaming matches that left her hoarse; the back of her head thudding against the wall as he loomed over her; tiptoeing in bare feet among the discards of broken glass. "I learned it was just easier to go along with what he wanted. Especially since I felt so isolated. I mean, I didn't have any good friends to confide in anymore. And when my parents called me every week, they spent half the time talking to him. I didn't know how to leave."

A clanging of pots interrupted from downstairs, followed by thin strains of conversation. Behind her, the sun gained strength and shone through the bay window, giving the library a lemon glow. "Everyone's waking up," said Dava, brushing away a fleeing tear.

"Don't worry about it, Amma." Sita hurried to her side and squeezed her hand. "They'll be okay. Just continue." Arvie looked up and nodded his agreement, then resettled his eyes on his feet.

"At some point I gave up trying to end it with him, because I was already set to study abroad at Cambridge for my junior year. So I just counted down the days until I flew out to the UK." She stayed with Panit through the summer, then broke up with him on his answering machine as soon as she landed at Heathrow. A few weeks later, she told her parents Panit had dumped her because he didn't want to do long distance.

"I thought I had plotted the perfect escape," Dava said, snapping her fingers, the pads of them too sweaty to make any sound. "But by that time, I was already pregnant. I actually didn't realize I was pregnant until I was six months along, because I didn't know enough about my body to understand the changes happening to me." Lonely and depressed during her first few months abroad, she had attributed her weight gain to eating her feelings. "Once I knew, I had to quickly figure out what to do about this baby. Because there was no possible way to tell him or your grandparents."

Dava looked from her youngest child to her eldest, all staring at her with wide, unblinking eyes. In that moment, they seemed so young to her, with their hair mussed and still in their pajamas, as if she had just told them a bedtime story with an unhappy ending.

"It was . . . a difficult time," she said, her voice trailing off. Envisioning her adult children as four little people she needed to protect pushed her to end the story on an upbeat note, as if concluding an inspirational speech. "And I was able to overcome and be better for it," she said with a grandness she did not feel. "Let my story be a lesson to you: choose the people in your life wisely, and don't let them ever make you doubt yourself or take advantage of you." She said this last part directly to Kali, who seemed confused by her mother's exhortation but nodded in return.

The sounds from the kitchen were growing louder and more distinct, and one of Sita's boys called out for her. Rev glanced at his watch and announced to the room it was 7:30.

"What now?" he said without addressing anyone in particular, his gaze pained and directed past his mother.

"We should go downstairs." Arvie stood up. "They're all stirring and no doubt wondering where we are. And there's a lot we need to figure out," he said pointedly in Sita's direction.

"Yes, let's go," she said distractedly, sweeping out of the room with her pink cotton robe trailing behind her like a cape.

"But there's more to the story, right?" Kali said, taking her sister's place at her mother's side. "How you gave her up, and how you reconnected again? And your relationship to Chaitanya now?"

Dava patted her arm. "Help me stand up, dear." Arvie watched as Rev and Kali assisted their mother in getting up from behind the desk. "Thank you." To Arvie, she said, "I hope it wasn't too shocking to hear about your mother's past."

He took a step back and appeared alarmed. "No, Mom, it was fine. I'm just sorry you had to go through . . . all of that."

"Me too," she said, wincing as the three of them walked toward the door. "Actually, boys, go ahead without us. I want to speak with Kali for a moment." The two brothers left the room, with Rev giving Kali an apprehensive glance before closing the door behind him.

⌒

Dava clutched the armrest with stiff fingers, her mood shifting between anxious and grouchy. Kali had helped her sit down on the leather sofa, only to rush out, claiming she needed to use the restroom. As her younger daughter's absence stretched longer and longer, the library shuddered with piercing silence, as muffled conversations played out downstairs, just out of reach. Tired of waiting, Dava stood up quickly but was struck by an overpowering dizzy spell. She slid back down onto the sofa, her body trembling with frustration.

The interminable quiet, coupled with an inability to leave the room, reminded Dava of when she became agoraphobic over two decades earlier. The twin shocks of her husband's death and the global pandemic, events that were only separated by a few weeks, froze her in a state of paralysis, as if cocooned inside her own terror and grief. Dava had listened to Anita the nanny tend to her kids in hushed tones while she fought to escape her mentally embalmed state, knowing how much her family needed her. As part of that inward battle, she had dreamed up what would become Beatrix Island, a lushly green and isolated space where she and her children could be safe. Almost a decade later, the fantasy she had conjured while adrift in a sea of balled-up Kleenex and unwashed bedding became a reality.

Once the Beatrix Island home had been completed, Dava immediately held a puja. The only other time she had a Satyanarayan housewarming puja was at the brownstone, at her parents' urging. Still smarting with guilt she had never given them the traditional wedding ceremony they desired, she acceded to their request and felt like a teenager again as her mind wandered while the priest chanted and passed around the aarti and poured holy water into her and Arvid's palms. But rather than sitting in the back surreptitiously reading V.C. Andrews, this was Dava's home being blessed, and so she had to sit cross-legged near the altar in one of her mother's saris, her legs cramping and her torso straitjacketed into a tight blouse that exposed her underarm fat.

She didn't have a puja upon moving into the penthouse, and eventually the calamities piled up: she lost her father and her husband, and then came the domino-like procession of the devastating events of that terrible year. So Dava had one at Beatrix Island, which she mandated that all her children attend. During the puja, she took a small satisfaction as they shifted uncomfortably behind her, wearing stiff salwar kameezes and kurtas purchased specifically for the occasion. From then on, Dava made sure her children held their own pujas each time they moved into new homes. Even if she couldn't attend, she paid for the priest, the altar, and all the accouterments.

Dava confided all of this only to Chaitanya, who had gone through her own succession of pujas throughout her adolescence. Perhaps noting the pain glinting in Dava's eyes as she recalled her children's bewilderment at their atheist mother demanding they follow this one religious ritual, Chaitanya had mischievously waggled her eyebrows.

"Well, it's a time-honored tradition to force your kids to sit through the story of Lilavati and Kalavati," she said, referring to the excruciatingly long morality tale told at every Satyanarayan puja about a mother and daughter punished with the loss of their husbands for not completing the ceremony.

Dava had burst out laughing, not just at the memory of the story, which Chaitanya recalled gleefully ("You didn't eat the prasadam? Sorry, this ship has sunk. Oh, now you ate the prasadam? Okay, here's the ship again; he's fine"), but also at the realization that Dava unwittingly had become a modern-day Kalavati, rewarded not with the miraculous reappearance of her long-lost husband and father but with the woman sitting across from her: her long-lost daughter.

⌒

Finally, the library door creaked open. Kali crept in carrying a red fleece blanket and draped it over her mother's knees.

"Just in case you were feeling cold," she said apologetically, the cloying scent of cherry-almond lotion wafting off her skin like guilt. Any other time, Dava would have scolded her for smoking, but she needed to hurry their conversation along. She beckoned Kali to sit down next to her, then spread the blanket over both their laps. For a moment, Dava thought Kali was going to lean her head on her shoulder, just as she had done as a little girl when they would read together at bedtime. But she seemed to stop herself and instead sat up rigidly against the sofa, as if correcting her posture.

"Amma, why didn't you invite Chaitanya here? Didn't you want to see her one more time? And maybe we'd like to meet her too."

Dava inhaled sharply. How could she explain that, even with her death close at hand, she was unable to blend these two distinct parts of her life? The East Coast was her responsibilities, her colleagues, her children. The West Coast was Chaitanya, warm conversation, and laughter. It was a binary that had served Dava well, and it simply seemed inconceivable the two should ever join—as unthinkable as Clark Kent entering the same room as Superman. So Dava decided she wouldn't even try.

"Do you know why I named you Kali?"

"But what about—"

"In a moment, dear. First, answer my question."

"Because she's a badass Hindu goddess?" she said with a nervous smile. "And you wanted me to be strong and powerful like her?"

"When I was at Cambridge, one of the things I did was study Hindu mythology." Dava gazed out the window, where she could see the ocean churning as two seagulls looped back and forth overhead. "And I learned Kali the goddess was deeply misunderstood. What she represented was misinterpreted because of what she looked like: black skin, tongue sticking out, a garland of demon heads around her neck. But Kali isn't merely the goddess of sex and death. She had this duality about her: fearsome and mighty, yes, but also deeply compassionate. I read a description of her I'll never forget: 'She has a mother's incomprehensible love.'" With great effort, Dava turned her head toward Kali, and brushed away the sleep crust under her eye. "You have lived up to your namesake."

"Thank you, Amma," she said, blushing. Dava felt her daughter relax, melting like a pat of butter on a hot pan. Kali linked her arm through her mother's and tightly held her hand.

"I know the events of the past twenty-four hours have been a lot to bear for all of you," Dava continued, reorienting toward the window to ease the strain on her neck. "But I worry about you most. Even with your strength, you can also be sensitive. I want to make sure you're okay."

"I haven't wrapped my mind around your illness yet, or that you...you intend to leave us soon." Kali sniffled. "I wish we had more time. I wish you had let us know what you were planning so we could have had weeks together, not days."

"I know," Dava said, keeping her voice measured even as her eyes briefly betrayed her again, and all she could see was a blur of shadows and glass. "I know it's hard. I'm glad all you children will have each other after I'm gone. I just wish..." She let her voice fade off, as if she was troubled by something she was unsure that she should share.

"What is it, Amma?" Kali said, lifting her head to look at Dava.

"Even with your strength, I think at times you might be too generous with your heart."

Dava sensed Kali tense up again just as a pair of clouds blocked the sun, changing the light in the room to the color of cement. Kali slipped her arm out of her mother's, a movement that caused the blanket to fall on the floor.

"Mattius James," Dava murmured as her daughter bent down to retrieve it. "How much do you know about him?"

Kali bolted up at the mention of her boyfriend. "I know how he makes me feel," she said as she laid the blanket across her mother's lap again. "How both of them do."

"He has a record, Kali," Dava said gently. "He's been in prison and—"

"I know," Kali said, swinging her legs onto the sofa and sitting cross-legged so she could face her mother directly. "I know all about it. It wasn't prison. He was in juvie when he was a teenager on some trumped-up drug—"

"Not just juvie. Actual prison," Dava said, her voice taking on a harder edge. "He served a three-year sentence for being the driver when his friends robbed a convenience store."

"Okay, fine. I didn't know that," Kali said, close to tears. "But not everyone went to college, you know. He made some mistakes when he was a kid, but now he's this amazing carpenter—"

"He got out of prison a few years ago. He's still on probation. And he's dealing again. I've seen photos, Kali." Dava leaned back slightly, watching Kali's startled face as she processed this information. Interrupting the weighted silence was a sharp knock at the door. Both of them snapped, "Not now," without breaking eye contact, as if locked in a staring contest.

"Breakfast when you're ready," they heard Rev say, and then footsteps receded from the door.

"I had someone look into his background. Once you children get serious about a partner, I always have them investigated because the family needs to be protected. We can't take chances." The library brightened again as the clouds drifted past the sun. "I had this done with Vincent, Bhaskar, and Colin. Sandi too. When you said you wanted to bring Mattius here for Christmas, I realized how serious you were about him."

"Them!" Kali shouted, followed by a loud, fake cough, which Dava knew was her way of trying not to cry. "I wanted to bring them. I'm in a relationship with *them*. Why can't you accept that?"

Because it's absurd and immature and they are beneath you, Dava wanted to say. Instead, she plastered on a soothing smile and voice to match.

"I'm not bringing this up to hurt you, dear. I'm bringing this up because I don't want you to be hurt." The chatter from downstairs had progressively become louder, as if someone were incrementally dialing up the volume every few minutes. "Listen, Kali." Dava cupped her daughter's face with both hands. "You always look out for everyone else. Now look out for yourself. Protect your heart. Don't be dragged down by these people. He didn't tell you about this crime. Who knows what else he didn't tell you?"

Dava dropped her hands and rested them on her daughter's knees as Kali bowed her head. She could tell this information had been illuminating in some way, the key to unlocking a mystery Kali wasn't sure she wanted to solve. Dava eyed her intently and debated whether or not to push further before deciding to double down on Mattius's unsuitability.

"Oh, sweetheart," Dava said. "My death is going to bring great scrutiny to this family. It is already happening in ways I did not anticipate, like with Chaitanya. I don't want a scandal with this couple to overshadow your talents or impact this family during such a difficult time." She reached out her arms and wrapped Kali in a hug. After a beat, she spoke softly into her ear. "Now would be a good time to end things with them. You can call using Sita's phone."

Kali let out a deep sob, then nodded. Dava let the hug continue for a few moments longer before finally pulling away. She had one more piece of business with her daughter before meeting with Dr. Windsor, and so she put on a sympathetic smile and tenderly stroked Kali's cheek.

"You will get past this. We as women endure so much, and we always survive. I did, and you will too. And you'll be better for it." Dava stood up and moved to her desk, and Kali, red faced and sniffling, followed close behind. Dava reached into the top drawer and pulled out a sealed envelope and placed it in her daughter's palm.

"I wrote this to Chaitanya." Dava told her that soon after receiving her terminal diagnosis, she poured out all her feelings about their relationship. "But I never intended to share it with her or anyone else. It was an outlet for me to express everything I had gone through, because I never confided in anybody about the adoption. Until now, of course. I had planned on being buried with a few items, including this letter."

"And now you want me to send it to her?"

"No. I want you to read it. Share it with your siblings if you like. So you can understand what I went through to be who I am today. And then when I die, I am trusting you to return it and let this story be buried with me."

"So you don't want her to know the truth?" She stared at the envelope in awe, then back at Dava.

"No." Dava squeezed Kali's arm. As she walked her mother back to her bedroom, Dava asked Kali to have Dr. Windsor and

Sita come up to see her. Just as she crossed the room's threshold, Dava called out to her daughter.

"Promise me," she said, her voice unnaturally high and strained. "Promise that letter doesn't leave this house, and to return it to me when I die."

"I promise, Amma." Kali closed the door and leaned against it, letting out some final sobs, as if wringing a wet sponge of all remaining water.

CHAPTER NINE

Biggest Regret and Biggest Relief

Dear Chaitanya,

My biggest regret, and biggest relief, was not holding you after you were born. I knew if I held you, my life would change, and I would not get to accomplish all I was capable of achieving. And each time something important and lovely happened in my life thereafter, I knew it was right not to hold you. Because of that choice, I was able to make so many other choices.

As the years went on, I was able to compartmentalize the fact you existed, make it small and hide it away at the bottom of a drawer, and so when I arrived at major family milestones—the births of my children, their first steps and first words—there was no sadness, no thoughts of you, just pure, unmitigated joy.

Yet when I first met you, I held you for a very long time, surprising even myself. I am not big on hugs, even with my own children and grandchildren. But did you notice each time we greeted each other or said goodbye, it was with a hug?

All those accumulated seconds when you were in my arms almost made up for when I turned away from you that first time and told the nurse I did not want to hold you.

—*An excerpt from Dava's letter to Chaitanya,*
dated December 1, 2044

"SHE SAYS IT'S ALL HERE."

These are the words Kali exclaimed upon entering Sita's room, only to find her prostrate in bed, a cold compress over her eyes and the shades drawn against the bright morning sun. Even with her conversation with her mother still stinging her ears, Kali glowered with resentment at her sister's sleeping quarters.

If Kali wanted to go off on an Arvie-esque rant about their mother's custom-built floating mansion, all her ire would have been directed at the varying sizes of the guest rooms. Kali's "cozy room" was located near the kitchen, a narrow space that only fit a full-size mattress and a chest of drawers and had a single porthole-like window facing the boathouse. Sita's upstairs guest suite, by contrast, shared the outdoor deck with Dava's room and the library, and had been designed to impress: a bathroom and closet equal in size to the master bedroom, and expensive, hand-stitched green-and-gold bedding that matched the Persian rug. If any dignitaries or celebrities visited Beatrix Island, that was the room they would have been assigned, but only Sita and her family had ever occupied it. As the only other sibling with a spouse and children, Arvie could have contested her but preferred staying in the guesthouse. But now that it was taken by Dr. Windsor and her wife, Arvie's family took over Kali's usual downstairs guest room, bumping her to what felt like the servants' quarters. The room assignments were an all-too-vivid reminder of the Shastri-Perssons' order on the totem pole, made worse by the fact that even if there were no Sandi, she likely still would have been given the cozy room over Rev. But her annoyance at the luxuriousness of her sister's suite disappeared when Sita remained unresponsive to her greeting.

"Are you asleep?" Kali said, hurrying to her side to check on her. Sita was like her mother and rarely slept for more than four hours at a time or took naps. "Or feeling unwell?"

Sita removed the compress. "I'm feeling…everything. Overwhelmed, mostly." She patted the right side of the bed. "Come sit. I heard Amma asked to talk to you." She paused, then said, looking at the envelope in Kali's hand, "Wait. What's all here?"

"Amma's story. About Chaitanya." Kali nestled next to her older sister and pulled the gold-and-green down comforter over them until it reached their chins. She then shared what her mother said about the contents of the letter and what Dava had asked of her. Sita took the envelope in her hand, turning it over and over, and then handed it back to Kali.

"Wow. Amma really said she wants to be buried with it?"

"Yeah. So can you read it with me?" Kali asked in the same whiny-hopeful tone she often employed when they were teens to convince Sita to let her borrow her clothes.

"I can't." She sighed again and swept her hair up in a tight bun, giving Kali a whiff of her shampoo. It was strong, with lilac and something odd and slightly unpleasant, like a muted skunk's odor, and was no doubt eco-friendly and absurdly expensive. "I have so much to do."

As she watched her older sister pinch her cheeks to rouse herself, Kali was reminded of when she first realized her mother was a public figure, and the costs of that role. At age four, she began noticing how often strangers approached Dava at restaurants, grocery stores, and even Kali's preschool. Dava accepted all of these interactions with a steely grace, nodding politely before ending the conversation by giving them a business card with her assistant's contact information. One time, Dava had been cornered at Fairway by a woman clad in a red jumpsuit and an enormous Chanel belt buckle, demanding in a screechy voice that she "help save the polar bears." After they returned home, Dava had asked her children to go watch cartoons while she took a shower. As her brother and sister watched TV, Kali snuck away to peek at her mother through her half-closed bedroom door. She was lying stiffly on the bed, wearing only a towel and noise-canceling headphones, with her phone balanced on her chest. When it vibrated, Dava let out a soft stream of expletives, glared at her phone, then tossed it aside. She stayed there a few minutes longer, pinching her cheeks with a grim determination, before finally removing her headphones and getting dressed.

To see her sister emulate their mother in this way made Kali feel a mixture of sympathy and irritation. Sympathy because perpetual exhaustion seemed like a trait that Dava had passed down to Sita along with her wavy hair and petite frame. And irritation because just once Kali wished that Sita could ignore duty so they could rip open their mother's letter and discover all her secrets.

"All right," Kali said, then exhaled, trying to contain her disappointment. "Actually, that's the other reason I came to find you. Amma wants to meet with you and Dr. Windsor now." Kali glanced at the mirror on the opposite wall and noted they both looked tired and wild-eyed, like insomniac children.

"Okay," Sita said, sounding both nervous and resigned. "You should go have breakfast; Vincent made pancakes. I think there are some left. If not, there might be some oatmeal."

"What's everyone doing right now?" The house was eerily quiet, especially in contrast to the chatter agitating in the background during her conversation with her mother in the library.

"Colin took the boys out to play in the snow to give me some alone time. I don't know what anyone else is up to." Sita started to move off the bed, but Kali reached for her arm.

"Wait. Take a moment. You said you were overwhelmed.

Talk to me." In truth, Kali wanted to talk about what Dava had told her about Mattius and Lucy, but she needed to be a good listener before unloading her own worries on her sister.

"I don't know where to start." Sita thought for a moment and then turned to her sister. "Actually, I do. I can't stop thinking about what Amma said about her ex-boyfriend. You know, it must have been worse than what she told us. Never in my life would I think that would have happened to her."

"That's not realistic," Kali said. "She was just a teenager."

"I know." Sita wiped away sweat from her upper lip. "I always saw her like this superhero. And I didn't realize how mythically I had built her up in my head until I heard her talk about her own 'dream Indian boyfriend.'"

"So this is also about Bhaskar?" Kali tugged at her braid thoughtfully. "I didn't even think about how Amma had her own Bhaskar. Is that weird for you?"

"Bhaskar was imperfect and made me unhappy, but he wasn't vile like this guy sounded. But I ended up with him for the same reason Amma dated Panit, in some misguided sense a 'perfect on paper' Indian husband would equal happily ever after. It just surprises me we had that in common." Sita got out of bed and began rolling up her sons' Star Wars sleeping bags rumpled in the corner next to her Louis Vuitton suitcases. "I know you and Rev and Arvie think I'm Dava Shastri Junior—"

"That's not—"

"Don't deny it. I know." Sita stacked the bags in the closet, then unzipped her suitcase, digging to the bottom. "But I don't think me and Amma have much in common. Just because I work for her doesn't mean I see myself in her." She pulled out a sleek purple device that resembled an anteater and sat down cross-legged on the rug. "This is a back massager, by the way. Don't go telling Rev I showed you my vibrator."

"Ha ha, okay," Kali said with a smile, shaking her head. "And I don't tell Rev *everything*."

"Sure you do." Sita switched it on and pressed it against her neck and then between her shoulder blades. "That's just who you guys are. You're like twins born a few years apart."

"Well, Rev doesn't know about this." Kali waved the letter in the air. "I told you first."

"Only to summon me to see Amma. That doesn't count." Sita let out a low whistle as she moved the massager down to her lower back. "This cost me— Never mind. I won't say; you'll gag. But trust me: it was worth every penny."

"I didn't tell Rev what Amma said to me, though. In fact, I was only going to ask your advice." Kali threw off the covers, moved to the foot of the bed, and lay on her stomach, burying her bare feet under one of the pillows. "Amma wants me to dump Mattius and Lucy." When her sister noted that was hardly a surprise, Kali told her what Dava's background check on him had uncovered.

What she did not share with Sita was the flush of pained recognition after her mother's revelation. The weekend before coming to Beatrix Island, Kali had made a trip out to Poughkeepsie to celebrate an early Christmas with them. Upon her arrival, Mattius and Lucy had asked her to watch Jicama while they went Christmas shopping. When the little boy had begun complaining of stomach cramps after eating Christmas cookies, Kali feared he was having an allergy attack and called both of them, but neither picked up. When they finally returned close to dinnertime, they profusely apologized and blamed their lack of response on spotty reception. They had seemed frazzled at the time, glancing constantly at the door and each other as if they were worried they'd been followed. She didn't get a chance to speak to them about their strange behavior, because Jicama's symptoms turned out to be a severe food allergy that needed medical attention, and so she had departed quickly with a promise to see them again in the New Year. But even though she now understood that those events were tied to something troubling and she wanted no part of, the idea of cutting them out of her life pained her deeply. She missed how Mattius's intoxicating scent of wood shavings and musk would envelop her when he kissed her neck, and the way Lucy would intertwine her legs with hers as the three of them nuzzled in bed. To be the sole occupant of the creaky, uncomfortable bed in the cozy room only intensified her loneliness.

"I hate that she's right about them. But I wish she could have acknowledged them as my partners, like Colin or Sandi." Kali crossly kicked up one of her legs, and the pillow resting on her feet flopped to the floor. "I bet she loves Chaitanya's husband. I'm sure she found the dream Indian boyfriend."

"PhD in biochemistry, tenured professor at Berkeley, volunteers at an afterschool program," Sita rattled off. "So yes." When Kali looked at her with surprise, she replied, "I couldn't sleep last night after we all talked, so I spent a lot of time online."

"Is he cute? Like, on a scale of one to ten, he's a what?"

"A solid seven." She held out the massager to her sister. "Want to try?"

"So she really did find the perfect Indian guy. Figures." Kali got out of bed and joined her sister on the floor, letting Sita roll the massager up and down her back. The device was as amazing as promised, kneading into her tense muscles like soft, giant thumbs, but Kali couldn't relax. Because what Sita had just shared sent her into an emotional tailspin. While she was relieved, even heartened, that Sita also seemed intimidated by Chaitanya, the information Sita discovered only deepened Kali's sense of inferiority—with not one, but now two sisters.

"So what are you going to do about Mattius and Lucy?" Sita swung Kali's braid to the side and guided the massager over her left shoulder blade.

Kali bowed her head. "I . . . I'm supposed to break up with them today. And I need your phone to do it."

"But Amma told me not to share—"

"She's the one who told me to use your phone. That's how urgent she thinks it is." Kali took a beat and then added, "What do you think? Should I hear their side before making a snap decision? I love them, Sita. They're *my* Colin."

"I honestly don't know," she said sadly. The two fell silent and let the hum of the device fill the room. After a few moments, Sita turned it off and Kali looked at their reflection in the mirror again. This time, they no longer looked like children but themselves: confused and angry and weighed down by the complexities of their adult lives.

～

When Sita entered her mother's bedroom, Dr. Windsor was already seated at Dava's bedside, and the two were talking quietly as they sipped tea. She winced at the sight of her mother, so small and frail in her enormous bed, as if cast adrift in a sea of lavender. Sita swallowed hard, then forced herself to proceed inside.

"You must be Dr. Windsor. Nice to meet you," Sita said loudly in order to announce her arrival.

"Pleasure as well, Sita," said the doctor, who was wearing a light-blue jogging suit, as if she had just stopped in to visit her mother on the way to the gym. Sita was surprised Dr. Windsor seemed to be a few years older than her mother, with her gray buzz cut and lined face giving her the appearance of a grandmotherly soldier. They shook hands, and Sita sat down at the foot of her mother's bed. "Your mother and I were just discussing her end-of-life treatment."

"We have agreed on when to schedule it," Dava said tersely,

squinting at them through her smudged glasses. "Dr. Windsor will commence treatment tomorrow morning at ten."

"Is that okay?" Sita wasn't sure what to say. It was such an odd conversation, discussing when the doctor would end her mother's life.

"It's what she has requested," Dr. Windsor said, setting down her teacup. "I hope you don't mind my frankness, but your mother said I can speak candidly in front of you." She cleared her throat. "Before all of you arrived, she ceased taking her migraine medication." Her tone was neutral until speaking the final two words, which then hinted at concerned disapproval.

"It made me foggy," Dava replied with an edge of stubbornness. "I want to be clear minded until the end."

"Yes, Mrs. Shastri, of course." The doctor nodded at Sita. "I've given instructions to Victor—"

"Vincent," Dava and Sita said in unison.

"Yes, Vincent, right. I've told him how he can prepare an herbal tea to help with your mother's pain. She has been experiencing migraines of varying intensity, as well as dizzy spells. And she's also beginning to have vision problems." The doctor lowered her voice. "Without medication, her condition will only worsen to a grave degree. So the timing of tomorrow, it really is for the best."

"Oh," Sita said. All the tension returned to her body, as if she were gripped in a vise. She glanced at her mother, who was unfazed by her doctor's words and was instead focused on cleaning her glasses with her pajama sleeve. She then abruptly looked up and stared at her daughter so intensely Sita had a brief flashback to when her mother had discovered her making out with her boyfriend Milo in the hospital chapel, while her father was undergoing what turned out to be his final chemotherapy treatment. After Milo had scampered away, a T-shirt only half covering his back, Dava had stared at her with an expression

Sita found impossible to read but that made her cower. Dava had wordlessly beckoned her daughter to follow her out of the chapel, then walked away without saying a word. Just as Sita was about to stand up from the pew, she heard her mother call out, "Light a candle before you leave." And Sita, tears streaming down her face, had dutifully done so before rejoining her family in the waiting room.

After the doctor left, Sita took her chair by her mother's bed, the cushion still warm. They must have spoken for a very long time, she mused. Then she turned to face her mother, who had put her glasses back on but was still gazing at her with that inscrutable, intense expression.

"Amma, what is it?" she said with alarm.

"Nothing, dear. It's just I'm finding it hard to see you," Dava said, her voice unsteady. "I find if I concentrate and stare like this, I can make out your features better."

"Oh my God. I'm so sorry. What can I do?"

Dava shook her head. "There's nothing you can do. Like Dr. Windsor said, my eyesight is failing me. But I still have my mind." She tapped both of her temples with two fingers, as if sending Morse code. "A mind is a terrible thing to waste." Dava looked at her daughter knowingly, as if this were a private joke the two shared.

Sita nodded numbly. She longed to lay her head on her mother's lap and sob until her tears turned the lavender bedspread a dark, mirthless purple. But there was simply too much to do. Sita pulled her notepad out of her pocket and rapped it with a pen as if it were a gavel.

"Amma, Kali said you wanted to be buried with...well, buried. But you always told me you wanted to be cremated."

Dava didn't answer and instead transferred her fervent gaze to something behind her daughter. Sita briefly turned around to see that it was a painting of her and her siblings, the one that caught her in a gawky preadolescent phase, with bushy eyebrows and a bowl haircut.

"Amma," she began again gently, "I know it's not pleasant to think about, but there's so much we need to discuss between now and tomorrow. I want to make sure I follow your final wishes." Dava turned toward her daughter with a start. At last, Sita had said something that caught her attention. "Okay, so what would you—"

"Your grandparents—your dad's parents—died in a car accident when he was thirteen," Dava interrupted. "You know that, right?"

"Yes, I do. Amma, listen—"

"They died because of a teenager named Jorgen." Sita was taken aback, not just by her mother's words, but by how her tone had changed. She now sounded feverish, agitated. "He was homeless because his father was abusing him, and he said he would rather live in his car than stay a second longer in that house. But he still had two younger brothers who lived there, and so he would secretly come over at night to visit them after a long day's work at a manufacturing plant of some kind—I don't remember what. He was working long hours because he wanted to afford an apartment where he and his brothers could live together." Dava furrowed her brow. "Was the mother living with them too?" she said to herself. "I don't remember. Anyway.

"After a twelve-hour shift at the factory, he was driving back to go visit his brothers, hoping he could see them before their bedtime. Jorgen had all his clothes in a duffel bag in the passenger seat and was exhausted from a long day at work. He had just pulled into his neighborhood when he drifted off for a second, and then when he woke up, he braked hard, and the duffel bag flew up and hit the windshield, blocking his view. And if the duffel bag hadn't obscured his view, he would have seen he was driving in the wrong lane and would have swerved to avoid the car driving toward him. Your grandparents were in that car." Dava paused, and then when she resumed speaking, she sounded like her normal self. "Do you know why I know this?"

"Why?" Sita's notepad dropped from her lap.

"Because Jorgen gave a TV interview about the accident. Your dad showed it to me."

Dava explained the teenager became a minor news sensation in Sweden when he gave an emotional interview after he had been sentenced to five years for vehicular homicide. Jorgen said if a single person had listened to him about the abuse he and his siblings were enduring, then he would not have been forced to leave home and work long hours to try to secure a safe place for all of them to live.

"He said if one person had helped him, his life would have been different, and the whole tragedy would have been averted." Dava sighed. "Your father was haunted by this interview. The domino effect. How one life can affect another in ways we might not even understand." Seeing her daughter's confused but stricken face, she groaned. "You think I'm rambling. I'm telling you this for a reason, Sita." Dava beckoned her daughter to move closer.

"My philanthropy work, and his work as an educator, was always about the Jorgens of the world. That was our touchstone. Each time we came across someone in need—either an individual, like one of his students, or an organization—we thought about what kind of good could be done if we got involved. And we'd think of the positive domino effect that could happen. By helping Person A, we'd be helping Person B, or maybe a whole family, or a community." Dava reached out to

Sita, and the two held hands. "And I'm telling you this because as the next CEO of the Dava Shastri Foundation, I'm entrusting you to continue my vision and your father's."

"CEO?" Sita tilted so far in her chair she nearly fell backward. "We...I..."

"Surely you knew this was the plan?" Dava raised an eyebrow and smiled.

"No." Sita's armpits tickled with sweat. "The plan is for the board to vote on who should replace you. And I think most of them will choose Vash. I know I planned to."

"I love Vash. She is wonderful," Dava responded grandly, invoking her boardroom voice. "But she's not me. Nor is she you. You are a Shastri." She paused, then added with an affectionate emphasis, "Sita Shastri."

Dava fixed Sita with a proud gaze. "When I had Chaitanya, there was a doctor who helped me through it, both before and after I gave birth. She was lovely; I often thought of her as a guardian angel. I wouldn't have survived the experience without her." Another pause, another knowing smile. "Her name was Sita."

Sita absorbed this revelation through her entire being, like a full-body tremor. She had never admitted it to anyone, not even Colin, but she had always been jealous that Arvie's name had been chosen with deliberation and care, while she had merely been named after the most famous and long-suffering spouse in Indian mythology. To know her namesake was an important figure from her mother's past floored her. Sita was so awed by this information she initially didn't realize her mother was still talking.

"...and after the debacle in the press with Chaitanya, plus the gossip over that song, I realize you're the only one I can trust to right the ship. If this gossip continues, the foundation will suffer."

And there it is. Sita slumped back down in her seat. How foolish to believe her mother shared this story without ulterior motives. That it had just been a tender moment purely between them, something her mother had longed to tell her and finally could. But Dava Shastri rarely shared a piece of herself without wanting something in return. This divulgence was meant to butter Sita up so she would feel compelled to acquiesce to her mother's final wishes. In relation to her foundation. Always her foundation.

Before this moment, Sita rarely dwelled on how Dava had been a hybrid of boss and parent for her entire adult life, simply because she hadn't known anything different. But now she wished their relationship could exist outside of her mother's ambitions, so she didn't have to feel like the gift of knowing her true namesake was also about maneuvering Sita like a pawn on a chessboard.

"I want you to announce you're taking over as CEO immediately," Dava continued. "That we had a conversation on my deathbed in which I had entrusted you with my foundation, and you were shocked by the stories that have come out after my death and are determined to defend your mother's honor. And so, you're starting a...um...starting some sort of grant in my name that will...I don't know. But something amazing. Something that will get people talking. I know: we're stopping the Medici grants and redirecting the money to women journalists who are on the side of truth. That's how insulted you are by this gossip and invasion into my privacy.

"Also"—and here Dava bolted up in bed, her voice taking on a strident tone—"I want you to look into buying the company that owns *The Takeover*. I looked up the net worth—it's only a few million. I want you to buy it and then dismantle it." She said this last part with glee, and her lips twitched in an unnatural way, making Sita wonder if her mother was beginning to lose her sanity.

"Amma," she said shakily, "you know there's no real way to change everyone's interest in your personal life. The immediate narrative can't be changed, but in time, we'll all work hard to—"

"It will mean less time with your family," Dava said, interrupting her.

"What?"

"Taking over the foundation. But it will be a worthwhile and worthy sacrifice." She leaned over until her hand connected with Sita's face and pinched her cheek. "You'll see."

CHAPTER TEN

Divine Radiance or Consciousness or Life or Knowledge

Chaitanya generally means Divine radiance or Consciousness or Life or Knowledge, is of Indian origin... [and] is a Unisex name, which means both Boy and Girl can have this name.

—*From IndiaChildNames.com*

DAVA FEIGNED A YAWN, then two more, as she responded to Sita's seemingly endless list of questions. When her daughter flipped to a new page on her notepad, she had to say the words "I'm tired, dear" before her daughter finally got the hint and left, urging her to get some rest. After Sita departed, Dava retrieved her tablet from under her pillow so she could complete watching the *90 Seconds* video about her life story, something she had been itching to do since her children had descended on her demanding answers about Chaitanya. She clicked Play and was unimpressed by all of it: the generic upbeat pop score, the unflattering photos emphasizing her squat height, and most of all, the narration, which lauded her as a "visionary" and "feminist philanthropist" but also threw in descriptors such as "buxom," "controversial," and "alleged muse."

Distressed that Chaitanya had seen her portrayed in such a vapid manner, Dava became more upset when she realized the clip had more than eight hundred thousand views, and she worried about what else was being said about her. The top search results for "Dava Shastri" didn't assuage her anxiety:

"Dava Shastri Dead at 70: A Timeline of Her Alleged Love Affair with Tom Buck"

"Dava Shastri's Alleged Secret Love Child: Everything We Know So Far"

"Industry Insiders Reflect on Dava Shastri's Pop Music Legacy: Medici Artists, MobileSong, and Yes, Tom Buck"

"'She Was Our Champion': 10 Women on How the Dava Shastri Foundation Changed Their Lives"

"'Dava,' 'Layla,' and 'Sara Smile': The Best Songs About Rock Star Romances"

There was only one positive article, and a second one that, if Dava was being honest with herself, would probably give her mixed reviews at best. As she scanned the headlines, she regretted never writing her memoir. She had been approached to do so several times, and while the prospect had intrigued her, Dava could never commit because she was reluctant to revisit her past in minute detail. Still, she always thought she would get around to writing her life story one day. But there was never any time, so she never did. And now a hundred breathless reporters were taking on the task for her.

Dava let out a stream of curses as she closed the device, anguished over the search results and frustrated that her vision was spinning again, this time accompanied by a flash of lightning behind her eyeballs. She felt almost physically pained to think that her name was rapidly becoming synonymous with sex, secrets, and scandal. That when a single mother in Fort Wayne or a college student at Princeton or a city councilman in Richmond thought of Dava Shastri, if they thought of her at all, it would be as the inspiration to that song.

She twisted her wedding ring on her finger and brooded over the unfairness of it all, convinced that a man with her accomplishments and wealth would not have his legacy eradicated in this way. *No matter what a woman achieves, she is always reduced to her sex life*, she thought as she covered her head with her pillow, sinking her face into its soft darkness. So her dream began in darkness too, an enveloping, black liquidity that surrounded her on all sides, as if she were floating in ink.

"You're right; there are no words," Dava heard a voice say. She looked to her right and saw Chaitanya standing next to her. They were standing on a vast platform, a thick bubble of glass overhead, and Earth, a spherical swirl of blue and green and white, in front of them.

A few years earlier, Dava had become the fifty-third person to travel into space as a civilian. She had purchased her seat on the *SpaceNautica* for an exorbitant sum, a price affording her a one-week ride on a luxury spacecraft orbiting Earth. A few days after she returned, she had visited Chaitanya to show her all five hundred photographs she had taken of her trip. As she scrolled through them, Dava noticed even as Chaitanya expressed delight at each picture, she seemed far away, her manner distant and thoughtful. Upon reaching the final photo, Chaitanya told her she hoped one day regular people could afford to take the journey too. When she saw Dava's chastened expression, she apologized and told her she had not meant to make her feel guilty to have had such a wondrous opportunity. The visit was one of the only times their vast income differences had become awkward for them. So, once she understood she was dreaming,

Dava thought it made sense that if she was going to reunite with her daughter, it would be on the rocket's observation deck to share this singular experience.

"I think if heaven exists, it must be like this," Dava said, tenderly stroking Chaitanya's cheek. "At least, I hope so. I'll find out soon enough."

"I'd like to think so." Chaitanya hugged her. "How are you doing?"

"I've been better. Have you read the news today?"

"Oh boy," Chaitanya laughed, finishing the Beatles lyric.

"Do you think less of me?" Dava looked away from her toward Earth, where she could make out the outlines of South America under a fuzz of clouds.

"Never," she replied gently. "I was thinking about your problem. And you know, pop culture always wins the conversation."

Dava jerked her head. "Where is that from? That sounds so familiar."

"I think you heard someone say that once. Maybe it's a telegram from your subconscious. Like me." She put her finger on the glass and traced the outline of the planet. "But to me, that quote means fight fire with fire. Because you know better than anyone the power of a perfect song. It can be hard to overcome. But it's not impossible."

Dava put her hand on the glass, too, and covered Central America with her thumb, something she had done often when she was actually on the spacecraft, winking out the existence of Iceland, India, and Japan with a single touch of the glass. "But those headlines," she sighed. "That song is erasing me. All the good I've done, and no one cares."

"Because it's much easier to connect with a star-crossed romance than the fact you helped thousands of people. They're faceless—they're abstract notions. And Tom Buck is, well...very attractive," she said in a teasing voice. "It's just a compelling story. So you need to craft your own compelling story." Chaitanya turned toward Dava and put her hands on her shoulders. "So, use me."

Dava shook her head. "I don't understand."

"Tell your story. How giving up your daughter instilled the desire to champion and protect every daughter on Earth. Or something like that, but less cheesy." When she saw Dava look away in shame, she grinned. "Even if that's not entirely true. Who needs to know?"

"So, you think I should have my own song?"

"Not at all," Chaitanya said, turning back to look at the view. "Think bigger. Much bigger."

As the rocket drifted past the Western Hemisphere, Dava ducked her head to avoid looking at the sun, which had started looming over Earth like a nosy relative. Then she remembered she was in a dream, where her eyesight was not failing her, nor would it be damaged by the sun's rays, and looked straight at it. The act of staring directly into its overwhelming light awakened her to what her daughter was suggesting.

"A movie," she said slowly. She considered the idea for a few moments, then asked, "Do you think a biopic would be better? Or a documentary?"

"Documentaries don't win Oscars for best picture," Chaitanya noted wryly.

"Very true." They both laughed, and Dava was flooded with happiness to be in her daughter's presence again. *I feel like flying*, Dava thought to herself, and just like that, the two were floating off the ground. Dava exulted in seeing Chaitanya experience zero gravity for the first time, observing her tumble and spin like a mother watching her child take her first steps. As Chaitanya zipped around her, Dava contemplated her advice.

"I need a movie that will present me as Eleanor Roosevelt or

Marie Curie," she told her daughter, her voice gradually rising in excitement. "Historical figures whose achievements drown out the noise of their personal lives." The continent of Asia started to come into view behind Chaitanya, and Dava could make out India under a whispery gold haze. "I remember my parents hated the biopic about Gandhi, because they said the beatific, sainted image of him erased how complicated he had been. He was no longer a man, just a symbol. A legend."

"So that's one idea." Chaitanya had abruptly stopped floating. Dava tried to drop to the ground, too, but remained fixed in the air. "The other is to merely accept that the media's current fixation on me and Tom Buck doesn't undo all the lives you changed." The sun became brighter as the spacecraft continued to circle westward, flooding the observation deck with intense light. "And if your foundation continues its mission, your story lives on in every woman who gets to make a choice to live the life she wants, just as you did." Dava was alarmed when she realized Chaitanya was getting swallowed up in the light, almost as if she were on fire.

"Wait," she called out. "Wait—don't go yet. There's so much more to see."

"It hurts too much to stay," Chaitanya said. And then Dava was awake, the blankets sweaty and her eyes throbbing as she called out for her eldest child, only to see her youngest anxiously hovered over her instead.

~

She's fighting the mirror
And she needs her space
Even from me, always from me
The sun's broken on the water
And we both know what that means

Yet her hand's still in mine
So right now, that's enough

"What does 'fighting the mirror' mean?" Theo asked Enzo as the two watched Tom Buck's music video for "Dava" on Enzo's tablet in the den. They had been out sledding with their dad for most of the morning and were hanging out downstairs while waiting to be called to the kitchen for lunch. When they plopped down on the couch, Enzo noticed that his tablet, which he had left in his parents' room, was jammed in between the cushions. When he had turned it on, the music video was open on the browser, and so they both sat down to watch it.

"I'm not sure," Enzo said as they watched the tall, scruffy man with the blue guitar strum passionately as a series of black-and-white images—a woman's eyes, her hands, her body in silhouette—were projected behind him. "I think it's some sort of poetry thing."

He noticed another tab in the browser titled "Dava Shastri over the years." When he clicked over, Enzo was surprised to see dozens of images of his grandmother taken several decades ago, in which she closely resembled his own mother. But Gamma had a looser energy, favoring fancier dresses, brighter lipstick, and much higher heels. All of the photographs were either snapped at charity galas or red-carpet events, with Enzo's grandfather by her side. The one exception was a picture that featured a very young Dava dwarfed by two tall blond women in white leather corsets and black jeans ripped at the knees, the trio gleefully sticking their tongues out at the camera. She didn't look like the stern grandmother he knew at all and seemed to have beamed in from an alternate universe. Stunned and slightly bewildered, Enzo returned to the music video.

"Hey, we were using that," the twins heard Priya say behind

them, as she and Klara came downstairs, each holding paper cups filled with popcorn. "Give it back."

"It's mine," Enzo said, holding it to his small chest. "Gamma gave it to me."

"Well, we're using it now," Priya said, sniffing. "Right, Klara?"

Klara set down her popcorn on the coffee table, then put one hand on her hip and stretched out the other expectantly toward them. "Hand it over," she said. Theo and Enzo looked at each other, and Theo shrugged. Enzo said he would give it to them, but only if she would let them all watch the video together.

"Oh, we've already seen that," she said, yanking it from his grasp. "Look, Enz, I'll give it back to you in a little bit, okay? Me and Priya are in the middle of something."

"What?" Enzo said suspiciously, while Theo hopped off the sofa to play "Three Blind Mice" on the piano.

"Just research. About Gamma." Priya and Klara settled on the couch, squeezing Enzo out so he was forced to sit on the floor at their feet.

"Any research you do, you should take notes so I can share with Gamma."

The girls rolled their eyes. "She doesn't want notes on what we're looking up—trust me," Klara said as her younger sister nodded. Theo continued playing "Three Blind Mice" with increasing speed, his fingers tripping and hitting the wrong note again and again.

"Can you not?" Priya whined at him. Theo abruptly stopped, then banged both hands on the keys and shouted, "Boom! Scared ya," before racing upstairs.

"He's a nut," Klara said, shaking her head. Priya let out a dramatic sigh and gave Enzo the stink eye, then urged him to follow his brother.

"Let him be, Pri," Klara said, crossing her legs. "If he wants to stay, whatever."

"What are you looking up?" he asked, sneaking a handful of popcorn from Priya's cup.

Klara said they wanted to "get the dirt" on Tom Buck, because they couldn't imagine their grandmother had secretly dated him, and wanted to figure out if the gossip was true. Priya nodded along with big, dreamy eyes and then said with a romantic sigh, "I wonder what he looks like now. Do you think he's still just as hot but, like, more wrinkly?"

"You know he's dead, right?" Enzo said, giving her an incredulous look. "He died a long time ago."

"Oh," Priya said with embarrassment. After a few moments, she asked Klara if they could watch the "Dava" music video again.

"Later," she snapped. "You've already watched it, like, ten times." Priya blushed and grabbed two handfuls of popcorn, some of which fell on Enzo's head. Klara told them she wanted to find gossip about his love life, and an online search showed he had been linked to several singers and actresses before and after he released "Dava."

"Wow, he dated so many blondes," Priya said. "They all kinda look like models. Nothing like Gamma."

"He married one of them," Enzo piped up. "She's on a TV show Amma and Papai watch. The one with the detectives who solve crimes and stuff. She's the wife of one of the detectives."

"That really narrows it down," Priya said, her foot knocking ungently against Enzo's back. He stood up and glared at her, then grabbed another fistful of popcorn and positioned himself behind the couch so he could see the screen.

"That one," he said, pointing at a brunette woman in a graphic titled "The Many Loves of Tom Buck," which depicted his face at the center of a bull's-eye encircled by the faces of fifteen women with different colored lines connecting him to each one. "Marie Antony. They were only married a year though."

"Look, there's Gamma," Priya said, pointing at one of the only two nonwhite faces in the graphic. "Her line is pink, though, which means"—she squinted at the fine print at the bottom—"rumored relationship."

"Wait—how do you know who Tom was married to?" Klara turned around to ask Enzo.

He shrugged. "I'm still collecting every article mentioning Gamma, like she asked. Some of them have stuff about him too. He and Marie had a son, and he's a few years younger than Rev uncle."

"Oh wow," Klara said. "Hope he's as hot as his dad. Show me."

Enzo took the tablet from his cousin, scrolled through his list of links, and clicked the one he had added right before he went out sledding. Before handing it back to Klara, he hesitated.

"Just promise me you won't mention this to Gamma, at least not until I talk to my mom."

Klara eagerly grabbed back the device and let out a "whoa" at the headline. A few moments later, her mouth dropped open in shock. "Holy shit, holy shit, holy shit," she said gleefully, handing the tablet to her sister. Priya piled on the gasps and "wows," trying to one-up her sister's reaction.

"Don't say anything to anyone, okay?" Enzo begged, hopping from one foot to the other. "I think we should keep it quiet." In response, Priya read the headline in a purposefully booming voice: "Tom Buck's Son Claims Long-Lost Lyrics Confirm His Father's Romance with Dava Shastri."

"What?" Kali shrieked behind them. "What did you say?"

~

As the latest revelation about Tom Buck slowly traveled and reverberated throughout the house, Rev sat at his mother's bedside, watching her gulp down a glass of water. Seeing his face still convulsed with worry, she gave him an encouraging smile.

"All better, sweetheart," she said. "I had a bad dream—that's all." Rev nodded, but his Adam's apple bobbed up and down as he swallowed nervously.

"What is it, Rev?" she asked, relieved in that moment her vision was on its best behavior and she could clearly see her handsome son. Even as he radiated a jittery energy and was clad in a simple gray T-shirt and dark jeans, to her eyes he was magnificent, as if he had been carved out of marble. If Arvid had survived to see their son grow of age, Dava imagined they would have had a private joke about whether Rev inherited his good looks from his father or mother.

"Well . . . you're dying," he said, his hands strumming on his lap, just as he used to do when he was a toddler waiting in his high chair to be fed.

"Yes, that's true," she said. "But that's not why you're here." She was always able to read Rev's moods better than those of her older children.

"No, it's not." Rev sighed and climbed into bed to sit next to Dava. She reached out her hand and he took hold of it. "I'm here because of Sandi."

"Oh," Dava said. Then, after a beat, "What of her, dear?"

"I brought her here so you could get to know her better. I want you to know the woman who's going to be my wife and the mother of my child. I wanted you to be able to meet our baby too," he added, choking up.

"I'm so sorry," Dava said, stroking his hair, her eyes welling with tears. She couldn't let herself dwell on the soul-incinerating pain of never knowing her grandchild. If she had known of Sandi's pregnancy earlier, Dava might have delayed her end-of-life plan. If news of her death hadn't already been made public, perhaps she would have even pursued treatments to prolong her life. There was a dark, shameful part of her that wanted to blame Sandi for this misfortune, but really it was just the cruelty of fate. To learn her youngest was going to have a baby of his own after she was gone could break her if she let it. So she couldn't let it.

"All we can do is be grateful I have a chance to say goodbye to all of you right now," she said gently, attempting to console him and herself. But Rev still looked forlorn, unbearably so, and she knew he had not expressed his true concerns. "What else, love?"

Rev's shoulders drooped, and he began to sniffle. "I'm scared, Amma. I don't know how to do this."

"Tell me," Dava said, keeping her voice tender, "are you marrying Sandi because she's pregnant?"

Maybe, he wanted to say. "Not at all" is what he told his mother. "I love her in ways I didn't know possible. And she's trustworthy," he added emphatically. In truth, one of the reasons he wanted to speak privately with Dava was because Kali had taken him aside after breakfast and told him about what their mother had disclosed about Mattius and Lucy, and that she had private investigators look into all the Shastri-Persson significant others, including Sandi.

"Don't be surprised if Amma asks for Sandi to give a blood oath swearing to keep silent about everything that's happened here," Kali said, stabbing at the air with a cigarette. "Or at least sign a nondisclosure agreement." But when Rev had seen his mother flailing in bed, crying out as if she was in physical pain, he was rocked by the idea he was soon to lose the only parent he had ever really known. And that made him feel gutted, alone, and frightened for the future.

His gaze traveled to the window, and he looked out at a grove of pine trees standing at attention as snow drifted from their needles in soft waves. When he started speaking again, his eyes remained fixed on the trees.

"I know you had a happy marriage with Dad. But I didn't really know him. Or even remember him all that well. Don't get upset"—he said this as he saw his mother tense up out of the corner of his eye—"I have some nice memories of him. But you basically raised me as a single mom. And you were a great mom. I feel like I had a different experience with you than Sita and Arvie did, because you were at home with me a lot. I didn't ever tell you I appreciated that, did I?" His voice cracked and faltered. "Well, I did.

"Kali likes to say there are two versions of you: Workaholic Amma and Working Amma," he continued, looking at her now. "Kali said she was lucky to experience both: she got to see you and Dad together but said the downside was you seemed stressed and tired and weren't always around. And then after he died, you were home much more, picking us up from school and eating pizza for dinner while we played UNO." Dava nodded, remembering how in the years after her husband's death, she gradually decreased her office hours so by the time Sita and Arvie were in college, she was working from home three times a week, a schedule she maintained until Rev began junior high seven years later. "But the three of them remember having a dad—and saw him be a husband. And I can't help thinking I won't know how to be either one, because I didn't have that."

He hesitated, desperate to share what else was on his mind. Rev had a central thought that ruled his life, which he never felt brave enough to articulate to anyone, not even Kali: nothing mattered. An undercurrent of unrest and global tragedy ran through his formative years, beginning with, but not limited to, his father's illness and death. He came of age during a time when "democracy dies in darkness," "defund the police," and "save the environment, save the world" were the prevailing outcries, as each day brought new headlines of casual evil and destruction. Yet his looks, coupled with his family's wealth, made life shockingly easy; he could have anything or anyone he wanted, which made him want nothing at all. By the time he reached adulthood, a bone-deep existential malaise lived inside him like an imaginary friend he never outgrew. And once he graduated from college, Rev decided to no longer pretend he was a person with ambition or focus. He would coast for as long as he lived, or until the planet imploded, whichever came first.

Then he met Sandi. Before her, Rev never had a relationship last longer than a month. But when they went out for drinks after closing on his condo, he could see the words *He's too pretty for me* in a thought bubble over her head as he charmed her with stories of his hapless modeling career. Seeing the inner conflict play out so plainly in her eyes, the way her leg brushed against him and then pulled away with a jolt, kindled a spark of desire in him, and he set out to conquer her defenses.

The hardest work Rev ever did in his life was beguile Sandi into thinking he was a catch. Maybe he had worked too hard, because within six months of meeting her, he was a soon-to-be husband and father. But for a while, he actually liked that he had these new roles to play, tethering him to the world at last. Yet every new adult decision—*We need to set a date; we should move to a bigger place before the baby arrives*—reawakened the darkness inside him, taunting he was incapable of domesticity. And while he had been grateful for Sandi's existence upon hearing his mother's shattering news, his hope his fiancée would help him bear his grief had been stymied by her obsession with Dava's will. *What about me?* was the thought bubble over his head throughout his time at Beatrix Island, but so far no one had noticed.

"I understand your fears, sweetheart." Dava leaned against her son, combating a wave of dizziness by squeezing her eyes shut. "I had no idea how to be a single mother, especially since your father was often the primary parent. He cleaned up your messes, handled the tantrums. And then he was gone and I was alone and you were so small. I was terrified to know I would be raising you alone. But what would center me is . . . you. And the specific love you were born from."

With her eyes still closed, Dava lifted a powder-blue tissue from the Kleenex box at her bedside table and placed it in Rev's hands. Then she took another one and crushed it inside her fist. "You know our story, right? How your father didn't propose to me, but we decided together before we left Argentina we wanted to marry?"

She heard him blow his nose. "Yeah. You camped on a cliff and talked all night."

"We did. And we also listened to an album called *Deserter's Songs* the entire time, for as long as the batteries would last on his Discman, then my Discman," she said wistfully. She recalled how the music—symphonic and magical, majestic and odd— had made the night seem even more otherworldly, as if they were the only two left in the world to watch the sun flood the sky with pinks and oranges as it set and then awaken the darkness into morning again.

"That album meant the world to us. It accompanied the most special night of our lives. In fact, it was so special to us we decided to never listen to it again. We wanted the memory to hold and the music to remain the soundtrack to that incredible view we witnessed together."

"I didn't know that," Rev said.

"Nobody does. It's something we kept to ourselves," Dava said, opening her eyes as the dizziness passed. "And it's the reason we gave you your name. Mercury Rev is the name of the band who made that album. Revanta was your father's idea. He knew—"

"Rev would be my nickname." Rev sat up in amazement. "Oh wow."

She nodded. "When you were born, he was in remission. It would be another year before we learned the cancer had returned. But I think your father knew by then his time was limited. So it was his gift to me. That our sweet little boy would be an enduring reminder of that beautiful night we shared." She dabbed her eyes with the crumpled tissue. "And it worked. After he died, each time someone said your name, or I said it myself, I felt this small jolt of joy. It helped me keep going." Dava rested her hand on her son's arm. "I didn't know how to be a single parent, but I muddled through and figured it out. You and Sandi will too."

"She keeps saying the same thing," Rev said slowly. "That it's all trial and error. But I know she's as lost as I am. Her parents divorced when she was two, and her mom—"

"So you'll muddle through together," Dava interrupted, trying to keep her irritation out of her voice. Why was her youngest so insecure? Why so many excuses? "Don't forget Sita and Arvie can help you out too. They've both been in your shoes. All of you have each other." Dava had a sudden flash from her dream, a quick moment in which she saw Chaitanya glowing on the observation deck, and remembered what she had advised. She observed Rev and noticed his chin quivering in the same way it did when he was a little boy and was about to erupt into a full-on meltdown. She couldn't decide whether to comfort him or insist he toughen up.

For Rev's part, the reference to his siblings being parents reminded him about Sandi's insistence on asking whether a trust would be created for their child. "Amma, I need to ask you something," he said, his voice so low it was nearly inaudible. "I need to—"

"What are you doing now, Rev?" she asked, looking at him

intently. "In terms of your day-to-day, what are you working on?"

"Well, there's Helping Perssons," he said defensively.

"Yes, but that only takes up two or three days of your time per month. What else?"

Rev turned away from her in embarrassment. "I'm kinda figuring a lot of things out right now. Personally and professionally."

"Then you have time to do something important. Something for me." Of course it should be Rev, her son with the movie star looks. "I have a project I want you to spearhead. And I need you to start right away."

CHAPTER ELEVEN

But You Never Dance With Me

I'm holding gold
But I might as well be holding shit
Because you're in that ruby dress
The sun glows at your feet
And your eyes are dancing
But you never dance with me

He discovered these lyrics in one of his father's notebooks and claimed Buck Sr.'s ticket to the 2013 Grammy Awards was tucked between the pages.

—Excerpt from "Tom Buck's Son Claims Long-Lost Lyrics
Confirm His Father's Romance with Dava Shastri,"
Musicala.com, *published December 27, 2044*

REV STARED AT DAVA. His light-brown eyes squinted, as if he hadn't heard correctly. As if his old, dying mother had also started going senile.

"A movie." He stood up and bumped into the bedside table. "A movie?"

"My story needs to be told and told properly." Dava leaned toward him, and in doing so, the bedroom leaned with her, as if she were riding over rough waters on a cruise ship. "Didn't you take a screenwriting class in college?"

"I dropped out midsemester." Rev's face glowed red, and a trickle of sweat fled past his temple. "I'm not qualified, Amma."

"Of course you are. You just haven't tapped into your potential yet. This will be good for you." Now Rev seemed to be leaning too. Dava frowned. She carefully reclined back against the raft of pillows amassed behind her, but the vertiginous sensation only increased.

"I'm about to be a dad." Rev sounded whiny and far away. "Maybe ask Kali? Or . . . well, anyone else?"

"It has to be you," she said, keeping her voice firm even as she began to understand that something was very wrong. Her arms and legs no longer belonged to her. It was as if Dava were trying to be the puppeteer for her own body, but the strings that controlled her limbs were hopelessly tangled. She tried wiggling her fingers, then her toes. Frozen.

"Are you feeling okay?" Rev peered at her as if she had just sprouted a second head. Dava's lips pursed.

"Of course!" Dava roared at him, glad that her voice still bent to her will. Whatever was happening was going to claim her soon. So she ignored her son's agitated expression and let the words pour out of her like an untended faucet.

⌒

"The movie should focus on my charity work with the foundation, I want to be seen as someone motivated to look out for all the world's daughters after I was forced to give up my own, ask Sita for a list of my colleagues to interview, ask Kali for the letter I wrote to Chaitanya, maybe that actress in the teacher's strike movie should play me, ask Doug to reach out to his contacts to see if they'd be interested, but after you write the script, of course, yes, that means I want Chaitanya acknowledged as my daughter, but maybe wait to reveal this until a studio green-lights it so the story will make a bigger splash, just retake a screenwriting class, you're so smart and it shouldn't be hard for you, this would mean the world to me if you could do this, you know what, you should form your own production company and produce it, that will give you something to focus on, you'll be able to balance this while raising your child, people work and have kids all the time, Rev..."

And then her tongue dulled even as her mind continued to race. She couldn't move. She couldn't even blink. Helplessly, she watched Rev repeatedly call out to her before running out of the room. She struggled to close her eyes and speak out loud. *Is this it? This might be it.* She tried to quell the rising swell of panic by reasoning the upside of death was an afterlife in which she would see Arvid again. Except there was a sourness even to this silver lining.

Dava did not know, and would never learn, about the article in which Tom Buck's son Indigo theorized to a reporter that his father's scrapped lyrics proved the two had an affair. But each time she reckoned with her mortality, her thoughts would eventually turn toward Tom Buck. Because if heaven was real and she would be reunited with her husband, how would she explain her time with him? Dava didn't consider it an affair, or a dalliance, or a series of trysts. She thought of it in terms of a trend that became popular in the late 2010s, especially with the women in her social and business circles: self-care.

If Dava had ever had to tell her husband about Tom Buck (and that was how she always thought of him—not as Tom but his full name only), she would have insisted he understand sex was much better with her husband. But with Tom Buck, she liked how much care and precision he took in pleasuring her, and when she was with him, she knew he was only focused on her. Not the kids, or waking up an hour early to squeeze in a run before work, or stopping by the grocery store to pick up milk, or just anything. Dava felt Tom Buck's single-mindedness when they were together, and that, in turn, helped her relax and think about herself and her pleasure, the rare time she wasn't thinking about taking care of, or being judged by, others. It was all release.

They had first met in her first month of her senior year at NYU, a time when Chaitanya's birth seemed like a dream, or at least a vivid hallucination. Throughout her last year in school, the events of those chilly months in the UK came to her in random bursts, and she pushed them away by thinking of recent fun times from her senior year, as if taking out pictures from a photo album. One of those memories involved Tom Buck. He had played a minor role in an all-night misadventure with her roommates, Tina and Ben, that spanned two boroughs, taking them from an open mic in the Lower East Side to a warehouse party in Greenpoint to a rooftop sunrise overlooking the Brooklyn Bridge. For years, the trio had fondly referred to it as "that crazy-ass night" because so many odd things happened: a missing bra, a junkie ballerina, a toilet clogged with Nokia flip phones. But for Dava, it also marked the night she met Tom Buck. She had seen him perform at the open mic, the two making eye contact repeatedly throughout his set as he sang The Replacements and Talking Heads covers.

After his performance, he had joined Dava and her pals at the bar and invited them to the party. During the cab ride to the warehouse, the two had sat next to each other, their legs touching as they traded stories about recent shows they had seen and their collection of concert bootlegs (he had a lot of Talking Heads; she had mostly PJ Harvey). Once the four of them had arrived, he and Dava did not speak again, as he was immediately drawn into a group of dudes who looked just like him—shaggy hair, ripped jeans, and black-framed glasses—and she and her roommates gravitated toward the dance floor. They left four hours later, sweaty and exuberant, after the ballerina had urged them to come see the magnificent view from her apartment (Tina's bra had gone missing at this point, but Ben's phone had yet to be ruined). Dava glimpsed Tom Buck as they left the party, and had been fascinated by his magnetic presence, the way his height and his handsomeness drew both women and men into his orbit. He seemed like the sun—he was several inches taller than everyone else—and the people around him the planets clustered for his warmth and attention. He and Dava made eye contact one last time, waving goodbye as Tina pulled her through the throng and out the door, but she could have sworn Tom Buck had shouted something to her as she left.

She didn't see him again until more than fifteen years later, at a very different kind of party. In 2012, Dava and Arvid were supposed to fly to Los Angeles to attend MusiCares's person of the year ceremony honoring Paul McCartney. They were both Beatles fans, but Arvid in particular was a superfan, and so Dava had secured the tickets as a treat for her husband. As someone who had an aversion to the sunny West Coast, Dava wanted to ensure any time spent in Los Angeles would also benefit the foundation, and so she had also arranged several meetings with female studio heads whom she wanted to speak with about funding the foundation's new filmmaking initiative. Many of these executives had been eager to meet with Dava since she had joined the list of the world's richest self-made women three years earlier. And after resisting their overtures for years, she finally had the perfect reason to fly west and sit down with them.

Anita, the Shastri-Perssons' longtime babysitter and future nanny, had been scheduled to stay with the kids for the duration of the weekend. So when eight-year-old Arvie came down with pink eye a day before their flight, Dava was surprised Arvid insisted she go to Los Angeles without him.

"There's no reason for both of us to stay here," he whispered to her, the two of them sitting on the far edge of Arvie's bed as they watched him sleep. Dava's heart panged at the memory of his tears as they struggled to give him his eye drops, and how he had batted their hands away despite their attempts to soothe him. "I thought he'd never fall asleep, poor thing. What kind of mother am I if I'm not here to take care of him?"

"Anita and I will be here, and by the time you come back, there's a chance we'll have three kids with pink eye instead of one. So you won't be missing any of the fun."

"What about Paul McCartney?"

"I'll just have to catch him next time he comes here," he said, shrugging. "And you have all those meetings in LA. If you don't go now, you won't have time again the rest of the year."

Dava closed her fingers around Arvie's bare foot, her thumb tenderly tapping each toe. "Are you sure, babe?"

"Let it be, dear," Arvid replied in a Liverpool accent, which made Dava giggle.

And so Dava found herself sitting at a table with record label executives—a few of whom had once openly decried Medici Artists as an enemy of the industry—watching Paul McCartney and artists like Alicia Keys, Norah Jones, and James Taylor perform his iconic songs, while her fingers clenched her BlackBerry, not wanting to miss a single message from Arvid about how the kids were doing. (Sita had complained of "eye itches" earlier that morning, while Kali seemed impervious to pink eye so far.) She knew she should be networking with the bigwigs seated with her, or at least enjoying the music, but her heart wasn't into it. Besides worrying about her kids, she detested Los Angeles—the snobbery and the sunshine and the inability to get anywhere without a car. The room was packed with industry heavyweights and A-list stars, and she was choking on the narcissism radiating from every tanned face. Dava's thoughts were interrupted by a burst of applause as a performance ended, followed by an announcement there would be a short break as the stage was reconfigured to include more musicians for the final number.

Dava had just pulled out her BlackBerry to text Arvid when she felt a tap on her shoulder.

She turned around and then looked up to see a very tall, handsome man looming above her with a friendly grin.

"Is this seat taken?" he asked.

She shook her head and he sat down next to her. He was casually dressed in a black T-shirt and jeans, which signified to her he was one of the musicians on the bill, although she could not remember seeing him onstage.

"I know you," he said, looking at her intently. "How do I know you?"

Dava held up her BlackBerry with a tight smile to indicate she was busy. But then when her eyes met his, he seemed familiar to her too.

"I have no idea. I'm not from here," she blurted out, as if the worst thing he could assume about her was that she lived anywhere within the state of California.

"Me neither," he said, chomping noisily on gum. "I'm from New York." He looked at Dava, sparkling in an emerald cocktail dress, and then at the similarly expensively dressed men and women on either side of them. "I guess I should have worn my penguin suit tonight."

"I can't imagine musicians like to play in tuxedos," Dava said distractedly, as she saw a message from Arvid come in. The kids are sleeping and I sent Anita home for the night. Everyone is fine. Itchy, but fine. Tell Paul I said hi. She smiled and let out a breath, then looked up from her phone to see the man watching her with a curious expression.

"Why would you assume I was a musician?" he asked, sticking his wad of gum underneath the table.

"The jeans—plus your table manners," Dava replied, shaking her head, although she was smiling. "And your fingertips are callused, which means you're a guitarist."

He nodded approvingly. "I played with Norah Jones tonight. Her guitarist dropped out at the last minute, and so a friend of a friend recommended me. A pretty sweet gig. Usually I play with four dudes who are dressed like me but smell much worse." He beamed at her, showing off his dazzling white teeth. "Tom Buck."

"Dava Shastri," she said, shaking his hand as she squinted at him, still taken by how familiar he seemed. "What's the name of your band?"

"The Jackmates," Tom Buck said with a mix of pride and disdain. "We have three albums, some critical acclaim, and not a lot of sales. I think our biggest claim to fame is appearing for five seconds on an episode of *The O.C.*" He looked at her expectantly, and Dava shrugged with an apologetic smile. She once had an encyclopedic knowledge of the music landscape, but in her late twenties she began ceding the space in her brain devoted to remembering song lyrics and discographies to wage gap statistics and the names of her kids' friends. Yet she appreciated that unlike most rock musicians, Tom Buck was not mortally wounded by her unfamiliarity with his band.

"We're actually going through a divorce," he whispered conspiratorially into her ear, giving Dava a whiff of his musky aftershave. "I'm recording my own album right now. Hopefully I'll be the Paul after we split up, and not the Ringo."

"Well, good luck," Dava said, beginning to turn back to the

stage. He was flirting with her and she might be flirting back. But she did not want the interaction to continue, even though she was fairly sure she had met him before.

"Thanks," he said wryly. "Here's my card." He handed her a silver guitar pick. "In case you're ever in need of an emergency guitarist." He winked at her and then got up and strode away with his hands in his pockets, and she watched his figure retreat in the vast ballroom until he disappeared altogether. Dava examined the pick and saw that his name was embossed in a tiny font on the front and his phone number on the back. She rolled her eyes and put it in her gold Fendi clutch and texted Arvid back. Happy kids are sleeping. Happy you're with them. Wish I were too. She paused for a moment, then added Love you so so very much! before erasing the extra "so" and the exclamation point.

It was only on the drive to the airport to return to New York that Dava finally recalled how she knew him. Her driver was listening to a classic rock station, and as soon as she heard David Byrne sing, "Oh, yeah, yeah, yeah, yeah!" from the Talking Heads' "Psycho Killer," she was instantly transported back to that fun night from her senior year with the cute guy from the open mic performing the song on a dimly lit stage and the invitation to the party in Greenpoint. She fished the guitar pick out of the inner pocket of her black Kate Spade purse (having transferred it there while packing her suitcase) and smiled to herself. What were the odds the two of them would run into each other again after so much time had passed? Dava wondered if he had ever figured out how they knew each other. Her first instinct was to fire off an email to Tina and Ben with the subject line "Crazy-ass night—you'll never guess who I ran into!" but then she remembered Tina was hiking Mount Kilimanjaro and Ben was in rehab for a painkiller addiction. She told herself that was why she didn't send her former roommates the email. In truth, the answer was something she was not ready to think about.

Exactly two months later, Dava found herself standing in her closet in the dark, the only light coming from the screen of her BlackBerry. She was examining her collection of handbags, her fingers traveling along the length of the shelf until she felt the stiff, curved handle of the Kate Spade. She dipped her hand in and took out the guitar pick. Then she slumped to the floor and hugged her knees, her shoulders shaking as her tears fell unimpeded.

Dava was hiding. From the world, from her children, from work and, more than anyone, her husband. Directly below her, Arvid was cleaning up a jar of tomato sauce that had fallen on the kitchen floor, as Arvie, Sita, and Kali were watching *Wizards of Waverly Place* in the family room, the older two avoiding looking at the big crack in the coffee table. Dava knew she should be downstairs with the kids to see who was responsible for damaging the table. But she was incapable of doing so.

Her mother had passed away the previous March. And while 2011 had been a profoundly difficult year, by the time Dava had reached the end of it, she thought she had begun to heal. But the first anniversary of her mother's death had set off a new, bone-deep melancholia that Dava refused to acknowledge, pouring water on the flames before they could be whipped into a conflagration. Even weeks after the anniversary date passed, the energy of keeping her grief at bay had Dava constantly on edge, prickly and remote and quick to yell over insignificant matters. All of this came to a head during a heated meeting in which Dava came perilously close to calling a board member a four-letter word, and Vash persuaded her to take the rest of the week off.

Dava had returned home at 7:15 p.m., starved and exhausted,

ready to fall into her husband's arms and regale him with her shitty day over glasses of wine and leftover Thai. Instead, she was shocked to see her children quietly nibbling on chicken nuggets and celery sticks at the kitchen table while Arvid sat with them, his face clouded and distant.

"Why are you eating dinner so late?" She leaned over to kiss each child and then her husband, whom she could feel slightly shift back after her lips met his temple.

"Go into the family room, and you'll see," her husband responded, looking up at her with irritation. Dava, taken aback by Arvid's cool tone, followed his directions and saw that the coffee table had an enormous, cross-like crack at the center. What on earth could have caused that? she wondered. When she asked her family after reentering the kitchen, Sita and Arvie exchanged guilty looks. Dava sat down with them and took a nugget off of Arvie's plate.

"How did you do that?" she asked, more curious than angry. The older children did not respond, only continued eating their nuggets as Kali licked the peanut butter off of her celery sticks.

"They won't tell me," Arvid said, still sounding distant. "And since they won't say, they're going to bed without dessert today, and no TV the rest of the week." The kids were still silent, their eyes not moving from their plates.

"Wow," Dava said. "Kids, listen: you must tell us what happened. Not telling us is worse than damaging the table."

"Not true," Arvid muttered. Dava gaped at him. She was not used to her husband contradicting her, especially not in front of their children.

"Go watch TV," she told them. "Take your dinner with you. I'll be in there in a moment. Go. Take your sister." After the kids had left the room, Dava reached for his hand and asked him if he was okay.

"I had a dinner meeting with the school trustees tonight," he said, letting his hand go limp in his wife's grasp. "You were supposed to be here at six. And I know you have a lot going on at work—"

"Oh, Arvid, I'm so sorry." Dava sighed heavily. "I had a bitch of a board meeting today and nearly cursed out Frank. Vash had to talk me down and then actually convinced me to take the rest of the week off."

"So you're going to listen to her and not me?"

She pulled her hand away. "What are you talking about?"

"I begged you to take time off," Arvid said, his fair skin turning a beet shade of red. "I told you first anniversaries are always the hardest." He stood up so sharply his chair fell to the floor. "And last year, I told you to join a support group. You think you're dealing with your grief, and you're not. And now it's affecting the kids again. Kali keeps asking me"—he choked up, then paused briefly to compose himself—"for the phone number for heaven. She said if you were able to talk to your amma, then maybe you'd feel better."

"Oh no," she said softly. In a daze, Dava watched a cockroach creeping over the white tiles near the trash can and was seized by the idea that as long as she kept the insect in her sights, she could prevent the flames of her grief from turning into a wildfire. "I'll . . . I'll talk to them. I know I need to do better. For them and for you."

"And for you too!" He picked up the plate of chicken nuggets and pointed it in her direction. "I've been urging you to take a breather. But then Vash suggests it, and you do it. Maybe I should ask Vash to tell you to hire a nanny, and we could finally have some help around here."

Dava threw up her arms in frustration. "Wait, I'm confused. What's the issue here? Just tell me why you're mad at me, and I'll fix it." She looked away from the cockroach to see her husband angrily clearing the table like a waiter who got cheated out of his tip.

"It's not that easy." He carried the leftovers and stacked them in the refrigerator, setting down each item with an accusing thump. "Your hours are long and getting longer, and I'm doing the best I can to be here for the kids, like I said I would. But they need you too. And you won't let me in to help you. Then on top of that, you're not physically here or emotionally here, yet you still think we don't need a nanny, because Dava Shastri can do it all. She's superwoman, right?"

She was cracking. The grief was getting ready to engulf her and stay for a long, long time. In vain, Dava searched for the cockroach, hoping that by spotting it she would prevent the inevitable, but it was gone.

"I'm so, so sorry, babe," she said, her voice trembling, and she went to stand behind him, placing her palm on his lower back. *Come back to me*, she pleaded silently. *I need your love and warmth and support without me giving you anything in return.*

Arvid continued standing in front of the open fridge, the frigid air blasting both of them in one solid wave. When Dava slipped her arm around his waist, he shook himself away and his arm knocked into a jar of tomato sauce, and it broke and spilled in a gory waterfall.

"Shit!" he erupted, his work slacks stained with dime-size red specks.

"Arvid, I got this. Just let me—"

"No," he interrupted her, his voice booming in an unnatural way that made Dava flinch. "I made the mess. I'll clean it up." He paused, then added, without looking at her, "I'm going to go out for a few hours, clear my head. You shouldn't wait up."

Dava backed away from him and fled upstairs, the loud canned laughter of the Disney sitcom that her kids were watching trailing her like an annoying odor until she shut her closet door. Which is how she found herself noiselessly sobbing with Tom Buck's guitar pick squeezed inside her fist. After a few moments, she opened her hand and shone the BlackBerry's light on it so she could see the phone number. Dava brushed away the thin river of snot flowing down her lips and then sent him a text message.

Twenty-four hours later, Arvid and Dava had made amends. He apologized for snapping at her, and she promised she would seek therapy and be more present for their children. Arvie and Sita admitted they had fallen on the table after bouncing on the sofa, which had opened up the unfixable fissure in the tabletop. And Tom Buck had responded to Dava's text—We met at the Paul Mc benefit (I said you had no table manners). Just realized we met at an LES open mic about 15 yrs ago. Then went to a party in Bklyn. Does that ring a bell?—with a much briefer message: 223 spring st. #4, 4/18 @ 7 pm?

During their yearlong "reacquaintance," and even after they stopped speaking, Dava never thought of her weekly visits to Tom Buck as romantic; she considered them a necessary indulgence, and occasionally as her own version of therapy. But when she reached out to him that night, she had merely texted him as a quick pick-me-up. At the most, it would result in a flirtatious text exchange, something fun and briefly thrilling that could numb her misery. And instead Dava received an invitation to meet him, which ultimately became an invitation to reconnect with herself. As she explained in a letter she wrote knee-deep into their time together but never sent, because she did not fully trust any of her friends to keep her secret,

Entering his apartment is like traveling backward in time. Each item of clothing removed is like taking off a part of my identity. When the suit comes off, so do my work responsibilities. When the heels come off, I'm no longer a wife. When I shake my hair out of a ponytail, I'm not someone's mother. All these layers are shed until it's just me, a person with vices and random opinions on consequential and inconsequential things. And he lets me be me. He asks nothing of me but my body, and the way he desires me is exhilarating because I know it's purely physical. There's no other need behind it. He has other women, he has his own life, and so he knows I need nothing from him too. And each time I leave, I feel refreshed and ready to resume my life, knowing I'm capable of being the best version of myself.

One week after contacting him, Dava found herself knocking on the door of Tom Buck's studio apartment. As she stepped inside, she was charmed by the interior's minimalist aesthetic, just large enough for an armchair, a queen-size mattress, and a small television perched on top of a steamer trunk, and there was a dark-gray rug that matched his bedding. An assortment of stringed instruments—an acoustic six-string and twelve-string, a Fender Stratocaster, a Rickenbacker, a banjo and bass— were lined up against a picture window facing a brick wall, all of them varying shades of blue. The only area that could be described as slightly busy was the opposite wall, featuring framed photos and papers in a perfect eight-by-eight grid, the latter of which Dava later learned were concert set lists from old Jackmates shows, plus concerts by his favorite bands. The orderliness of his apartment, and his obvious attention to detail, was immensely appealing to her. Tom Buck looked even more handsome than the last time she saw him, and she was especially taken with how the color of his stonewashed jeans matched his eyes. Dava's past attraction to him resurfaced like a tidal wave, and she did not try to escape from being submerged inside.

"Hi," he had said to her, reaching out his hand to shake hers once she had entered and he closed the door. "I feel like we should reintroduce ourselves now that we know who we are to each other. If that makes sense."

"It does," she breathed. In the cozy, closed-in space, the scent of his cologne, a mix of florals and sandalwood, was overpowering without feeling oppressive. A frisson of anticipation spun through her, and she surprised herself by stepping out of her heels upon entering.

"Do you still listen to PJ Harvey?" he said, his eyes twinkling as he gestured toward the camel-colored armchair, while he sat on the edge of his bed.

"No," Dava said with a nervous giggle. "But you're still a Heads Head," she added, nodding toward the framed *Stop Making Sense* poster placed at the center of the memorabilia grid on the wall.

"That I am," he said with a too-loud laugh, as his sneakered foot jittered noisily on the stone floor. "I have to admit I Googled you. And I'm impressed. And intimidated."

"Oh, right," she said. It was the first time reality had encroached on this fever dream of curiosity and lust. The immense weight of her life—Arvid, her children, the loss of her mother—slammed down on her like a hammer striking a nail. She began to hyperventilate, her thoughts rapidly ping-ponging in her brain: *What am I doing? Why am I here?*

"Are you okay?" Tom Buck said, jumping up as he saw her shakily try to stand. She nodded, then feeling jittery with panic, shook her head vehemently. He took her in his arms and wrapped her in a hug, holding her body close until her shaking subsided and she regained her breath. They stood together for close to ten minutes, which gave her the impression of being hugged by an oak tree, somehow sturdy and soft at the same time.

As Tom Buck held her, she realized that without her heels, she was so short her head only reached the top of his abdomen, and she could hear his stomach gently growl. It was a different feeling than when she and Arvid embraced, when she could lay her head against his chest. To Dava, hugging Tom Buck after being married to Arvid was akin to visiting Chicago after years of living in New York City: it was not as great as her hometown but enjoyable for being a different kind of big-city experience. She would never leave New York but did not mind going to Chicago now and then.

"Feel better?" He bent down to murmur in her ear. When she nodded, he asked her if she was sure. She looked up at him and said yes. And that was the last thing she said to him before he pulled her in for a kiss, and they quickly consummated their attraction. As he kissed her neck and slid his hand between her thighs, she idly wondered if sex with Tom Buck would also be like Chicago. When they finished, she likened it to Shanghai instead: exotic, intoxicating scents and an unfamiliar language. She liked it well enough but also felt culture shock. Yet she wanted to visit again.

Afterward, Dava brought her practical, business-minded self to the situation and laid out her ground rules, which she had come up with while standing under the rain showerhead in his bathroom: *Don't contact me unless I contact you, don't talk about me with anyone, and we'll only see each other here. If we ever see each other in public, we can acknowledge each other as two people who met at the MusiCares benefit and, in meeting, remembered we had briefly met in the mid '90s.* She included this latter rule because she did not ever want the possibility of conflicting stories, since they might run into each other again in the future. They discussed this while Tom Buck was still in bed as she got dressed, and she laid out these rules as she gazed at his tanned, naked torso, unable to look him in the eye. When Dava finally looked at him directly, she issued her final rule.

"Don't ever ask me about my professional or personal life when I'm here," she said in her boardroom voice, hoping to emphasize she needed to keep him walled off from the rest of her life. But when she saw he was nodding in a "sure, whatever you need" kind of way, Dava softened.

"I have to run," she said, glancing at the gold-and-silver Rolex on her wrist. "But I'll be in touch. Thanks for welcoming me into your home."

Tom Buck nodded, then stood up and wrapped the bedsheet around his waist. *He knows how handsome he is*, she thought, *and knows how to demonstrate it to full effect*. She appreciated that he seemed to use it benignly on the many women who had crossed this threshold before her and would after.

"Thanks for stopping by," he said, pecking her on the cheek.

When he closed the door behind her, Dava's first instinct was to reach into her purse and pull out her BlackBerry, but then that would break the spell just as Tom Buck's offhand comment about Googling her had threatened to do, blurring boundaries between the real world and this sort of dream state she was in. So she waited until she left his building before calling her driver, scrolling through the twenty-three emails and four texts she had received in the past hour.

⌒

What Dava liked most about Tom Buck was what she liked least in other people, and it was why she carved out time in her schedule for a weekly tryst no matter how busy her life became. Because while there was an undeniable physical attraction, what kept bringing her back to his SoHo apartment was the fact he was not fully engaged with the world. Tom Buck's incredible attention to detail only applied to matters of himself and his interests. Dava thought of him as being more self-contained than narcissistic yet also completely unaware of his white privilege. Tom Buck eschewed all social media and barely knew about what was happening in the news unless he saw it on the cover of the *New York Post*.

And in anyone else, Dava would have hated it. But in Tom Buck, it was a relief: he was like a void she could step into and not have to feel plugged into the concerns of a civil war in a third world country or an environmental catastrophe in a nearby state. Their hour-long liaisons rarely deviated from a pattern set by their second time together: Dava would arrive after work around 7:00 p.m., and after she'd step inside his home, Tom Buck would slowly undress her, then carry her over his shoulder to the bed, where he would gently lay her down and trail his lips down her body until he was between her legs. Then he would expertly train his tongue in places that made her eyes go wide until she came, half laughing as she begged for mercy from the intense pleasure of his touch. Sometimes she would reciprocate, but usually afterward they would have sex. Then Dava would take a shower—after a month she began keeping a second set of shampoo, soap, and perfume under his bathroom sink—and she would leave with a promise to text in a few days to schedule their next meeting.

When she had a little extra time, or when sex concluded in a short but energetic burst, they would lie in his bed and talk about music, exchanging anecdotes from their youth about favorite albums and concerts. Sometimes they would play a game in which she would look up lyrics on his laptop and he would have to guess the song, album, artist, music producer, and record label. (He always got it right.) Or he would play the guitar and she would try to recall the song and artist. (She got it right only about half the time.) And occasionally, he played her a new song he was working on for his album. But just as she kept her life separate from him, Tom Buck also did not share details of how his album was progressing, the musicians he was working with, or even where he was recording it. And that suited both of them just fine.

The closest Dava's two worlds ever came to colliding was three months before the 2013 Grammy Awards, on Thanksgiving Day. It turned out to be the final holiday the Shastri-Persson family celebrated in their brownstone, since they went to Disney World for Christmas and would move into an Upper East Side penthouse the following summer. Besides the family of five, the brownstone was crowded with relatives: Dava's father, Rajesh; Arvid's aunt Ebba and uncle Albin; and Arvid's graduate school pal Kenny, a high school geometry teacher from Seattle. Kenny had been a last-minute addition, since he was supposed to be spending the holiday with his fiancée and her parents for the first time at their suburban New Jersey home, but then the two broke up on Thanksgiving Eve, and Arvid felt he had to offer Kenny a place to stay until his flight on Sunday.

So the five-bedroom brownstone was overly crowded and bursting with noise and chatter in a way Dava found deeply claustrophobic. As the person assumed to be in charge of the Thanksgiving dinner, she also felt judged by all the visiting adults when Arvid explained he would be preparing the big meal to give Dava time to prepare for an important meeting that upcoming Monday. Over the course of the four-day weekend, when not gathered around their long oak dining table for meals, Dava's father sat in the La-Z-Boy in the family room and silently watched football and *Twilight Zone* marathons; Arvid's aunt and uncle took up space in the kitchen, anxiously peppering their nephew with questions in Swedish; and Kenny shut himself up in Arvie's bedroom, knocking back Miller Lites while binge-ing episodes of *The Sopranos* on his iPad, interrupted only by loud, intense phone calls with his ex-fiancée. The children had never been close to any of their relatives, save for their late grandmother, and so they mostly took refuge in their parents' bedroom playing UNO and watching Nickelodeon shows.

Dava had no refuge of her own. She did not feel any desire to sit down and chat with her father, who she knew was likely depressed and lonely in his life as a widower living in a retire-ment community in Phoenix. She had a cordial relationship with Arvid's aunt and uncle but was put off by their penchant for having conversations in Swedish with her husband, even if she or the kids were also in the room, as if they were hungry for Arvid's time and used their shared language as a way to keep him to themselves. Dava had told him she resented the way they were isolating her and the children from their family dynamic, but Arvid said he had "only child" and "I rarely see them" guilt, and it was easier to just let things be. So Dava kept her distance from Ebba and Albin and only spoke to them to ask them if they needed anything: tickets to a Broadway show, an extra blanket, more milk for their cereal (the answer was almost always a polite no). As for Kenny, she had never liked him much during Arvid's grad school days, and she liked him less now as a last-minute houseguest.

Despite the noisiness of having so many extra people in the house, Thanksgiving dinner itself was a weirdly muted affair, in which even the kids seemed lethargic as they all quietly ate turkey, stuffing, green beans, and raggmunkar, which were Swedish potato pancakes prepared by Ebba. Afterward, Rajesh wished everyone good night and went to sleep in Arvie's bed-room (during the nights, Kenny relinquished her son's room and slept on the family room couch), while Kenny helped Arvid clear the table and his aunt and uncle put the leftovers in the fridge and washed the dishes. Dava was grateful that she had the combined excuses of work and getting the children ready for bed to hurry away upstairs. After she had put the three kids to bed in Sita's room—with Arvie complaining about bunking on the floor in his Spider-Man sleeping bag as the sisters kicked each other under the covers—Dava exhaustedly dragged herself into her bedroom closet and shut the door.

She slipped off her black wrap dress and bra and threw on a purple NYU sweatshirt and boxer shorts, then sat with her back against the wall opposite the closet door, seated in the same position as when she had sent Tom Buck that first text several months before. Her first instinct was to pull out her BlackBerry to check work emails and go over her notes for the upcoming meeting. Instead, she sat cross-legged, the phone screen lightly pressed to her lips, and thought about how Tom Buck was spending the holiday. She knew exactly what he was doing, because he had told her about his annual Thanksgiving tradition: watching his second-favorite concert film, *The Last Waltz*. Dava had admitted she had only seen parts of it in passing when she had come across it on VH1 years ago, including a full clip of The Band's iconic performance of "The Weight" with the Staples Singers.

"All of it is iconic," Tom Buck had insisted as the two lay side by side in bed listening to a heavy rain crash and splatter against the windows. He explained it had been The Band's final performance with the original lineup, and they ended their decade-long run with an all-star concert on Thanksgiving Day. "Despite the infighting and squabbles, they came together one last time and invited some quote-unquote 'family'"—Bob Dylan, Van Morrison, Joni Mitchell, Neils Young and Diamond—"to help say goodbye. What's a more rock 'n' roll Thanksgiving than that?" Tom Buck said he was especially interested in seeing it this year, because it would be his first time watching since his own band had dissolved, and he wanted to see if it had extra resonance with him this time around.

"Do you make your family or whomever you're with watch it with you?" Dava asked as she sat up and reached for her clothes, wondering how many girlfriends and girls of the moment had sat through the movie with him.

Tom Buck shook his head as he approvingly glanced at her breasts as they disappeared under a lacy pink bra, then a pink silk blouse. "Just me. I don't do Thanksgiving with other people. I find it's the one time of year I can be by myself, because everyone I know will have plans. It's very peaceful. No expectations on my time."

Dava had nodded wistfully, perfectly understanding the sentiment. And as she hid in her bedroom closet, seeking refuge from the chaos and the judgment and the constant need for her attention, she envied his solitude. So when she found herself texting Tom Buck, it was not for a flirty pick-me-up. She simply wanted to see if she could have a small piece of what he was experiencing for herself. She texted him: How is The Last Waltz?

She bit her lip, wondering if she was intruding on his time and also being hypocritical, considering her cardinal rule about not texting unless to coordinate a meeting. Dava waited anxiously for him to respond, hoping he would write her back before Arvid came upstairs. Two minutes later, the BlackBerry vibrated against her chin.

T: Awesome. muddy waters is doing his thing

T: Can't believe robbie rob wanted to cut him out of the movie

T: How was ur turkey?

D: Fine

D: I have a question for you

D: Can you recommend one clip I should watch from Last Waltz?

T: Sure

T: What kind of mood are u in?

D: Exhausted. Need a moment's peace. The usual post-Thanksgiving emotions :)

T: Hold on

T: Okay first watch it makes no difference

T: It's the band at their most beautiful

T: It will put you in your feelings, make you feel what you're feeling even deeper

T: When you have to psych yourself up again and go outside

T: Cuz I assume you're in a bathroom or closet right now

T: Then watch caravan by Van the Man

T: When he sings he exudes so much power but makes it look so effortless

T: It will give you a kick in the pants

D: Thanks so much! Happy Thanksgiving

T: Sure! Hope that helps

T: Happy t-giving to you too

Dava brought up the YouTube clip of "It Makes No Difference" and let the song wash over her, then played it again and again for the next fifteen minutes. Listening to the band members harmonize gorgeously on such an achingly sad love song was an entrancing experience. She had not sat by herself and listened to a track on repeat since the kids were born, and she missed the days when she had the time to devote several hours to falling in love with a single song.

When she heard Arvid's footsteps outside her door, she switched to the "Caravan" clip by Van Morrison. A wedge of light interrupted the darkness as he stepped inside and closed the door behind him. Dava motioned toward him and showed him the screen.

"Van the Man," he said before settling down next to her. "This version is so much better than the one on the album. The purple suit, his high kicks. It's magic."

Dava laughed. "I can't wait to see the kicks."

They watched the video together, and she realized she knew "Caravan" from Arvid's days of listening to *Moondance* over and over while studying for his graduate school exams. Dava was then reminded of Kenny, which reminded her of all the day's stresses and tension, but she decided to banish those thoughts and focus on the fact she and her husband had a rare moment's peace. "Let's watch the whole thing from the beginning," she told him.

"Sure," Arvid said, surprised. As he started to stand up, Dava tugged on his arm.

"No, in here." If they left the closet, she was paranoid the others in the brownstone would somehow intrude on their solitude.

"On your phone? In the dark?" She nodded, and he laughed and sat back down. Dava crawled into his lap and leaned her head against his chest. For the next two hours, they watched *The Last Waltz* and marveled at the performances and cracked jokes about the rugged '70s aesthetic and Robbie Robertson's tendency to fake sing into the microphone. When Neil Diamond appeared onscreen, Arvid groaned and lamented he was the worst part of the lineup. Dava was about to fast-forward past the lesser Neil when Arvid revealed he had talked to her father.

"Just for a few minutes, though," he added. "He asked how you're doing."

Dava paused the video and looked up into Arvid's eyes, even though she could barely see them in the darkness. "What did you say?" she asked, shocked.

"That you were taking things day by day and starting to sleep better. Still working hard, of course, doing a lot of good things for a lot of good people. I told him I'm proud of you." He wrapped his arms around her and kissed her on the shoulder.

"And he said in response I'm a bad daughter and a money-obsessed workaholic?" Dava groaned.

"Why would you even say that?" Arvid said, his breath warm against her neck.

"Because that's what I see from him each time he looks at me."

"All he told me was to take care of you and make sure you don't work too hard. And I told him I would." Arvid kissed her other shoulder. Dava was touched to hear her father express concern for her well-being, something he had never voiced to her in person. That feeling lasted all of five seconds, when Arvid mentioned Rajesh also advised that Dava spend less time at work and more with the children.

"And there it is," she said, sighing in exasperation.

"Well, you're not the only one he had advice for. I overheard him tell Kenny he should go to New Jersey and apologize to Darlene."

"You're kidding!"

"I'm not. For some reason, Kenny confided his romantic woes to Rajesh rather than me. And apparently your dad thinks it's fixable and is urging him to take the first train to Secaucus tomorrow and pull an 'In Your Eyes' outside her window. Okay, well maybe not that last part."

"My dad is full of surprises," Dava said, laughing, her first genuine moment of happiness since all their relatives had arrived one day earlier. She nestled in closer to Arvid's chest and inhaled the woodsy scent of his cologne.

"Speaking of surprises, guess who's finally venturing out of the house tomorrow?" Arvid chuckled.

"No way! How did you do that? I've been trying to get Ebba and Albin to explore the city since they got here."

"I've finally convinced them to go to the Met. Your father— we should start calling him Mr. Surprise—volunteered to go with them. He said he's been to the city a dozen times, and he'll be able to make sure they won't get lost."

"Does that mean…we'll have our house back to ourselves tomorrow? For, like, a few hours?"

"Yes, dear." Arvid held out his hand for a high five. "It's a Thanksgiving miracle."

"You're a Thanksgiving miracle," Dava said, high-fiving it and then pulling his hand toward her lips to plant a kiss inside his palm. They then resumed watching the movie, and after it ended, she set down the phone and turned around to face him while still sitting in his lap.

"I love you, baby," she whispered in his ear. "I want you so much."

"In here? In the dark?"

"Mm-hmm," she said, moving her lips down his chest as she unbuttoned his shirt.

"But first let me go downstairs and double-check the doors are locked and that Ebba loaded the dishwasher properly. Plus, I think Kenny—"

"Baby, it can wait," Dava said softly as she unzipped his pants and straddled him, and he sighed with pleasure.

And so their bodies melted together as they made love in the dark, surrounded by their clothes and shoes and purses and neckties, the peaceful aroma of cedar floating over them. This stolen moment together—before Sita had knocked on the closet door complaining Kali had peed in her bed, and before Arvid had learned via a phone call from the police that Kenny was five blocks away, drunk and shoeless—salvaged the holiday for her and made that final Thanksgiving in the brownstone one of her most cherished memories.

And the fact her and Arvid's romantic night came after a song recommendation from Tom Buck did not compromise the memory for her in the slightest. As she told the therapist she began seeing a month after Arvid's death, "I was always able to separate that part of myself from everything else." She was trying to deal with the fact that even as she was grieving for her husband, she still did not regret her time with Tom Buck, even after the whole situation had imploded. And she felt guilty over *not* feeling guilty.

"Dava Shastri is Wonder Woman, and Dava, the woman who went to SoHo every week, is Diana Prince. The two never inhabited the same space. One wanted to save the world, and the other was a human being who needed to eat and take naps and have sex. They were truly two different people," Dava had said.

"But the thing is, Dava, they are the same person," her therapist, Theresa, pointed out. "Diana Prince was Wonder Woman's alter ego. It's just that Wonder Woman kept the fact she had an alter ego a secret."

"So it's not a perfect metaphor," she shot back. "But the thing is, I was fine with the duality. I never allowed the two parts of my life to overlap."

"And what happened when they finally did?" Theresa asked, peering at her over her tortoiseshell glasses.

"Well," Dava said, exhaling bitterly. "You've heard the song."

CHAPTER TWELVE

We Still Have the Spark

"Dava"

Music & Lyrics: Tom Buck

She's fighting the mirror
And she needs her space
Even from me, always from me
The sun's broken on the water
And we both know what that means
Yet her hand's still in mine
So right now, that's enough

Well, it's you and me
In the light and the dark
It's you and me
We still have the spark (x2)

The guitar is in her hands
And she's playing me perfectly
No notes hit the sky
But the melody lifts her
Into my arms
And she sings, oh, she sings

Well, it's you and me
In the light and the dark
It's you and me
We still have the spark (x2)

She's taking a bath but her eyes have run dry
I stare at myself through her eyes
And know I'm not enough

Well, it's you and me
In the light and the dark
It's you and me
We still have the spark (x2)

A FEW DAYS AFTER Thanksgiving, Dava asked her assistant, Parvati, to get her two tickets to the upcoming MusiCares benefit after hearing that Bruce Springsteen would be the honoree. She had been hoping the MusiCares' person of the year for 2013 would be someone of stature on par with a Beatle so she could whisk Arvid to LA for the weekend as a makeup for missing last year's event. And while her husband was not as die-hard about The Boss, she knew Springsteen was one of his favorite live performers.

So when Parvati informed her not only had she been able to get the MusiCares tickets, but she had also been offered Grammy tickets too (since MusiCares was on Friday and the Grammys were on Sunday), Dava said yes without thinking too much about it. They had recently begun a monthly tradition of "sleep-ins," which saw them checking into a luxury hotel for twelve hours of uninterrupted sleep, and she had intended the three days in Los Angeles to be an extended version of that ritual, save for their attendance at the MusiCares event. When Parvati had asked about the Grammy tickets, she thought they would be a nice option if they were in the mood before their flight home the next morning.

While Dava recognized the oddness of bringing her husband to an event where she had become reacquainted with Tom Buck, she was not bothered by it. For starters, she could not imagine he would attend two years in a row, since his appearance at the McCartney ceremony had been a fluke. And more crucially, even if he happened to be there, Arvid already knew the story of their initial meeting and their later run-in at the benefit. Soon after her first visit to his SoHo apartment, Dava had dashed off a breezy email to Tina and Ben—the one she had initially intended to send them two months earlier when she heard "Psycho Killer" on the drive to the airport—and claimed the mystery man's identity had only just occurred to her. She had made sure to casually include the anecdote in her conversation with Arvid that same night as they were watching *Doctor Who*, adding, "Isn't that random?" as he good-naturedly nodded and then asked her what she had done with all of her PJ Harvey bootlegs.

The month of December had been so hectic with work and family obligations that Dava and Tom Buck didn't see each other again until a frosty Sunday in early January; it was, in fact, the only time during their yearlong "reacquaintance" that they met for more than one hour's time. Christmas in Orlando had been particularly stressful, wrangling three young children hopped up on Disney princesses, rides, and sugar, all the while trying to stay on top of foundation work that required fielding phone calls from two different time zones, and it had led her to finally concede to Arvid's request to hire Anita as a full-time nanny. So Dava asked that Anita's first day coincide with the same day she had scheduled a spa retreat, which, in her mind, was what the languorous fourteen hours in Tom Buck's bed would actually be.

After a morning of sex and lazy conversation, Dava was eating lunch in bed, something she never did at home. She wore his V-neck undershirt and gray sweatpants as she ate shrimp lo mein and listened to Tom Buck, naked except for a towel around his waist, strum an acoustic guitar. Behind him the window was coated with heavy clumps of snow, but she didn't mind the lack of sunlight, because to her it made the apartment even cozier and more womb-like than usual. As Dava slurped the last of the noodles, she heard Tom Buck say her name.

"I know we don't talk about our work or our lives outside of these four walls, but my schedule is going to start getting crazy," he said apologetically as he walked over to sit beside her, guitar in hand. "My album's coming out soon, so we won't be able to meet as often."

Dava set down the bowl and chopsticks and patted him reassuringly on the leg. She had known at some point soon his music career would take him out of their weekly routine, and told him as much.

"I'm excited for you," she said. "And I can tell you've been working hard on your album"—she couldn't, actually, but thought it would be a nice thing to say—"and of course you'll be hitting the road to support it." Tom Buck thanked her for being so understanding as he placed the guitar on the edge of the bed. He then delicately picked up her arm and began landing soft kisses up her wrist. Just as he reached her elbow, she pulled her arm away, then turned down the covers and invited him to climb in next to her. "You didn't even tell me anything about your record," she said with a laugh. "Like when it's coming out."

With a shy smile that did not mask his bursting pride, Tom Buck told her his album was self-titled and his label was excited by the luck of having scheduled it to be released the Tuesday following the Grammys. When he saw Dava's confused expression, the words sprang from his lips with the joyous rat-a-tat of fireworks.

"I'm nominated! I guested on Feli Navarro's record, and we're nominated for best rap/sung collaboration! Haven't you heard 'Blind Night'? We're performing it during the pre-telecast!"

"Oh!" Dava leaned back against the headboard, feeling dazed by his news, as well as mildly alarmed. Because when she had told Arvid about the Grammy tickets the night she secured them, he had confessed he was actually more excited to attend the awards show than see Springsteen.

"Kanye, Frank Ocean, Jay-Z, Chuck D!" he exclaimed as he scanned the list of performers on his iPhone as they cleaned up after dinner. Unlike his wife, Arvid was a fan of hip-hop. It was a love dating back to his teenage years, when he felt like the only kid in school who loved LL Cool J and A Tribe Called Quest and despaired he would never see them perform live.

"You're such a hipster," she teased him, patting his butt as she scooted by him to load the dishwasher. "Well, it looks like I'll need to pack two dresses, then. Maybe I should go shop—"

"Oh wow, there's going to be a tribute to Levon Helm too," Arvid said, showing her the story on his phone. "Mavis Staples will be on the bill! If she's going to be there, that means they'll be doing 'The Weight,' don't you think?"

At the time, Dava had found it strange but also sort of funny the Grammys would include an all-star jam dedicated to The Band's late drummer, a band that had only recently become linked in her mind to both of the men in her life. But as Tom Buck looked at her expectantly, Dava realized the coincidence should have given her a premonition that her two selves were on a collision course. In the abstract, she had not been worried about the idea of running into Tom Buck while with Arvid, but now that the possibility had presented itself, she was unnerved.

"Congratulations!" Dava told him, even as she believed the tone of her voice was strained and her smile obviously fake. "I'm sorry I didn't even know. That's great, Tom."

He beamed at her. "It was a surprise to me too, for sure. I never thought an impromptu seventy-two hours in the studio would lead to a Grammy nod. It's really for Feli—she's a genius. I'm just lucky she invited me to be on the song with her."

"Yeah...wow." Dava's smile strained her cheeks, but she continued wearing it. For months, Tom Buck's home had become her respite from the world, a place where she could drop off her life like a piece of luggage at the front door. And now she no longer felt at peace in his apartment, or his bed, and never would again.

But Tom Buck did not seem to notice her change in mood. He leapt out of bed and grabbed his guitar, playing the same chords he had been noodling with earlier but this time with a more manic energy.

"What is that?" Dava asked in an attempt to change the subject, as she debated whether to tell him she and Arvid would be attending the Grammys. "It's pretty. Reminds me a bit of The Velvet Underground."

"I can't get it out of my head. I wrote it for the album, but I couldn't get the bridge to work." He strummed the same chords again, making each note ring out distinctly. "I have the verse and chorus, but the bridge just didn't come together, so maybe it'll make the next one."

"I like it a lot." And she truly did. "It's so warm yet melancholy...but like a sweet melancholy. Teenage me would have definitely had this playing on repeat while dreaming about the boys she had crushes on. Unrequited, of course."

"I find that hard to believe," Tom Buck said, raising an eyebrow as he stopped midstrum.

"Believe it," Dava said with a laugh. "Teenage me also used to dream she would one day be beautiful and interesting enough to inspire a great song. Like Linda McCartney or Pattie Boyd. It's a little pathetic, actually."

"Pattie inspired several great songs. I think 'Layla' even won a Grammy." Tom Buck grinned. "And it's not pathetic at all. Maybe," he added, lowering his voice, "if I figure it out, I can make this song yours."

"Sure," Dava said distractedly, her thoughts drawn out of the past and firmly back on her Grammys dilemma. Tom Buck lay down his guitar and pulled her into his lap, which caused his towel to come undone.

"We don't have much time left," he said as he picked up her arm again and moved his lips down her wrist. "So if you don't mind, I have to finish what I started."

⌒

In the end, Dava had chickened out about telling him in person, and texted him a week before the Grammys that she and her husband had been invited. He had quickly responded— a little too quickly to Dava's liking—with Very cool! Maybe will see u there. And so that entire February weekend, which was supposed to be an oasis of Egyptian cotton sheets and room service, turned into one of simmering unease. Ironically, Dava and Arvid skipped the event that had brought them to LA in the first place after they realized they preferred staying in to continue bingeing the fourth season of *Breaking Bad* rather than, in Arvid's words, "getting dressed up just to see The Boss sing 'Born to Run' for the millionth time." But the series, which featured characters trying to keep secrets in increasingly dangerous situations, only stoked Dava's sense of dread about Sunday night.

And yet for all her worries, she and Arvid ended up having a fun night out at the awards show, with little drama or awkwardness even when they did run into Tom Buck. The Grammy Awards ceremony clocked in exhaustively long at close to four hours, prompting the couple to leave the show early, after Arvid saw the performances of his favorites, in favor of the post-Grammys parties. As she had expected and feared, Dava spotted Tom Buck at one of these soirees, a record label bash at a swanky hotel. Before she could decide if she should say hello or hide, he had seen her and waved.

"Who's that?" Arvid had shouted as a pop song screamed through the speakers. "Is he a former Medici Artist?"

"That's Tom Buck," Dava said loudly back. "Remember? Open mic night, PJ Harvey? MusiCares?"

"Look, he won a Grammy!" her husband said with delight. "Let's go over and see it up close."

And so they did, with Tom Buck giving Dava a kiss on the cheek and murmuring, "You look gorgeous," into her ear before saying hello to Arvid with a friendly handshake. Just after she introduced the two men, Feli Navarro had come by to hug her fellow Grammy winner, and it was at this moment a photographer asked the foursome if he could take the photo that would one day accompany the 7,482 articles written on the topic of Dava Shastri, Tom Buck, and "Dava." The photographer's image captured the following: Arvid, in a fitted light-gray suit, beaming at Dava with his arm wrapped around her waist; Dava, wearing a Mona Lisa smile and a jewel-toned, beaded dress; Tom Buck, casually dressed in a leather jacket, white T-shirt, and black jeans, holding his Grammy like a mug of coffee and snapped midlaugh; and Feli, in a feathery green gown, looking quizzically at the three people standing next to her while clutching her Grammy to her chest. Afterward, Dava had regretted she was standing between both men in the photo, as it made it too easy to crop out Arvid and Feli, or only Feli if the story was aiming to illustrate a love triangle.

But at the time, the photo had happened so fast Dava didn't even recall posing for it. There was just a bright flash and the next thing she knew, Tom Buck had handed Arvid his Grammy so that he could feel its weight, and Feli had disappeared into the crowd as quickly as she had emerged from it. So Dava stood there stunned and bemused as she watched Arvid heartily clap Tom Buck on the back while the rocker shouted something into his ear. The two then turned to face her, and Dava was overcome at seeing Arvid's giddy expression and Tom Buck's intense blue eyes. *Teenage me would never believe this. Then again, neither can I.* She was flooded with shame as Arvid unknowingly palled around with a man who knew his wife as intimately as he did. To her immense relief, a trio of women in silver dresses chose that moment to engulf Tom Buck with their squeals, and both she and her husband stepped back and watched him with the women who had come by to congratulate him.

"Nice guy," Arvid had said. "The Grammy's heavier than I thought. Can you make friends with Robert De Niro sometime so I can hold an Oscar too?"

"I'll see what I can do," she replied, giving him a kiss on the lips as she led him in the direction of an outdoor bar on the patio. Once they were outside and had sat down near a fireplace with martinis in hand, Dava asked, in a tone she hoped sounded light and casual, "So what did you guys talk about?"

"He said you were the most beautiful woman in the room," Arvid said, toasting her glass.

"Ha," she said, her eyebrows rising. "But really."

"We were just talking about what a crazy night it's been. He said Elton John invited him to his Oscars party. He also told me that five years ago he was working as a bartender while gigging with his band at weddings. And now, all this. Can you imagine?"

"Yeah. How crazy," she said, then downed half her martini.

A stir went through the two dozen guests huddled under heat lamps on the patio, and Dava and Arvid watched as they began to hurry back inside. Dava thought she heard someone say "Drake," while Arvid was sure he heard "Beyoncé." In either case, the rumor of a surprise performance left only the two of them on the patio, along with the fireplace and a faint drizzle pinging softly on the cement floor.

"I don't care who's in there. I'm ready to go." Dava leaned down and took off one of her gold stilettos. "My feet are threatening to go on strike. Remind me never to wear six-inch heels again."

"Okay," Arvid said, setting down his barely touched drink. "But first, indulge me." He stood up and extended his hands. Dava groaned as she slipped back on her stiletto and rose into his embrace.

"What are we doing?" she said. The sound of cheers erupted in the ballroom, followed by a song Dava didn't recognize. "Maybe that is Drake in there."

"Maybe. But I'd like to dance with my wife," he said, gazing at her with affection. "You look so beautiful tonight. And this weekend has been so amazing. I just want to have you all to myself a little longer."

Dava's eyes welled with tears. "You always have me, Arvid."

As a light rain fell around them, the two slow danced to the cacophony of wild screams and several songs Dava never was able to identify. She would always remember that night as the bookend to their night on the cliff in Argentina, another perfect snow globe moment preserved in time and memory, even as the dark cloud of illness was hovering outside of it, waiting to shatter the bubble.

~

Dava first learned about Tom Buck's song from Vash. Five years had passed since the Grammys weekend, and her relationship with Tom Buck had ended not long after. Just as there was a marked and startling difference between what the world looked like in 2013 compared to 2018, so, too, was it for the Shastri-Perssons. The shape and trajectory of Dava's family had been so drastically altered since their time together that Tom Buck rarely entered her thoughts. So when she returned from a work trip at sunrise on a wintry Saturday morning after a long flight from Ho Chi Minh City, bleary-eyed and feeling in desperate need of a shower, Vash's text didn't alarm her but merely left her confused.

I'm at Sundance and I swear there's a movie that has a song with your name? Google Sundance & The Skylight. Dava reread the text over and over as she waited for her suitcase at the luggage carousel. Her brain was fuzzy after the seventy-two-hour trip and cross-continental flight, and she couldn't comprehend Vash's message. A song with her name? Connected to a movie at Sundance? Vash is at Sundance?

Dava decided she would not investigate further until she had a combination of sleep, caffeine, and snuggles with her baby. She had been so exhausted by the time she arrived home she barely remembered the ride up the elevator or Arvid greeting her at the door with a yawn and a kiss. Dava woke up from a dreamless sleep abruptly at noon, with her older kids' incoherent yelling acting as an unwanted alarm clock. As her mind adjusted to the fact she was home again, she buried herself deeper in the glorious warmth of the goose down comforter, longing for the noise to stop long enough so she could hear herself think.

Arvid, wearing a baggy polo shirt, jeans, and newsboy cap, entered the room with a coffee and her iPad on a breakfast tray. He was followed by a three-year-old Rev, who toddled in wearing only tiny green shorts and blueberry smears on his cheeks.

"Hi, baby! And hello, my sweet baby," Dava said, feeling refreshed by the sight of both of them. She picked up Rev, took him in her lap, and covered him in kisses. She looked up fondly at Arvid, who placed the breakfast tray near her, and then sat down on the edge of the bed. "I missed you so, so much," she cooed. To Arvid, she said, "Thanks for letting me sleep. I really needed the rest."

"I know," Arvid said, holding out his thin arms to his son, and Dava carefully passed him over. "Anita's going to take the kiddos to the library after they finish lunch. And I'm going to take Rev with me on my walk. I figured you could use an afternoon to yourself."

"Have I told you lately that I love you?" Dava smiled gratefully as she took a sip of coffee.

"Only if you mean the Van Morrison version, and not Rod Stewart."

"But of course," she laughed.

Arvid winked at her and grimaced as he stood up with Rev in his arms. Before Dava could ask if he was okay, he mouthed the words "I'm fine" and walked out of the room with their son, closing the door behind him. Dava closed her eyes as she took another sip of coffee and enjoyed listening to the house's clatter—the kids' arguing, Rev's squeals, Anita's musical voice calling out, "Let's go; shoes on," Arvid's whistling—slowly diminish before being completely replaced by crisp silence. Dava ordered herself to finish her coffee before checking her devices for news and any new messages but managed to finish only half the mug before reaching for her phone. A new text from Vash immediately jumped out to her, reminding her of her friend's previous message.

Did you read about skylight yet? The song is named for you! Why didn't you tell me? Dava sat up with a start, the coffee close to sloshing out of her mug. She finally followed Vash's suggestion and Googled "The Skylight + Sundance." After a brief hesitation, she added her own name before hitting Return. The first item that popped up was a headline that made her heart want to tear a hole in her chest so it could jump out the window: "*The Skylight* Director Jinna Azure Talks Sundance Premiere, Oscar Buzz, and Tom Buck Ballad."

Dava scanned the story, hoping against hope her name was not contained inside. But she found it in the second-to-last paragraph of the article:

Azure let out a laugh when asked about the ballad "Dava," written by Grammy-winner Tom Buck. An instrumental version plays during significant moments throughout the film, but the actual track isn't heard until the film's end credits. The musical refrain is a major part of what makes the film's aching love story resonate so deeply with audiences, and Azure said the music was due to "Tom's mystery and magic." Azure said she had asked Buck, a longtime friend, if he could write her a song that could act as the musical theme for Marguerite's yearning for Luisa.

"He sent 'Dava' back to me exactly 24 hours later. Exactly! I had to compare timestamps on our emails to make sure. And it was this amazing, heartfelt piece of songwriting. He is so gifted." She added she was not quite sure why Buck had named the song "Dava," since no character in the film bears that name, and it does not even appear in the lyrics. Buck himself answered the question when reached via email.

"I wrote the song from the perspective of the main character singing to her unrequited love, and in a nod to 'Layla,' I named it 'Dava.' I asked my friend [philanthropist] Dava [Shastri] if I could use her name, since it was so unique. And she was kind enough to give me permission."

After reading this, Dava opened an incognito browser to search "Tom Buck song + Dava," leading her to a clip of him performing the song at a Sundance Festival party. She was transfixed, her stomach doing somersaults as she listened to the song, fairly sure this was the same melody Tom Buck had played for her five years earlier. When she heard him sing, "She's taking a bath," Dava immediately knew what he was referring to, and she was shattered by the weight of the memory and their last, emotional night together. Until that moment, she had completely forgotten about this song and their joke that he would name it for her if he could figure out the bridge.

"I can't believe he did this," Dava said out loud, her shock consuming all the oxygen in the room as her thoughts traveled back to that terrible, terrifying day at the doctor's office, and how she had coped with the news.

A few weeks after they had returned from the Grammy Awards, Arvid began complaining of abdominal pain. Initially, he had dismissed the discomfort as food poisoning, then severe indigestion. But when Dava found him on a day in late April looking green and glassy-eyed after having vomited in the toilet bowl for several minutes, she had immediately taken him to see a doctor. After several tests were conducted, they had learned Arvid had stomach cancer, he needed to be admitted to the hospital immediately, his type of cancer had a 40 percent survival rate, and the best possible outcome postchemotherapy was a maximum life expectancy of ten years. Dava could not remember much after they received his diagnosis beyond the blur of activity involved in getting Arvid checked into Lenox Hill's oncology wing, calling Anita to tell her to stay with the children overnight, phoning her father and then Arvid's aunt and uncle with the news, and finally firing off a series of messages to Parvati and Vash about her need to be out of the office for the rest of the week and what work needed to be handled in her absence.

By the time she had emerged from the hospital thirty-six hours later, with the order that she go home for a few hours' rest, Dava could not bear to do so. The idea of being with her children and trying to explain that Dad was sick and needed to stay in the hospital for a while, and seeing how Arvie would respond with stoicism even as his chin would tremble and how Sita would cry and put her arms protectively around Kali, wasn't something she could handle yet. Even though Anita and Dava's father were with them, she knew her children needed her. But she also needed some time to put her armor back on after it had been so badly damaged by each piece of bad news and had nearly disintegrated upon seeing Arvid look so frail in his hospital bed. And so she had texted Tom Buck, even though she had not seen or spoken to him in a month, to let him know she was heading to his apartment.

After the Grammys, the two had only seen each other twice more in February and twice in March. The last time they had met, Tom Buck was days away from going on his first solo North American tour. As Dava was about to leave his apartment, he pressed something into her hand but told her not to look until she had left, adding, "In case of emergencies, for when your emergency guitarist is out of town." In the elevator, Dava had opened the tiny manila envelope to see a set of keys. Dava had not been back to Tom Buck's home since then, but now it seemed like the best place for her to process all that had happened and all that she knew would eventually be lost.

Upon arriving at his home, she had peeled off her clothes as she walked to his bathroom, and stood naked and shivering as she waited for his bathtub to fill with hot water. She had never taken a bath there, but she wanted the sensation of being surrounded by lacerating heat. Plus, curling up in Tom Buck's bed would also remind her too much of all the times they had spent there together, and she did not need to feel the steely-eyed guilt of her infidelity on top of all else she was experiencing at that moment. Before getting inside the bathtub, she dragged a chair from the main room so she could put her phone beside the tub for easy access. Then, Dava submerged herself, and for a few moments, all time had stopped, and there was no world at all.

Dava did not know how long she had been soaking in the bathtub with her eyes closed, her ears half-attuned to her phone in case it vibrated with calls or texts, before she heard the front door open and Tom Buck say her name. She had put her phone on "Do Not Disturb" mode, save for calls from Arvid, Anita, and the hospital, and the silence of her device, coupled with the soothing warmth of the bathwater, had lulled her into a light sleep. Upon hearing her name, Dava jerked up and, forgetting where she was, let out a small scream as she flailed in the water. Tom Buck rushed in and dropped his bags on the bathroom floor, then enveloped her in a hug, nearly lifting her out of the tub.

"Are you okay? What's wrong?" She felt smothered from his embrace and the aroma of tobacco and burgers emanating from his breath against her cheek. Dava gently pushed him away and submerged herself back inside the tub, wrapping her arms around her knees.

"I'm fine. Sorry—you just startled me. What are you doing here? I thought you were on tour."

Tom pushed the chair away and knelt by the bathtub. "I had wrapped up my show in Philly when I saw your text…and, well, we hadn't seen each other in a while. So I thought I'd surprise you." He looked at her closely. "But maybe I shouldn't have. Maybe you were expecting time to yourself."

Dava shook her head. When she had decided to make a beeline to Tom Buck's apartment, she had done so knowing he would not be there. But now that he was, Dava felt comforted by his presence. "That was so nice of you. I had a shitty day, and I needed a place to be alone. Thank you for letting me come here."

"Do you want to talk about it?"

"If I do, it makes it real." Dava splashed water on her face to hide the incoming onslaught of tears. She paused, then blurted out with a sob, "My husband is sick. Very sick. He's in the hospital."

Tom Buck looked at her, his blue eyes radiating concern and alarm. "Oh my God. Dava, I'm so sorry." He reached out his hand to take hers but then seemed to think better of it, and instead he steadied himself by grasping the edge of the tub. "I really liked him."

"Thank you," she managed to say between sobs, her shoulders shaking as the reality of the past few hours began to settle in. Tom Buck sat there silently as she cried, and after several minutes, he reached over and placed his hand on her arm. After the initial eruption of emotion started to fade, she asked if she could stay a little longer.

"Of course," he said soothingly, stroking her arm. "Can I get you something to eat? Or—"

"But I'd like to be alone." Dava raised her gaze to his. "I

would never ask you to leave your home, but I'd like to be by myself in here."

Tom Buck seemed taken aback by the request but nodded his affirmation as he stood up. "Take all the time you need. I'll be outside."

He left with a sympathetic backward glance, leaving the door cracked open. Dava heard him settle down on the bed with a soft groan, and the mattress creaked under his weight. She then closed her eyes and began taking deep breaths, inhaling deeply and then exhaling slowly, counting her breaths until she reached one hundred. Dava had first done this during a flight to Arizona after her mother had died. She did not want to cry on the airplane, and so for the entire five-hour flight, she had focused on her breathing, wearing a sleep mask and noise-canceling headphones to keep her grief at a distance.

For over an hour, she repeated this practice in Tom Buck's bathtub, ignoring how the water was gradually cooling and how her skin was becoming painfully wrinkled from oversaturation. She envisioned herself as a skeleton who was meticulously reassembling her body, starting with her heart, her lungs, her eyes, and her kidneys before finally putting on her skin, one long piece she reattached to herself like applying Scotch tape. And then on top of the skin, she began putting on armor, sheathing her arms, legs, torso, and finally her head with thick metal until no pain could possibly penetrate inside. For the days and weeks to follow, as she spoke with Arvid's doctors, paced urgently in the waiting room during his surgery, interviewed home health-care aides, and argued on the phone with their health insurance provider, Dava saw herself as wearing armor, a warrior that would protect her family while remaining unscathed in the midst of battle.

Her eyes snapped open when she heard her phone vibrate, and she saw it had lit up with a text message. Dava called out to Tom Buck and asked if he could pass her the phone and a towel. Entering with a hangdog expression on his face, he handed her the phone and then stood at the side of the tub with a blue towel. The text was from Anita, saying Arvie had woken up crying from a nightmare and could not be calmed down. Will you be home soon??? Anita had the grace and patience of an angel, so those three question marks told Dava how much her nanny was panicking.

"I have to go," she said, struggling to stand up. "My kids need me." She had never mentioned her children to him before. In fact, she had no idea if Tom Buck knew she had a family. He handed her the towel and she stepped out of the bath, her teeth chattering as she dried off. He watched her with a longing she didn't quite understand, her mind already out the door and back at home, as she began to think of what to say to her children and how she could prepare them for the hardships to come. Her mind was so consumed with thoughts of Arvid and her kids she nearly left the apartment without saying goodbye. She was shaken out of her thoughts by Tom Buck's halting voice calling her name as she opened the front door.

"I'm sorry; I'm all over the place," Dava said, turning around, her hand still on the doorknob. "Thanks for letting me come here and for giving me space. I don't know what I would have done otherwise."

"Of course." Tom Buck cradled her face with both hands. "I'm glad I could help."

Dava took her hand off the doorknob and placed it on his chest. "You...this..." She didn't know what to say, so she let the words fall off her lips without adding more. They stood together for several minutes, his thumb stroking her cheek. Then she shook her head back and forth, as if waking up from a dream. She dug into her purse and took out the keys he had given her a few weeks before.

"Here," she said, pressing them into his hand and closing his fingers over them. She gave him a quick kiss on the cheek, then rushed out.

"Take care of yourself," she heard him call out as the door swung shut, the last words she ever heard him speak.

⌒

When looking back at her last night at Tom Buck's apartment, she thought she had gotten into the tub as one person and emerged as another. A woman who was no longer split into two selves but who was one dominant self who would be entirely devoted to her husband and children. It was not accidental she became pregnant with Rev once Arvid had a brief remission. Having another child was her "fuck you" to the specter of death. So that even as the Shastri-Perssons had to endure watching Arvid suffer, they could also celebrate life by welcoming a new member of their family, bringing joy into their home even as the darkness encroached ever closer. And she would be her family's champion. They would know they would never lose her: not to her work, not to her need for a moment's peace, and not even to death.

But Dava had no idea as she mentally readied herself to embark on the most profoundly difficult chapter of her life that Tom Buck had been watching her. *She's taking a bath but her eyes have run dry*, she had heard him sing in the YouTube video. *I stare at myself through her eyes / And know I'm not enough.*

She remembered how, on that long-ago January day, Tom Buck had mentioned he was struggling with the song's bridge, and she recalled his promise to her if he was able to complete it. Her stomach dropped with a sickening thud: one of the worst nights of her life inspired him to finish the track. Dava shoved away the comforter with her feet and jumped out of bed, panicking at the implications of a song like this bearing her name and earning attention from the media. He had betrayed her. Betrayed her privacy for the sake of a song and some glory.

Dava seethed as she strode toward her bedroom window, scanning the view of the East River as if she could find someone out there to help her with this problem. The river was gray and swampy, and the clouds were so low they were skating on the water, a view that accurately reflected her despondency. She held her iPhone tightly, and the constant vibrations of incoming messages seemed like a warning she needed to act quickly. She had never intended to interact with Tom Buck again. But now Dava wanted to reach out and scream at him until she lost her voice. She hated seeing herself through his eyes, knowing with every moment that passed, her private self was gaining more attention like a cotton sweater attracting lint. What could she possibly do to combat this? The song was such an intimate distillation of their time together she knew chatter and rumors were inevitable.

In the end, she did nothing. Because as she was pacing back and forth in her bedroom, staring at her iPhone and debating whether to call Tom Buck or her lawyer, she heard Arvid and the children return home. The bedroom door flung open as Arvie, Sita, and Kali scrambled up onto the foot of the bed, with Arvie turning the television on to a tween sitcom, as their father walked in holding Rev. Dava held out her arms to her little boy, and her spirits lifted as she inhaled the sweet scent of his baby shampoo.

"How was the library?" she asked her older children.

"Fine!" Sita yelled to be heard over the TV show. "I got seven books. Arvie only got two."

"Shhh! I'm trying to watch," Arvie whined.

"Turn that down, please. And who said you could watch

in here?" Dava asked as Rev squeezed her cheeks with his tiny hands.

"Um...we missed you," her older son said with an impish grin. "Now can we watch?"

"Please, Mama," Kali said sleepily, snuggling with one of the gold-and-silver throw pillows.

Dava's fierce grip on her iPhone loosened, and she smiled. "Okay, sweetie," she said as she returned to bed, indicating Arvid should climb in with them. As the kids watched television, Arvid softly broached the topic of Tom Buck's song.

"How did you hear about it?" Dava said, blinking rapidly. She held Rev closer to herself, almost as if he were a shield.

Arvid removed his cap and ran his hand over his pale, sweaty head. "I ran into Deacon at the park. His sister-in-law is a studio publicist who's at Sundance, and he said that she said everyone was buzzing about *The Skylight* and its amazing song. I pretended I knew what he was talking about when he mentioned your name and the movie in the same breath." He pulled his wallet out of his pocket and threw it on the bedside table, knocking over a few of his prescription bottles.

Dava sucked in her breath before responding. "This whole thing is crazy, Arvid. I'm starting to have some real regrets." She told a version of events fusing truth and fiction: Tom Buck had randomly reached out to her a year ago, asking if he could use her name for the song he was contributing to a little indie movie, and she assented without thinking too much about it. And she had forgotten about this until she had received Vash's text but had been too jet-lagged to look into it more closely.

"Do you think it's too late for me to ask them to take my name out?" Dava fretted, biting her thumbnail. Rev wriggled out of her grasp and crawled over to Kali, who was dozing at her parents' feet. "I had no idea it could turn into something like this. Why did I ever say yes?" She looked at her husband out of the corner of her eye to gauge his reaction to her explanation.

Arvid readjusted his weight so he was able to sit up straight in bed, his back ramrod against the upholstered red headboard. "I have to admit I was surprised." Dava gripped her phone again with so much force she thought it might break. "But it's also kind of cool," he added, looking at her closely. "Who wouldn't want a song named after them?"

"So I shouldn't sue?" she said, trying to keep her tone playful. She placed her bare left foot on his right white-socked one.

"Nah," he said, putting the cap back on and pulling it low over his eyes. "I'm going to snooze a bit. All the cool kids are doing it," he said, pointing at their children, who were curled into little commas, snoring softly. "You should get some rest too."

Dava stayed wide awake, her heart thrumming fast in her chest as she watched her family slumber and the sky deepen into evening. Her instinct was telling her Arvid believed there might be more to the story, but he wasn't going to probe further. But from that day until the end of his life, Dava never knew how much, if anything, her husband knew about her and Tom Buck. Because by the time Tom Buck had won the Oscar one year later and given a quick shout-out to the "uniquely named and uniquely beautiful Dava Shastri" in his speech, generating a whole host of articles about their friendship and rumored relationship, Arvid's cancer had returned, leaving him homebound as his faculties slowly failed him. And Dava at the time darkly thanked God he was not well enough to pay attention to or recognize the gossip that trailed them in the outside world like a swarm of angry bees.

〜

Dava was pulled out of ruminating on her past when she realized she could move again. She blinked a dozen times, and her vision gradually regained focus. The next thing she did was try to open her mouth and found she could also speak again. It almost felt as if she had been on the verge of a stroke but that the stroke had gotten distracted and ambled away, leaving her with barely any residue of the immobilization that had convinced her she was dying. Her mouth parched, Dava sat up in bed, reached for her teacup, and gulped down the leftover tea as if it were water. As Rev, Sita, and Dr. Windsor rushed into her room, Dava raised her finger as she finished the final sips, then told them with a small, satisfied smile, "My time is not up yet."

CHAPTER THIRTEEN

Not Easily Forgotten

Dava Shastri was a beast and never let anyone get in the way of all she wanted to accomplish. I am sure she left this mortal coil with the satisfaction of knowing she gave her all to the world. Dava, and all she stood for, will not be easily forgotten.

—Indra Voorhies, cofounder of the Reginald and Indra Voorhies Foundation, ranked number eighteen on the 2044 list of world's richest women (personal net worth: $3.13 billion), in a quote from Feminist First's *tribute to Dava Shastri*

THE ANGEL HAUNTED KALI. Specifically, the painting of the rat-faced cherub hanging over the bureau in her bedroom. As she spoke with Mattius and Lucy, she wondered how something better suited to a roadside motel found its way onto a multimillion-dollar estate. Even if it was the worst room in the house.

Before calling them, Kali had decided she would not accede to her mother's demand to end the relationship until she had asked their side of things. But as she listened to their murmuring condolences and Jicama's sweet voice burbling in the background, Kali despaired to bring up the topic. The angel judged her with septic green eyes, and the crude outlines of his wings were a visual depiction of Kali's mental state. And so just as Lucy was about to put Jicama on the phone, Kali bluntly informed the pair she knew about their illegal activities.

Kali steeled herself for proclamations of innocence or outraged denials. What she had not expected was the pair outlining their financial difficulties over the past year: several months behind on mortgage payments, a damaged solar shingle roof, and a panicked ER visit after Jicama fell off his tricycle.

"We worried you'd think we were asking for help," Lucy explained in between hiccups about why they had not told her earlier.

"And we didn't want our domestic problems to interfere with our relationship," Mattius added. "As for . . . well, it's like a part-time job. As soon as we've covered our debts, we're done."

Kali did not know what to say. She had never been in such dire straits and forced to make tough decisions to support herself. So while she could not judge them, she couldn't stay with them either. But what agonized her most was Mattius and Lucy inadvertently making clear she was a satellite to their marriage. Would they have confided their troubles if she was not a Shastri sitting on a trust fund? Or was the fact she didn't wear a ring or live with them full-time mean she would always be the odd one out? She had believed they were in a three-way partnership, but their thoughtfulness at not wanting to drag her into their personal affairs only highlighted her outsider status.

And so Kali shared her regret about their circumstances and then explained her inability to be in a relationship with them. "At least until you quit your part-time job," she said. As the two expressed their dismay, there was a knock at her door. Grateful for the distraction, she shouted, "Come in!" not caring who was seeking entry. To her surprise, it was Arvie, and her eyebrows shot up at the sight of her older brother, his forehead as pink as a sunrise, and his crisp blue jeans torn and stained at both knees. She waved him in, and with the flourish of a magician, he produced two glasses and a bottle of whiskey from behind his back.

"I'm sorry; I have to go," she said. Arvie sat down next to her and mouthed, *Who is that?* at her. She mouthed back, *One sec.*

"Can we talk again after the New Year?" Mattius asked at the same time Lucy implored, "If you need us, we're here. We're always here for you."

She thanked them, then hung up the phone and flopped back onto the bed with a sigh. Arvie chuckled and lay down next to her, placing the alcohol and tumblers between them. She wrinkled her nose at her brother's faint stench. He smelled like he had washed his hair with day-old beer.

"Was that your couple?"

"Yeah," she lamented as she loosened the rainbow scarf wrapped artfully around her neck, which had been knitted by Lucy. "That was me sort of breaking up with them."

"I thought you loved them," Arvie said, scratching at the auburn stubble dotting his chin. "You said you wanted all of us to take your relationship seriously, and now you're dumping them?"

Even though she had already shared the news about Mattius and Lucy with her other siblings, she didn't want to divulge it to Arvie. "It's a long story. Don't feel like going into it right now." She turned to face him, knocking the sealed whiskey bottle on its back. "Liquid lunch?"

"It's been a wackadoo day, Sis," Arvie said, raising his right leg and rotating his sneakered foot. "First Mom tells us that Helping Perssons woman is her daughter with that awful guy. Then Sita said Mom asked her to take over the foundation after she dies."

"Wait—what?" Kali sat up so quickly she nearly bounced Arvie off the bed. "She didn't tell me."

"Well, that's because after you told me the girls read that Tom Buck's son has proof our mom screwed his dad—"

"Arvie, don't say—"

"Rev came running downstairs crying that Mom is dying, and I take that stupid tunnel to the cottage to find the doctor and slip and fall and rip up my knees, and bring her back here, and now I'm here with you."

"Wait, so Amma is—"

"Still kicking." Arvie snickered. He abruptly dropped his leg, then grimaced as he clutched his knee. "The doctor said she had some kind of focus pocus seizure, but she's fine for now. At least, that's what it sounded like." He began giggling to himself, then reached for the glasses. "Drink?"

"What . . . are you . . . what?" Kali placed one hand on her forehead, then both hands, and bowed her head. "I need a moment."

Arvie nodded understandingly. "Yeah. Like I said, wackadoo." He clinked his glass to the whiskey bottle. "Cheers."

Kali glared at him. "How long have you been drinking? Did the girls see you like this?"

"Vincent's with them in the gigantic room. I think they're watching a movie. He said he wanted to give me some space to process." He laughed bitterly to himself. "That's the word he used. Our marriage counselor likes that word a lot."

Kali slid off the bed, then pulled at Arvie's feet. He yelped. "Get up, Arvie. You need to eat something. Sober up. If Amma came close to dying, we need to start . . ." She trailed off, searching for the right word. "Doing things," she added lamely.

She marched him next door to the kitchen, sat him down at the counter, and forced a mug of coffee under his nose, then made him a Monte Cristo sandwich. Kali watched her brother eat noisily, first stripping the pieces of bread of their crusts and then dipping the sandwich in a dollop of ketchup before each bite.

"You still eat sandwiches like that?" Kali said, shaking her head.

"It's the only way to eat sandwiches. Grilled cheese, hoagies,

Philly cheesesteaks, good old Monte Cristos," he responded, smacking his lips. "You know who taught me that?"

"Dad," she said with a sad smile.

"This is how he used to eat them. He said the trick is getting a bit of ketchup with each bite for maximum impact. And crusts are useless. They're like eating cardboard." Arvie delicately dabbed a napkin at the corners of his mouth, then looked around the kitchen as if looking for a waiter. "Can I have another?"

"Yeah, but only if you drink water for the rest of the day." He nodded eagerly and tapped his small belly as if telling it to be patient.

After he finished the first sandwich, Kali set down a second one in front of him. As she watched him eat, she thought about the series of events of the morning, including her mother's near-death experience that apparently lasted the length of her phone call. Arvie had mocked the word "process" (and divulged he and Vincent were seeing a counselor, which she found intriguing), but that is exactly what she needed to do. But just as she was able to grasp that her mother was dying and had faked her death to the world, other bombshells dropped. Secret daughter. Illicit love affair. Mattius had a criminal past, and he and Lucy were dealing drugs to pay their bills and save their house. Kali wanted the world to stop for a moment, so she could hop off and at least work through her feelings about losing her mother and being parentless. But her loss was being crowded out by anxieties about her relationship, the swirl of gossip surrounding her mother, and her feeling of uncertainty about her own future in a post-Dava world.

"What will it be like without Amma?" Kali said, half talking to herself. "When Dad died, there was a hole, a blankness. It just kept growing and growing. In time, I think we learned to live with it. But without Amma, it's going to feel like...a crater."

"I never learned to live with it," Arvie replied, sounding more sober, but with that came a more focused anger. "It always felt like a crater to me. Like a goddamn abyss." He banged his hand against the plate, making it rattle and spin on the marble counter. "And now that article makes it clear Mom cheated on Dad . . . it sickens me. How could she do that to him?"

"We don't know the whole story, Arvie." Indigo Buck had revealed that his father's notebook contained the lyrics to "Dava," including an excised section referencing a "ruby dress," which Indigo believed was in reference to the gown Dava was wearing during the duo's run-in at the Grammy Awards—especially since Tom Buck had folded his awards show ticket inside the page. And while this theory was titillating to the media, since their articles could feature the Grammys photo showing Dava in a ruby-colored gown, his proof was still speculative. Yet unbeknownst to Indigo, it was another part of the song that confirmed to the Shastri-Perssons their mother did have a long-term liaison with his father.

The article featured a snapshot of Tom Buck's handwritten "Dava" lyrics, and there was another verse, also edited out of the final version, that had caught Kali's eye, which she had reluctantly shared with her siblings: *I spent a year staring at your skin / Tracing your crescent moon with my tongue / You say your scars are obscene / I want to make you feel seen*. When their mother was ten, she had badly gashed her leg after she fell off her bicycle into a front yard filled with cacti. As a result, she had been left with a discolored, crescent-shaped mark stretched over the entirety of her left thigh. And even though their father, and later Kali and her sister, tried to convince her the scar was not that bad, Dava was so self-conscious about it she never wore swimsuits and avoided skirts and dresses with hemlines above the knee.

"We know enough," he said gruffly. For the first time since

their father died, Kali saw her brother cry. His sobs came out like sad belches, as if he were unused to expressing difficult emotions. She reached over and gave him a hug, which he did not immediately return. But as he cried harder, Kali felt Arvie's arms grasp her tightly, and then she started crying too. They held each other for a long time, her face buried in his shoulder, his tears staining her sweater, as the noises of the house swirled around them: the muffled sounds of conversation from upstairs, and the tinny audio of a movie soundtrack from across the foyer. When Kali heard the loud patter of footsteps descending the staircase, she pulled away from Arvie and whispered to him, "Let's go back to my room." Their faces still wet with tears, they hurried away from the kitchen and back to Kali's room, shutting the door and sitting on the floor, leaning against the bed.

"I just needed a moment," Kali explained, wiping her face with her sleeve. "I can't talk to anyone yet. God knows what new thing will be revealed next."

"I don't like her," Arvie said quietly. He kept his gaze fixed on the floor, on the space between his feet.

"Do you mean Amma?"

He nodded. "I love her, in the way you're supposed to love your mother. But I don't like her as a person. I don't respect her. This weekend has convinced me I'm right to feel that way. Knowing how many secrets she kept, the things she's done . . . I'm done with her." Arvie looked up at his sister. "I had to say it out loud. I hope you don't mind I said it to you."

Kali was shaken to hear the matter-of-fact way her brother expressed his disdain for their mother but did not want him to feel judged for sharing his feelings. She grabbed his hand and squeezed it. Outside, they heard Vincent, Sita, and Rev talking and the clamor of cabinets being opened and pots being clanged on the gas stove. When they heard Rev say both their names, they looked at each other with alarm. Kali had an idea and grabbed the phone on the bedside table. She opened up a blank email, typed a message, and then passed it to Arvie. He saw what she wrote, typed a response, and gave the phone back to her. They kept up their conversation this way, the noise outside expanding as Vincent prepared something that had the distinct, vibrant smell of spices, red chilis, and mustard seeds sizzling in hot oil.

K: Let's just stay here a little longer. What do you think?

A:

K: I think it's good you opened up how you feel. You shouldn't keep stuff bottled inside. Does Vincent know?

A: Probably. Haven't said the words but sure he knows in some way

Arvie was about to return the phone, then hesitated before typing one more message: I'm about to write a lot of stuff here. Can you make sure to delete this when we're done? After she nodded, Arvie, his forehead creased and his breathing heavy, wrote for several minutes before passing it back.

A: The truth is I haven't felt close to mom since dad died. And the gap just kept widening. I don't know if she ever noticed or cared. I always thought her favorite child was her foundation (followed 2nd by Sita). This became real to me after I found something in her office. I was there to talk about taking on a lead role at Helping Perssons, and she was called out of the room. I asked if I could use her laptop, and while she was out, I saw she had a file on her desktop called Shastri-Persson résumés. I had this weird feeling, so I opened it.

Upon reading this last part, Kali made a "tsk" sound, and when he looked at her with confusion, she pointed to the sentence and mouthed, *Snoop*. He merely shrugged and began massaging both of his knees, pressing hard on them as if they were pizza dough. She continued reading.

> She had written résumés for each of us. Well first our strengths and weaknesses, then her thoughts on where we'd best fit in the foundation. Like we were freaking employees of The Great Dava Shastri. I won't tell you what she wrote about all of you, but I was disgusted. What she said made me feel like shit. That she could be so calculating, treating us as pawns to prop up her "dynasty," was the height of her bullshit. But despite what she did, I still agreed to head up Helping Perssons to honor Dad, and honestly the HP salary is hard to pass up. Living in Stockholm is even more expensive than NYC these days. But now knowing she really did cheat on Dad, and it wasn't even like a one-time thing, I'm so humiliated for him. He didn't deserve that.
>
> I'm done with her. I want to quit HP. I want to quit being a Shastri.

Kali gasped. She showed Arvie the sentence she had just read, then mouthed, *What?* He nodded emphatically and indicated she should keep reading.

> HP does great work; I want it to keep going. But it doesn't need me. I want to do my own thing. Mom is way obsessed with her name, to the point she practically offered bribes so that we keep the Shastri name and pass it on to our own kids. But I want to give my daughters what mom never gave us. A chance to be their own person, not her grandkids or future

"employees." She wants a Shastri dynasty. Well she can have it without me. I'm going to change my name to Persson-Lindqvist and let my girls know they can do the same. I want to give them the gift of being their own people and not feel like they have to continue HER legume.

She looked up from the phone and saw Arvie was closing his eyes, his head resting against the mattress. Kali wrote something, then tapped him on the shoulder and handed it back to him.

K: Legume?

A: I meant legacy. Stupid autocorrect

K: That's one of the reasons why I didn't have children

A: Because of legumes?

The two looked at each other and smiled, with Kali mouthing, *Ha ha*, at him. She was relieved to notice her brother seemed softer somehow. He didn't seem happy, exactly, but he no longer gave off the energy of a volcano forever on the verge of erupting. She softly slapped him on the arm, then continued typing.

K: I didn't want to ever worry about Amma's expectations re: next generation. Plus, you and Sita gave her a respectable amount of grandkids, so I never felt pressure to come through in that way. I thought Rev felt the same way as me, but guess he changed his mind.

Kali paused for a moment and thought about the letter to Chaitanya, which she had hidden in the pages of her sketchbook. She debated whether to tell Arvie about it. Once she made up her mind not to, she wrote one more sentence and then gave the phone to her brother.

K: I kind of feel like calling her.

A: Who?

K: Chaitanya. I just want to know what Amma was like with her. I have so many questions. I know we can't though

A: Why not?

K: You know why. Amma doesn't want us to

A: She's not the queen. And she's going to be dead soon

Kali slapped him again, but this time hard and on his knee. He let out a howl that he immediately muffled by screaming into his arm.

A: I'm NOT wrong though

K: Have a little respect for her. And for my feelings. I'm so torn about this

A: How about this: I'll give Chaitanya my seat at the table. HP, I mean

K: Shut up

A: It'll give you a chance to get to know her

K: Stop with the jokes. We have a sister. That's weird. But also amazing, don't you think?

A: What if we have more than one?

K: Don't slut-shame her. What happened with Chaitanya and what happened with Tom Buck are two different things.

Kali paused as the rich aroma of rasam drifted under the doorway and made their stomachs rumble. A triangle of sunlight slid between them, dividing the floor into two pieces of shadow, as the day reached peak afternoon. She wondered why Vincent was making rasam when lunch had passed hours ago. Arvie interrupted her thoughts by reaching for the phone, but she gestured she wasn't done writing.

K: I could have had a Chaitanya, but I didn't. What Amma chose to do was hard. What I chose to do was hard too. I feel like if you're judging her, you're judging me too.

A: I don't mean to do that. I'm sorry.

To emphasize this, he clasped his hand on her shoulder and gave her an apologetic smile. She accepted with a curt nod and typed as fast as she could, as she heard Rev loudly say, "Where are they?" and knew someone could come by and knock at any moment.

K: Reading the story about Tom Buck and his son, and those lyrics...it's the closest I've ever felt to her. To know she has a messy past. A messy and sexy past. I have a messy, sexy past, present, and future. All of you made me feel like I'm a weirdo because of my relationship with Mattius and Lucy. You don't take seriously the idea we could love each other and fit together in a way that makes me feel a part of something real. I might be breaking up with them, but I don't regret dating them. And I bet Amma doesn't regret him either.

A: How can you tell she doesn't regret it, even though her precious legacy is in danger from all the gossip?

K: I know because in her shoes I wouldn't have either. Whatever she had with Tom sounded intense. He might have given her something she needed. I just can't judge her.

A: Aren't you hurt for Dad's sake? She cheated on him!!!!

K: She had something truly special with Dad. I used to watch them together and it was like watching a comedy act, they were so in sync. But maybe she had something special with Tom too.

I know you're all about the sanctity of marriage bonds, but I've never thought that way. Maybe one person isn't supposed to be the be all and end all for everyone. It doesn't mean I don't love Dad. Or that she didn't. It's like . . . she had room for both. Or needed both. Love works differently for everyone.

Arvie pointed at her last sentence and made a huffing noise, his face twisted with annoyance. He waved away the phone when she tried handing it back to him. So instead she showed him she was deleting their conversation, and he made a muttering noise as he stood up on shaking legs. Just then, they heard Rev calling her name outside her door, and Kali told him he could come in. When he saw the two of them inside, he looked at his siblings askance, obviously not expecting to find both of them in her room.

"What is it, Rev?" she asked, standing up herself as she watched Arvie stalk away without a goodbye to her or acknowledging his younger brother.

"What's up with him?"

She sighed. "Long story. Is everything okay?" Kali sniffed the air. "And is Vincent making rasam?"

"Sita is, actually. Vincent is helping. Did you hear about Amma and . . ."

"Arvie told me. How is she?"

"Right now, she's okay. Hanging in there. That's why the rasam. She asked for it because it might be her final"—he pushed the last word out as if it tasted sour on his lips—"meal."

"Oh, Rev," Kali said softly, hugging him. "What can I do to help?"

"Are you done with Sita's phone? I need a device with internet access. I want to play something for her."

CHAPTER FOURTEEN

Of Husbands and Legacies

Arvid Persson was a lovely man. A wonderful husband. An amazing father. A dedicated educator. I believe he changed the life of every person he ever met, in both small and significant ways. And so I have created an organization I hope encapsulates his warmth, his quirkiness, and the generosity of his spirit. He is no longer with us, but his legacy will live on.

—An excerpt from "Of Husbands and Legacies," an essay published in the New York Times *on September 16, 2022, to announce the founding of Helping Perssons*

DAVA WAS COMFORTABLE. PERHAPS the most comfortable she had been since arriving at Beatrix Island five days earlier, which at that moment, looking out at the evening sky over choppy waters, seemed forever ago. After her medical episode, in which Dr. Windsor told her she had suffered a seizure that likely signaled the worsening of her tumor, Dava had asked for the blue sofa in the den to be brought upstairs, so she could recline in front of the sliding glass doors and take in the outdoors in all of its wintry glory.

Vincent and Rev carried it upstairs, and Sita followed with an ottoman from her room. As her son-in-law, eldest daughter, and youngest son arranged the furniture, Dava noticed the latter two would not look her in the eye.

"Is there anything else we can do for you, Dava?" Vincent asked as Sita draped a cashmere blanket over her mother's lap.

She thought for a moment, then cocked her head. "Rasam?"

"Is that the soup with tamarind and tomatoes?"

Dava nodded, amused by Vincent's description of the South Indian staple. "My amma used to make it for me when I was sick, and so I think it would be very fitting." She looked at him expectantly. "Is that possible?"

"I can make it," Sita said, tapping Vincent on the back. "I've made it dozens of times. As long as we have garlic, tomatoes, and Amma's masala dabba, I can at least approximate it." Vincent said he would be glad to help her so he could learn how to make it himself. "Then one order of rasam coming up," Sita said cheerfully, even as she continued to dodge her mother's gaze. "But maybe one of us should stay with you . . ."

Dava waved away her concerns. "Nothing's going to happen between now and tomorrow morning. I'll be fine."

After they departed, Dava settled into a worn groove in the left cushion, the spot she had always favored during her time at the brownstone. The fabric still felt as soft as suede, and as she nestled in, the sofa let out a familiar squeak, almost like a greeting from an old friend. With a happy sigh, she rested her legs on the ottoman as her eyes traveled sleepily toward the sky. Winter Storm Imogen had officially departed the East Coast to fizzle out over the Atlantic Ocean, leaving a clear blue canvas ideal for showcasing sunsets. Even though Dava's bedroom faced east, she could still see the aftereffects of the sun's swan song, with tendrils of peach, yellow, and pink fanning out in all directions. As she contemplated the view, she heard someone walk into her room.

"It's me, Amma," she heard Rev say behind her. "I'm setting something up for you. I thought you might like this while you rest."

"Okay, dear," Dava said, wiggling her toes contentedly. During a consultation with Dr. Windsor, Dava admitted that in going off her migraine medication before her children arrived at the island, she had also neglected to take her anti-seizure meds too. The doctor explained she seemed to have experienced a focal onset aware seizure in her occipital lobe, which would explain why she remained conscious even while briefly frozen. Whatever it was, Dava didn't care. All she cared about was she felt near normal again, like a device that had been given a hard reset and restored to factory settings. Dr. Windsor had cautioned that this feeling of renewal was temporary, which made Dava all the more determined to enjoy her autonomy and unclouded vision for however long it lasted. As she listened to her son bustle about behind her, she remembered asking him to write and produce a film based on her life story. Just as she was about to raise the topic with him again, he spoke up.

"Okay, all set. I hope you don't mind." She turned around to see a pair of apple-size speakers set up behind her. "I connected them to Sita's phone. If you want to hear it, all you have to do is press Play." Rev handed her the device with trembling fingers. "I thought you might want to hear it again," he said softly, before hurrying out of the room and shutting the door.

Dava looked at the phone in her hand and saw the screen showed the Mercury Rev album *Deserter's Songs*. So many emotions hit her at once: love and nostalgia surged inside her but also a deep melancholy at the idea of hearing this again, at this point of time and by herself. As she glanced at the surrounding ocean view, with the sunset beginning its gorgeous fade along the horizon, she realized why Rev had decided to do this for her. Dava let out a long sigh and then pressed Play.

Behind her, the first song burst joyously out of the speakers, as if it were a genie let out of its lamp for the first time in centuries. Dava was surprised by how immediately familiar it was, as if she had listened to the album on and off for years, rather than hearing it for the first time in nearly half a century.

"Can you believe it?" Dava whispered to her husband, as if he were sitting beside her. "How lovely to hear this again."

Watching the sky dim into a deep shade of peacock blue, Dava thought back to her and Arvid's pivotal final night in Argentina, seated side by side on their backpacks as the fire crackled in front of them. They hovered together so they could easily share the single pair of earbuds plugged into Arvid's Discman, with the left one in Dava's ear and the right in his. So she had never listened to the album with both ears, let alone in surround sound. She was incredibly moved to hear the music again, with a similar view that had greeted her and Arvid all those years ago, and let herself weep with pleasure.

There had been a time Dava could recall everything they had spoken about that fateful night. But as she thought back to that time now, she could mostly only recall how it felt. The encompassing happiness of sharing those hours together, coupled with the heart-fluttering stakes of having to determine their future within that time. But one conversation they definitely had was about starting a family. As only children, both had longed to have siblings when they were growing up—Dava to share the burden of her parents' American Dream aspirations, and Arvid so he could have felt less alone after his parents died—and decided that night they would have three children, close in age, preferably two girls and a boy.

They made the decision with so much optimism, as if it were as simple as choosing items from a restaurant menu. And for a few years, their post–Peace Corps lives did come together easily. They smoothly progressed from cohabitation to marriage to first-time parenthood, all the while pursuing their respective careers. Of course there were times of stress and struggle, marked by too many nights of cheap wine and ramen, and later, dirty diapers and a lack of sleep. But overall, Dava's early years with Arvid in New York City were content veering on blissful—and that was before Sony bought Medici Artists for an absurd amount, turning the couple into millionaires overnight. The highs were so high that neither knew how to cope when the bottom inevitably dropped out.

◦

Suede gray pumps. Tasseled loafers. A sneaker with a cracked heel. Neon-yellow flip-flops. These were just a few of the shoes Dava threw at Arvid when he came home late at night two months after Sita was born, her pajamas splattered with spit-up and her long hair tangled in a careless ponytail. Arvid, slightly inebriated, cowered in shock as the shoes bounced off his knees and chest. When Dava ran out of things to lob at him, she barreled past him muttering, "I want a divorce."

Although she did not know at the time, she was in the grips of postpartum depression, which she hadn't experienced with Arvie. Dava had attributed her darkness and anger to the drastic changes in her life after selling her company. At the beginning of 2006, she was chosen as one of *Fortune's* "40 Under 40" and attended private dinners with Ira Glass and Laurie Anderson. Exactly one year later, she was a stay-at-home mother with a hemorrhoid pillow and an empty inbox. Meanwhile, the only substantive changes to Arvid's life were a work promotion and a small bald spot on the back of his head he couldn't stop soothing with his fingers.

Besides the birth of their daughter, their lives had been altered in another significant way: they were massively wealthy. Dava viewed her new wealth the same way she viewed full-time motherhood—as swiftly and painfully disconnecting her from her old life. The disconnect was made worse by the torrent of negative press following Sony's purchase and subsequent dissolution of Medici Artists, and Dava thought of her previous self, the one running out the door in beaded dresses or sweating exuberantly at the front of a stage in a tiny club, as someone else entirely, a close friend who was now a stranger.

She was momentarily cheered when she and her family moved from a cramped one-bedroom near Columbia University to their own five-bedroom brownstone on the Upper West Side. But her dream home—the one that reminded her of Jess and Marie's in *When Harry Met Sally* and that was only a five-minute walk from Central Park's Strawberry Fields—eventually became a tomb sealing her in with her babies and her unabated sadness and rage. That Arvid seemed perpetually cheerful, going on morning runs and after-work drinks while she slumped on their new sofa in the living room, making halfhearted shushing noises to their children, only intensified the blackness corroding her from within.

In the early wintry months of 2007, she tried to shake herself out of her stasis by launching the Dava Shastri Foundation, an idea born the moment she saw the number of zeroes in Sony's offer. Her reasons for creating the foundation were so deeply personal to her she never confided it to anyone, even Arvid. Instead, she had written them in a late-night frenzy in her journal, hours after she signed the paperwork that finalized the sale of her company.

This just has to be mine. Not Arvid's. It has to be the Dava Shastri Foundation, not a Shastri-Persson foundation. I made the money. I earned the money. I'm Bill Gates; he's my Melinda. But I don't need a Melinda. I don't ever want to be mistaken for the Melinda. Indra Voorhies is even worse, a mere accessory, only there for the photo ops. There should be no mistaking that this vision is solely mine.

For its inaugural year, she only wanted to award three $25,000 grants. Because even though Dava had earned $45 million in the sale of her company, the major bump in income had made her weirdly more frugal than when she had a regular job, causing Arvid to nickname her "El Cheapo." Every cent spent or socked into savings or investments made Dava fearful her family was running out of money, watching the figures in her bank account statement dissipate like a slowly draining pool. And as much as she wanted to create a foundation and have something in the world bearing her name, giving away a major sum of money as quickly as she had received it made her deeply anxious. Dava could still recall with aching clarity the year the '87 stock market crash threatened to decimate her family's stability, and she never wanted to feel that again, or ever have her children experience it.

So she launched small in scale and stature, and with medium fanfare. In a press release publicizing its formation, she had given a March 31, 2007, deadline for musicians to apply. Dava had done so with the idea she would spend her maternity leave reading the applications and announce the grantees in the fall, because as the sole person vetting them, she didn't want to get inundated. Yet the furor surrounding the Sony sale had raised the Dava Shastri Foundation's profile to a degree she had not anticipated, so instead of receiving a few hundred, she received close to 6,500.

And as each day passed, the stack grew bigger and harder to sift through. Even after hiring a night nurse and having her mother move in with them, Dava was still able to do little but sit in a rocking chair near the bedroom window and hold Sita in her arms, willing her squalling, red-faced baby to sleep for a few minutes as she felt tremendous guilt for not spending more time with Arvie, largely leaving him in the care of his father and grandmother. The worst part of her day was the early afternoon, as she rocked back and forth, waiting for the mailman to arrive. Each day at 2:30 p.m. she watched as he deposited a crate filled with manila envelopes on their doorstep, crying quietly as she watched him leave, knowing what that meant for her. She had arranged to have the applications forwarded from the foundation's PO box to their home address, and she described it to Arvid as having her "misery hand delivered to her each day."

Her darkest moment was with the shoes and throwing out the word "divorce" at Arvid like a grenade, hoping he would wake up to how she was not just over the edge but dangling her entire body over the railing. She later learned her husband had been wrestling with his own identity crisis as a father of two who was no longer the family breadwinner, blinding him to his wife's depression. After the incident, he urged her to see a doctor, and a few weeks before the March application deadline, she received a diagnosis of postpartum depression and was prescribed antidepressants that gradually lifted her out of her fog. One day before the deadline, she made the decision to postpone the announcement of the grant winners and put her foundation on hold until the following year.

She wrote about this decision in an essay for *Mothers without Borders*, a private online newsletter for "high-achieving New York City mothers." After receiving several requests to write an essay about the "joys and complications of modern-day motherhood," Dava finally did so in September 2008, not long after discovering she was pregnant with Kali, and as she watched cable news out of the corner of her eye, with the channel's

chyron screaming "LEHMAN BROTHERS CRASH PLUNGES
MARKET INTO CHAOS."

Here's the truth: I always wanted to have children, but I
didn't want to be a mother. I wanted the family portrait, the
rosy cheeks and sweet smiles for the camera. I wanted the
heart-swelling pride of watching them wave their diplomas
in the air on graduation day. I didn't want the stickiness, the
stink, the tantrums, and above all, the horrifying, overlying
worry about keeping them alive every single day.

I had to confront this truth about myself during the year
I had no identity beyond wife and mother. At the beginning of last year, I had two children—a newborn and a
two-year-old—but I no longer had my own company, and
my foundation existed in name only. I had been on the move
since I was eighteen years old, going from college to the
Peace Corps to starting my own business, and had thrived on
the pace of it. Moving so fast, leaping from Thing to Thing
meant I was Important and doing Something Important with
my life. When I had my first child, I was still leaping, but it
was much smaller, more like leapfrogging from one lily pad
to the next. I was a sweatshirt-stained zombie for the first
several months, unaccustomed to having to adjust my way
of being and thinking to this little person, but with the help
of my mother, I was able to get back into the rhythm of my
old life by his first birthday.

But being at home with not one but two tiny people felt
like the difference between jumping off a two-story building
and jumping off a cliff.

So you have the stinging loss of identity coupled with
the realities of full-time motherhood. And I was drowning. I
couldn't admit I needed help to anyone, or what kind of help
I needed. Eventually a diagnosis of postpartum depression

let the sun in, but it didn't quell my existential angst. Here's what did: an audiobook of *Titan*, a biography of John D. Rockefeller.

I listened to it on repeat for five solid months, overcome by how this man's contradictions and ambitions mirrored my own. And in learning about him, I learned about myself. Because like Rockefeller, I want to make a lot of money. I want my name to be a synonym for success and accomplishment. I want to give away as much money as I make. And I want my family to carry on that legacy, so it's not just Dava Shastri who helped people in this world, but the first person in a long line of Shastris to have done so.

Because, personally, I did not want a family so I could enjoy the sweet, intoxicating scent of my baby or cuddle with my little boy. It's been a bonus. Transcendent moments to be sure, but they come with the aforementioned stickiness, and also, sleep deprivation.

As I said, I never wanted kids. I wanted children.

Children who are a reflection of their parents' values while becoming individuals shaped by their own interests. I wanted to create good people who would make the world a better place.

That is what Rockefeller achieved. After completing the audiobook the first time, I did some research to see how his grandchildren have been able to continue his philanthropic vision. And I discovered to my great joy they are not mere recipients of his largesse, but the keepers of the flame. They didn't simply maintain his wealth; they expanded it. They give and give and give, and have given for over one hundred years. They are a force in this world. And by "they," I mean his family. Not just his direct descendants, but the family tree—children, grandchildren, spouses, cousins, stepchildren, etc. Each branch extending on and on.

That is a real legacy. A legacy that did not end when one man's life did but was only the beginning. A dynasty.

Midway through *Titan*, I made the decision Rockefeller would have never had to make (let's try not to dwell too much on the unfairness of that) but that was crucial to my well-being. I chose to take a full calendar year off from working, including taking time off from my foundation just after its launch, to be with my kids. So I could learn how to be comfortable in my role as their mother. So I could learn to enjoy having kids, while helping them to be the children I envisioned.

Because I recognized something important about myself: I had the luxury of making my own rules. I had enough money so I didn't have to worry about rushing back to the workforce to ensure I still had a job. My maternity leave could last as long or as little as I wanted. And if I had to put my foundation on hold—something so integral to my identity—I was going to make it count. And emerge from the cocoon as the rarest kind of butterfly.

But the essay was rejected because it was deemed "not relatable," especially in the wake of a financial crisis rapidly sweeping through the country like wildfire, even singeing the newsletter readership of upper-crust mothers. Dava was actually delighted by the rejection, because the last thing she wanted to be was relatable. After all, with the sale of Medici Artists, she had built an ark for her entire family in which they could survive the catastrophic crash threatening to overwhelm every single person she knew. Beyond that, Dava also no longer had the daily mundane concerns of living: paying the cable bill, saving for the kids' college tuition. She could be *bigger* than all of that. And Rockefeller gave her the blueprint for how to achieve that kind of benevolent immortality. His life story—his ruthlessness in his success, his core belief of giving away as much as he earned, how he ensured his passion for philanthropy was passed down to his heirs—had impressed itself on her deeply, almost as if it had changed the contours of her brain.

She had never shown her *Mothers without Borders* essay to Arvid, and she kept her Rockefeller-inspired thoughts to herself until she was offered an opportunity she instinctively knew would propel her to his heights.

⌒

"I want to be this great."

Dava said this to Arvid as he was splayed out casually on the sofa in the family room, his Yankees hat pulled down over his eyes, his legs balanced precariously on an empty laundry basket, bookended on one side by a tall pile of towels and on the other by a stack of bed linens. The windows in the family room were open, letting in the warm spring air and the overly sweet, enticing aroma of candied nuts from the Nuts4Nuts cart parked around the corner, as well as the cries of her two children, who were sitting on the front steps with their grandmother. Upon hearing her voice, he stirred and saw his seven-months-pregnant wife standing over him, holding a hardcover edition of *Titan* in one hand and her BlackBerry in the other.

"What, honey?" he murmured sleepily, swiping off his baseball cap and running his fingers through his light-brown hair.

"I want to be this great," Dava reaffirmed, holding out the book in front of her.

"Okay," Arvid replied, his eyes squinting in confusion. "I'm still not sure what you're asking me, though." He had known she was obsessed with the Rockefeller biography, but he did not seem to understand the manic gleam in her eye, or why she was dressed in a blue suit jacket and matching slacks, with a black top barely fitting over her stomach. "Are you going somewhere?"

"I want to be this great," she said again, emphatically pointing at the portrait of the billionaire on the cover. She then took a deep breath and let out eighteen months' worth of thoughts in one unbroken torrent.

"And to be this great, I'm going to need a wife. I'm going to need for you to be my wife. I know it's not what you signed up for. But this is what I want. And to get to that level, I'm going to need you to be the kind of person who will be in charge of all this—laundry, playdates, dinner parties. You get to say no, and I'll let it go and figure out another direction for myself. But you don't get to say no five days or five years or thirty years from now. I need a wife for life. It's what it's going to take for this family to always be secure. For our children's children to not just be okay but thrive. I don't need an answer now. But I'm going to need an answer soon."

After she was done speaking, breathless and exhausted, she sat down next to him and inadvertently toppled the tower of towels onto the floor. He looked at her expectantly, and then they both glanced in the direction of the window, where they heard four-year-old Arvie and two-year-old Sita singing "Wheels on the Bus" in between peals of laughter. Arvid opened his mouth to speak when Dava unleashed her second wave.

"MobileSong. They've asked me to invest in their company. I know you love your iPod, but their MP3 player is so much better...and I believe in it, Arvid. It's going to be big. Maybe as big as the iPod." Dava carefully placed her copy of *Titan* on the table, and as she continued speaking, her eyes did not meet her husband's but locked in on the cover photo of Rockefeller instead. The philanthropist seemed to be staring back at her with impatience, his eyes skeptical and his lips pursed. "I've asked for a fifteen percent ownership stake. I know, I know—

this is a big risk. But my gut is telling me to make this leap. And by taking this leap, I think I can take my foundation to the next level." She took a deep breath and looked up at Arvid. "I'm on my way to sign the papers right now. And I know I should have discussed this with you first, but—"

"Okay," he said softly. "Yes."

Dava's mouth dropped open; this time it was her turn to be surprised. "Wait. Are you saying yes to MobileSong or the wife thing?"

"MobileSong we'll talk about in a minute. I'm saying yes to being your wife."

"You are? So quickly? Why?"

"Because you asked. There are two ways this could have played out," he said as he gathered up the fallen towels and placed them on the coffee table. Arvid then turned toward Dava and spoke to her in a measured, almost resigned tone. "The other way is the one I feared would happen. That you would just decide something like this—'I need Arvid to be my wife'—and start treating me like, I don't know, your personal assistant. And then there would be tension, and you'd resent me for not understanding the strain you were under or what you needed from me, and I'd feel resentful because I'd feel like you were taking me for granted . . . it's a slippery slope." He chuckled and placed his hand on her belly. "It's much better that you asked and sort of a miracle you even gave me an option to say no."

"And so . . . you're okay with what I'm asking? You're sure you don't need to think about it?"

"I don't." He moved his hand to her face, and she vibrated from the warmth of his touch. "We have our gang of three. Well, we will soon. I'm where I want to be. I have the family I wanted. I have the career I want. I have the partner I want. But your ambitions have always been much bigger. I knew what I was signing up for. So I can do this for you." He looked at her tenderly. "Easy peasy."

"Easy peasy," Dava repeated as she pulled his hand back to her belly so Arvid could feel their baby kick.

"So explain to me, El Cheapo," he said after a few moments had passed in which they quietly listened to their children's squeals and ambient conversation drifting through the windows. "What are you investing in, and for how much?"

CHAPTER FIFTEEN

Mission and History

The Dava Shastri Foundation has awarded over $500 million in grants to over 8,000 organizations to date promoting causes aligned with our two core tenets: supporting the arts and women's empowerment.

Originally founded by Dava Shastri in 2007 to award grants to musicians in the spirit of her previous enterprise, Medici Artists, the foundation expanded its mission in 2011 to fund and invest in groups supporting women and girls across the globe. As part of that expansion, Shastri invested her own personal fortune to raise the endowment to $100 million...

—An excerpt from the "Mission and History" page on
ShastriFoundation.org

THE OFFICIAL STORY, THE one that would be retold at cocktail parties and magazine profiles and eventually in her obituary, is that Dava was inspired to make women's issues the main priority for her foundation after saving Independent Woman from bankruptcy. And she could afford to do so on a global scale: six months after her investment in MobileSong, Apple's acquisition of the company earned her upward of $500 million. She earmarked a fifth of the amount for the endowment and in the process raised her own profile among the philanthropic elite.

But in truth, Dava had been spurred by the death of her mother.

From a young age, Dava considered her mother to be everything she was not: sweet, introverted, and delicate, reminding her of Snow White. She loved her mother but never confided in her, because Dava thought she was wholly incapable of understanding her struggles as an Indian-American kid in a largely white town. Once she entered high school, the arguments between Dava and her father were frequent and explosive. Aditi never spoke up during their clashes—over dating, over driving, over applying to liberal arts colleges—except to gently ask her daughter to calm down and listen to her father. If Aditi had opinions different from Rajesh, she never expressed them.

She did not express much of anything, at least not to Dava. Aditi was a homemaker and seemingly had no interests outside of running the household. The only time Dava glimpsed her inner life was when she would find her absorbed in an episode of *As the World Turns*, sitting so close to the television her knees would touch the TV stand, and especially during her weekly phone calls to her aunt and cousins in India. Aditi would beam as she chatted with them in Telegu, and her way of speaking in a happy rapid burst of words was just as foreign to Dava as the language itself. Because whether asking her to clean her room or demonstrating how to roll out dough for chapatis, Aditi was always polite and doting with Dava, even a little shy.

She and her mother had continued their relationship of smiles and silences into adulthood, even as Aditi divided her time between Calliston and New York City to help out with the children. And so one of the biggest shocks of Dava's life was when she learned her mother had registered to volunteer at a women's shelter. Her parents had come to celebrate Christmas with them in 2010, yet Aditi did not share her news until she was packing her suitcase the morning of their flight back to Arizona.

"Independent Woman is still operating? You were able to save it?" Aditi asked as she neatly arranged her slacks and sweaters alongside the forest-green sari she had worn on Christmas Day.

"Yes, Amma." Dava usually avoided discussing her finances with her parents but weeks earlier proudly informed them she had donated $5 million to the nonprofit, and she had been surprised her father did not respond by lecturing her about mismanaging her money.

"I'm so glad. I... did you know there is a domestic violence shelter in Calliston?" She tilted her head, and her gold earrings shook like tiny, ringing bells.

"I didn't. But I'm glad to hear it's there."

"Me too." Aditi smiled at her daughter. "I applied to be a volunteer last month. After the holidays, I'm going to begin my training. It's forty hours. There will be a lot to learn, I imagine."

"You did?" Dava squealed. Just then, all three kids descended on them, Arvie asking for oatmeal, Sita begging her grandmother not to leave, and Kali wrapping herself around Dava's leg.

As they took the children downstairs for breakfast, Aditi explained she had researched Independent Woman after learning about her daughter's actions and had been so moved by its mission she wanted to help in kind.

"That's so unlike you, Amma," Dava said as they buttered toast side by side. "I'm... wow."

"That was your father's reaction too," Aditi replied, and they both laughed. Dava looked at her mother and felt like she was meeting her, the real her, for the first time.

From that point forward, Dava and Aditi's weekly phone

conversations were charged with warmth and intimacy. Rather than a dutiful litany of updates on herself, Arvid, and the children, their calls centered on Aditi's work at the shelter. Dava had loved how bubbly her mother sounded as she shared stories about the other volunteers, or what she had learned in her training, reminding her of how Aditi had sounded during her phone calls to relatives in India. Dava was immensely proud of her mother, but even though the words were on her lips each time they spoke, she never actually said them.

And then, three months after she began volunteering at the shelter, Aditi died of a heart attack.

Up until that time, death had been a stranger to Dava. She could count on one hand the number of people she knew who had passed away—a high school classmate, the spouse of a friend from the Peace Corps—but it had never felt personal to her. The closest she had come to experiencing it viscerally was during the events of September 11, but even then she and Arvid had not known anyone who died in the terrorist attack. Dava had been psychically wounded by the tragedy happening in the city she loved so fiercely but had also found solace in the city's collective grief and fortitude. This was the first time death had come to her doorstep, snaking away a loved one, and she was completely unprepared to handle it.

When she had given up Chaitanya, Dava had buried the experience so deeply it was as if it had happened to someone else. At first, she handled Aditi's death in the same way. The funeral in Arizona had been a blur of triple-digit heat, Rajesh's shaking hands, and condolences from near strangers. Forever after, she would always think of grief as the claustrophobic sensation of sweating in a black dress, the polyester fabric fusing with her damp skin. After she returned home, she coped by refusing to think about or discuss Aditi with anyone, including her children. Perhaps sensing their mother's fragility beneath her business-as-usual exterior, the three gravitated to their father for comfort. And since he had experienced loss at a young age, Dava was grateful to have Arvid guide them through the unanswerable as she numbed herself with busywork. Because unlike with Chaitanya, reminders of Aditi were everywhere, especially because she had visited so recently: her beige cardigan accidentally left behind in the hall closet, the trio of red woolen caps she had knitted as Christmas gifts for her grandchildren. And so Dava was forever on the precipice of falling apart, even as she insisted to Arvid she was fine, she was coping, and she just needed time and space.

Fifty-four days after Aditi's death, Dava was standing in a swanky bathroom across from a gold-framed mirror, her chin wobbling as her false eyelashes glinted with tears. Minutes earlier, she had been applauding the honorees of the Manhattan Center of the Arts silver jubilee. The performance arts center was celebrating its twenty-fifth anniversary by paying tribute to the families who had been patrons since its inception. Dava had been excited to attend, since the Rockefellers were among those being feted ("Your version of the Beatles," as Arvid had joked). But when Julianne Moore took the stage to pay them tribute, Dava gasped. The actress had starred on *As the World Turns* in the mideighties as Aditi's favorite character, Frannie Hughes. When the movie star briefly reprised her role on the soap, Aditi had been so excited she left Dava a voice mail exclaiming, "Frannie's back!"

"I can't wait to tell Amma about this," Dava whispered to Arvid, who looked at her with confusion and, after a beat, immense concern.

Then she remembered.

Dava fled the ballroom so quickly one of her heels flew off, and she heard someone crack, "What's wrong, Cinderella?" as she exited. Once she reached the bathroom, she stared herself down in the mirror, widening her eyes as big as she could, willing herself not to cry.

A toilet flushed, and she spun around to see a tall, willowy woman in her midforties exit the stall, patting at the pleats of her perfectly arranged gold sari. It was Indra Voorhies, who, along with her husband, Reginald, represented the Voorhies family, another of the night's honorees. The first time the two women met was at that moment, when Dava fell to the floor crying, her strapless purple gown rippling around her in a puddle of silk. As sobs racked her body, she was aware of a faucet being turned on, then the whir of a paper towel dispenser. Dava felt clammy hands patting her bare back, a "there, there" whispered hurriedly into her ear. Indra's perfume, citrusy with a touch of cardamom, reminded Dava of her mother, and she let out a guttural moan that felt deep and ancient, as if it represented all the unspoken grief from her thirty-seven years of life.

"I have to go, dear; I'm so sorry," Indra said to her with a hint of impatience. "Is there someone I can call for you?"

"No," she managed to say, her hands covering her face. "I'm fine." Dava had been so embarrassed to have a witness to her dam breaking, especially Indra Voorhies, that she had added, more harshly than she intended, "Please go."

Twenty minutes later, Dava was back in her seat, mascara and lipstick reapplied, her shoe recovered, her hand in Arvid's, watching Indra beside her husband as he accepted the award on behalf of the Voorhies family. She disdained Indra's pencil-thin eyebrows, her equally thin lips, and how she was basking in the glory of her husband's family's accomplishments. She disdained Indra for knowing how to wear a sari and move about gracefully in a way she had never been able to master. And above all, she disdained Indra for seeing Dava at her lowest and most broken, which even Arvid had never witnessed.

The new phase of the Dava Shastri Foundation had been

born in that moment, a fusion of sorrow and anger, tribute and revenge. Aditi Shastri would not be remembered beyond her immediate family. Indra Voorhies's obituary was prewritten from the moment she married her husband. And Dava was determined that of the two, no matter whose name was remembered and whose was lost to time, Aditi Shastri would have the bigger impact on the world, because of what she gave with what little she had, and what she had inspired in her daughter.

"Are you sure you're okay?" Arvid whispered as Reginald walked off the stage, only for his wife to take his place at the podium with a speech of her own.

"I am, baby. Thank you." She linked her fingers through his, and their wedding bands clinked together as if they were champagne glasses. Listening to Indra read a laundry list of thank-yous, her gold sari nearly blinding in the spotlight, Dava was grateful. *I love my husband, but I don't need him. Not for my name to mean something. Not to feel whole.* Years later, Dava would remember that moment and would berate herself for tempting fate—and losing.

CHAPTER SIXTEEN

Of Husbands and Legacies, Part 2

Arvid shouldn't have forgiven me for taking most of our nest egg and investing it in a music tech company without talking to him first. Maybe he did because it all worked out, and Apple's acquisition of MobileSong gave us true financial freedom, enabling me to expand my philanthropy work to a global scale.

But even if MobileSong had tanked, I imagine he would have been just as understanding. Arvid didn't hold grudges. He forgave mistakes. It might seem like I'm describing a saint. But he was not that. I'd like to think he was more evolved than the rest of us.

—An excerpt from "Of Husbands and Legacies"

THE SUN DIPPED PAST the horizon, and Dava's bedroom dimmed into the darkness of an early evening. Sita had already delivered the rasam to her, distractedly kissing her on the cheek before saying she would return after checking on the twins. Dava was so focused on the music she barely noticed Sita come and go, only registering her brief appearance as Dava stared at the bowl of rasam on a metal tray, which she had left on the ottoman. Dava knew she should drink the rasam while it was still hot, but *Deserter's Songs* was nearing its midway point, and she listened with her hands folded on her lap, eyes closed with a faint smile on her lips, lost in a reverie. Each new song awakened a memory from that night on the cliff with Arvid and sent her searching for more memories, like a fisherman casting his line despite the choppy currents. When the opening notes of "Opus 40" began, delicate and celebratory, Dava's eyes opened in recognition, and she let out a laugh. She remembered during their fourth listen of the album, the sun long gone and night surrounding them like a warm blanket, he had asked her to dance. So they had swayed slowly back and forth, the Discman pressed between their bodies as they took care not to trip into the fire crackling next to them. She had just laid her head on his shoulder, her lips relaxing into a smile of pure happiness, when she heard Arvid say, "Whoops."

"What is it?" Dava lifted her head and saw Arvid looking startled and bug-eyed.

"I think I stepped on something. I felt a crunch. But I'm afraid to look."

She sucked in her breath. "Let's look together on the count of three. Okay?" He nodded reluctantly, and Dava stifled a giggle. After two years of greeting lizards and frogs in her bathroom like they were her roommates, and once waking up to find a snake at the foot of her bed, Dava no longer scared easily. "Okay. One, two . . . and three. Let's see. It might be nothing."

Arvid lifted his left foot, and they both spied something vividly green oozing down the tread of his boot. He let out a yelp and jumped back on one foot, but since they were connected by the shared headphones plugged into the Discman that was sandwiched between them, Dava had jerked back with him and they both fell down onto each other, creating a circus of dust and leaves upon colliding with the ground. They had laughed until they couldn't breathe, the chorus of "Opus 40" spilling into their ears as they lay on their backs and stared up at the blinking stars in the welcoming darkness, and they had listened to the rest of the album in that position, tangled in each other. In the seconds as they were falling and before they hit the ground, Dava worried that if something dangerous was lurking on Arvid's foot or in the jungle beyond, or if one of them twisted an ankle, they could be in serious trouble, especially since they were miles from the nearest town and had neglected to bring a first-aid kit. That fear was accompanied by a thought that gave her solace. *If something bad is about to happen, he's the one I want to be with.*

Now, as "Opus 40" faded from the speakers, she remembered there had only been one other time she had tried to relive every detail of that night with Arvid on the cliff: when she had been seated at her husband's bedside at the hospice center as he was dying.

At the beginning of what turned out to be his final day alive, Arvid was lucid but in debilitating pain and unable to speak. Seeing his intelligent eyes flash with agony, she had screamed for a nurse to give him more morphine. After he had been administered a heavy dose, and Arvid's expression communicated his pain was diminishing, Dava somehow sensed he would not live until tomorrow. So she had phoned her assistant and ordered her to have the kids picked up from school and driven to the hospice as soon as possible.

As she sat beside him, waiting for their children to arrive, she found herself babbling about all their shared memories: the day they had met at the Peace Corps orientation and she asked him about the Camper Van Beethoven patch on his backpack, because she couldn't believe there was someone else who loved the band as much as she did; the first time they danced together, which was on a sidewalk while listening to an Argentine jazz combo perform at a street festival; the ways the colors of the sunset seemed to emanate from the fingertips of Mother Nature herself during their cliffside conversation, as Mercury Rev echoed majestically in one ear apiece; the births of their children, all lasting for at least fourteen hours of labor that Arvid had eased her through with silly jokes and by whistling her favorite songs; their all-too-rare sleep-ins at the most expensive hotels in New York City and London; their last Thanksgiving at the brownstone; and every other memory she could recount, whether meaningful or banal, of their two decades as a couple and eighteen years as husband and wife.

Dava barely took a breath as she cycled through every remembrance that entered her consciousness, as it dawned on her that with her husband's death, she would never be able to talk about these memories with him again, and she would be the sole repository of their shared history. As she spoke, her sentences always starting with "remember when" and her voice taking on a singsong quality, Arvid smiled beatifically and occasionally nodded. She held his hand the entire time, and he would press hers after each new memory, as if to indicate he, too, remembered. After two hours had passed, she sensed the life fading from him, the smile withdrawing from his lips, his eyes becoming cloudy and unfocused. So Dava sang his favorite song back to him, hoping her shaky rendition of "Brand New Day" would give him comfort in the same way his had done for her so many times before.

Just as she had finished singing, their children arrived. Arvie and Sita were wearing their high school uniform of blue slacks and white collared shirts, while Kali was in purple overalls, still wearing the artist's smock from her after-school arts program. Little Rev, in red shorts and a Superman T-shirt, was carried in by Sita, and the little boy gave his father a kiss on the forehead before erupting into confused tears. So Dava bestowed her own kiss on her husband's lips, whispered, "I love you," and left the room with Rev in her arms. She had stood outside the door and listened as her older children bid their own hesitant, tear-stained farewells. Ten minutes later, Kali had rushed out of his room, tripping over her feet as she did so. And Dava knew her husband was dead.

~

Years later, when the wound of his absence had scabbed over and felt less excruciating, Dava would ruminate about the extended nature of Arvid's passing. And she couldn't help but think death by illness was almost a blessing. She had been given the gift of knowing their days together were numbered, rather than having him violently yanked out of their lives, as had happened with her parents and his. Arvid had been declared cancer-free in 2015, two years after his initial diagnosis. They had been celebratory about the news but cautious too, since 90 percent of the patients diagnosed with his type of cancer experienced a recurrence within five years. So to Dava and Arvid, the news was more like a signal that time was in a finite supply.

To that end, Dava urged her children to not take time with their father for granted and to find something meaningful they could share with him. For Arvie, it had been a fascination with Sweden and his Swedish heritage, and so father and son had traveled to the country together three times in the final years of Arvid's life, which acted as the springboard for his son's eventual move there after college. With Sita, the two were dedicated readers and would have their own book club–type discussions in which they went back and forth selecting books for each other to read: Ellen Raskin, William Faulkner, Suzanne Collins, Anita Desai, Jennifer Egan, Jenny Han. Arvid and Kali made a point of dedicating each Sunday afternoon to visiting a museum or art gallery in the city, logging the most visits at the MoMA. And for as long as he had the strength to walk, Arvid would take Rev on long strolls through Central Park, with the hope Rev would always fondly associate his father with the park, in case he was too young to remember specific memories of their time together.

After Arvid had learned in fall 2018 the cancer had returned, he devoted two months crafting letters to each of his children that he instructed be read on their twenty-first, twenty-eighth, thirty-fifth, and forty-fifth birthdays. He chose each year because those years were significant in his own life: official adulthood, the age he got married, the age he became vice principal, and the age he learned the cancer had returned. The letters were personalized to each Shastri-Persson for each milestone. The twenty-first-birthday letter was an assortment of memories and anecdotes about each child; the twenty-eighth letter was advice on love, friendships, and relationships; the thirty-fifth letter was Arvid's thoughts on the importance of kindness and generosity, on both a grand scale and small; and the forty-fifth was simply a list of songs Arvid asked that they listen to on their respective birthdays at a location of great significance to them. He signed off with the same sentence in all four letters: "Celebrate each remaining birthday in a way that is meaningful to you. Each one is precious and extraordinary, and so you are to me. I love you, and I am with you always. Take care of each other. Love, Dad."

Arvid had not sealed these missives before giving them to Dava to pass along to them after his death. So in her lowest moments during his illness, when she was gutted he was in so much pain and terrified his death was approaching, she would read his letters and find comfort in them. And she was incredibly touched by how much time and care Arvid had put into these missives, with the goal of wanting to remain a voice and presence in their lives. In her *Times* essay, she mentioned these letters to their children.

One of the final conversations we had when he was still himself, all twinkling eyes and warm humor, was about what he thought about when he wrote these letters to our kids. And he responded, "I'm planting seeds in a garden I'll never get to see—well, that I won't get to see grow to fruition." I knew he was quoting something—Arvid loved to insert song lyrics into our conversations; it was just one of the things that made him so endearing to all who knew him—but I had not quite figured out where it was from. And so when I asked, he answered with another quote coupled with a devilish smile: "Best of wives, best of women."

What she did not include in the essay was their experience watching *Hamilton*, which in many ways had inspired the *Times* essay and her decision to found Helping Perssons. They had seen it twice: first at the Public Theater during its off-Broadway run, and a few years later on Broadway, one week before they had learned his cancer had returned. The ending of the musical had left them both sniffling, just as it had the first time they saw it. But this time, Dava was also bothered by the show's conclusion: the fact that Eliza Hamilton had completely devoted herself to her late husband's legacy.

"Would he have done the same for her if she had died first?" she complained as they left the theater arm-in-arm.

"He would have done something for her in his own Hamilton way. I could see him having written a two-hundred-page pamphlet about her wifely virtues."

"But the dedication to preserving his work for the remaining fifty years of her life? The *orphanage*?" She blew her nose into Arvid's handkerchief, which he had given to her at the start of act two. "He wouldn't have done the same for her. Trust me."

"Yeah, probably not," he said, laughing. "Just so you know, if by some miracle I outlive you, I would do the same for you. I would dedicate myself to upholding your legacy."

"Oh," she replied. Her emotions, already rubbed raw by

having watched the musical, were now exposed and gaping upon hearing her husband's words. Because she knew he meant it. Right there on the street opposite the theater, she broke down and cried, collapsing on the curb and not caring if anyone saw her. Arvid sat down by her side, put his bony, hairless arm around her, and waited for her tears to pass before saying gently, "I'm sorry."

"Don't be sorry. What you said is so beautiful," she croaked, wiping her eyes with the handkerchief. "Honey," she said hesitantly, "I'm not cut out to be an Eliza. There's so much I still want to do . . . for me." She let the words flap there, out in the open, and ducked her head, ashamed.

"I know," he said, gazing at her with kind, sad eyes. "I've never had a problem being the Eliza to your Hamilton."

It had been the only time during their marriage she had hinted at the motivations behind her philanthropic work, revealing the dark heart of ego that beat underneath. And he had not judged her for it. It was this conversation Dava had in mind when she decided to write an essay about her late husband. Not just as a way of announcing she was founding a nonprofit in his honor, but also as a monument to their marriage. She wanted to fight the cloud of infidelity rumors plaguing them since *The Skylight*'s premiere and intensifying after the Oscars, reducing him to a footnote in the public's fascination with her and Tom Buck. Dava wanted to celebrate his personhood. And in doing so, she began to research.

She read about the ways notable men and women were honored by their spouses: statues, buildings, scholarships, charities. But what she uncovered was a dispiriting imbalance. Because women tended to outlive their husbands, there were so many Elizas: women who worked tirelessly at the meticulous curation of their husband's legacies at the expense of their own sense of self, so that their own identity would always be "Mrs."

or "The Wife Of." She did not want Arvid to only be "The Husband Of" in the public consciousness, especially not "The Husband of That Woman Who Allegedly Inspired That Song by Tom Buck."

And so in 2022, two years after Arvid's death, Helping Perssons was born. As part of her *Times* essay, Dava announced a website in which people could apply for a $2,000 grant for their projects, no matter their size, scale, or ambition. After the Helping Perssons employees reviewed the applications and narrowed them to the top ten most worthy or interesting candidates, they would be forwarded to Dava, who would then decide that week's grantee. In its early years, the program averaged about one hundred applications per week. But by the time Dava had asked twenty-six-year-old Arvie to head up the program eight years later, the applications had swelled to three thousand per week, and so Dava ceded decisions to her son.

Chaitanya and her community garden were the fifth-ever Helping Perssons grantee chosen by Arvie. Dava could still distinctly recall the day she had received his email listing that month's grantees and spotted Chaitanya's name on the list. She had been attending a summer cocktail party held on a yacht circling Liberty Island, shivering by herself on the lower deck after fleeing inside when the winds buffeting the boat became too intense for someone clad in a whispery pink-and-green summer dress, which she had worn even though she worried that at age fifty-six, she was too old to wear such a flirty confection. Dava had inelegantly plopped down on a bench facing an oval-shaped window that gave her a view of the sun glinting off the water and the Statue of Liberty in the distance, far away enough that she looked like a woman trying to hail a taxi. With a sigh mixed with a harrumph, regretting she had agreed to attend a party in which everyone seemed at least two decades younger, Dava retreated to her phone, checking her email for the eighth time since boarding the yacht.

And there it was, third on the list of Helping Perssons grantees: Chaitanya Rao, Oakland Springtime Community Garden. Dava had blinked her eyes several times, then enlarged the email so that Chaitanya's name took up all the space on the phone's screen, as if that would help her determine whether this person could possibly be her daughter. After staring at her name for a few moments, Dava quickly searched for the garden's website and gasped when she saw that Chaitanya's pictureless bio stated she had been born and raised in London. Even with insistent, facile chatter and a synth-heavy song that sounded as if it were trying to break the speakers rattling above her, Dava thought she could hear her heartbeat, loud and wild and shocked, above the noise. She looked up from her phone and noticed the yacht had sailed closer to the Statue of Liberty so Dava could now make out her features, her green-blue lips pressed firmly together and eyes resolute to the sky.

Dava then recalled what Arvid had said to her about flying into New York City for the first time, when he was arriving to attend graduate school and move in with her. As the plane began its descent into John F. Kennedy International Airport, he had spied the Statue of Liberty outside his window.

"When I saw her, that's when it became real to me," he had said. "The life we had planned together on our cliff was really happening. And we'd finally be together."

In particular, he had singled out her torch, joking that the statue's raised arm was like "a wave hello from the official ambassador of your country." And in that moment, seeing Lady Liberty was almost as if her daughter were now waving at her, inviting her to connect.

What she could have never anticipated was that by losing Arvid, she would regain her daughter. Since the day she had signed the paperwork waiving all legal rights to her firstborn child, she never reached out to her, letting that chapter of her life stay in the past along with everything else she associated with Panit. In an alternate reality, she could have lived her whole life knowing Chaitanya existed somewhere in the world, without knowing anything about her beyond her name and those of her adopted parents. So for her daughter to apply for a Helping Perssons grant was an incredible coincidence and a joy—something she didn't even know she wanted, but ultimately needed.

I'd like to think it was Arvid's gift to me, in a way, she would have said to an interviewer if she had ever thought about going public about Chaitanya. *It was my goal to honor his life, and in doing so, she came back into mine. It was a real, healing way of coming full circle.*

⌒

Dava was shaken out of her thoughts by hearing the final song on the Mercury Rev album. She had forgotten *Deserter's Songs* ended up on an upbeat note with a sunny jam called "Delta Sun Bottleneck Stomp." It reminded her of the early grace notes of a sunrise, when the sun first emerges and effortlessly shows off its ebullience. The song put her in a light, even festive mood, and she longed to be around her family. Why, in her final hours on Earth, was she spending so much time by herself?

She looked toward the door, to the noise of conversation dancing outside, just out of reach. Dava thought about standing up and walking downstairs, but that felt like it would take enormous effort, and she feared triggering another seizure after finally regaining her equilibrium. The sun had disappeared completely, and darkness was rapidly overtaking her bedroom, the shadows slithering in like snakes. And then the album concluded. Dava had forgotten it did not end with "Delta Sun," but on an ominous note—an eerie bouquet of sounds akin to a ghost story mixed with a car crash—that made her feel alone, and a little afraid.

CHAPTER SEVENTEEN

Siblings

I was so blessed to know Dava and have her as a mentor and friend. If she truly is my mother, then yes, I would like to have that confirmed so I can learn about my family history and possibly meet my siblings.

—*Chaitanya Rao, when asked for comment about whether she intends to reach out to the Shastri-Persson family*

WHEN KALI SAW THAT Rev's parka and snow boots were missing from the mudroom, she immediately knew he was at the boathouse. She carefully walked down the hill to go join him, Dava's letter and her last three cigarettes hidden in the inside pocket of her purple, ankle-length puffy coat. Kali was thankful her brothers-in-law had shoveled several feet around the perimeter of the house earlier in the day, making it easier for her to get to the two-story boathouse, which to her eyes had always resembled a doghouse expanded to five times its normal size. The first floor of the wood-shingled building was home to a speedboat and several rainbow kayaks hanging along the walls, although the oars had long gone missing. Kali ascended the staircase to the attic floor, in which she saw her brother standing in front of the octagonal window, the sunset's last blast of light illuminating him so that he cut a slim, dark figure in silhouette.

"Rev," she called out as she walked toward him, navigating through a maze of weathered boxes and summer patio furniture.

"Hey, Sis," he said as he turned around, his leather-gloved fingers twirling a long, thin white stick.

"How long have you been out here?" She partially unzipped her coat to pull out a cigarette. She held it out to him, but he shook his head.

"It was too hard to quit; I can't go back." He stuck the white stick in his mouth and held it between his teeth. "I'm trying to make do with a lollipop stick."

She shook her head in amazement. "I don't have your will-power. Especially after everything that's happened today." She lit her cigarette with a zebra-striped lighter, then blew the smoke over her shoulder, away from her brother. "I didn't get to say this earlier, but I'm sorry you had to see Amma in that state. That must have been awful."

"I don't want to talk about it. I came out here because I needed to be away from all of that, all of them." He clenched his teeth so that the stick, which had been dangling from his lips, was now pointing sharply at attention.

Does that include Sandi? Kali wondered. Instead she asked, "How is Sandi? I haven't seen her since yesterday."

Rev kicked at a loose nail sticking out of the wall with such force that he bent it sideways. "She's been dealing with morning sickness, so she stayed in bed most of the day. She's fine." In truth, Rev didn't know if Sandi was fine. Each time he had stopped by their room to check on her she had been sleeping, but he wondered if she was pretending so she could avoid talking to him. After he had gone to bed the night before, stinking of tequila after the siblings' meeting about Chaitanya in the den, he found Sandi waiting up for him, her black sleep mask pulled up above her eyes like one giant, questioning eyebrow. She had heard about Dava's alleged secret daughter, but rather than ask him how he was doing in the wake of such stunning news, Sandi had instead laid into him about the urgency of making sure their own child was represented in Dava's will.

"I hope you know it's not about the money," she told him as he climbed into bed that night. She rested her head against his bare chest, then picked up his arms and wrapped them around her. "These past few days have been so shocking. And lonely too. Of course your family is busy and upset, so I haven't had a chance to get to know them, and I'm not a priority, but it'd be nice to feel like I belonged here, and so in my crazy brain this would help me feel like the baby and I are a part of all of this. Does that make sense?"

No, he wanted to respond. "I'm dealing with a lot right now" is all he managed to say. She gave him an irritated look and withdrew to the other side of the bed. They had slept with their backs to each other, although he had barely slept at all.

"So Amma and Tom Buck," Kali said, changing the subject to the first thing she could think of that had nothing to do with Sandi. "You know what's the most surprising thing to me? Not that she had an affair. But how she found the time."

"I should add that to the movie too. Shoehorn in the Tom Buck stuff before I end with the big reveal about Chaitanya."

Kali exhaled a big cloud of smoke, then coughed. "What are you talking about?"

Rev sighed as he explained Dava's wish for a biopic, penned by him, that included sharing the story of giving up and later reuniting with her eldest daughter. Kali continued coughing incredulously, then stubbed out her cigarette by emphatically smashing it with the heel of her boot.

"I don't get it! She told me the exact opposite."

"Opposite of a movie?"

"She told me she never wanted Chaitanya to know the truth." Kali pulled the letter out of her coat pocket as she finally told him about what their mother had said about its contents, and how she had pleaded with Kali to ensure she was buried with it. "Only you and Sita know about this. I didn't tell Arvie, because ... well, he's having a rough time."

"So now what?" Rev groaned. "Amma keeps changing her mind every other second. Not to mention I don't want to work on some movie. I'm not a screenwriter. I'm just trying to focus on how to be a good dad. And Sandi ..." He trailed off and muttered something unintelligible under his breath.

Kali returned the letter to her pocket, then dragged an iron patio table closer to the window and sat down on top of it, beckoning him to join her. "Sandi what?" she asked delicately.

"Sandi keeps asking me to check if Amma can create a trust fund for the baby, like the ones she set up for the other grandkids. She said it's not about the money but about fitting in here or something. I don't get it." Rev turned to his sister. "I mean, I get that this is important for our child. But Sandi seems more preoccupied with Amma's will rather than the fact that I'm about to lose her. Not to mention the unending wall of shit we're dealing with."

"Sandi's not completely wrong, though," Kali said, fighting the urge to light another cigarette. To quiet her craving, she took out the lighter again and flicked it on and off repeatedly. They both stared at the flame as she continued to speak. "That is definitely something that needs to be figured out, preferably before Amma passes away. But I think that in case it doesn't, the rest of us will make sure it's taken care of somehow. I know Sita planned to speak to Amma's lawyer." She extinguished the flame and held the lighter tightly in her fist, absorbing the latent heat into her palm.

"I'd appreciate that—thanks," Rev said dully, then shifted his weight to sit farther back on the table so they were right next to each other. "I just wish Sandi cared about what I was going through, you know?"

"I'm sure she does. I saw her when Amma told us the news, and she was devastated for you," Kali said. She recalled what Dava had told her, how the goddess Kali, her namesake, was described as having "a mother's incomprehensible love." She squeezed his arm. "But at the same time, she has a maternal instinct to look out for her child, and I imagine that comes before anything else, even you."

He snorted, even though she could see tears welling up in his eyes. "I didn't know you were such a big fan of Sandi."

Kali pulled her hand away, startled. "What do you mean? I've always been supportive."

"I mean, in words, yeah. But you've never shown interest in her as a person. You've barely spoken to her since we got here."

"There's been a lot going on," she retorted. "But I like her just fine. I don't know what you want from me, honestly." *Fuck it*, she thought to herself as she dug into her pocket and pulled out the second-to-last cigarette, dismayed to see that it was creased in the middle. She lit it anyway and this time didn't take care not to blow in Rev's direction.

Rev glared at her, then pulled the lollipop stick out of his mouth and pointed it in her direction. "Admit it, though: you'd prefer if there were no Sandi. That it was still you and me against the world, mocking Arvie and Sita and the rest of the normals."

"Grow the hell up." Kali jumped off the iron table, and the sudden movement rattled it, causing Rev to slide off and nearly fall. "I miss our closeness, sure. But I'm never going to begrudge you having a marriage or a family. It's just that I never realized you wanted it," she added, her cheeks turning red. "But now that you do, I'm happy for you. I've always been happy for you." Her eyes landed on the sideways nail and she kicked it in the other direction.

"Are you, though?" Rev said. He had fully expected sympathy from his sister, after coming up short from his mother and fiancée. But since he didn't get it from her either, Rev wanted to hit a nerve. "Arvie mentioned to me yesterday you were upset you weren't able to bring Mattius and Lucy. That you didn't have anyone in your corner. We used to mock the normals, but maybe you were mocking it so much because you secretly wanted it."

"Who doesn't want companionship, Rev?" Kali leaned against the wall opposite him and railed at him through chattering teeth. "That doesn't mean I want to do the marriage-and-kids thing like you guys. There's more than one way to have a meaningful relationship. And I can be fine on my own too." Her eyes flashed. "My point to Arvie was that I was in a real relationship with them and wanted them here with me, and none of you took it seriously. From them, I can't say I was surprised. But you?" Kali shook her head. "I always—*always*—have your back. One thousand percent. Can't say the same about you."

"Maybe because you're not number one in my life anymore. Think of that?" Rev knew he was in the wrong, but he couldn't stop himself. He felt hurt by Sandi, by his mother, and desperately needed to lash out against the one person he knew would forgive him.

"Of the two of us here, I'm the only one who's accepted that. Because guess what, Little Brother. You're not number one in your life anymore either." Kali swung her braid over her shoulder, then tugged at it for emphasis. "You've been floating through life, not giving a shit about much of anything. Because you don't know how to do anything but be taken care of and adored." Rev staggered back, as if her words were a bullet to his chest. She had taken the worst things he thought of himself and given them air. "It's time to step up and take care of your family."

They both froze as they heard someone coming upstairs and turned to look behind them to see Sita emerge from the doorway, shivering in a thick red turtleneck and matching beanie. "There you two are. I should have looked here first."

"What's going on? Is Amma okay?" Kali asked as she cast a sidelong glance at her younger brother, who had moved back to face the window.

"She's fine for now." Sita paused in the center of the room, turned on the ceiling fan light, and let out an "oh shit" as both the light bulb and the fan switched on simultaneously. "I just checked in on her and she seems better. But she's also not budging about having the treatment administered tomorrow morning, which means we only have today to figure out some logistics. Starting with being on the same page when it comes to her."

Sita pulled out her phone, retrieved from Dava's room, and showed them the interview with Chaitanya, in which she said she wanted to get to know her siblings and learn more about her family. "I know Amma doesn't want her to know—"

"Well, now she does," Rev muttered, his eyes still fixed on the darkening sky.

"Long story," Kali cut in. "Go on."

"But I think this story is bigger than Amma's wishes. Like the Tom Buck news, this eventually will be confirmed with or without us. We need to be in control of this going forward. I think the four of us need to be a united front about several things, including her." When neither responded, Sita gave them a quizzical look. "Um, everything okay? Were you guys fighting?"

"Long story," Kali repeated. "If we need to hash out a few things, let's do it here, then, in private. I'm sure Colin and Vincent can watch over things in the main house for a bit."

"It's freezing out here," Sita protested as she pulled at the ceiling fan rope multiple times, discovering to her frustration that she could only turn off the fan if she switched off the light too. "I don't think I can stand out here for more than a few minutes."

"How about this? I'll go get Arvie and tell the guys where we are and why. Take my jacket in the meantime, and I'll go inside to get yours," Kali said.

"All right, then," Sita said with uncertainty as Kali unzipped her jacket and handed it to her. Kali looked at the back of her brother's head for a moment, then rolled her eyes, not trying to hide her irritation from her older sister as she exited the room.

━

Sita watched Kali's retreating figure and then let out a low whistle. She hopped onto the table, then cupped her hands over her mouth and blew into them for warmth. When Rev still didn't speak, she finally broke the silence with a nervous laugh.

"Were you guys fighting? I didn't know that was possible."

Rev swung around, tears running down his face. Sita rushed over to hug him and soon realized he was shaking, as if he was completely letting himself give in to his grief. She had a sense of déjà vu, remembering little Rev trembling in her arms when they were standing at their father's deathbed, sensing something was terribly wrong but not comprehending what was happening. One major difference was Sita was now several inches shorter than her younger brother, and so trying to hug him felt akin to clinging to a sailboat mast buffeted by heavy winds.

"Rev, Rev," she whispered until his body stilled. "It's all going to be okay. We're going to be okay."

"How do you know?" he asked earnestly as he pulled away from her, staring down at her with watery eyes, one teardrop still balanced on his long lashes.

"Because we lost Dad, and we got through it. We're going to lose Amma, and we have a lot of crazy things we have to figure out once she actually passes. But—"

"I'm not just talking about her," he said in a near whisper. "I'm talking about me. I don't know if I can do it."

"Do what?"

"Marriage." His voice cracked. "I've been worried about being a good husband and father because I didn't have Dad in my life. But it's more than that. I love Sandi—don't get me wrong. But I don't love the idea of . . . it." He said this last word as if he were spitting out a hair he had found in his dinner.

Sita's eyes widened, but she kept her voice gentle and steady. "It's natural to have doubts, Rev. Especially since Sandi's your first real relationship."

Rev shrugged and sat down on the patio table. He pulled the lollipop stick out of his pocket and held it between his two front teeth. Sita eyed this odd gesture but did not comment. Instead she sat down next to him, her feet barely touching the floor.

"I always wanted to be married," she said. "Maybe too much. I wanted what Amma and Dad had, but even better. Bhaskar was my—"

"But that's the thing about Amma," Rev interjected. "When she talks about Dad, she sounds like she's completely in love with him. Earlier today she told me a story about the night they decided to get married and . . . it was so sweet." He decided to keep the story of the Mercury Rev album to himself, since Dava had confided it only to him. "Anyway, if Amma and Dad had this amazing relationship, but she still cheated on him, what does marriage mean anyway?"

Sita nodded knowingly, touched to see her little brother asking the same exasperated questions she had asked when she was twenty-four and newly divorced from Bhaskar. She had met him in graduate school, and they so immediately clicked she had referred to him fondly as her "mirror image." She saw in Bhaskar her own ambition and determination to carve out a career distinct from a dominant parental figure (in his case, a grandfather) while still hoping to please them. The two also shared the same values and interests, the kinds of traits one would list in an "About Me" blurb on a dating app: *I'm socially liberal but fiscally conservative, and I love Thai food and snowboarding.* Her parents' marriage had been foremost in her mind when she had decided to wed Bhaskar, because she believed their similar qualities guaranteed her a similarly happy relationship. In fact, Sita secretly thought she had one-upped her mother because Bhaskar was Indian. She knew it wasn't logical to feel that way, except for the fact that Dava had hinted at her parents' disappointment in her marrying a white man, with their absence from her wedding a glaring example. In Sita's head, she had been able to accomplish something her mother could not.

As they sat there shivering in the boathouse attic, weakly lit by a single light bulb, Sita relayed this information to Rev. Even in the growing darkness, she could see Rev's eyes go big when she mentioned looking at her marriage as a way of being better at something than their mother.

"Is that why when Amma told us about Panit, you seemed so uncomfortable?" he asked tentatively.

"Yeah. Her story hit so close to home for me, because we had essentially done the same thing. We were both in love with an idea—Mr. Perfect, and Indian too—instead of a person. The only difference is I was stupid enough to marry mine." Sita shook her head at herself, her diamond stud earrings sparkling as she did so. "But to be clear, Bhaskar never was terrible to me. He just wasn't right for me. We fought constantly about stupid, useless things and didn't know how to stop hurting each other."

Sita noticed Rev open his mouth to speak but she continued

on, wanting to hurry out her words before the other two
arrived. "After we divorced, I felt adrift. Ashamed, embarrassed,
and completely skeptical of marriage. You would have thought
I was Kali," she said with a small laugh. "And then maybe
like a few months after the divorce, I read an amazing quote:
'Compatibility is an achievement of love. It shouldn't be its pre-
condition.' Well, that hit me in the gut. And it made me rethink
everything about Bhaskar and why it hadn't worked."

By this time, Rev had accidentally dropped the lollipop stick
from his mouth and was now instead chewing on his chapped
lower lip. As he did so, he thought of Sandi. Were they com-
patible? He had never thought about his relationship in those
terms. He had won Sandi over, and then her lease was up, and
he liked waking up next to her every day, and so they were soon
living together, spending most of their time curled up on the
sofa, a paperback in her hands and a video game controller in
his. Once she became pregnant, he had proposed in a fit of joy
and panic, and their honeyed days of sex and laughter instantly
switched to planning and logistics. They hadn't disagreed on
anything major yet, because Rev found it easier to agree to what
she asked for. When he imagined a future with her, he saw it as
an endless to-do list scrolling before him like the opening crawl
in the *Star Wars* movies.

"Ouch," he yelped. In gnawing on his bottom lip, he accidentally ripped off a large chunk of dry skin. Rev pulled off
his glove, touched his fingers to his lips, and felt a tiny button
of blood.

"You okay?" Sita asked, looking up at him. *Is he even listening
to me?* she wondered crossly.

"Yeah, just tore through my lip a little." Noticing his sister
rubbing her hands together, he took off his other glove and
handed both to her. "I hope you know I'm ready to step up
and be a father. It's just that anytime I think about marriage,

I feel miserable." He groaned. "It's no slight against Sandi. I'm the defective one."

"After Bhaskar, I thought I was defective too. What helped me was changing my whole concept of marriage and seeing it for what it is." Sita explained she had discovered that the quote was from a *New York Times* essay by a writer named Alain de Botton titled "Why You Will Marry the Wrong Person."

"Can you imagine? That the quote was from an essay with *that* title?" Sita told Rev. "I had only been divorced from Bhaskar for about three months and had just met Colin and was starting to really like him. But it seemed too soon to be falling for someone. I was also nervous about making the same mistakes. So this essay found me at the right time."

"Is it true that you met on a dating app?" Rev asked. In the dim light where they could barely see each other's faces, he felt brave enough to ask the question he had wondered about for years. Sita had always claimed she and Colin had met at a bookstore in Union Square, but her vagueness about the details of their meet-cute led him and Kali to speculate she wasn't telling the truth.

Sita groaned. "Is that what Kali told you?"

"We, um, both assumed that was the real story. Is it true?"

"Fine. Yes, we met on an app, okay? I was embarrassed that we met on HitMeUp—"

"Wasn't that mostly for hookups and one-night stands?"

"Shut up. I'll have you know Colin was the first and only person I matched with. I deleted it right after." Sita thought back to how, after running into Bhaskar's cousin and learning he was dating again, she had come straight home—their former home—and downloaded the app. Colin's face was the first one she saw. He had seemed impossibly beautiful, but what she had found most intriguing was that his "About Me" blurb had featured only one word.

"Books," she told Rev, unable to stop a smile from blooming on her lips.

"That's it? Just 'books'?" Rev thought of what he knew of Colin and did not know he was much of a reader. And then realized he did not know much about him at all.

"Yes. Written in all caps. Followed by an exclamation point," Sita gushed. "I just had to know more. We texted and sent emails for weeks before meeting, because he was traveling for work. Even before I met him, I felt like this could be my guy. But that also freaked me out. I didn't want to start seeing someone new and make the same mistakes I had with Bhaskar. So I remembered that quote, searched for it online, and found the Alain essay. It honestly changed my life. There's a reason we eloped after only nine months of dating," she said triumphantly, sounding a little smug to Rev's ears. If Kali were with him, the two might have traded eye rolls. But in this moment, there seemed to be a concrete solution to his crisis, and he was desperate to know more.

"What was it called again? 'Why You Will Marry the Wrong Person'?"

"That's right. It's not meant in a judgmental way, but pragmatically. We all pretty much marry the wrong person because we're inherently flawed people, and somehow we don't expect our partners to notice and call us on it." Sita took out her phone to look at the time. "Let me see if I can sum it up pretty quick—they'll probably be here any minute.

"The gist of it is that before we enter serious relationships, we don't have to look in the mirror and see our true, flawed selves. So the first time you get called out regularly for being annoying or stubborn or odd is when you're in a relationship. It's like you're taking off the designer dress and letting someone see you in sweats. Sweats that you haven't washed in a week."

Rev, delicately dabbing his lip again, let out a laugh of

recognition. Sita smiled in the darkness and pushed forward, glad that her words were resonating with him.

"And so no wonder marriages are hard work, right? Because you're taking the mess that is you and expecting your spouse to just embrace it. And by the same turn, you expect the person you love to change into the person you want them to be. Conflicts are inevitable."

"Way to sell me on marriage, Sis," Rev said, chuckling darkly.

"I'm not trying to sell you on it," Sita said. "I'm trying to say it's *work*. It's recognizing that the husband who brings me breakfast in bed every morning also neglects to clean up in the bathroom unless explicitly told. It's recognizing that he has a point when he tells me I overschedule every inch of my life." She shook her head knowingly. "Like Alain says, it's about understanding there will be conflicts between you and your partner but that the conflicts don't matter as much as how you resolve them. Wait—hold on a second. Let me quote from him directly."

As Sita searched for the essay online, Rev looked at her face illuminated by the blue light. How much did he really know about his older sister? This surely was the most time they had talked seriously about their lives in years. Possibly ever. Since she and Arvie were already out of the house by the time he was a teenager, he had always seen them as pseudoparental figures, their lives established in the adult spheres of jobs, mortgages, and dinner parties. Even though he saw Sita more often since they both lived in New York, he only knew the broad outlines of her life and none of the specifics. She had always seemed like a less playful and interesting version of their mother. Whenever Sita had scolded him or Kali, they would laugh about how they had gotten in trouble with "Dava Junior." *But maybe that's what we need right now*, he mused to himself. And as he sat next to Sita, he thought about how much both she and Colin had done in the past few days—spearheading laundry runs after discovering a dearth of bedding and towels, helping Vincent prepare meals, tidying up the kitchen and common rooms at the end of every night—acting as a quiet, steadying force in all the chaos.

Sita handed him her phone. He read out loud:

Marriage ends up as a hopeful, generous, infinitely kind gamble taken by two people who don't know yet who they are or who the other might be, binding themselves to a future they cannot conceive of and have carefully avoided investigating.

"That's exactly it," he said on an exhale. He looked at Sita with beseeching eyes, the light from the phone giving his boyish face an alien glow.

Sita nodded as she took back the phone and pocketed it in Kali's coat. "Don't fault yourself for thinking marriage was the next step once Sandi got pregnant. But maybe now think about the work you both need to do by yourselves, and together, before going forward."

She hopped off the table and started jogging in place. "Okay, where are they? It's too cold to stay out here much longer. Honestly, I don't know why Kali insisted we talk in the boathouse."

"Probably because she knew Arvie won't have access to any alcohol out here," Rev mused. He smiled when Sita let out a long, boisterous laugh. "You gotta admit that's the only thing that makes sense."

"True," she replied as she headed to the other side of the room to the octagonal window facing the house, to see if she could catch sight of them trudging through the snow.

"Before they get here," Rev called out, then hesitated.

"If they get here." Sita turned back toward her brother. "What, Rev?"

"What's your secret?" He needed more facts, more answers. "You guys are rock solid. Watching you together these past few days...it's like what I imagine you guys saw with Amma and Dad."

"Oh wow, really?" Sita said from afar. "That's so nice of you to say." She rejoined him again on the table. "Well, after Bhaskar, I made it a point that our fights don't last longer than twenty-four hours, no matter what. And absolutely nothing comes first except for the kids and each other." She stopped speaking, lost in thought. "I don't want that to change," she murmured to herself. Before Rev could ask what she meant, two pairs of footsteps clamored up the stairs. "Is that them?"

"We're here, we're here," they heard Kali panting.

"What took so long?" Sita asked as she saw Kali, wielding a large flashlight and wearing her red woolen coat, and Arvie trailing behind her. "Did you see the boys? What are they up to? Is Colin with them?"

"So many questions," Arvie sniggered. Kali sighed and placed the flashlight on the table, with the golden light beaming upward like a reverse waterfall.

"Arvie and I got sucked into watching this documentary with the girls," she said. "The boys are fine; they're playing some sort of card game. I think Colin and Vincent are making dinner."

"What was the documentary about?" Rev asked.

"Tom Buck," Arvie spat out. "She wouldn't let me watch to the end so I could see him die."

CHAPTER EIGHTEEN

Someone Else's Story

I'll never be a footnote in someone else's story. Everyone I meet is destined to be a footnote in *my* story.

—*From a diary entry by Dava Shastri, age fifteen*

SANDI WAS SHOCKED THAT it was already close to evening when she woke up from her nap. Sleep and nausea had been her primary worlds for the past few weeks, but since arriving at Beatrix Island, sleep had been winning out.

She was barely three months pregnant, but felt like she had been experiencing morning sickness and fatigue for an eternity. If she had felt close to Sita, Sandi would have asked her for pregnancy advice. But Sita had only said six sentences to her since arriving at the island, and two of them had been to ask her if she had seen the twins. On the one hand, Sandi understood they were all handling a lot on an emotional and practical level. But she also could not help but feel resentful toward Rev and his family for looking at her as if she were a stowaway on the SS *Shastri-Persson*, still trying to determine whether she would be granted passage or asked to disembark at the next port.

Sandi's stomach rumbled, and she knew she could no longer hide in the guest room. She glanced at the clock on the nightstand and saw it was half past six, which meant the In-Laws—which is how she thought of Colin and Vincent—were likely preparing dinner. As for Rev, she hoped against hope he had taken the time to sit down with his mother and spell out the need for a trust fund for her fifth grandchild. If that happened, then Sandi could finally relax, knowing he understood why this was so important to her.

After trading her pale-pink pajamas for a white sweater and black jeans, sweeping her hair into a loose bun, and applying lip gloss, Sandi cracked the guest room door open. Her and Rev's room was located adjacent to the great room, and so as soon as she exited, she was awash in noise. After patting down flyaways and smoothing out the wrinkles in her sweater, Sandi headed toward the great room. But then she spotted Colin entering the kitchen and decided to go there first, because Colin was the second-nicest person in the house after Vincent. Also, her stomach rumbles had become full-on earthquakes, and so she quickened her steps past the great room into the bright warmth of the kitchen, which featured a small checkerboard of pots and pans on the stove, each expressing delicious, unknowable aromas. Colin and Vincent were speaking to each other in low tones, with Colin pausing to pat his brother-in-law sympathetically on the back. Sandi didn't want to intrude, but her hunger pangs urged her forward.

"Hi there," she called out. "How's it going in here?"

"Hi, Sandi," Vincent responded jovially, his face glistening with sweat and his eyes watery and sad. "Haven't seen much of you today. Hungry?"

"Yes—starved, actually. I'll eat anything, even frozen pizza." The three of them laughed. Sandi sat down at the kitchen island as Vincent handed her a bowl of thin soup from a pot that had been warming on the stove. "What is this? Is it Indian?"

"Yeah, it's rasam. I figured it could fill you up a bit until dinner is ready. Tonight we're having…should we call it an international feast?"

Colin nodded warmly. "We're having spaghetti Bolognese, red pepper risotto, Swedish baked potatoes—"

"They're hasselbackspotatis," Vincent noted, smiling.

"Yes, what he said. Plus the last of the rasam." Colin placed a tumbler of water in front of Sandi before tending to the risotto. "It's basically all the food we have left in the kitchen except for some canned items. But since we're leaving tomorrow, we can survive on this until then."

"Oh," Sandi said with surprise. How could Rev have neglected to tell her? "Does that mean... what does that mean for Dava?"

Colin and Vincent exchanged glances. "Dr. Windsor is administering the treatment tomorrow morning," Vincent told her as he ladled an extra spoon of rasam into her bowl. "Rev was pretty shook-up after Dava's seizure. Is he doing okay?"

"Yeah, he's hanging in there." Sandi hoped her face didn't express how hurt and baffled she felt at hearing this. How much had she missed? "Have you seen Rev? I haven't seen him since... then."

Colin turned around to respond to her, and for the first time she noticed the men were wearing nearly identical black zip-up pullovers. Sandi was reminded of a very old movie poster that showed a tall, muscular actor and short, bald one standing next to each other dressed in the same outfits. The differences in height and build were not quite as striking with the brothers-in-law, but seeing them made Sandi feel even more of an outsider, that the two had a bond she could not hope to share in.

"They're having a family meeting in the boathouse. They're trying to figure out some logistics, like funeral arrangements," Colin said, lowering his voice on that last part. "I was about to run over there and let them know dinner's ready."

"I'll go," Sandi said as she quickly slurped down one last spoonful of rasam. "I need the walk anyway."

"Don't go out there by yourself—it's freezing," Vincent said, his eyebrows creased with concern.

"I'll be fine. It's only a two-minute walk. I'll just pop over and pop right back." She backed out of the kitchen and hurried over to the foyer, where she grabbed her hooded jacket and boots from the mudroom and rushed out the front door, shivering on the doorstep as she put them on. Sandi did not want to be stopped from going. Yet as she made her way to the boathouse, with only the wan presence of a crescent moon to guide her, cursing under her breath each time her foot slipped on a patch of ice, she knew it was a dumb idea to be outside by herself. But she was determined to intrude upon one of the incessant Shastri-Persson meetings, because she refused to be kept outside the loop any longer. She entered into a wall of pitch black and a chorus of overlapping conversations from above. Sandi stood at the bottom of the stairs and clung to the railing to anchor herself in the darkness. Despite the chill rapidly numbing her fingers, she took down her hood so she could better hear them speak.

"It's the 'is,'" she heard Sita say.

"What are you talking about?" Arvie's high-pitched whine was accompanied by a stamping of feet and the sound of something being dragged across the floor.

"When talking about Amma, she didn't say 'if she truly was my mother.' She said 'is.' Like Amma is still alive to her, like she can't process that she's gone. That tells me she's genuine. This isn't a money grab for her."

"So based on one stupid word in one stupid interview, we're going to let her into our lives? Makes real sense."

"What makes sense anymore?" Sandi's ears pricked up at hearing Rev's voice, sullen and listless. "Meet her, don't meet her—doesn't matter to me."

"Okay, so Rev and I agree about this, then," Arvie proclaimed. "Next topic."

"I'm not agreeing with you, Arvie. I just don't care. But if they want to have a relationship with her, I'm not going to stand in their way."

Sandi did not like hearing Rev sound so beaten down. For the first time, her anger cooled toward him and was replaced by concern. She wondered if she should go upstairs and invite them to dinner, and then the two of them would have a chance to speak privately. But she hesitated when she heard Sita speak again.

"So Kali and I will get in touch with her after we leave here," Sita said. Several seconds of silence passed. "Okay, good. Now we should really talk about what happens after Amma passes."

Sandi's eyes widened as Sita told her siblings she had finally spoken with Allen Ellingsworth, Dava's lawyer, and learned Dr. Windsor knew about her patient's plan to prematurely announce her death before coming to the island, and planned to backdate the death certificate to yesterday, which is when the news had reported she died. The doctor had agreed to the plan because Dava had promised her a seven-figure sum, half of which would go to a charity of Dr. Windsor's choosing.

"Amma..." Rev said. Sandi desperately longed to hear what he was saying, but could not make out the rest of his words. She cautiously took one stair up but paused midstep, afraid the creaks would give her away. Instead, she blew into her hands and pressed her palms against her cheeks to warm her frozen face.

"This is so fucking unethical," Arvie bellowed, interrupting what Rev had been saying. "Mom sure surrounds herself with the best people, doesn't she?"

"It's not ideal," Sita admitted. "She didn't think through how this could potentially backfire on us. But it is what it is. Which is why it's all the more important we're on the same page, not just with family matters but also the foundation, and the face we put forward to the world."

"Except that I'm quitting"—Arvid let out a hiccupping belch—"Helping Perssons. I'm going to be a Persson-Lindqvist. Kali knows."

"Omigod, c'mon, Arvie. Now is not the time." Sandi had never heard Kali sound so angry before.

"If we're figuring out logistics," he said, then belched again, "I have things to say too. I'm quitting. Add that to your to-do list, Dava Junior."

"Don't call her that like it's an insult," Kali snapped.

"Why is it okay for you and Rev to say but not me?" Arvie said.

"Call me Jesus if you want. Can we please just get back on track?" Sita pleaded.

"Of course you want to be called that."

"I'm so sick and tired of your bullshit!" Sita said as Sandi heard steps banging toward the north end of the attic. "No wonder Vin— Never mind."

"No wonder Vincent what?" Arvie hollered.

Sandi heard Rev let out a stream of words he sputtered so quickly she could only make out a few expletives and the word "drama." More stomping, and all four of them yelling. Then her fiancé's voice sliced through the tumult, vibrating with rage, silencing everyone else.

"This is so fucked. FUCKED." Sandi held her breath as the wind let out a low howl, the only noise to be heard inside and outside of the boathouse.

"Rev—" Kali began to say.

"I don't care about lawyers. Or Helping Perssons. Or Chaitanya. I care that I'm about to become a dad, and my baby won't ever meet his grandmother. That's all I care about."

"Oh, Rev," Sita said, sounding close to tears.

"I only have, like, four distinct memories from a time when Dad was alive, and he was always sick. So I can't really remember a time when this family was ever functioning, let alone happy. You don't know how lucky you are to have had the two of them together, and you have those memories you can revisit. All I have is hospital waiting rooms and whispered conversations that stopped when I entered the room. And now, here's a chance—a chance I never expected—to have my own child and maybe re-create some of...I don't know, that sense of unity, belonging. Not this. I don't want this."

Sandi almost burst into applause at hearing Rev sound so defiant and protective of their family.

"This anger, Arvie, it's toxic, and no one wants to be around it. It's poisoning everything. You're hurting Sita and Kali and Vincent, and I've had enough. Sometimes I don't think you're mad at Amma. You're mad because you love her, despite whatever wrongs you think she did to you."

The silence was heavy and portentous. Outside, the wind was picking up and was gusting enough to slightly rattle the kayaks hanging on the walls. Sandi held her breath, wondering what was happening upstairs that would allow the quiet to extend so long without a single word from any of the siblings. Just then, Sandi heard slushy footfalls at the doorway. Without thinking, she slipped outside and saw Colin and Vincent pointing their flashlights at her.

"Are you okay? Are they okay?" Vincent said, looming over her like a giant.

"They're in the middle of something intense." Sandi pointed upward toward the second floor. "I didn't want to interrupt."

"Oh no—I hope there isn't yelling," Colin said, beaming his flashlight to the upstairs window.

Sandi relayed how there had, in fact, been a lot of yelling, and now there was just an eerie lull. But she did not reveal what Sita had said that triggered it, not wanting to embarrass Vincent.

"I'd rather they not know I was here. I overheard some things...and I don't want to make it, um, you know, weird," she said. "Anyway, I'm going to head back to the house."

They both insisted on walking her back before checking on their respective spouses, and after escorting her to the main house, they walked back side by side on the icy path toward the boathouse. The phrase "good eggs" came to mind as she watched them go, her late grandmother Mary Josephine's way of indicating whether she liked someone enough to ask them to her house for Sunday dinner. Of all the Shastri-Perssons, only the In-Laws would have received an invite from Mary Jo.

In the foyer, she took off her winter gear and returned it to the mudroom closet. As she did so, she was struck by how empty it was, since all the adults except for her and Dava were now in the boathouse, and so the closet only sported two slender puffy jackets, one light pink and the other silver, plus two smaller parkas, both pumpkin orange with matching beanies. She decided to finally enter the great room and see what the kids were watching, as a way to distract herself from whatever was happening in the boathouse.

The kids were on the gray sectional, rapt in front of the television. Sandi heard the words "On November eighteenth, Tom Buck and his girlfriend, Isobel, set sail from Long Beach, California, to Baja on his sailboat, *Orion*." The screen showed a photo of a deeply tanned, silver-haired Tom Buck with his arm around a younger blond woman with a gap-toothed smile.

"What are you watching?" Sandi asked tentatively. The girls' glossy hair and shaded smiles reminded her of a trio of teens who had bullied her throughout high school.

"Shhh!" Klara said, her eyes fixed on the TV.

"Excuse me?" Sandi said, reminding herself she was the adult and a soon-to-be mother and shouldn't let a teenager shush her. "That's not nice."

"It's almost over and we're going to learn how Tom Buck died," Priya said breathlessly without looking at her.

"Oh. Okay." Sandi sat down on the far end of the sectional near Theo and Enzo, their playing cards splayed out between them and ignored in favor of what was happening on the screen. She was soon drawn into the narrative, learning that on that night, *Orion* had encountered a storm that had left the ship capsized and its two occupants missing. After an exhaustive four-day search, the US Coast Guard recovered Isobel's body but never found Tom Buck. A photo of the smashed-up boat faded from the screen, replaced by an interview with his son, Indigo. He was sixteen when his father died, and he said it took him two years before he fully accepted that his father was gone. "I couldn't help imagining he had washed up on an island somewhere, and nobody had looked hard enough for him."

"Wow," Klara said. "I want to, like, cry. But omigod, could you imagine if he's actually been alive all this time?"

"How sad," Sandi said as she rubbed her socked feet, which were aching after standing in the cold for so long. "I had no idea."

"Maybe sharks ate him!" Theo cried as Enzo let out an "eww" and shook his head.

"Shhh," Klara said again. They all continued to watch the final minutes unspool, as the narrator discussed Tom Buck's legacy and impact on the music world. Sandi gasped when the photo of Dava, Arvid, and Tom Buck from the Grammys party popped up on screen. She had yet to see any of the obituaries or videos related to Dava's death, so this was her first time seeing the two of them together. The frail woman in the silk pajamas seemed a pale echo of the striking woman who drew focus with her hypnotic gaze and mysterious smile, and she was flooded with longing to know more about her future mother-in-law.

When she had first learned who Rev's mother was, Sandi had read a 2030s-era *Forbes* profile of her to absorb as much as she could. She had come away from the article thinking about how much she and Dava had in common: self-made women who had been estranged from their parents at times and prided themselves on not needing another person to support them. All of Dava's children had her wealth as a safety net, but Sandi had never had that cushion, and she had daydreamed of having a conversation about their similarities as a way for the two of them to connect.

"I bet Gamma was so sad when he died," Priya said dreamily. "I would have been. I would have listened to the song he wrote about me and cried and cried for days."

Klara stood up and stretched her arms. "Well, Gamma sure seems to hate him now."

"I'm sure she was a little sad," Enzo said as he and Theo returned to their card game.

"Why don't you ask her?" Sandi heard herself say. All four faces turned to her and looked at her confusedly, as if they had forgotten she was there. As she had listened to the grandchildren speculate about Dava, it occurred to Sandi how strange it was that no one was with Dava during her final night alive.

"We can't do that," Klara said, even as her face brightened at the idea. "She hates being asked about him. And our dads said we should stay out of her way as much as possible."

"What's the point of that?" Sandi was standing now, even though her feet still throbbed. "She's dying very soon, and you'll never get to know anything about her if you don't talk to her now."

"But she's recovering from a—" Enzo began.

Sandi waved away his objections with the flick of a hand,

then glanced at the grandfather clock on the opposite side of the room. "It's not that late. She's not sleeping yet." Sandi walked away from them and headed toward the stairs.

"Where are you going?" Klara called out, scandalized. "You're really going up there?"

"You want to know about Tom Buck? Ask her. What do you have to lose, except her?" Sandi thought of Rev and his voice breaking as he shared his pain over losing his mother. Since he was unable to broach the topic of financial inheritance for their baby, then she would take up the mantle on behalf of their little family. When Sandi began ascending the steps, Dava's grandchildren exhaled a collective noise of wonder, then followed her.

CHAPTER NINETEEN

Charity Should Be a Family Business

I always thought charity should be a family business, and my ultimate goal is that the name Shastri become synonymous with giving and generosity. My most ardent wish is that my children do not just accept the baton and continue my work after I'm gone, but that they ascend to new heights.

—From Dava's acceptance speech after being named philanthropist of the year by New York Cares in 2032

DAVA WAS DOZING ON the blue sofa when she heard her bedroom door open, and awakened by the door's squeak, she called out, "Sita? Is that you?" So she was shocked to see Sandi come to stand before her in front of the window, followed by Klara, then Priya and the twins.

"Is something wrong?" Dava stammered. "Did someone die?" Then she laughed at herself, and the five nervous figures, arrayed before her from tallest to smallest like Captain Von Trapp had just summoned them to meet Maria in *The Sound of Music*, laughed too, albeit hollowly. "Everything is okay?" she asked, her hawklike gaze trained on Sandi.

"Yes...um, Dava." Sandi remembered during their one and only prior conversation that she preferred to be called by her first name. "We...the kids...we just wanted to check on you." Sandi's courage was about to fade until it dawned on her that lined up before Dava was the next generation, including the one growing inside her. And remembering her child, and her need to secure its future, helped Sandi rediscover her resolve. When she spoke again, her voice was assertive and strong, because she was not speaking for herself, but the fifth Shastri grandchild.

"I hope you are feeling better."

"I am." Dava was still staring at her, unblinking. Sandi called on all she had within her to match that unsparing gaze.

"I am so glad. Because we wanted to spend some time with you, while we can. Isn't that right?" Sandi said to the girls and the twins, and they nodded, their fearful eyes fixed on her rather than their grandmother.

"Well, that's wonderful." Dava's shoulders relaxed slightly and she gave the hint of a smile. "Sit down here," she said, patting the couch next to her. "Sit with me. With all that has happened, we haven't had a chance to speak, have we?"

One by one, each of them sat down, until Dava was flanked by one of Arvie's girls and Sita's boys on either side of her, and Sandi at the end. After a long, uneasy stretch of silence, Sandi was about to say something, anything, to get the conversation rolling, when Dava did so herself.

"How much do you know about my foundation?" she asked, turning left to look at Priya and Theo, then right at Klara, Enzo, and Sandi. Theo answered first, saying with a shy shrug that his mother worked there. When asked what Sita did, he shrugged again, then looked at his brother. Enzo responded with, "Helps people and travels a lot?"

"But how does she help people?" The twins shrugged again and averted their faces from their grandmother, as if she had caught them taking cookies from the kitchen.

"How about you, girls?" Dava said, and Sandi could hear how much she was straining to keep her voice steady. "Surely you must know something."

"Dad travels to the States once a month to help award money

to people who need it," Priya said, beaming that she was able to answer correctly and before her older sister. Klara rolled her eyes and flicked an impatient look at Sandi.

"Yes, that's Helping Perssons. The nonprofit I founded in honor of your grandfather Arvid. But what do you know about the Dava Shastri Foundation?" More blank stares. More shrugs. The whole enterprise was going south, and Sandi racked her brain to figure out how to improve this summit between the oldest and youngest members of the Shastri-Persson clan. Then Dava asked a question that surprised all of them.

"Are you happy, children?"

The question balanced precipitously in the air as the group traded uneasy glances. Sandi thought of responding, just as a way of clearing the awkwardness. But Enzo answered first.

"I am, mostly. I'd say seventy-five percent. No, eighty percent. No... seventy-nine percent."

Dava beamed at her grandson. "That's a good percentage, Enzo. What makes you happy seventy-nine percent of the time and unhappy twenty-one percent of the time?"

Enzo furrowed his brow. "Our home is really nice. I always feel safe there. And when Amma or Papai read us books before bedtime, that's my favorite time of day. And on Sundays, Amma lets Theo and me choose something to eat that's yummy but not very healthy."

"I usually get French fries," enthused Theo. "They're my favorite."

"And the twenty-one percent?" Dava was focused on Enzo with an intensity that intrigued Sandi.

Enzo blushed. "Um, sometimes I get called names at school. I get teased for being a nerd. But not as much now. And when Amma travels for work, I miss her. We miss her. Her trips seem to be getting longer."

"I see." Dava gave him a bland smile, but her eyes were

unreadable. "Theo, Priya, Klara: Do you feel the same way? Do you feel happy most of the time?" The other three looked at each other, then each nodded their assent. For the first time, Klara seemed to be paying attention to Dava the same way Sandi was, sensing these questions were leading somewhere important. The two exchanged glances.

"That's good. I'm glad to hear it." She cocked an eyebrow. "And what have you done to make someone else happy?"

Silence was filling the room again, a guilty silence so enveloping that Sandi could have sworn the temperature in the bedroom dropped several degrees. Then Priya hesitantly asked Dava what she meant.

"I mean, have you ever volunteered your time? Or donated to a cause you believed in? Have you ever given to someone in need?"

Enzo nodded. "At our birthday party last year, Amma asked our friends that, instead of bringing us presents, they each bring a toy we can donate to a homeless shelter."

"That's nice of your amma. But have you boys done anything? Something that was your idea?" Shamefaced, the twins shook their head. "How about you, Klara and Priya? Anything?"

"Um," Klara said, twisting a lock of hair into little curlicues, "we help Dad and Poppy package leftovers from Poppy's restaurant to give to the needy. We've done it for the past two years." Klara sat back satisfied, as if her response was the correct answer in a trivia game.

"And we get paid to help!" Priya chimed in. "I saved up to buy this necklace," she said, proudly raising the thin gold chain off of her neck and holding it out so Dava could see.

Dava let out a little *pfft* as she gave her granddaughters an appraising look. Then she turned her gaze to Sandi. "What about you?"

"My parents divorced when I was two, so it was mostly

me and my mom." Sandi composed her features into a calm expression, even as her heartbeat accelerated. "But she took care of me the best she could." She explained how she and her mother lived in a one-bedroom apartment in Queens and how her mother worked as a health-care aide at a nursing home across the street from their building. "My mom was thrilled about the lack of commute," Sandi said, smiling at the memory. "She was so grateful for not having to take the subway that she wanted to do something worthwhile with the time saved. So an hour every evening after work, she would knit hats and scarves for the people at the nursing home. I learned knitting from her, and I used to knit scarves for my friends for Christmas gifts to save money on buying actual presents. But I'm not sure why it never occurred to me to follow my mother's example."

Originally, Sandi was going to share her mother's story and end it by saying she, too, knits for people at that same nursing home. She wanted to endear herself to her future mother-in-law. But in the end, Sandi could not go through with the falsehood, because the memory of her mother's generosity sparked real shame in her, and the truth spilled out.

"I appreciate the truth," Dava said, breaking into her thoughts. Her eyes were glassy, and her mouth grim. "From all of you." Dava stood, shaky on her feet, then sat down again. "Just a little dizzy spell. It will pass. Theo or Enzo, can you retrieve my glasses and tablet from the bedside table and hand them to me?"

Theo and Enzo both stood up and each retrieved one item and handed it to her. After they sat down on either side of her, Dava began speaking in a warm but formal tone, beginning a conversation the five of them would distinctly remember the rest of their lives.

"I established my foundation with a simple goal: to help the less fortunate. And I had assumed because I have dedicated my life to this cause, and asked your parents and aunt and uncle to work at the foundation, that they would feel the same way." Dava crossed her legs and put on her red-framed glasses with shaking hands. "Instead, you know nothing about the foundation and little about the act of philanthropy. I have to blame myself.

"Let's be straight with each other. You barely know me. I barely know you." Upon hearing those words, Klara's face exploded into a shocked grin, and she mouthed, *Oh shit*, in Sandi's direction. "We've spent a total of, what—a few weeks together in the past few years, a few Christmases and Thanksgivings? I can't imagine how you see me. Old, imposing, maybe cranky." Dava's expression grew wistful. "I never knew any of my grandparents. They all passed away before I was born. And here I am, almost to the last moments of my life, continuing that sad tradition.

"My philanthropy work is my pride and joy, and yet in your eyes, it's the thing that takes your parents away from you—makes you twenty-one percent sad," she said, nodding at Enzo. "I have no doubt my children feel my work took me away from them too." Dava paused and closed her eyes. When she resumed speaking, she sounded less formal and more vulnerable. "I wanted to read what the world had to say about me before I died. But maybe I should care more about what you have to say about me.

"So let's get to know each other better. Everyone gets to ask me a question. Think long and hard about what you want to ask. Sandi will ask a question on behalf of her child. And the answers I give don't leave this room. Keep in mind I'm an old, dying woman," she added with a dry laugh. "So don't make me too sad."

The doorbell rang, and the six of them all jumped. The

children looked from Sandi to Dava, and Sandi shot up from her perch at the end of the sofa.

"They were all in the boathouse," Sandi said hurriedly. "Everyone who's not in this room, that is. I must have accidentally locked— Anyway, I'll go open the door."

Dava held up a hand to indicate she should wait. "Come back afterward. Bring something for us to eat too. Klara, go help her. And let them know we should be left alone until we're done. In fact, they shouldn't even come upstairs."

Sandi nodded, wide-eyed, and beckoned Klara to join her. When Sandi looked back on this night, and she did so fairly often, the only part she could not recall with clarity was when she briefly left Dava's bedroom. She remembered opening the door to let in Rev and the rest of the family and then foraging in the kitchen with Klara and returning upstairs with Vincent's Swedish potato dish, a gigantic tin of popcorn divided into three flavors (caramel, cheddar, and wasabi), and a box of sugar-free Christmas cookies. What she said to Rev and the others about where she was going and where the grandchildren were, and how they were not to be disturbed, she could not recall. But she did remember a sense of melancholy and peace shrouding them, an almost trancelike state, which could have been the reason why she and Klara were able to collect a hasty dinner from the kitchen and return upstairs with minimal questions and pushback.

When she and Klara returned, the duvet from Dava's bed had been spread out on the floor in front of the couch, with Priya and the boys seated on pillows. No one was speaking when they came in, but it was a thoughtful silence, not an uneasy one. Sandi and Klara joined them on the floor, while Dava remained seated on the sofa. As she eased down onto a stiff throw pillow, Sandi already knew the question she wanted to ask. She just hoped she would not lose her nerve to say it when the time came.

But first Dava announced a caveat: "I'm going to ask for one thing of each of you before you ask me a question. Give me an idea about how we can help others. It can be to help one person or a million people. And I'll fund it through the foundation. Think big. But think practically too." She handed her tablet to Sandi and looked down at her through her red-framed glasses. "Sandi. Take notes."

And for the next half hour, Sandi did take notes. This is what she wrote down and emailed to herself and cc'd Sita, at Dava's request:

Theo: Gym scholarships. "Papai (sp?) goes to a super-hero gym. Best one in NYC. He says it costs as much as one year of college tuition." Helped him recover after shoulder surgery, says he feels stronger and more fit now than when in Olympics. "Papai says he wishes more people had access to his kind of gym—if they did, everyone would live ten times longer."

Priya: Unlimited art supplies for underprivileged kids—paint and canvas is expensive. "I don't like drawing on a screen. It feels better when I use paints and pencils. But I don't experiment as much as I'd like to because I'm afraid of running out and have to use my allowance to buy more."

Enzo: All-expenses paid trips on the SpaceX shuttle for foster children and children in orphanages. "I can't imagine feeling unwanted by my mom or dad. If I was them, this would help me to not give up. I'd believe my life could change for the better."

Klara: Free private walk-in counseling centers, a cross between a drive-thru window and a church confessional. "Sometimes my friends and I feel like we can't talk to anyone about how we're feeling. And we have nice homes, good lives. What about kids who have less?"

Sandi: Affordable (or free if possible!) day care for parents who earn minimum wage or under $25K per year.

Dava listened intently and respectfully as each of them haltingly shared their ideas. Sentences that began with "Um, I don't know; how about..." would eventually transform into free-flowing thoughts building enthusiastically until a sound concept was achieved. Sandi appreciated Dava's approach of letting each of them talk without interruption, and that continuous monologue allowed them to come up with ideas they had not known were percolating in their minds. After they had gone around the room, Sandi was touched to see how each of the grandchildren seemed refreshed, almost like wilting plants who had seen sunlight for the first time in days.

After they each shared their thoughts, Dava thanked them for their ideas. She then beckoned Theo to pass her the tin of popcorn and took out a handful of the wasabi ones. "I should have asked you to bring me a drink," she muttered, more to herself. "Okay, let's begin with the questions. Who wants to go first?"

Klara's and Sandi's eyes met across the room, and the teenager's hand slowly went up. "I'm sorry to ask this, Gamma. Because I know you don't like talking about him. But how did you feel when Tom Buck died?"

Dava made a low humming noise, her eyes flicking from Klara to something just out of sight over her head. As she ate the popcorn slowly, one kernel at a time, Sandi was amazed to see Dava react by giving her granddaughter a bemused grin.

"So of all the questions you wanted to ask, that is what you want to know? Are you sure?" Klara nodded, biting her lip, her cheeks turning scarlet. "You are a brave one," she remarked with another dry laugh. "Okay, then. I made a promise. But let me reiterate: nothing said in this room leaves this room. All I have is your word. And all you are in this world is your word. I hope you can honor me in this way . . . because this isn't easy for me. But I haven't given you a lot of my time, and I'm trying to make amends. So, can you do this?" Each of them solemnly nodded.

"We'll pinky swear," Priya cried out, half on her knees, her hands clasped together almost in prayer. When Klara dismissed it as childish, Dava declared that it was exactly what she wanted to do.

Each of them stood up, one by one, and linked their pinky fingers with Dava's. Theo went first, shyly extending his finger without standing close enough to reach her outstretched arm. So Dava quickly leaned forward and surprised him by snagging his pinky with hers, as if they were playing a game, leading him to erupt into giggles. Then came Priya, with all the solemnity of taking a church vow, followed by Enzo, who wiped his sweaty hand on his jeans beforehand, then red-faced Klara, who couldn't quite look her grandmother in the eye as she did so, and finally Sandi. Dava held out her pinky, the nail perfectly manicured in a deep maroon shade, and Sandi caught it in hers. When she and Dava linked pinkies, both of them looked at each other as if they were really seeing one another for the first time. Dava's eyes then traveled to Sandi's stomach, and Dava gently unlinked her pinky to tap her belly. Sandi let out a little "oh!" and they both laughed at the gesture, which struck Sandi as sweet and odd in the moment but deeply meaningful in the days and years to come. Stifling the urge to hug Dava, Sandi instead pointed to the space on the couch next to her, and Dava nodded her assent for Sandi to sit beside her.

"Okay," Dava said, as if she had been holding a long breath until then. "Let's go."

Between handfuls of wasabi popcorn, Dava unwound her complicated feelings about Tom Buck's death. She described it to her grandchildren and Sandi as "anger and grief braided together," a complex knot of feelings she did not have time to process at the time and so never did.

"When he died, I hadn't spoken to him for many, many years. And I never forgave him for that song. He never apologized for it. Maybe he didn't think he had done anything wrong, but how could he not?" Her voice rose at those last words, and with shaking hands, she took off her glasses and balanced them on her lap. "There was a time... when he was important to me. Not in any way that resembles what I had with your grandfather." Dava briefly touched the white streaks of hair framing her face. "But there was affection there. So yes, I was sad when I heard that he died and how he had died. And I wished we had one more conversation so I could have told him how betrayed I felt. So I could have let that anger go." Dava paused for several moments, then popped the last kernel of popcorn into her mouth. "But life isn't tidy that way. What can you do?"

She put her glasses on, then pointed at the box of cookies. Klara, who was closest to it, grabbed the box and held it out to her grandmother. "Wow, Gamma, so you and he did..." She choked on her words, apparently unable to say more.

Dava gave her a hard stare. "Why else would you ask if you didn't already think so?"

The tension in the room swelled, and Klara stared beseechingly at Sandi. But before Sandi could attempt to smooth things over, Dava took the cookies with one hand and held up the other in Klara's direction, as if she was about to give her a fist bump. "Don't forget," she said, winking at her, then raising her pinky in salute.

Klara swallowed, then laughed nervously. "I won't."

"Okay. Next."

Theo tentatively raised his hand and asked his grandmother if she was afraid of dying. In response, between delicate bites of a Santa Claus–shaped cookie, Dava explained she was not, because she had had a very good life, experienced love and pain and success, and exquisitely made martinis, and a child's face light up in happiness, and watched the best musicians in the world play songs that had fortified her days, and had seen Earth from a rocket ship like some sort of movie from her childhood.

"If I hadn't lived the life I did, met and married your grand-father, been able to help so many people, had a family, and seen my children have their own children, then maybe I would be afraid to have it end. Life has done well by me, but life did not happen to me. I had the ability to make choices, and it led to all of this." She took a bite of Santa's foot, leaving only his torso and one arm. "Next."

Enzo spoke up almost immediately. "Were you happy with what you read about yourself?"

Dava tore off the arm and crunched thoughtfully. "This brings me back to him. Tom Buck," she responded, nodding at Klara. "It's not easy in this world to make your mark as a woman, to be seen as succeeding on your own merits. Especially if you are not a great beauty. I had a vision about how I wanted to help other people, and through a combination of hard work and luck, I was able to largely achieve that. By myself," Dava added, lightly slapping her thigh for emphasis. "Because often when a woman succeeds on a grand scale"—Dava said this while giving a pointed look to her granddaughters—"many people, mostly men, want to presume she had help in some way. Arvid was my

partner in life and family, but not in business. Not in the *work*.
And the reason I named the foundation after only myself was so
everyone would understand that distinction. And yet, despite
my best efforts..." Dava's voice faltered, and her eyes took on
a faraway expression. She finished the cookie, took a sip of
water, and then continued. "And despite my best efforts, based
on what I've seen from Enzo, all anyone can focus on is this
one man's connection to me. Which is ironic, actually. Because
pop music is what allowed me to dream myself into thinking
I could do great things. And now, a pop song—something I
did not help create and did not want—is what seems to define
me. Honestly, I would have rather not known I would be
remembered this way."

The wind's intense keening halted soon after she finished
speaking, so everyone absorbed her words in absolute silence.
Sandi did not know how appropriate it would have been to
follow up this stark admission with the question she wanted
to ask, but then Dava continued on, after bending to pick up
the bowl of hasselbackspotatis and picking out slices of baked
potatoes to pop in her mouth.

"Regrets—I've had a few," Dava murmured. "Do you know
Frank Sinatra? Any of you? No? Sandi, not even you? Ahhh,"
she said with a faint smile. "Someday you will. Well, he had this
song in which he looks back on his life, and what I appreciate
about it is that the lyrics admit to regrets. Because it's hard to
live a real life without making mistakes. Even at the very end
of it." She cleared her throat. "But if nothing else, this exercise
has allowed me to spend more time with all of you. So that is
something to be grateful for, right?" She said this last sentence
as if she wanted to switch on the lights in a dark room. "Now,
who's next?" Dava passed back the potato dish to Theo and
looked at Priya, then Sandi.

"I haven't been able to come up with a question," Priya

admitted, her lips flecked with bits of cheddar from the popcorn. "I'm still working on mine."

"Ask me the first thing that comes to mind." Dava sat back against the sofa cushions, her eyes closed. "Go. Now."

"Um...did Grandpa Arvid know about Tom Buck...or your other daughter?" Priya seemed horrified as the words came out of her mouth, the sentence tumbling out in a whimper. She glanced at her older sister, who nodded back at her, apparently impressed by her boldness.

"No. To both." Dava said this with her arms folded, her eyes still closed. "But I'd like to think if he had lived longer, I would have told him eventually. And that's all I have to say about that." She opened her eyes and turned toward Sandi sitting beside her. "It seems you have the last question."

Sandi squirmed next to Dava, torn between asking her about a financial inheritance and something else that had been weighing on her mind. Thinking about how time was quickly elapsing and Rev and the others waiting downstairs, she swallowed hard, taking a big gulp of air as if she were about to dive off a cliff into the ocean, hoping she took enough oxygen with her to last the minutes she would be underwater.

"How were you able to give her up?"

CHAPTER TWENTY

Chaitanya Rao

Name of applicant: Chaitanya Rao

Organization/project title: Oakland Springtime Community Garden

Organization/project description: The community garden was founded to give residents of the Oakland neighborhood of Kinghope an opportunity to grow their own organically farmed produce in a clean and accessible space, as well as forge bonds between neighbors, made up of refugees and non-English speakers, through the communal act of gardening.

Where will the funds be allotted? To the building of a gazebo to establish a public square that can serve as the heartbeat of the neighborhood.

Is there anything else you would like us to know? Kinghope is a neighborhood that deserves the chance to grow beyond its tragic foundations. (For more info, please go here: WeAreKinghope.com/history.) The garden was the first time many residents had a chance to gather together, not to protest or mourn, but to smile and do good for each other.

—From Chaitanya Rao's application
form for Helping Perssons

SHE HAD A LARGE head, and a shock of wavy black hair that struck out in all directions like octopus arms. Her face was tight and scowling, eyes squeezed shut as if she did not want to know what world she had been born into, and her cries had the intensity and consistency of an alarm clock that refused to be shut off. These were Dava's first thoughts as she saw her newborn child held in the arms of a nurse—"A darling baby girl!" she said in an accent that reminded Dava of a Monty Python sketch—and was asked if she wanted to hold her. Dava loved her first by sound, then sight. Which is why she shook her head, as much as she could manage, and mouthed, *No.*

"In giving birth and seeing I had actually created a child, it cemented for me I had to give her up," Dava answered Sandi. "You are carrying a child you want, with someone you love," she continued, her voice taking on an almost melodic quality. "Neither of those things applied to me. But it only deepened my responsibility to make sure she found people who did want her and would be able to give her the best life possible, because I knew I could not."

To Dava, those nine months in England were akin to a shattered mirror, fogged memories that she could remember only in fragments: Discovering she was not just pregnant, but six months pregnant. The shock over how her body had betrayed her, and the shame of not realizing sooner. Feeling bloated and lonely and that her body no longer belonged to her, now possessed by an alien entity. Breaking down, as if a tsunami had been unleashed from her mouth, in a pub bathroom after drinking three glasses of red wine and then vomiting it in a toilet stained with scum and other people's fluids, until a woman—a freckled redhead with Freddie Mercury buckteeth—found her, helped her clean up, and sat down with her on the curb afterward until 3:00 a.m., persuading her she didn't mind her vomit breath or holding her hand while she cried. She never knew her name or saw her again. If she had been more religious, Dava would have thought she had been visited by an angel. Instead, she knew it was something perhaps even more miraculous: a good-hearted stranger who made time to help another person in need without asking for anything in return. In many ways, even if she had not consciously realized it at the time, that was the moment the Dava Shastri Foundation was born.

That night also represented the moment when Dava chose not to run away or deny what was happening to her but become an active participant in her own life again.

Which meant telling her university roommate, Lalita, she wanted to ask her older sister, an emergency room physician at a London hospital, for advice on a medical issue; confiding in Lalita's sister, Sita, that she was pregnant and wanted to give her child up for adoption; lucking into Dr. Sita being close friends with an Indian couple looking to adopt; meeting with them and Dr. Sita at a kebab restaurant in Cambridge, in which the couple, the Raos, brought photo albums and letters of recommendation to prove they could be a good family to her baby; Dava deciding ten minutes into the dinner they were the right parents for her child but only agreeing to let them adopt if they agreed to keep the name Dava chose for the baby; taking a temporary leave of absence from school and staying in a hotel room in London, paid for by the Raos, on March 8, her twenty-first birthday and one week before her due date; giving birth; recovering from the birth by staying with Sita in her flat for several days; reluctantly accepting several stunning pieces of gold jewelry as a thank-you from the Raos, but only after several firm refusals of their offers of a check; returning to Cambridge and burrowing herself in her studies, avoiding the thick, gray depression hovering over her like a wind-whipped flag; flying home to Calliston in June and staying in bed for a month, subsisting on a diet of candy-colored comedies from Blockbuster (*Sister Act*, *Wayne's World*) and power pop (Weezer, Matthew Sweet) to help lift her out of her malaise; selling the jewelry to buy a used car and driving it cross-country back to New York City in July.

"I was able to make my peace with giving up Chaitanya because I gave her two crucial things: good parents and a good name," Dava told Sandi. "If you start out with them, then you are miles ahead of everyone else." Seeing Sandi open her mouth to ask a question, Dava cut her off with a flinty smile. "Why Chaitanya? I liked what it meant, that it had multiple meanings, all good ones: life, knowledge, consciousness, divinity, some other things, all very positive. And it's a very Indian name. It can't be shortened into an Anglo nickname. Davinder easily can become Dave; same with Jesminder and Jess. Not so with Chaitanya. You have to accept her as she is."

"Wow! You put so much thought into a name?" Priya marveled.

"I put thought into everything," Dava declared with a gravity that made Priya so nervous she shifted in her seat, causing her to fall off the throw pillow with a loud thump.

She looked at her granddaughter, whose name she had never liked, and wondered if Arvie had put as much thought, or any thought, into his younger daughter's name. To Dava, it seemed he had just picked the most common, ordinary names for both daughters, something that would help them blend in rather than stand out. And that mentality rankled her. Dava had no idea why her eldest son was so intent in his need to fade into the world, rather than risk anything to make his mark. But this quality in him is why she believed there had always been a coolness to their relationship, which had started in his teen years and fractured into a cordial estrangement once he moved to Stockholm after graduating from college.

If Dava was honest with herself, she had never contested the Americanization of his name because he hadn't proven worthy of the name she had so lovingly chosen for him. Both she and Arvid agreed that they would not name their children after themselves because their kids deserved to have their own identities. So when Dava discovered the name Arvind in an on-line search for Indian baby names, she insisted on the name for their firstborn child, because it was a perfect combination of both parents yet let him fully be his own person.

Yet Arvie had gone through most of his life with a permanent posture of slumped shoulders and a surly visage, the complete opposite of his father's sunny yet pragmatic personality. Especially after Arvid's death, she and her son's dynamic was one of wheedling, angry silences, and ultimatums. This included having to coax Arvie to take on a lead role in Helping Perssons, including paying him a salary for a few days of work per month, covering his airfare to and from Stockholm, and renting him a pied-à-terre in the city. At the time, she had been so into the optics of Arvie overseeing a nonprofit created in honor of his father and semi-namesake that she didn't think about how much she had to indulge him in order to get him to grudgingly agree.

In fact, she considered Arvie's biggest accomplishment to be vetting Chaitanya's application and awarding her a Helping Perssons grant. And if nothing else, she was grateful something so miraculous, so serendipitous, had taken place on her son's watch. When she had learned about Chaitanya and her life in Northern California, Dava had been at what she thought of as a stagnant juncture in her own life. At age fifty-six, she felt like a thirtysomething in her mind and spirit and believed her looks were still largely intact, with some aches and pains as a result of too much time spent sitting at desks, conference tables, and first-class airline seats. "Well preserved" is the term she liked to think of herself physically, and to a stranger's eye, she would not have looked like a mother of four young adults or someone who was nine years away from being regarded as a senior citizen. But she was edging closer to being a full-time empty nester, with high school junior Rev rarely at home, Kali in college, Sita in graduate school, and Arvie settling into his life as a young newlywed with Vincent in Stockholm. The future stretched out long and lonely for her.

She had not expected to be a widow longer than she was a wife.

When the children were still young, Dava often daydreamed about the time when her children would be grown-up and out of the house, so she and Arvid could take extended trips to far-away locales, lazing around in hammocks and sipping cocktails out of coconuts. A sort of semiretirement in which they could work on a few projects at their leisure. But in the first few years following Arvid's death, she had divided herself in two. While she reduced her hours at work so she could be more present for her children, especially the younger two, all her remaining time was spent immersed in new initiatives and grant investments. Dava rarely socialized but instead focused on work and parenthood so she did not have to confront the gaping hole in her life, in her bed, and by her side, and learn who she was without him.

She also remained celibate after Arvid's death. Men, sex, and romance swiftly lost their appeal for her, in the same way she forever swore off chocolate after a single bout of food poisoning from a slice of her sweet-sixteen birthday cake.

"I lucked into meeting Arvid," she told Vash close to a year after his passing, after her friend tried to gently prod her into dating again. "I don't think life will let me be that lucky again."

When Vash insisted that she could date casually to have a little fun, Dava shook her head, tears in her eyes. "I just can't. He was it for me. He was enough."

What she could not explain was that she could not bear to know another man in an intimate way like she had known her late husband: his scent, light and woodsy; the smoothness of his muscular thighs; the oval birthmark on his left shoulder blade; his hairy blond belly that protruded slightly on his slender frame, which she lovingly called "my pillow"; his pale, enormous hands with rounded fingernails that looked like opals; the soft, perfect texture of his lips. She ached for his physicality and his presence, and to try to be with someone else, even for a brief time, would only throw into enormous relief what was missing. For a time, Tom Buck had been her vacation spot, where she was familiar with the tourist attractions and local haunts. But Arvid had been her home.

So rediscovering Chaitanya was a series of small earthquakes reverberating inside her, reviving the part of her that wanted love, to know someone deeply and be known in return, without the complications of a romantic relationship. Loving her children was different. This was something she had to admit to herself following her first session with her therapist Yuisa (her third of eight overall). Dava had begun seeing Yuisa in March 2030, soon after Arvie had started working at Helping Perssons but before Chaitanya was awarded a grant. Dava was seeking help dealing with her anxiety and restlessness—"I refuse to call it a midlife crisis"—as she faced beginning a new phase of her life as a widow whose children had left the nest.

Professionally, Dava was at the top of her game, with no more heights to climb, having accomplished everything she wanted as a philanthropist. So to distract herself from no longer having a foundation or family that actively needed her, and to give the ambition and drive that still lived inside her a new outlet, she wanted to focus on legacy building by spurring her children into getting involved in her life's work. As part of this idea, Dava had explained how she had drafted warts-and-all résumés for each child, when Yuisa pointed out she could not extricate her love of them with her own conception of herself and the Shastri name.

"That's not true," Dava had sputtered, her left foot slicing the air as she crossed her legs. "My three eldest are adults now, and the youngest will be soon. I'm just trying to figure out where they would fit within the organization. And the best way for me to conceive of that was thinking of them as potential job candidates."

"So, you want them to be your employees."

"Not literally, no," Dava said, aghast.

"Let me ask you this," Yuisa said. "What if one of your children decided not to work in your foundation? Would that impact how you felt about them?" She cocked an eyebrow, which to Dava resembled a woolly mammoth raising its head. "Be honest."

Dava's nostrils flared. "Well, that wouldn't happen. They know how much their involvement means to me."

"But what if one of them did?"

"Then I wouldn't be happy, but I'd have to learn to live with it." Dava sat up in the sunken leather chair and pointed in her therapist's direction. "That doesn't mean I'd stop loving them."

"But would you love them less?" The statement hung in the air between them, with a knock at the door saving her from having to answer the question, for her therapist and for herself.

I might. That answer echoed in Dava's head whenever she thought about that discussion, but she would never allow herself to say those words aloud. She didn't want to feel that way, and yet she had to acknowledge that her desire to be a force of good in the world was equaled by her desire to have her name stand tall and resolute through generations, similar to Rockefeller. Dava needed her children to be the pillars on which her legacy could live on for decades to come. And for that to happen, it would mean transforming them from unformed marble to intricately carved statues, even if they ended up not liking the scalpel that shaped them. Once Yuisa had said the word "employees," it was all Dava could think about in relation to her children, creating a distancing effect in how she viewed them that she could never quite overcome.

And so Chaitanya had entered her life at a time when she was starved for human connection and had not fully realized it. Right after she disembarked from the yacht after learning Chaitanya had been named a Helping Perssons grantee, she called her assistant and told her to clear her schedule and book the next available flight to Oakland. Now that she knew her daughter, her eldest child, was walking the same continent as her, Dava needed to see her immediately.

From the moment that her flight took off from John F. Kennedy International Airport to the moment she stepped foot on Chaitanya's doorstep and rang the doorbell, Radiohead's *The Bends* was on a loop in her mind. It was the album Dava purchased the day before she went into labor and the music she listened to nonstop for months after. The surreal nature of that time of her life, in which she gave birth to a child she planned on never seeing again and then returned to university as if she were an ordinary American exchange student, came flooding back to her as the music burrowed itself in her brain. "It was like being in a beautiful depression," she had told Arvid about how her memories of her time in the UK were inextricably linked to the album, her feelings of alienation laid bare in her headphones on a daily basis. Dava wished she could get the music unstuck from her head as she made the cross-country trip, but Thom Yorke's yearning yowl wouldn't leave her be, and the album's lyrics would pop out to her at random. She could not understand why the soundtrack to a particularly miserable time in her life was accompanying her on her way to do something so extraordinary.

The music stopped the moment Chaitanya opened the door of her sun-shaded bungalow. A wild mass of frizzy curls and a radiant smile framed by faded lipstick was Dava's first memory of meeting her daughter, a vision that stayed with her the rest of her life, as if burned in her retinas from staring too long at the sun.

⌒

"What was it like to meet her?" This question came from Priya, as she readjusted herself on the floor sans throw pillow, her wire-thin legs stretched out before her as if she were about to do sit-ups. "I'm sorry, Gamma; I know I already asked a question. But this one is better than my other one."

"Maybe her question can be on this one's behalf," said Sandi, pointing at her stomach. "And in a way, it's the flip side of what I asked."

"True," Dava said. "But I'm not sure I can find the words. It was overwhelming." She paused, and the image of Chaitanya from their first meeting flashed before her again. "It was as if I were meeting someone I had known forever, but for the first time."

"She kind of said the same thing," Enzo piped up. "About you. In her private conversation that got published online. I can find it for you," he added, gesturing toward Dava's tablet, still on her lap. Dava nodded and handed the device to her grandson. Maybe she should feel a little pathetic about her desperate urgency to know what Chaitanya thought of their first meeting, but the phrase "time is fleeting" actually meant something now. She was mere hours away from the end, the actual end, and she needed to know. Enzo found the story and read it aloud, his voice shaky at the start but resolving itself at the end.

"I had received a call from the office that Dava Shastri wanted to meet me, because she had personally read my Helping Perssons application for the garden. I was told she happened to be in the area on a work trip, and she had a small window of time to meet. Of course I was flattered! She's a legend, especially with my Indian friends. I swear, not ten minutes after I hung up the phone, she was at my front door. I hadn't even brushed my hair yet. But there was nothing to do but open the door and welcome her in. And it was like welcoming the sun itself to sit down on your sofa and have some tea. Dava had such tremendous energy from the moment I met her. I don't believe in reincarnation, but if I did, then that's what it felt like to meet her. It was as if I had known her in another life." Enzo looked up from the tablet. "There's more if you want me to keep going, Gamma. But that's the part I meant. You both had the same feeling."

Dava coughed and pressed her hand to her throat, as if that would hold the tears at bay. Her daughter had thought she was a legend. Before they had even met, Chaitanya had used that word to describe her. She was speechless. At that moment, there was nothing she craved more than to be back in Chaitanya's bungalow, seated in the high-backed chair that faced the bay window overlooking the back garden, with a view of two rows of pink and white roses forming a semicircle around Old Moses, the affectionate nickname given to the weeping willow. In her hands would be a cup of chai, the aroma of cardamom mingled with cinnamon reminding her of the chai Dava's own mother would make for her every day after school. Chaitanya would be sitting opposite with her droopy-eyed cat, Opie, on her lap, her husband Ram's musings at the piano tinkling in the background. And during the moments when Chaitanya was occupied with her cat or bustling about her home, Dava would flat out stare at this person she created, this person who looked nothing much like her, yet was very much of her own flesh. She could not help reveling in the fact she had given birth to a person so lovely, so genuine, and so Indian, more so than Dava herself.

Even though they were both only children, Chaitanya's upbringing had been very different than Dava's: cosmopolitan and diverse, yet anchored in family and community. Chaitanya had been raised by devout Hindu parents who had immigrated to London from the northern state of Bihar five years before they had adopted her. Fluent in Hindi and English, she spent her childhood and young adult years steeped in Indian culture, with weekly visits to the Neasden Temple in London, bharatanatyam training that began at age nine, and Shah Rukh Khan movies playing on the TV at all times.

"There were always people at our house, or we were always at other people's houses," Chaitanya had said about the close-knit North Indian community in which she was raised. "I didn't know there were other ways to live, because that's how all the families I knew operated." She had said this to Dava on her fourth visit, while the two were sipping chais as Opie, having finally warmed up to her, nestled at Dava's feet and timidly licked her ankle.

"If I hadn't known from an early age I was adopted, I would have learned from all of those uncles and aunties who couldn't keep from commenting on my skin color. 'Stay out of the sun today, beta,' or 'Lakshmi aunty has a new lightening cream you should try; I'll give it to your mother.' They looked like this," Chaitanya said, pointing to her cup of milky chai. "It made me even prouder to be as brown as I am. But living in London helped me with that, the incredible diversity of people and faiths. Sometimes I loved the insularity of my community and felt safe inside their care. Because they always cared, even if they didn't articulate it well, or in the nicest words. And other times I was desperate to be free of all of them knowing my business, and so I would take the tube to Chelsea or Covent Garden and melt into the anonymity."

All of these details were fascinating to Dava, who lapped them up as Chaitanya dropped them offhandedly like bread crumbs. Because she had this craving to know every single thing about her, an inquisitive hunger comparable to her relationship to The Replacements. They were her first teenage love, and so her devotion burned bright and quick and deep, just like the band itself. To love The Replacements was to overly identify with them and their music, and so their highs were her highs, and their legendary, shambolic split was as devastating as if she had suffered her own breakup. If Chaitanya were a band, then Dava would have her posters adorning the walls of her room, her albums lined up in chronological order on her desk next to her stereo, her bootlegs meticulously curated in her desk drawer, the magazine articles organized in a three-ring binder (also in chronological order) with Chaitanya's photo taped to the front. She simply needed to know *everything*. But unlike The Replacements, with whom she preached the gospel to everyone she knew, Dava could not talk about Chaitanya with the people in her life. And so she burrowed inward, an obsession she nurtured with equal parts discipline and zest.

When teenage Dava fell for a band, she would read every article, music review, and profile she could get her hands on. Chaitanya did not live her life online, with little social media presence Dava could stealthily monitor, and so in a way Dava created her own fanzine. After each monthly visit to Chaitanya's, Dava would write down notes from their conversations, something she could revisit and pore over for days afterward, marinating in the details and marveling once again that this person was made by her. The greatest hits, anecdotes, and stories Dava would reread again and again when she missed her daughter's company:

On being adopted: "When I was young, I never felt like this other part of me was missing. Mum and Dad made me feel like I was their child in every way."

On her birth parents: "I did find myself daydreaming about them. They were mythic to me, like the Beatles or Princess Diana. When I was growing up, I would look at every South Asian person I saw on the street and try to see myself in them."

On moving to America: "I wanted to move here for three reasons: Beyoncé, Lady Gaga, and Rihanna. They were my everything when I was young, and the reason I applied to college in the States. I came to Berkeley and never left."

On meeting Ram: "This is scandalous. He was my professor! Can you guess the age difference? Twelve years. Can you tell? His beard makes him look even older, but he's attached to it. Anyway, I was madly in love with him, full stop. I came to Berkeley intent on medical school and was enrolled in one of his labs. I dropped out of the class after five weeks and asked him out right after. And that was that. Maybe I should have dated more. There are tiny regrets here and there that I didn't have more of a romantic history. But then I see the life we've built, and I wouldn't trade it."

Chaitanya had confided this to Dava on their seventh meeting a few months later, the first time Ram had not been home.

There was more that her daughter was not saying, and she wanted to excavate what was buried underneath without over-stepping boundaries. She didn't feel like Chaitanya's mother—more like a cool auntie type, the kind you could ask for dating advice and who would buy you beer. Dava's own children—her other children—rarely confided anything of their personal lives, and she was introduced to their significant others begrudgingly. She liked that one of her offspring felt close to her, and so Dava thirsted for even more intimacy. Which is how she and Chaitanya ended up having their first disagreement.

"I had a colorful romantic history in college," Dava said, licking the crumb from a lemon scone off of her lip. "There were a lot of ups and downs, a lot of craziness. Looking back now, I wish I had met Arvid much earlier so we could have had more years together."

"That's a good point," Chaitanya said with a sympathetic grin. "I'll remember that next time I have one of my what-if moments." She tugged at the top button of her white button-down blouse. Dava could tell that it was a nervous tic, and she had worried that button so much that it was close to falling off.

"Do you have a lot of what-if moments?" Dava was trying to get a better sense of how her daughter felt about being adopted. She knew that adoptees often struggled with the fact that their parents had given them up, and so Chaitanya's sanguineness about it had surprised her. "You're so young still; there's no reason to look back with regrets yet."

"I'm not sure I'd call thirty-five young, but thank you," she said with a laugh, throwing back her head so her curls shook like wind moving through leaves. "I don't know if I have a lot of them, but they surface now and again. I'm very content with my life. Ram is a treasure, and I'm so fulfilled by my work and my friends here. I just . . . I can't define it. Maybe I think I should want something more?" She shrugged sheepishly. "When I was a little girl, I idolized Belle in *Beauty and the Beast*. She has this line about wanting more than a provincial life. And anytime I'm having this tiny ounce of what-if, that lyric sings out to me."

"Well, it seems you do have a very lovely life here." Dava nodded at the room, with its sunny, mint-green interior and wicker furniture. "But there's nothing wrong with having more ambition, if that's what this malaise is."

"I wouldn't call it a malaise, exactly." Opie purred on her lap and flipped on his back, and Chaitanya scratched his patchy black-and-gray stomach. "It's more like maybe I should be doing more. Maybe I'm not pushing myself enough out of my comfort zone? Coming here from the UK was the biggest risk I've ever taken, and that was, oh Lord, more than fifteen years ago." She sighed. "And I meet someone like you who has done such amazing work and traveled to thirty countries—"

"Thirty-two," Dava corrected.

"That's almost one-fifth of the whole world! And me, I can count how many places I've been on two hands." She shook her head at herself. "I've always been a happy homebody, but lately I'm wondering if I'm...I don't know if 'settling' is the right word?"

Dava set her teacup down on the crocheted orange doily draping the side table next to her and then looked at Chaitanya. She was trying to decide whether she would talk to her as if she were a Shastri-Persson, which would be the verbal equivalent of taking her by her shoulders and gently shaking her to see reason. Seeing Chaitanya's confused, self-flagellating expression and how her fingers were clutching her top button so hard it threatened to come off, Dava took a breath and dove in.

"If you don't mind, dear, I have some thoughts." Chaitanya nodded and set down her own cup. "Okay, then. I was thinking about the garden, and what an amazing little nonprofit you have created. Kinghope has thrived by having such a wonderful

community space. I just wonder...what if you took yourself to
the next level?"

"What do you mean?" Chaitanya stopped scratching Opie,
causing her cat to look up at her in annoyance, then jump off
her lap and scamper to the kitchen.

"I mean that you are so bright and compassionate, and
so many more people could benefit from that. You are limit-
ing yourself by not looking toward expansion." Dava's phone
vibrated next to the teacup but she ignored it as she became
revved up in discussing her favorite topic with someone who
had quickly become her favorite person. "Kinghope can just be
the beginning for you."

"But Kin—"

"What if you took what you did there to other refugee communities? There's a wonderful school called The Philanthropy
Workshop run by the Rockefeller Foundation. You can take
the strategies you developed so far and learn how to do more
integrat—"

"Dava." Chaitanya had her palm up, as if she were a crossing
guard commanding traffic to halt. Her eyebrows were knitted
together, giving her a jagged crease above her nose. "I appreciate the advice. And the compliments. But I'm not talking about
my work. I'm very happy with what we've done in Kinghope
and want to focus on it exclusively. There is still so much that
needs to be done." Dava drew back, realizing that she had
hurt her daughter's feelings by basically calling the community
garden "provincial." When she tried to speak again, Chaitanya
stood up from her armchair. "It's getting late, and Ram will be
home soon."

On the drive to the airport and then on the flight home,
Dava ruminated on their conversation and wondered if she had
overstepped her bounds, and if so, whether it would cause
a permanent break. One of the songs from *The Bends* snaked

its way back to her brain, and Dava fretted she had pushed Chaitanya too far by expecting too much from her. If Sita had reacted to Dava's advice the way Chaitanya had, Dava would have waved it off as Sita being too sensitive and not thinking big enough. But Chaitanya had seemed so upset by what Dava had honestly thought of as constructive encouragement. Upon landing, she saw Chaitanya had texted her a lengthy message in which she expressed remorse for her reaction to Dava's words. So sorry for how I spoke to you. I'm very protective of Kinghope. Any perceived slight to K I take as a slight to me. But you should know the one aspect of my life I'm 100 percent about is my work. My what-if moments apply to my personal life, individual goals, bucket list, etc. Apologies again for my crossness. Would love to talk & explain more when you have a moment.

Dava immediately texted back, writing and deleting several times before sending: It is me who should apologize. I shouldn't have assumed you were talking about your work. I never meant any slight to Kinghope or what you have achieved. No need to explain more. I understand. I'll call in the morning. XOXO to Ram & Opie.

A minute later, Chaitanya replied with Phew, then a smiling-face emoji, followed by Goodnight and then a heart emoji. Dava stared at the heart until her vision blurred, tears of relief streaming down her cheeks.

⌒

During their twelfth meeting, which took place in March 2031, close to a year after their first, Dava treated Chaitanya to a three-day stay at a luxury spa in Sonoma. She surprised her with the weekend trip by arriving at her home in a cherry-red Ford Mustang convertible.

"I thought we'd go celebrate our birthdays together." She was pleased by Chaitanya's stunned expression as she took in the sight of Dava, wearing red cat-eye sunglasses and matching handkerchief tied around her head, next to the classic car.

"No!" Chaitanya clapped a hand over her mouth. "Is this the car? The one you drove cross-country back to New York?"

"Not the exact same one but the same model," Dava called out merrily. She leaned into the driver's side and honked the horn in three quick bursts. "Pack a bag, darling, and let's hit the road."

As they had gotten to know each other better over the past year via near-daily text exchanges and twice-weekly phone calls, Dava found herself edging closer to the similarities between her and Chaitanya, hinting at their connection as if daring herself to tell the truth. The closest she came to admitting it was this birthday weekend, which Dava had planned after their eighth meeting, in which, during a conversation about astrology, they learned (or in Dava's case, "learned") that they were both Pisces and their birthdays were one week apart. After consulting with Ram and making sure it was okay to whisk his wife away the weekend prior to her birthday, which happened to fall on Dava's birthday, she had booked the spa's most expensive adjoining suites and three days' worth of spa treatments. She might have overdone it, she realized, as the hotel concierge handed them their personalized schedules and Chaitanya's eyes widened at the back-to-back-to-back appointments.

"Oh wow. Will we have time to breathe? Can we pencil in breathing between the seaweed wrap and the lavender tea facial?" she joked. Then she added with awe, "This must have cost a bomb." Dava laughed but inwardly chastened herself for going overboard. Dava had once planned a similar weekend for herself, Sita, and Kali as a college graduation present for the latter, but the sisters had bickered the entire time over every detail (who got the most comfortable bed, who took too long getting a massage), and so Dava had never attempted a girls' trip with them again.

"I'll cancel a few," Dava said, smiling through gritted teeth as the two followed their luggage and the bellhop to the elevator.

"No need. They all sound heavenly. I only want to make sure we have time for my little birthday present for you." Chaitanya did a little skip as the two entered the elevator, her yellow sundress rippling around her. "Don't worry—it's no big thing. Nicked it from Ram on my way out the door."

And so the two soon found themselves wearing white bathrobes and avocado masks, watching the sunset from Dava's balcony as they enjoyed Chaitanya's gift: Ram's weed.

"Are you sure he won't mind?" Dava said as she took a hit from the joint before passing it to Chaitanya. She was fond of Ram and the way he doted on his wife, and she secretly thought of him as one of her own sons-in-law.

"He was planning to go to the dispensary next week anyway to replenish—this was just the last of it." She raised her hand that was holding the joint, toasting the air. "Cheers, Dava. Happy birthday."

"And happy birthday to you too, dear," she said, eyes twinkling. She hadn't smoked pot since her Peace Corps days, and so taking a few puffs already had her fizzy and giggly. Dava stood on her tiptoes as she leaned over the stone balcony and looked down five flights below at the spa's circular driveway, lined with poplar trees with fairy lights strung up in the branches. For a moment, as she watched the sun dip behind the Sonoma Mountains, she almost felt she was with Arvid and that this was one of their sleep-ins. If she turned around, Dava thought she would see him inside the room stretched out on the bed in his red boxers and Hüsker Dü T-shirt, flipping the channels on the widescreen. When she actually did turn around and instead saw

Chaitanya next to her, staring off thoughtfully into the middle distance, Dava was surprised to feel at peace, rather than the old familiar sorrow whenever a memory of Arvid resurfaced.

"How are you and Ram doing these days, if you don't mind me asking?"

"Much better. I think having the discussion about children has been a relief to both of us." Over the past few months, and with the help of a therapist, Chaitanya had realized her vague stirrings of discontent were largely related to her ambivalence about starting a family, and that by not making a decision one way or another, she felt stuck in her life and unable to move forward. She and Ram had a whirlwind romance and married just a few months shy of her college graduation, and in their thirteen years of marriage, both had assumed that if the other person wanted children, the topic would have come up. When Chaitanya at last broached it with Ram, he said he would be willing if she was, but he believed he was too old to be a father. To hone in on if they wanted a family, each created their own pro/con lists and shared them with each other. When they saw that their "con" lists had more items than the "pro," they broke out into weepy, relieved laughter. So the couple agreed the two of them were enough but added one more member to their family: a bulldog puppy named Belle.

"It feels like a weight has been lifted, for both of us. The worst part was breaking it to Mum and Dad, because I know they want grandchildren. It's almost criminal not to give Indian parents a grandchild, right?" Dava chuckled exaggeratedly, trying to ignore the tingle of recognition running down her spine. "Once I was able to break it to them and let all that go, poof!" She let out a laugh, slapping her bare knees. Dava wondered if being adopted had also played a role in her ambivalence, but she did not ask. Chaitanya handed the joint back to Dava and touched her green face. "This hardened so fast I can barely move my lips." She let out a little melodic laugh. "Am I doing this right?"

"That's how face masks work," Dava said, chuckling, as she sat down in one of the two reclining patio chairs, stretching out her legs so that her tangerine pedicure peeked out of the complimentary spa slippers. The pedicure had been an impulsive choice, and she was starting to regret the bright orange-pink color. "You don't think all of this is too girly, do you?"

"I could stand to be a bit more girly, to be honest. I was always a bit of a tomboy. I didn't wear lipstick until I was fifteen."

"You and me both," Dava said between clenched teeth as she held the joint between her lips while tightening the belt of her robe. She then took it between both fingers and took an extra-long hit, then let out an elaborate "ahhh," as if she had just stepped inside a hot tub on a winter's day. "Last time I attempted a spa weekend was with my girls, and it was a mess. I don't think you're supposed to leave feeling tenser than when you arrived."

"Oh no—that bad?"

Dava nodded. "Oh yes. In their early twenties when they could barely stand each other. Now they're friendlier, but..." She paused.

"But what?" Chaitanya pressed gently.

"Neither Arvid nor I had siblings. And so we wanted a big family so our kids could be each other's best friends, have each other's backs, the whole deal. But it didn't happen in the way I had envisioned." Dava stubbed out the joint on the chair's arm, the ash leaving a sun-shaped mark on the plastic. "At least the younger two have that relationship. But I want all of them to be close. They take each other for granted, and I would have done anything to have had just one brother or sister."

"Oh, me too, me too. I begged for a sibling from everyone I thought could give me one: my parents, Santa, the tooth fairy,"

Chaitanya said, touching her face with all five fingers. Her lips, which looked even rosier when contrasted with the greenness of her skin, curled into a smile of wonder. "Wow, we seem to have a lot in common, don't we?"

"Seems that way," Dava said sheepishly, averting her eyes from her daughter.

"What else, do you think? Besides our birthdays, being tomboys and only children, plus our rubbish taste in telly." One of the first things they had bonded over was a mutual love of a Korean reality show about pop stars training to be astronauts. "I'm sure there's more."

Dava giggled. She couldn't remember the last time she had gotten this high, but she embraced the floaty sensation that swam through her. Even as she luxuriated in her high, she knew she should be careful about what she said in her heightened state. But the daredevil side of her, long dormant and recently awoken, longed to test boundaries and see how much she could push toward the truth. Maybe even say the words aloud.

"We're both Indian," Dava said with a straight face. "Add that to the list." After a beat, they both laughed hysterically.

"Check, and check," Chaitanya said in a clipped, posh British accent. "That's a big one. How did I forget that in my exhaustive list of all the ways we're alike?"

"Ah, but you're way more Indian than me, my child," Dava replied, feeling a thrill surge through her at saying the last two words. "I never learned Hindi or my parents' mother tongue. I've only visited India three times in my life, and it was always for work." Not wanting to get too heavy on a subject she had never delved in deeply within herself, she changed the subject. "How is your mask feeling?"

Chaitanya knocked on her cheek with her knuckles. "Hard like a coconut shell." Their stomachs then rumbled at the same time, which they responded to with more hysterical laughter. "Even our hunger pangs are in sync," she noted.

They agreed to freshen up and meet in the lobby in thirty minutes to go to dinner at the spa's on-site restaurant. Dava walked into her suite's bathroom, feeling frothy and light-headed. After washing the avocado mask off her face, she interrogated her suitcase in search of an outfit, and went through three different looks before choosing a black linen jumpsuit and red leather flats, which she had custom made for herself after spotting a petite actress wearing a similar ensemble on a TV series, because it had an elegant simplicity that did not advertise its costly price tag. Dava was always careful about not flaunting her wealth too much in front of Chaitanya, because it inspired in her a latent guilt that she had chosen not to raise her and, in doing so, had deprived her of having a privileged, comfortable life. Whenever she came to Chaitanya's to visit, she did her best to ignore the water stains on the ceiling, the peeling paint in the bathroom, the clutter of bills on the coffee table that had NEEDS IMMEDIATE ATTENTION stamped in red. The birthday weekend was no doubt an extravagance but also the only way Dava thought she could take care of Chaitanya just like she did her other children.

By the time Dava arrived in the lobby, she was fifteen minutes late. As she scanned the room, she heard Chaitanya before seeing her.

"It's been lovely, Mum. I can't believe how much she is spending! She has been so wonderful to me."

Dava's knees shook, and she leaned on a brass pillar for support. She followed Chaitanya's voice and spied the back of her head near the entrance, where she was seated at an ottoman facing away from the elevator. Just like that, she had lost her buzz and freewheeling spirit, and all fifty-seven years of her life hit her in the face. Still, she couldn't help creeping closer to where her daughter was seated so she could overhear her conversation with her adoptive mother.

"Yes. I know. Yes," Chaitanya said, sounding amused, as if she was hearing something from her mother she had heard many times before. "Of course. Mum, I told you that already."

For the first time, Dava wondered if Chaitanya's mother had seen a photo of her. When Dava had met with the Raos, she had given them a fake name because she had been paranoid that news of her pregnancy would somehow hop across the Atlantic and reach her parents. So she was fine if Chaitanya had talked about her with her adoptive mother but prayed that she never wanted to introduce them to each other. Then again, would either woman recognize the other after their sole meeting more than thirty-five years ago? Dava hoped she would never have to find out.

"Oh no, Dad really did that?" Chaitanya laughed long and loud. "I can't believe it; I wish I had seen it." She sighed softly. "Miss you too."

Dava backed away, feeling she was intruding on a personal moment. She hid behind a pillar and composed herself, tucking away her feelings of jealousy and inadequacy, and then walked the ten steps toward Chaitanya, tapping her on the shoulder. She jumped up, elated.

"Mum, she's here. I have to run. Yes, I will. I said I will! Kisses to Dad. Good night; get some sleep, please." She hung up her phone, her face shining. "Mum says hello."

"Hello to her," Dava murmured, then linked her arm through Chaitanya's, something she had never done before. "I'm starving. Ready to eat?"

⌒

The restaurant was called Delight, and the cuisine was described by their waiter as "heart-healthy, cruelty-free vegan Asian/

Caribbean fusion," but the menu showed this meant different kinds of tofu and vegetables coated with soy sauce and jerk flavors, all priced at double digits. It was the worst kind of food possible for two people who had not eaten all day and just shared a joint made up of the second-strongest marijuana sold at Pot of Gold.

"Should we get out of here and order a pizza?" Chaitanya said, glancing at Dava over her menu. "Because this...doesn't seem...good."

"I know," Dava said, dismayed. Her stomach felt like a yawning chasm, and she was so hungry she could barely focus on reading the menu. "Let's just order one item so we can eat something immediately, and I'll order us a pizza right now."

"Brilliant!" Chaitanya said, setting down her menu on top of her plate. "You choose. I'll eat cardboard at this point." The two exchanged grins, and Dava beckoned their waiter. She told him they would share a plate of the hoisin jerk tofu nachos. When the waiter stood there, waiting to hear more, she told him that was all and to bill it to her room. His eyes went hard and his face screwed up in a sickly sweet smile.

"Okay, then," he said, looking her dead in the eyes and sounding as if he were talking to a child. "But we have a fifty-dollar minimum, so I won't be able to place that order for you unless you choose something else."

"Is that so?" Chaitanya said, her voice rising.

"Yes," he said, continuing with the same condescending tone. His eyes swept over Chaitanya, taking in her skin color and the white cardigan she was wearing over her sundress, which was unraveling at the sleeves. "So, might I suggest you and your mother order a bottle of wine as well? Or three orders of baked bread with lemon aioli? That would take you to the minimum."

Dava was so awestruck at hearing the word "mother" that

she didn't know what to say. Chaitanya, seeming to think that her friend was paralyzed by anger, stood up from their table with a dramatic backing of her chair, which made a loud scraping sound that caused the other patrons to look in their direction.

"We're bloody well not going to eat here," she spat out, her North London accent emerging full force.

"Chait—"

"You can take your aioli and shove it up your bum. Let's go, *Mum*," she said, winking at Dava. Still in shock, she followed Chaitanya out of the restaurant and back into the lobby. Once outside, Chaitanya began laughing so hard she doubled over and put her hand on a pillar for support.

"I'm so sorry, Dava, but the nerve of that man," she said, her body shaking with laughter. She then drew herself up and the laughs gradually petered out of her. "When I get really upset, I laugh like I'm being tickled. I don't know why."

Dava, to steady herself from the stir of emotions ricocheting within, focused on ordering a pizza via a delivery service app on her phone. "Pepperoni, olives, and mushrooms," she said with a sad smile.

"Oh dear, I hope I didn't embarrass you," Chaitanya replied.

"Ha ha, not at all," Dava said. "He was an ass. I'll be lodging a complaint with management. I'm..." She trailed off, placing her hand on her forehead. "I'm feeling a bit unwell."

Concerned Dava was feeling ill effects from the pot, she escorted her back to her room and insisted she lie down on the bed. Just as Dava got under the covers, her phone pinged with an alert that their pizza arrived and was waiting in the lobby, giving her time to collect herself while her daughter went downstairs to retrieve it.

"That was fast, wasn't it?" Chaitanya said in an overly de-lighted tone. Dava nodded tiredly and insisted Chaitanya join her on the bed as they ate, and so they both were soon under the covers eating slices while a dating show played in the background.

"It was so bizarre for me," Dava said abruptly, "when he called me your mother." She turned to see Chaitanya looking at her expectantly, and swallowed hard. Here was the moment she came closest to revealing the truth. Her mouth was open, the words forming on her lips. But then she saw Chaitanya's phone light up with a text message on the end table, reminding her of her connection with her other mother. And she couldn't do it. Dava could not radically upend her daughter's life just to make herself feel better.

So instead, she told her something else that was also painfully true. "Because when I was younger, and I'd be out with my children, eight times out of ten I'd be mistaken for their nanny."

"No!"

"Oh yes. My kids are much fairer than me and have lighter hair. My oldest in particular looks just like his dad, more Scandinavian than Indian. At restaurants, at parks, at stores, I was often assumed to be the nanny while their actual mom was in the restroom. It happened so much we all got used to it. Sometimes I'd be upset; other times I'd shrug it off." She set her pizza down on the end table and dabbed at the corners of her lips with a napkin. "It's new for me to be mistaken as someone's mother for a change."

"Oh wow, Dava; that must have been tough." Chaitanya finished off the last of her pizza and took a sip of white wine straight from the bottle. "I can somewhat relate. I'd get so many confused looks when I was out with my parents, especially from other Indian people. When we walked down the street, we kind of looked like a reverse Oreo: butterscotch cookies with chocolate filling in the middle." She passed the bottle to Dava, who shook her head. "But I'm sure your kids didn't care.

Because for me, I felt even more bonded to them. Stare all you want—this is my mum and dad, and no, we don't owe you an explanation."

Dava nodded, tears filling her eyes. The two continued to eat in silence, watching as the couple on the show navigated an odd first date that involved trying archery while blindfolded, as Dava reflected on why the waiter's words had made such a stupefying impact on her. She was chagrined to realize how much joy she experienced in that initial second when he had called her Chaitanya's mother, and it was because the visual of them together made that a natural assumption. They didn't look that much alike in terms of their physical characteristics, but their ease with each other, coupled with their age difference and how they shared the same skin color, was not a random or vaguely racist assumption to make about their relationship. But the initial joy was followed by tremendous guilt, like having an anvil fall on top of a red balloon floating in the sky. Not just the guilt of keeping the truth from Chaitanya, but also that, by taking such pleasure from the waiter's assumption, she was somehow slighting her other children.

And then there was the worst idea of all, the one that curdled in her stomach as she robotically ate slice after slice, focusing all her energy on the television screen so she wouldn't have to look at Chaitanya. The idea she had been avoiding and pushing away for the past several months but that kept encroaching on her until now it was practically leaping on top of her, just how Belle greeted her each time she came for a visit. Dava had always known her decision to give up her daughter for adoption was the right one, and she had never once regretted it, even after meeting her and developing such a close friendship.

And yet.

It had dawned on Dava that of all her children, the one she had no hand in raising was the one who seemed the happiest and most well-adjusted. And, perhaps most heartbreaking of all, the one who was the most high-minded, the most giving. The one who was most like her.

"Bull's-eye!" Chaitanya cried out, raising her half-eaten slice in triumph.

"What?" Dava said, nearly dropping her own pizza on her lap.

"Somehow she just hit the bull's-eye blindfolded. Isn't that amazing?" She pointed at the TV, which showed the woman jumping up and down in excitement as her date beamed at her.

"Yes, amazing," Dava replied softly.

CHAPTER TWENTY-ONE

All I Can Be Is Grateful

Since learning about her passing and seeing the photograph of her mum, I have to grapple with the fact I might never know the truth. The only people who can confirm this for me are my parents, but they, too, are gone. So I have to live inside this uncertainty, this official not knowing—even as my instinct tells me she was actually my mother—and ponder what that means. That she would seek me out, form a friendship with me that at times made her feel like a second mother, but never tell me the truth about who she was.

I should be angry. Right? I should be. And there's a strong possibility I will be tomorrow or a year from now. But at this moment, all I can be is grateful. That I got to know her at all; that I learned what a tremendous, giving person she is; that Kinghope directly benefited from her largesse; that philanthropy was what brought us together in the first place.

I might never know the truth. And without a doubt that is a major loss. But I also received so much from her. That might have to be enough.

—An excerpt from Chaitanya's message posted in the
Oakland Reading Club thread

"SO, GAMMA…NOW WHAT?"

Enzo's question hovered over the six of them as Dava set down the tablet, having finished reading Chaitanya's entire post, which had taken great effort, since the light from the device had left her with a stinging sensation behind her eyes. But she was glad she had done so, knowing that Chaitanya's words were written for a private audience and therefore were what she genuinely felt about her. She was leaving Chaitanya in a good place in her life, and their relationship was loving and stable until the end. But could she say the same about her four other children? The answer, weighty and burdensome, hung like an anchor around her neck.

As to how to confront this painful reality in the time she had left, she thought back to *The Last Waltz*. Not about the memory she attached so vividly to Arvid from that final Thanksgiving in the brownstone, but about the movie itself, which she thought of as a self-conscious act of mythmaking. By saying goodbye in such a grand, cinematic fashion, the film had enshrined The Band in rock 'n' roll history, ensuring their music lived on long after they had disbanded. Their public farewell ended up defining them in the public consciousness, casting a glow over all that came before.

"The film ends with The Band playing their own swan song," Tom Buck had once told her. "It doesn't get more epic than that."

And now here was her chance to say goodbye and attempt her own kind of mythmaking. Not only for herself, but for Arvid too. For the whole family. She wanted this night to be remembered by her grandchildren, to be mythologized even, so if one day someone decided to tell the Shastri-Persson story, then this time together, her final night of living, would be a part of it.

"There are letters," she started as her head began to swim and her thoughts momentarily lagged. Dava pushed through with gritted teeth, willing herself through the tumor making its presence felt again. "There are letters," she said louder, causing the other five to sit up sharply. "Your grandfather wrote them for each of them. I mean your parents. My children." The words stumbled out of her mouth like a drunk trying to exit a bar. Still, she pressed on. "Arvid wrote letters for each of the kids before he died. Messages he wanted them to know about himself, his life." Dava noticed the emotional, almost uncomprehending expressions of her grandchildren and turned to her right and saw Sandi's sympathetic gaze.

"Gamma..." Klara said, her hazel eyes widening. Dava held up her finger, the boardroom gesture, and her granddaughter nodded deferentially.

"When he learned he was dying," she continued, "he wrote each of his children four letters. Ask your parents and Kali aunty and Rev uncle to share them with you, and read each one. You barely know about him," she added, choking up, "and you should. He was a wonderful man. He would have been a wonderful grandfather too."

"Okay, Gamma," Klara said. "We will. We promise. Right?" she said, and her sister and cousins nodded. They all looked anxiously toward Sandi as the only other adult in the room, as they sensed their grandmother was ailing, if not physically, at least emotionally. Sandi placed her arm around Dava's slim shoulders, and realized she was trembling.

"Dava? Are you feeling unwell? Should—"

She held up a finger for the second time. Getting the words out about Arvid had been a struggle, and now that she had conveyed them, her mind relented and allowed her thoughts to come out evenly. After reassuring everyone she was fine, Dava cleared her throat and then delivered the following thoughts in a soft but steady monologue, her voice taking on a rhythmic quality so when the rest of the group recalled what she said, it was not just what she said to them, but how she said it.

"Arvie," she said, directing her gaze at his daughters. "When he was seven, he told me he wanted to be a superhero. And he

asked me where he could go to college to study to be a superhero and learn how to fly and climb walls. His favorites were
Superman and Spider-Man, you see. And so I had to break it
to him, just as your parents had to break it to you that there
was no Santa Claus, that he couldn't be one. And his little chin
wobbled. I had devastated him, and I felt terrible." Dava winced
to recall the way his face slowly turned red, from his chin to his
ears to his nose and finally his forehead. "He cried all day long.
And there was nothing I could do to reassure him. I sometimes
think that was the moment we lost something between us. Our
closeness. He was my first child I saw grow up before my eyes,
and he was my first child I saw act as a sibling for another.
There's so much that is meaningful to me about that." She saw
Klara reach for Priya's hand. "But I had shaken his faith in something he held dear, and I had nothing to say to make him feel
better. And I carry that as a regret, one of the few. I should have
had an answer for him, a better answer." Dava briefly took off
her glasses so she could dab at her eyes with her pajama sleeve.
"He's a good man. When I see him, sometimes it's like Arvid has
come back to life again. All he ever wanted to be was his father,
and I think he's capable of it. But maybe help him get there."

"Sita," Dava continued, now glancing down at where Enzo
and Theo were seated cross-legged at her feet. "Your mother
has always been the one in charge. From the moment she
could speak and form sentences, she was the leader and Arvie
and Kali followed her path. Not always happily, or willingly,
but they did it," she noted fondly. "She always had that natural
self-assurance. For the longest time she wanted to take after her
father and become a teacher. But then I asked her to work at the
foundation, and she did." Dava did a sharp intake of breath as
another memory sprang up and came into focus. "And when
your grandfather died, she was about the same age as Klara. But
she did her best to take care of me. Even as she was grieving

herself. She was the one who saw me at my worst, you know," she said, her voice taking on a near whisper. "On the days I couldn't get out of bed, she would peek her head in, and see me gray and exhausted, and without a word she would shut the door and look after the other kids for me. Sita took on a lot. I leaned on her so much. I don't know if I ever thanked her. It was something that had been unspoken between us. But each time I see her running a meeting, or even talking with the two of you, I think back to when she was just a young girl, and she was taking her whole family on her shoulders." Theo nodded in recognition at his grandmother's words, and Enzo's mouth curved downward as he rubbed a small fist past his eye.

"Your aunt Kali loves so much and so deeply. I can't help but worry for her, you know, because she feels things so intensely. Perhaps that's what makes her such a good artist. Her empathy is all right there, all the time. She's constantly observing. It can be unnerving, at times, honestly." Dava laughed, but it sounded more like a shiver. "Kali has always been the glue. It's this intangible thing. Maybe it's the fact that she's a middle child, so she has no choice but to hold us all together," she said, the words sounding as if this idea had just occurred to her. "She goes out of her way to keep in touch and stay close to each of your parents and, of course, Rev," Dava said, absently patting Sandi's hand. "If she didn't make an effort, I don't know how close they would be. I admire that in her. I...I never thought how important that could be. Every family needs someone like her." Dava smiled sadly. "Take care of her. Look after her. I know she'll do the same for all of you."

"And Rev, my baby," she said, a note of finality stretching through the melancholy in her voice. The room was lit by a single lamp near her bedside table, and all she could make out were shapes of furniture and people surrounding her, so she felt like she was talking to shadows, which allowed her to break herself open a little more. "He was pure joy in the darkness. When Arvid was dying, and then after he died, I knew I couldn't just hide away, because this little boy needed me. Your grandfather loved music, all kinds. You'll find out when you read his letters. And I wanted to keep that love alive in Rev. When he was having a particularly difficult time, and I wanted to lift his spirits, I'd play 'Yellow Submarine' or 'My Girl.' And we'd sing it at the top of our lungs, sometimes dance around the room. He asked me once after we did that, 'Why does that make me feel so much better, Amma?' And I said it's a little bit of free happiness." The shadows moved around her, but she did not know if that was the children moving or her eyesight starting to fail her. "There was a time when it was just Rev and me at home—all the other children had gone off to college. And I'd start to feel lonely. He was a teenager; he didn't have to think about me or recognize I was going through the empty nest phase. But he did, and once in a while, he'd come find me and he would say, 'How about a little free happiness?' And we'd sing out loud to the same songs from his childhood. That was his way of checking on me, which I appreciated."

The shadows were now floating throughout the room, and the light from the single bulb was fading. One final sunset, she thought sadly, but without fear. "So," Dava said, as Sandi squeezed her hand. "This is how I'll remember my children and what they gave me. I wasn't always easy on them. Because I accomplished a lot in my life, through my own hard work and merit. And I wanted them to do the same. So I could be tough. Exacting. Maybe not as . . . motherly as others could be, or what they would want from me. But I tried my best. And I love them dearly. And I love you dearly. Because the only thing I wanted, ultimately, was to leave a mark, to have had my life and my presence matter. In the world, yes. But with all of you also. I hope I have, but it's out of my hands. It lies within yours." Dava gave them what she hoped was a reassuring smile. "That's it, dears. That is what I had to share. And now I should get a little rest. I know your parents are waiting for you."

She stood up, her legs wobbly and stiff from sitting for so long. Sandi leapt up and, with Klara's help, escorted her back to bed. Dava tried her best to not give away the fact her eyesight was failing again, and at a more rapid rate. As the two settled her in bed, bringing the comforter to her chin, she heard Enzo say something, his voice urgent.

"What is it? What did you say?" Dava asked.

Klara and Sandi exchanged confused looks as they saw Dava look in the exact opposite direction of where Enzo was standing.

"Tomorrow is when you're going, right?" he repeated.

"That's right," she replied hesitantly. "The doctor will be coming tomorrow morning to administer the treatment." Even in the descending darkness, she could feel the sadness enveloping the room, strong and thick like fog. When Dava had first had her idea about having her family around her as she died, she thought about how much it would mean to her to be surrounded by her loved ones. She had not thought through what it would feel like for them, especially the children. When she had to go through the rituals of grief for each parent and then Arvid, each time was more heartrending than the one before. Whether death visited her suddenly or the visit was a long time coming, the grief always felt the same: heavy, suffocating, impermeable. She didn't want that for her children or grandchildren. She did not want to be at the center of a living wake, having them crumple-faced and sobbing as she took her final breaths. She wanted joy.

"How many days until New Year's Eve?" she asked.

"It's in four days. But it'll be midnight in a few hours, so really, three days," Sandi answered. She knelt down at Dava's bedside and whispered, "Are you all right? Should I get the doctor?"

Dava shook her head. "Let's have a party. New Year's Eve is my favorite holiday—did you know? The renewal of each year. I always liked saying goodbye to the past year and welcoming a new one." She smiled and hoped her smile was big enough that all of them could see it. "I'm not going to be able to celebrate this one. But I'd still like to have a party. Because these have been a tough few days. The days to come will be hard too. In between, let's try to have a little happiness."

"Free happiness!" she heard Theo call out from a distance.

"Yes, that!" Dava laughed in genuine surprise, momentarily forgetting her vision was receding. "Is that possible, kids? Should we try?"

She couldn't see it, but she knew all five of them were standing around her bed, nodding.

CHAPTER TWENTY-TWO

Our Happy Gang

To our happy gang, our gang of three
I watch your smiles and hope for four
And that we grow and grow and grow
Until we're the whole show
So many names we fill the marquee
We play until the lights come up
Then keep on playing anyway

—*An excerpt from Arvid Persson's journal, age thirty-nine*

ONE BY ONE, THEY came downstairs, Priya first, followed by her older sister, then the twins walking together step by step, with Sandi bringing up the rear. When Sita heard their footsteps echoing down the staircase, she was the first to rush out of the great room, where she had been waiting with everyone else, and met them at the landing. As she hugged her sons, they remained standing at the foot of the stairs, all in a bit of a daze, with the group looking to Sandi as their spokesperson as they were inundated with questions.

"Is she okay? Are you okay?"

"What happened up there? What's going on?"

"What did she say?"

"Is she still awake?" This last question was from Kali, who was gazing upward while the others were focused on the kids and Sandi.

"We just settled her into bed," Sandi told Kali. "But she might not be asleep yet if you wanted to visit with her." Kali nodded, began walking upstairs, and then reversed herself and sped toward the mudroom, where she took her mother's letter out of her coat pocket. She emerged again with envelope in hand and went back upstairs, going two steps at a time.

"Your mother is fine," Sandi continued once Kali disappeared. "But she did make a special request, and I think we'd all like to honor it." She turned to look at the grandchildren, who nodded solemnly.

"It's late," Sita said as she glanced at her watch. "You kids need to go to bed."

"But, Amma—"

"Whatever you want to plan, we can talk about it in the morning. Right?" she said to Sandi, not unkindly.

"Right," she said, smiling big at the twins. "Let's get some rest tonight so we can do it up properly tomorrow." Sita nodded her thanks, and she and Colin took them upstairs, with the girls, Arvie, and Vincent soon following behind. Rev and Sandi watched them go and then looked at each other before heading to their own room.

⌒

As soon as the door closed, Sandi peeled off her clothes and crawled into bed. Only then did the extent of her exhaustion make itself known to her, and she let out a colossal yawn. Her mind and body longed for rest, but she fought against her sleepiness as she watched Rev also disrobe down to his blue boxer briefs.

"Long day, huh?" she started tentatively as she sat up and reclined against the pillows.

"Long night too," Rev responded, reaching for her bare feet and absentmindedly massaging the right one. But he wouldn't look at her, instead his eyes focused downward, where he pressed the ball of her foot so intently she howled in pain. "Oh God, are you okay? Is the baby okay?"

"We're fine. But you were massaging really...hard." *I'm not a stress ball,* she thought crossly. But then Sandi remembered Rev's near meltdown in the boathouse with his siblings, and she reached over to him and buried herself in his arms.

"What's wrong?" he said, returning her embrace, even as she sensed his mind was elsewhere.

"I was in the boathouse." She explained she had overheard his conversation with his brother and sisters, the last thing being Rev taking Arvie to task for his anger toward their mother. "It was all noise and yelling, and then silence. A long silence. But I was so proud of you, baby, for speaking up for yourself and saying how you felt. What happened after that?"

Rev pulled away from her embrace so that he could face her, and he sat half off the bed so one foot was on the floor. "We hugged, actually. I don't remember if he moved in to hug me first, or I did, but before I knew it, we just were. He kept whispering, 'I'm sorry,' into my ear—I'm not sure why. We both got choked up." Rev's voice caught in his throat as he recalled holding his older brother, whom he had not hugged since he was a child. "And then after a little while, Sita and Kali joined us too." He added he and his siblings had their arms around each other for what seemed like several minutes. When they finally broke apart, they noticed Colin and Vincent standing nearby, watching them with misty looks on their faces.

"It felt deep, powerful. I wish I could explain it," Rev said, shaking his head at the memory. "I'm not sure it's going to solve anything long-term, but I think we're all a little healed."

"That's great, Rev," Sandi replied, taking his hands and rubbing them between hers for warmth. She leaned in and kissed him on the lips, which felt cold against hers. "I'm so happy you've had the chance to spend time with them in a meaningful way. And that you were able to express yourself."

Rev shivered and stood up to find his sweatpants. As he searched the closet, with his back to his fiancée, he wondered if he should talk to her now about his insecurities about getting married and wanting to put the engagement on hold. He was close to raising the topic when he heard Sandi start to cry behind him.

"What's wrong?" Rev found his sweatpants and quickly put them on, but he hadn't pulled them up completely over his feet, and so he tripped and fell on the bed in one big swoop, like a tree felled by an axe.

"Omigod, are you okay?" Sandi asked. His head had landed on the mattress with a thud next to her knees, and she reached down to touch his face. Slowly, Rev stood up, and in doing so, he broke into a chagrined grin.

"Yeah, I'm fine. Just tripped over my own feet." Seeing her concerned eyes and her cheeks stained with tears, Rev felt a resurgence of protectiveness. He sat down next to her, and she rested her head on his chest. "Why were you crying?"

"I was thinking about your mom." He waited for her to say more, but when she did not, he asked her what had happened upstairs. She apologized for not being able to go into specifics— "I know this sounds odd, but we pinky swore we would keep it to ourselves"—but noted how their time together made her feel like a part of the family for the first time.

"Your mother—there are no words to describe her. She is a legend; that's the closest thing I can think of, but even that doesn't do her justice. I just feel so happy and proud I get to be a part of this family. A Shastri." Sandi's eyes shone as she looked up at Rev and ran her thumb over his stubbled chin. "I'm happy that our child gets to be a Shastri, and all that it means."

Rev was astounded by Sandi's words but did not say anything, just let the sentiment wash over him. For the first but not the last time in his life, he wondered what transpired among Sandi, Dava, and his nieces and nephews. And he would never truly know, although Sandi would share her remembrances of that night with their son many years later.

"You can't give me a hint? Just a little one?" he teased, but he was being serious.

"I can't, babe. I'm so, so sorry." Her stomach rumbled loudly enough that they both laughed. "The little one is starving, it seems. I never really had dinner."

"He's going to have a big appetite like his papa." Rev decided for the moment he would table his insecurities about marriage and just focus on this time with Sandi. "But I know he's going to—"

"Or she!"

"All right, or she." He nuzzled his lips against her neck before continuing. "How is our peanut doing, by the way? Besides being hungry."

"He or she is wonderful," she said, beaming at him. "Now, bring us some sustenance, please." After Rev retrieved a bowl of risotto from the kitchen, he sat next to her, stroking her hair as she consumed it with big spoonfuls.

"Based on your appetite, I'm going to guess Rev or Sandi Junior will be a football player. Or a sumo wrestler. Or both." He stopped midchuckle when Sandi paused chewing to shake her spoon at him. "What?"

"No to Rev or Sandi Junior. If there's one thing I've learned from your mother, it's that names are very important."

"Really?" Rev let out a long breath, overcome with emotion at the thought of his mother witnessing her final sunset, and the soundtrack that accompanied it. "Me too, actually."

⌒

Sita was taking laps around the leather couch as she waited for Colin to return from the bathroom. Her pink robe fluttered behind her as she glanced at her watch, her impatience growing with every minute that ticked past 10:00 p.m. They had decided to convene in the library to discuss the day's events after they had settled their children into bed, but the task had taken more than forty minutes, since Theo and Enzo were hyper and chatty as if hopped up on sugar, asking them question after question, first about Dava and Arvid, then about Colin's parents. The questions ping-ponged between inquiries about family history ("Where in Sweden is Grandpa Arvid from?") and inquiries about their own family unit ("How come we don't speak Swedish or Portuguese?"). When she tried asking them what they had talked about with their grandmother, they had firmly shaken their heads. "You don't get it. We pinky swore," Theo had said to her earnestly. "We can't tell you."

"Did you notice they only asked about speaking Swedish and Portuguese? Not Hindi, not even Japanese." This was the first thing Sita said upon seeing the door open and Colin walk in.

"Hold on. Let me sit down one moment." Colin collapsed onto the sofa with a gentle groan, grimacing as he placed his hand on his lower back. "I might need your massager. I think I overdid it playing with the kids in the snow today. Feels like someone's been doing jumping jacks on my spine."

"I'll go get it now." Sita kissed his forehead before leaving the library to enter their room next door. Just as she was about to turn the doorknob, she heard the boys talking. Sita pressed her ear to the door and tried to listen.

"How do we find out Gamma's favorite song? If we want to surprise her, we can't ask her."

"Maybe Rev uncle would know, since they used to sing together." Sita was confused. She had no idea what the twins were talking about. When did her mother and Rev ever sing together?

"But how do we ask him if we're not supposed to talk about what she said?"

"I don't think asking about her favorite songs will give anything away. All we need is one song. I can stream it on the tablet. But it has to be a good one. The perfect one."

Sita's hand slipped on the doorknob and she accidentally turned it, alerting the boys to her presence. They immediately clammed up and pretended to be asleep. *Shit*, she thought to herself as she crept inside to retrieve the massager from her suitcase. Before she left, she took one last look at her children, who were curled up on the floor in their sleeping bags but had their backs to each other, the same way they had slept as babies. Sita sighed again and shut the door behind her. She waited for a minute to see if they would resume talking, but they did not. She returned to the library and handed the massager to her husband, who took it from her gratefully and got to work on his lower back.

"I'm so mad at her," she muttered, pulling her robe tightly around herself.

"Who?" Colin asked, raising his voice to be heard above the massager.

"Amma. She has the boys keeping secrets. I don't like that. What could she have possibly said that would make them want to not share it with us?"

"The girls might be more forthcoming. I hate to say it, but they're a little gossipy."

"That's not the point." In irritation, she took the massager out of his hands and pressed it against his back for him. "She shouldn't be encouraging *my* children to keep things from me. From us." Sita told him how she had overheard part of the boys' conversation, and how they had been so adamant on keeping what their grandmother said private. "I can't help but feel hurt. By her mostly, but them a little bit too."

"Are you ready for a few more 'silva' linings?"

"Oh God. Not really."

"Too bad—you're getting them anyway."

Sita switched off the device and folded her arms, still gripping the massager.

"For starters, whatever Dava told them piqued their interest not just about her and your father, but also about my own parents. They seemed genuinely interested in our families. So I think whatever Dava said, at least it has them thinking about family. That means something, don't you think?"

"True," Sita said, sniffling. "Go on."

"Whatever they experienced tonight, with their grandmother and cousins—"

"And Sandi! Freaking Sandi. How did she get to be a part of that?"

"In any case, they all seemed to have shared something very special. It might bond the kids in a beautiful way. I treasure the time I spent with my cousins when we were young." Sita rolled her eyes as she heard Colin talk for the umpteenth time about his cousins' annual summer trek to a tree house built on their grandfather's property. "These kids have never been close, Sita. So maybe let them have this. At least for now."

Sita scowled but nodded reluctantly. She believed that in time, she'd be able to wear at least one of them down—likely Theo—about what had transpired in Dava's bedroom. And she would get a few crumbs over the years, a dropped anecdote here and there, but like Rev, she would never learn the full story. But feeling left out of her sons' time with Dava only strengthened Sita's resolve in terms of her own future.

"Colin," she said, unfolding her arms, "I think I'm going to take a leave of absence from the foundation."

He mock-clutched his chest as if having a heart attack. "I'm sorry. I think I heard you say you wanted to quit your job?"

"Not quit. Take a leave of absence." She explained she had decided she would not take over as CEO of the foundation, unless the board voted for her. "And they won't. I know Vash has the votes. As she should."

"Okay," Colin said, running his hand through his hair. "What will you tell your mother?"

"Nothing. She doesn't have to know. It doesn't really concern her anymore. It's what she wants for me, maybe because if I take over, it's like she's still in charge, at least in spirit. Dava Junior and all that," Sita added. "But it's not what I want."

What Sita wanted instead was a life that did not tether her and her family to the foundation, with her work schedule dictating their lives. She outlined her vision of a six-month sabbatical the following year, in which their family would journey around the world, with the idea she would homeschool them as they traveled.

"The boys are growing up so fast, and before we know it, they'll be in college and out of the house. I want to wake up in the morning and know I won't be pulled in a million different directions. I want them to be my focus for a while."

"Plus, it seems they're starting to express interest in their heritage."

"Exactly!" Sita responded. "We could stay for a few weeks or so in Brazil, India, Japan, Sweden. And make it educational, exploring our genealogy, our family trees." Sita's resentment toward her mother lessened as she continued naming all the cities she wanted to visit with Colin and the kids. "I want them to have a real global education," she said, beaming. "I want all of us to have this great family adventure, something they'll never forget."

"You don't have to sell me, honey," Colin said, smiling as he kissed her. "I'm all aboard. I'm ready to go now." Sita noticed him wince in pain, so she turned the massager back on and pressed it against his back. "Thanks, honey. So...I guess visiting your brother in Stockholm is a real option, now that you're on better terms?"

"I'm not sure if you can call it that. I'm not sure what to call it. But I hope he and Vincent can work things out." Sita recalled the moment in the boathouse in which the four of them had embraced and broke apart to see Colin and Vincent watching them. Her brother-in-law's expression seemed pained and sad, which surprised her because she thought the sight of the siblings getting along, at least for a moment, would have made him happy.

Colin hesitated for a moment, seeming to not want to puncture her good mood. "And you and Arvie?"

"Tonight was a start, but we have a long way to go." The massager abruptly stopped buzzing. "Oh crap—the batteries just died." She tossed it on the floor.

"That's all right. I'm already feeling better." He nudged it with his big toe. "And to give my two cents, I think Arvie might be a changed man. In fact, I think..." Sita raised an eyebrow at him. "Okay, I'll shut up now."

"Yes, do that." She pulled him down next to her, and they spent the remainder of the night on the sofa, their arms around each other as they daydreamed about their future in an effort to not think about the hours to come.

⌒

Kali furtively let herself into her mother's bedroom and sat at her bedside to watch her sleep. Her posture was as rigid as a watchdog's, trying to soak in the memory of her mother, living and breathing and sleeping, so she could retain it long after she was gone. Just after midnight, Dava stirred, murmuring something as her legs danced underneath the covers.

"Amma, it's Kali," she said as she switched on the bedside lamp. "Are you all right?"

"I'm fine, yes," she croaked, sounding a bit hoarse. "Is everything okay?"

"Yeah, we're all fine. I was just checking on you. And I wanted to talk to you about a few things if you're up to it."

Dava opened her eyes and sensed there was a light illuminating her room but could barely make out her youngest daughter's shape or her features. She reached out her hand so Kali would hold it, as that would help Dava know Kali was really there, rather than being caught between waking and dreaming.

"I am up to it," she replied. "But I'm going to lie here. I don't have the strength to sit up," she added apologetically.

Kali bit back the tears waiting to flow, ordering herself to not succumb to her emotions, because there would be time to cry later. At this moment, she needed to be clearheaded and not have anything fog up her mind. To keep herself from giving in to her grief, she pinched her arm each time she neared the abyss.

"Rev told me you wanted Chaitanya to know the truth. Something to do with a movie about your life. I don't remember the details." She gave herself a quick pinch. "So I just need to know what you really want. Do you want her to know about you or not?" Kali tried to ask this question kindly, but the words had come out sounding too accusatory.

"I did? Oh, yes... I did." To Dava, it seemed her conversation with Rev had taken place weeks ago, not earlier in the day right before she had her seizure. "I'm not sure anymore." Every word uttered now felt like a small effort, akin to doing sit-ups.

The more she said, the harder speaking became. "She's happy. I think she's happy."

"But what does that mean? Should we tell her or not?"

"I think she will be fine not knowing." Dava looked in Kali's direction. "I'm trying to spare her, you see."

"No, Amma, I don't see." Kali tried to not feel frustrated with her mother and her seemingly willful crypticness. "I've decided I want a relationship with her. I want to know her better. I think you should know I plan on reaching out to her . . . after."

"You do?"

To Kali's surprise, her mother seemed touched by the idea. She gave herself another, harder pinch on the arm. "I do. But I would rather have your blessing. Which is why I'm here." She took the letter, which had been on her lap, and placed it on the bedside table. "I want to get to know her, but on my own terms. Because as much as I want to read this letter, it feels too personal for me to read. You deserve for your private thoughts to remain your own. Especially given what else has happened, with the media and . . . you know."

Dava nodded, hoping her daughter could sense her gratitude. It now thrilled her to think of Chaitanya and Kali becoming acquainted, perhaps becoming friends, even if she felt an acute loss that she would not get to witness it in person. "You have my blessing. But—" Dava had said the last word so faintly her daughter did not hear it, and Kali interrupted her.

"There's one more thing." And now Kali was pinching both of her arms, trying to maintain control even as the tears had reappeared again, and this time she knew she would be help-less to stop them. "I need you to know I'm okay. That the way I navigate the world in terms of my relationships, it works for me. I'm not this sensitive girl who feels too much and gives her heart away at a moment's notice. My relationships aren't traditional compared to what you're used to, but I thought you of all people could relate to having feelings for more than one person at the same time." She bit her lip at that last part—she could no longer censor herself. "I'm not sure if I'll stay in a relationship with Mattius and Lucy. At this point, likely not. But in my future, there might be another couple. Or there might be no one. I'm comfortable with either possibility. I just... I need you to know I've experienced love too. Mind-bending love, soulful love. You've had a great love story. I've had several." Kali sat up straight in her chair and leaned toward Dava, pressing her hand in between both of her mother's for emphasis. "So I beg of you, please stop invalidating how I live my life. I need this from you; I need you to understand this, before you go." And then she was weeping, even though she had thought she had run dry of tears by this point.

"Okay, Kali." Dava was desperate to say more, to comfort her. She dug into whatever reserves of energy she had left, even as her vision dimmed completely, and she only knew Kali was still there because of their clasped hands and the sound of her hiccupping sobs. She hurried through her next words, barely taking a breath until she was done. "I understand, dearest. I am so glad you have known love." She blanched at how Kali had misconstrued her time with Tom Buck as anything to do with love or feelings but had to sacrifice clarification to expend her energy on a more pressing matter. "I want you to do something for me. Related to Chaitanya."

～

Arvie sat on the marble island facing the dining room, his legs idly swinging back and forth, even as his face was ruddy and anxious. Vincent was standing at the microwave, heating up the remaining hasselbackspotatis, his finger hovering next to the power button so that he could turn it off before the seconds ticked down to zero. Arvie heard him press the button, and hopped off the counter and walked toward his husband, who handed him the bowl of potatoes and a spoon.

"I thought we had some leftover risotto too, but I guess not," Vincent said, shrugging. After their daughters had returned from Dava's bedroom, he had settled the girls into bed while Arvie took a long, hot shower, partly to wash the hangover stench from his pores and partly to decompress from the intense meeting with his siblings. He had exited the bathroom to see that Vincent was waiting for him, and asked him if he was hungry. Then the two had quietly decamped to the kitchen, where Arvie knew that Vincent wanted to say something to him, and dreaded what that might be.

"That's okay. Thanks." The two stared at each other uncomfortably until Arvie broke the stalemate by pulling out a stool to sit at the counter, the scraping noise against the tile sounding especially harsh in the house's bedtime quiet.

"It's late," Vincent said, checking his watch. "Let's go downstairs instead," he added, already walking in that direction without waiting to hear Arvie's response. The two made their way to the den, each step down making a loud creak. His heart seized with every footfall, because Vincent's demeanor—silent, intense, deep forehead creases—meant they were about to have a very serious conversation.

One of the main reasons Arvie had fallen in love with Vincent was that he reminded him so much of his father. His dad had once told him Swedes were generally reserved and taciturn and prone to walling off their emotions. As someone who considered himself the opposite of these traits, Arvid had told his son he had felt like a misfit in his native country while growing up and rarely returned after moving to America. But since Arvie had expressed an interest in his Scandinavian roots, Arvid had obliged and traveled there with him when he was fifteen, and

Arvie had immediately felt at home, thinking at last he had found his people. Yet he had still gravitated toward Vincent upon first meeting him a few weeks after moving to Stockholm in his early twenties, where they had shared a table at a crowded café. Vincent had struck up a conversation with him, immediately recognizing him as an American, and was eager to test out his English skills. For his part, Arvie had been feeling lonely and homesick, but most of all missing his father with an intensity he could barely stand. Vincent's carefree, chatty demeanor had stood out in vivid contrast to the other Swedes he had encountered, and their first meeting had eventually turned into a first date. They would marry exactly one year later.

Throughout their marriage, and after they started their family, Vincent rarely got upset. He would always find a way to put a positive spin on disappointments and carefully steer a spousal disagreement back to harmonious accord, with most of these centered on child raising, since Arvie considered his husband too lenient and forgiving. So whenever Vincent was visibly angry, Arvie, Priya, and Klara reacted as if they had seen a hurricane hurtling in their direction and they'd run for cover, each one praying he or she had not provoked his wrath. Because Vincent did have one quality in common with his countrymen: a tendency to bottle up his feelings until they exploded messily like a shaken soda can, so the person he was angry at had no idea until the moment he expressed it. In this particular instance, however, Arvie not only knew it was directed at him but also had an idea of what his spouse would say. Arvie understood he deserved the hurricane about to bear down on him, but that only made him fear Vincent's words more.

With the sofa moved up to Dava's bedroom, they awkwardly squeezed together on the coffee table, and Vincent's size and height meant he took up most of the space even as he shrank his body as much as possible. Sitting side by side with their legs forced to be pressed together, Arvie ached for his husband's touch. So he decided to make a strategic move and preempt Vincent's diatribe by sharing news he hoped would please him.

"I've decided something big, *käraste*," he began. *Käraste* was Swedish for "dearest," which is how they often addressed each other, although not recently. "I'm quitting Helping Perssons. I already talked it over with Kali. I want to be able to spend more time at home, help out with the restaurant, and be there more consistently for the girls. What do you think?"

While waiting for his response, Arvie took a big bite of the potatoes, which were so hot they burned his tongue. For a half second, he wondered if Vincent had overheated them on purpose but waved away the thought as silly and paranoid. And yet, Vincent had still not responded to his announcement, so Arvie continued filling the room with his voice, brimming with fake positivity. "You know Helping Perssons is a big deal to me, but this way, I can focus more on our life and the—"

"What life?" Vincent was staring at him, exhaustion and a hint of regret in his tone.

"What do you mean?" Arvie said, setting down the food. He moved to sit closer to Vincent and was pained to see his husband recoil.

"Colin was the first one to notice. Which I guess shouldn't surprise me." Vincent said this in Swedish, which he switched to when he wanted to feel more comfortable conveying his thoughts. That signaled to Arvie he was in for a long speech, and he began to worry. He pulled his long legs in and hugged them to his chest, something he had seen Kali do since she was a little girl, in the hope doing so would give him solace. And he was surprised it actually did. Not that it made it any easier to hear what Vincent said.

"Colin took me aside the second day we came here and asked if we were doing okay. He noticed we weren't speaking. And I only spoke to you after you said something to me." He shook his head and brushed a gob of sweat from under his nose. "I thought we had been hiding this pretty well. But Colin picked up on it immediately. I hope the girls aren't nearly as perceptive."

"They've had a lot to preoccupy them lately," Arvie offered up meekly.

"I'm glad. I really hope they haven't noticed your behavior this weekend, but maybe it's old news to them at this point. You're getting worse at hiding the bottles and the breath." Vincent looked at the hasselbackspotatis cooling on the table. "This morning, after Dava's health scare, I asked Colin if I could use Enzo's tablet. I wanted to read what was being written about your mother, because maybe then I would understand your anger better." Arvie opened his mouth, and Vincent glanced up at him and shook his head. "I understand about your father. But I don't believe your anger is just about the rock singer. I used to believe you, you know. How you would go on and on about your mother's ego and about how any good works she did was for the applause and the accolades. But how much do you actually know about what she's done?"

Arvid shrugged, his mouth set in a petulant pout. "She's done a lot. I've never denied that. I've just questioned her motives."

In response, Vincent began rattling off statistics: how much the Dava Shastri Foundation had given away since its inception, how many Medici grants had been awarded over a forty-year span. And then he began telling stories: the schoolgirls in a tiny Afghan village who received an all-expenses paid trip to NASA's headquarters, several of whom later attended college in the US with scholarships funded by the foundation; the mother of five from San Diego who graduated summa cum laude from

Stanford Law after being provided legal and financial resources to help her leave an abusive marriage; the seventy-two-year-old folk singer who used half of her Medici Artists grant to build a revolutionary water purification system. On and on, Vincent went, until the names and numbers began to blur together and Arvie found himself tuning out. Then Vincent insistently tapped him on the knee.

"I said, what do you think?"

"Um," Arvie replied, hugging his legs tighter. "I think my mother did good things for others—no question. But like I said, why did she really do them?"

"What does that matter?" Vincent roared, and in response Arvie cowered on the other side of the table. "I don't care if she built a gold statue of herself in the middle of Times Square. Because she's actually made a real difference in the world, Arvie. It's not mere lip service. She's helped hundreds, maybe thousands of people."

Arvie nodded, wondering how long the rage storm would last. He was used to being the raging one, expelling his anger with tossed-off asides and smirks, but he was not used to being yelled at for an extended period of time, especially by his own husband.

"Sita has a theory. I wasn't going to tell you, because I didn't want to hurt your feelings."

"You talked about me with her?" Arvie sputtered. He found his own anger rising, and his voice along with it.

"So what if I did?" Vincent shot back. "I needed to talk with someone about how I was feeling."

"Why did it have to be her? You could have talked to Kali or Rev, at least. You know how much—"

"How much what?" Vincent glowered, his arms folded over his round, solid stomach.

"Never mind. Go on."

"She calls it King Edward syndrome." Named for the king of England who famously abdicated his throne so he could marry the woman he loved, Sita had explained that many believed he had other reasons for giving up his title: Edward famously hated his royal duties and would rather smoke cigars and travel to posh locales than shake hands and give speeches. "She said it's about wanting all the perks of being wealthy and privileged without doing any of the work. That you actually recognize you have little inclination to help others, and that makes you ashamed of yourself, so you take out your self-loathing on Dava."

"Hello, what do you think I was doing with Helping Perssons?"

"The amount of times you've complained about working there far outweighs any good things you've said about it."

"That's because my mother guilt-tripped me into taking the job. But I've done some good things there too. Things I'm proud of. And without me, Mom would have never known about her alleged secret daughter. So I don't want to hear about this bullshit syndrome."

"I know it's hard to hear. I don't like throwing your sister's words in your face, considering your relationship. But I've told you about my father, and how he vibrated with fury all the time. I recognized self-loathing in him, and I see it in you. I'm sorry it took your sister's words to pry that insight out of me, but there it is."

These last words from his husband resounded like a slap in the face, the kind that left a red, stinging mark for a long time afterward. But before Arvie could rebut it, Vincent had one more thing to say.

"If you want to quit Helping Perssons, fine. We'd be okay without your salary for about six months, eight months tops. And I guess we'd have the funds from your mother's . . . will," he added uncomfortably.

"You mean the hush money," Arvie said, unable to help himself.

"I just need you to get your act together, okay?" Vincent raised his hands in exasperation. "Quitting Helping Perssons isn't going to make you a happier person. You need to fix whatever is going on inside of you. Maybe that means checking into rehab, taking anger-management classes, or both. Whatever it takes. Because you can't come home until you do." Vincent stood up, and in a daze, Arvie followed his lead. "I'm not going to be the happy husband anymore and pretend everything's okay. The girls might not say anything in front of us, but they know."

"But . . . wait. You can't drop this on me out of nowhere! That's not fair." He grabbed Vincent's hand and pressed it to his own chest. "Let's try counseling again. We could get a new therapist. Or go on one of the marriage retreats you told me about last week. Just . . . just hold on about this."

Vincent gently removed his hand from Arvie's and then kissed him on the forehead. "I need you to go back to being the person I first met," he said in English. "I want to be married to him, not the person standing here." And with that, he picked up the bowl of hasselbackspotatis and returned upstairs, his husband in shock as he watched him leave.

Arvie collapsed back onto the table in exhaustion, clapping his hands over his eyes. It was the worst fight they had ever had. Vincent's ultimatum had been the cherry on top of a shit sundae of a day; in fact, he could not keep track of how many people had yelled at him in the past twenty-four hours. Arvie let out a low groan and licked away the salty tears that trickled from his closed eyes onto his lips. He remained in that position until he drifted off to sleep, awakening several hours later with a start. Arvie had been dreaming his father was giving him a piano lesson, the two sitting side by side in the den as they played "Heart and Soul." But their duet had not been blending properly, with Arvie playing the melody too fast in comparison to his father's more measured pace.

"Take your time, son," Arvid said affectionately. He took his hand off the piano, but the keys continued playing on their own, as Arvie still struggled with keeping pace with the music. "You'll get there—it just takes practice."

These words echoed in Arvie's ears upon waking up, as he glanced at the piano in the room as if expecting his father to still be sitting there, watching the piano keys dance without touching them. Arvie went and sat on the bench, resting his own hand where his father's had been in his dream, tentatively pressing a white key, then a black one. To his ears, it sounded woefully out of tune. No one in the family actually knew how to play the piano, yet the cherrywood Yamaha upright had been a fixture in the Shastri-Persson household for as long as he could remember. Dava and Arvid had acquired it upon moving into the brownstone after it had been left behind by the previous owners, and so it had been absorbed as part of the home's interior, even as it mostly functioned as a place for framed photographs and stacks of old magazines.

Arvie glanced at the family portrait on top of the piano, his eyes jumping from his father to his mother, then back again. He could not remember posing for the photo, although he could tell by his father's fragile frame that it was taken in the months before he died. For a few moments, he gazed at his mother and her tight, overly lipsticked smile, taking in the way her arm locked protectively around her husband's slim shoulders. Arvie then stared hard at his father, his hollow cheeks, wan smile, and unfocused eyes. As Arvie got older and his hairline receded, he would sometimes catch a glimpse of himself in the mirror or a window's reflection and see his father looking back at him. But now as Arvie looked at the portrait, the opposite was true:

when he gazed at this sickly version of his father, it was as if he were seeing his own face instead.

The piano made a rude, discordant sound, and Arvie realized it was because his hand had tensed into a closed fist and banged against the keys. He stood up from the bench and backed away as if he had seen a ghost, then hurried upstairs, surprised that bright bands of sunlight lit his way back to his room, back to Vincent and their girls.

CHAPTER TWENTY-THREE

All You Can Be Is Grateful

I wish I could protect you from so much. Especially grief
and loss, starting with mine. But when you lose someone,
or are about to lose someone, all you can be is grateful
for the time you had. Death takes so much, but it never
will rob you of your memories.

*—An excerpt from Arvid Persson's
final birthday letter to his children*

SUNDAY, DECEMBER 28

SHE HEARD THE MUSIC first. Lilting violins and delicate
harps, the volume set to a low hum. Dava wasn't sure exactly
what was playing, but to her ears and unseeing eyes she imagined this was what played over the speakers while waiting in
an endless queue to enter heaven. Dava did not or could not
know she was hearing a song called "Strings in Bee Major" by
the Klassical Kids Orchestra, which was what her grandsons
had picked as the music to accompany her "going away" party,
as they were referring to it.

Kali helped her walk down the stairs, bracing her on the left,
her arm sturdily around her mother's waist. Dava had insisted
on walking rather than being carried, because she had never
once thought of herself as an invalid and did not want to begin

her final day on Earth as one. Over the pretty but slightly hyper string music, she heard voices calling out to her, and at her. *Amma. Dava. Gamma, hi! Hi, Amma. Gamma! Hello, Dava. Mom, good morning. How are you, Dava? Almost there, Amma.* This last one was whispered to her by Kali, who also counted down the number of steps as they took each one, until at last, with slightly shaking legs, Dava reached the foot of the staircase.

Only her youngest daughter knew Dava's eyesight was all but gone, equivalent to a TV with bad reception, mostly static interspersed with random bursts of clarity. But she wanted to prevent this information from being revealed to the rest of the family for as long as possible. Dava gave a small wave to acknowledge her family's greeting and then let Kali continue to carefully lead her into the great room, to the same rocking chair she had sat in two days earlier—how long ago that seemed, another lifetime—and after she was seated, she felt a blanket cover her lap and a small ottoman being placed underneath her feet. Her hair was still slightly wet from the shower Kali helped her take. As she had stood underneath the bright, cascading heat from her rainfall showerhead, she had relished the warmth of the water on her skin and had lifted her face to it, a contented smile resting on her lips. She tried to summon that smile now, in order to help reassure her family, but she could not bring about much more than a nervous twitching of her lips. In not being able to see any of them, Dava fretted about how she could provide them comfort in her final hours and prevent this gathering from being awkward and sadder than it had to be.

"I feel like the host of the world's worst party," she whispered to Kali, believing she was still in earshot.

"The kids are trying to do something special for you," Arvie responded. Dava sat back, stunned. The two of them had not spoken to each other since she told him and his siblings about Panit, and she found herself momentarily at a loss for how to respond.

"I'm glad," she said as the volume of the music went up several decibels and then abruptly cut off. "I enjoyed spending time with them yesterday. Your daughters are...lovely," she added. "Intelligent. And perceptive."

"Yes, they are. Thanks, Mom."

"Of course, dear." She turned her head in his direction, then realized several things at once: that Arvie had moved from standing next to her chair to sitting next to her; that there were hushed, angry words erupting to her far right, perhaps near the Christmas tree; and that a cup of chai had been placed on her right, which reminded her of the many cups of chai her mother and Chaitanya had prepared for her throughout her life. Upon realizing all of this, she actually relaxed. Maybe this would not be so ghoulish or maudlin. Maybe today would be less a living wake and more like a family reunion, at turns heartwarming and bumptious. She could scarcely believe her eldest son was actually engaging her in conversation without sounding annoyed or defensive. "How are you doing, Arvie?"

"I don't know. Is it possible to feel a lot and feel nothing at all at the same time?"

"Yes. Definitely." Dava briefly turned away from Arvie to reach for her chai, carefully guiding her hand until her fingers brushed past the handle, and she heard the cup rattle.

"Let me help you." After a beat, she felt the mug warming her hands. "Got it?"

"I do. Thank you." She took a sip, then asked him if he was taking care of himself. He said yes, but without emotion, and so the two of them sat together as the argument grew more animated.

"What are the kids arguing about?"

"I'm not sure." Dava sensed Arvie was about to stand up and walk toward them. She reached toward him, a few drops of tea spilling on her lap. "Wait. Sit for one moment."

"I am sitting, Mom. Are you all right? Can you see—"

"I loved your father. And I love him still. He is the only man I have ever loved."

⁓

Priya and Klara were insistently calling for their father, and Dava heard Arvie say, "One sec, Mom," as he joined them at the Christmas tree. But before he had spoken, she had heard a catch in his throat, and she hoped her words about his father made an impact on her firstborn boy, whom she could still remember meeting with a shocked, amazed grin when the nurse placed him in her arms. *At last, I can hold my child*, she remembered thinking as she looked up at dumbstruck Arvid, then at her newborn Arvind, to whom she murmured, "Welcome," against his soft cheek, the first word she had ever said to him. So if their brief conversation was to be their last one, Dava believed it had led to a reckoning of some kind, a shifting of their relationship, and for that, she was relieved.

She turned her head in the direction of the arguing, so she could try to make out what was going on. "What is it?" she said, hoping someone would hear her question. "What is this commotion about?"

"I'll go find out, Amma," she heard Rev say, followed by feeling his lips brush against her cheek, his breath heavy with caffeine. She nodded and took tiny sips of chai, letting the sweet, milky taste punctuate her tongue. Frustrated by her obscured vision, she willed herself to instead focus on the tea's comforting warmth, until she noticed Rev's voice cut through the discordant chatter, replacing it with burbles of laughter.

⌒

What Dava did not know was that her grandchildren were arguing over what kind of music to play for her. Priya and Klara had seized Enzo's tablet from their cousins, with Priya holding it above her head, as the boys jumped up and down, vainly trying to remove it from her grasp.

"Don't you get it?" Klara said. "This is the last music she'll ever hear. And you want it to be that weird classical stuff? No way."

"But we couldn't think of anything else. We stayed up all night but realized we didn't know any songs she'd like, so we thought we'd at least start with something that reminded us of angels," Theo said as his brother rose on his tiptoes, his fingertips touching the screen.

"Girls, give Theo back his tablet," Arvie said as he joined the group. "What's going on here?"

"It's Enzo's. And we're trying to decide what music to play for Gamma," his oldest daughter told him, her cheeks pink and determined. "Do you have any idea what she likes?"

"I see," Arvie said, taking a step back from the group, which caused him to step on a reindeer ornament that had fallen off the Christmas tree. "Ouch! Shit! Sorry, didn't mean to swear." He kicked away the ornament. "Um, have you asked her yet?"

"We want it to be a sur-prise," said Klara, expressing her eye roll in the way she elongated the word.

"Ah, I see. Well, um, maybe...I don't know, how about—"

"There he is!" Enzo cried, pointing across the room. "We've been waiting for Rev uncle so he could tell us."

"Tell you what?" Rev said. Arvie was both disappointed and relieved to see the four children turn their attention toward their uncle.

"Free happiness!" Theo said. "You and Gamma."

"Oh!" Rev's mouth dropped open at hearing his nephew say two words so specific and unique to his childhood. "Well . . . how do you know about that?"

"Dava shared it with us yesterday," Sandi said, linking her arm through his, then turning to look at Dava, whose eyes were squeezed shut as she sipped her tea. "It was a sweet story about the two of you, how you would sing with each other."

"Right, so since it is her last day," said Klara, lowering her voice conspiratorially, "we wanted to play something fun for her, not church music. But we can't agree on what that would be. Except that it shouldn't be church music."

"We need your help," Priya said as she beamed a smile at Sandi, who nodded back warmly.

"Any thoughts, sweetie?" Sandi said to Rev, batting her blue eyes at him with so much affection he was strangely disconcerted. Sandi felt truly a part of his family to a greater degree than he did at the moment, considering his fight with Kali in the boathouse the night before, which they had not discussed when they encountered each other in the kitchen getting refills of coffee. He banished his continued uneasiness over his rocky relationship with his sister as he took in the eager faces of his nieces and nephews, gratified to think one day his own child would be among their number and, like him, would be the baby of the family.

"Give me a moment; I'll think of something." Rev shifted his weight from his right foot to his left and back again, giving him the look of someone walking in place, as he thought back to his mother's sing-alongs. When he was around six, they had sung a song he knew from a cereal commercial. Rev had enjoyed singing it so much—"It lights me up inside!"—he had asked his mother about it, which led to a musical awakening on YouTube, in which Dava introduced him to The Temptations, The Supremes, and many more.

"Motown," Rev told the group with a grin. "Amma told me those songs used to make her happy when she had to take road trips with her parents, because it was the only music that the three of them could agree on. She has a lot of good memories from her childhood associated with those songs, I think," he added wistfully.

"Who's Motown?" Theo asked, wiggling a finger in his ear. "Is that a person?" Rev caught Arvie's eye and they both stifled smiles. This was the first time the two of them had seen each other since their own moment in the boathouse, and unlike with Kali, Rev felt no awkwardness with his older brother.

"C'mon over here—I'll show you." He beckoned them to the sectional, and his nieces and nephews followed, as Sandi and Arvie, now joined by Colin and Sita, watched them as they stood drinking coffee near the Christmas tree. Mirroring a moment that had taken place more than two decades before, Rev delighted in introducing his nieces and nephews to Motown songs, and they were amazed they knew a few despite the songs being "so, so, so old." As he played them snippets and arranged the tracks into a playlist, his gaze would often seek his mother, who had moved from the rocking chair to the sofa facing the fireplace. Kali was sitting next to her, and he could see their heads were bent toward each other as if in deep discussion. Rev wondered what the two could be talking about that would cause Kali to take their mother's hand and place it on her own face, not once, but twice.

"It's all so happy and beautiful," Enzo said with awe, his eyes transfixed on Ronnie Spector belting out "Be My Baby," breaking into Rev's thoughts. He affectionately ruffled his nephew's hair. Rev was surprised how much he liked playing music for them, and watching their eyes light up and their smiles of recognition reminded him of how he and Dava had once shared a similar bond. After he helped the children put together a playlist and the music began to play, starting with "My Girl," he excused himself to go visit with his mother. When Kali saw him draw near, she gave him an uncertain smile and rose up from the sofa.

"Rev's here, Amma," she said in a near whisper. "I'll leave you two alone for a moment." Kali passed by her brother and gave him a squeeze on the shoulder. Rev put on a cheery expression and sat down near Dava and asked her how she was feeling.

"About as well as to be expected," she said with a sigh, turning toward him. "May I?" she asked, raising her hand and feeling through the air for his face. Before he could nod in assent, Rev felt Dava's fingers trace the outline of his features, drawing her finger from his eyebrows to his jawbone. She then pressed her palm against his cheek.

"You need a shave, son," Dava said with a little laugh.

"Yeah, well." He shrugged but laughed with her too. "Do you hear what the kids are playing for you?"

Dava cocked her head, and the glasses that had been perched on top of her head fell on her lap. "My goodness, The Temptations!" She was pleased her story about Rev had impressed so firmly on her grandchildren, resulting in this sweet gesture. "You helped them choose it."

"And you told them about free happiness. I had totally forgotten about it." Rev picked up his mother's glasses and held them out to her. When she didn't register this but just continued blinking in his direction, it dawned on him she had lost her eyesight, something Dr. Windsor had warned about when he visited her in the cottage. "Amma..." But he found himself at a loss of what to say.

"Kali and Sita have informed me you have a few concerns related to your child," Dava said, reaching her hand out unsteadily until she found his knee. He looked at her hand, delicate and blemish-free, with only the veins standing out against her brown skin like mountain ranges viewed from a great height. They did not seem like the hands of an old woman, of a woman who was dying, and very soon. Rev was so focused on Dava's imminent passing that he missed what his mother said, and had to have her repeat it. And what she told him was that while her initial directive was that her penthouse and the Beatrix Island property were to be kept as part of the Shastri-Persson assets, she had asked Sita, as the executor of her will, to sell both and put the proceeds in a trust for Rev's baby.

"I had hoped that you would all keep returning and continue the tradition of gathering here, but with Arvie making his home in Sweden and the rest of you living such busy lives, maybe it's not meant to be." She patted his knee. "What's most important is that your baby is well taken care of in the same way as my other grandchildren. Please let Sandi know, okay? I hear she was especially concerned."

Rev promised he would, just as "My Girl" faded from the speakers and was replaced by "Sugar Pie, Honey Bunch." He was struck by how much Motown's heart-pleasing harmonies were at odds with this long goodbye they were all experiencing. The upbeat melodies weren't cheering him up but were instead exacerbating his own dread and melancholy, especially now that he knew his mother was blind. But he swallowed his sadness when he turned toward the other side of the great room and saw the girls and the twins heading toward him and Dava. Before they arrived to interrupt what could be his final private conversation with his mother, Rev struggled with whether to tell her he had no plans to fulfill her request to produce a biopic about her. In the end, he decided not to say anything, because he saw no good outcome in informing his terminally ill mother he could not bring himself to do what she had asked.

As the grandchildren came over, sitting on the floor around

her in a semicircle, Rev thought about standing up to give the kids a moment with their grandmother. But he could not get himself to leave, because he wanted every last moment he could have with her, and so he remained there with them, trying his best to smile and keep that old, terrible grief from claiming him completely for a little longer.

Dava beamed as her grandchildren's chatter reached her ears, nodding as each of them spoke at the same time, asking if she liked the music and if they had made a good choice for her going-away party.

"I wish I knew the words," Enzo mused as the Four Tops song reached its euphoric chorus. "I'd like to sing along." A bright swath of light cut through the windows and hit the semicircle. He turned around to gaze outside and saw the snow dripping off the trees with big, fat drops of water. "I think the snow's melting."

"That's good, since we're leaving soon, right?" said Priya, before realizing what her words meant in relation to their grandmother. Red faced, she clapped both hands over her mouth and looked to her older sister in distress. Klara shook her head, but not unkindly, and mouthed, *It's fine.*

"That's probably true," Dava said, her voice sounding cracked and distant. She had awoken to Sita and Kali whispering to each other in her bedroom, as they debated which of her personal items to pack and take with them that day and what they would come back for later. And so even though she knew her family was preparing to leave the island after her treatment, for some reason hearing her granddaughter's words walloped her with the reality that she would never see the outside world again, her home in New York City, the office, her friends, Chaitanya. And then she laughed bitterly at herself, because not only would she not see any of that again, but she would also not be able to see anything again—period. Feeling Rev's hand on her arm, she realized she was betraying her own anxieties to her grandchildren.

"So many possibilities await you once you leave here. Take advantage of all you can," she said in an attempt to sound serene yet feeling like a Hallmark card, full of empty platitudes she imagined people expected from the noble and dying.

"We will, Gamma—promise," she heard Priya say, but Dava remained unsure if all of them were just saying what they thought she would want to hear. She would have been shocked and heartened to know that Klara, Priya, Theo, and Enzo—and eventually their cousin, Rev and Sandi's son—would one day have a tradition of taking an annual weekend trip that almost always included a night of snacking on hasselbackspotatis, Christmas cookies, and three kinds of popcorn, and during which they would lovingly and not so lovingly grouse about their parents and, on occasion, relive the weird, wondrous night they shared with their grandmother.

A brief silence charged the room as the next song from Rev's Motown playlist refused to play. The quiet coincided with the hum of conversation taking place near the Christmas tree coming to a standstill, and Dava's senses were attuned to the flourish and crackle of the fireplace, and a ray of sunshine skipping over her face, as if she had received a brief kiss from the sun. In that moment, she was overwhelmed with a suffocating sensation of warmth that tipped from bewilderment to fear. How does one prepare one's self to say goodbye, not only to loved ones, but the act of living itself?

"How are you, Dava?" This was Sandi now coming to sit next to Rev, who had just returned to the sofa beside his mother after turning on the fireplace. The music slipped back into the room like a whisper, after Arvie fiddled with the tablet and skipped to the next song on his brother's playlist, the dreamy, languorous "Just My Imagination."

"I'm here," she replied. She was running out of ways to answer that question, even as she knew they all meant well. "I'm happy to be here for a little longer."

"Oh, good. I mean, uh, so are we." Sandi paused, then said in an overly cheery tone, "Your earrings are so beautiful. I can't believe I didn't notice them before."

"They were my mother's," Dava said as she briefly touched her earlobe. "She was wearing them the last time I saw her." She felt a bubble of emotion pierce her throat, and she swallowed hard. "How are you doing, dear?" Dava asked hurriedly. "The first trimester of pregnancy can be hard at times."

Sandi blushed, touched that her mother-in-law was asking about her, considering all that was about to happen. "I'm fine, thank you." She paused. "Always hungry, always nauseous, but fine," she added, leaning her head on Rev's shoulder.

"Take care of her," Dava said to her son. She wanted to say more, to be a fountain of advice about the months to come and how to cope after their child arrived, but she was rapidly losing energy, and speaking was starting to become difficult again.

"I will," Rev said, his eyes shining and chin wobbling as he clasped Sandi's hand. "We're going to take care of each other."

~

"Dava, would you like another cup of chai? Or I can bring out your breakfast." Vincent had bent his enormous frame down all the way toward her, so she could feel his breath directly on her face. Unlike the previous few days, Vincent did not prepare breakfast for anyone that morning, with everyone instructed to finish the remaining boxes of cereal and uneaten fruit. As for Dava, she had already informed her son-in-law two days earlier that she had brought her final meal with her to the island, wrapped in foil in the freezer, and so his last task in the kitchen would be to defrost this for her.

"Yes, dear, both, thank you. But also please come sit with me after. In fact," she added, hoping her voice would carry to wherever the rest of the group was in the great room, "tell everyone to join."

And soon the fireside area of the great room became filled with voices that drowned out the music, the majority of them doting and fussing over her, which was the exact opposite of what she wanted. Citing Dava's shaking hands, Kali fed her bites of strawberries and honey-dipped waffles from her favorite Upper East Side diner, as her family members took turns asking her how she was feeling and if she needed anything, until they gradually realized her vision was gravely impaired. She could hear their loud whispers—*Wait, is she? Why do her eyes look like that? Oh my God, she can't see*—and was mortified. It was not that she knew she'd be able to hide it from them, but Dava did not like being witness to their collective realization that she was losing her faculties.

"Amma, you've lost your sight." Dava sensed her oldest daughter's presence first, the scent of lilac from her freshly washed hair. Sita told her this as if she were gently breaking the news to her mother, as if she were not already aware of her impairment.

"I have." Dava felt the cool sweetness of a strawberry touch her lips. She bit into it and chewed slowly, feeling all eyes on her and hating it. Now she wished she had not called them over, if it was to make her feel like a specimen under a microscope. "But I'm fine," she added frostily.

Dava could not see it, but Sita drew back as if her words had been a slap. "Okay, then. I'm going to check in with Dr. Windsor and see if she needs anything from me."

Hearing the name of her doctor sent a chill up Dava's spine, and the strawberries went sloppy in her mouth. She swallowed hard. "Sita," she said loudly, clearing her throat.

"Yes, Amma?"

"Thank you." Dava felt her daughter's wet kiss on her cheek, then her temple, before the scent of lilac evaporated as quickly as it had come.

⟋

Sita knocked on the door before entering the downstairs guest room that Rev and Sandi had been sharing. Upon hearing "Come in," she entered and saw Dr. Windsor and her wife talking quietly in front of a side table, where the doctor was prepping a device connected to an IV bag that stood innocuously next to the bed like a coatrack. Seeing Dr. Windsor in her white coat, and the IV bag that was waiting to be connected to her mother, made Sita feel faint, and the reality of the situation bore down on her. The doctor and her wife spun around and both immediately reached for her and guided her toward the bed.

"Breathe, Sita, breathe," Dr. Windsor told her, wrapping her arm around her shoulders as she shivered uncontrollably. "It can be a lot. Take the time you need."

Sita was flashing back to seeing her father in hospital beds, then the hospice bed, his body shrinking and losing mass each time he transferred to a new one. The antiseptic smells, the marks on his arms from the constant insertion of IVs, his skin getting paler and paler until he nearly matched his sheets. All of those memories came to her like a fast-moving fog that draped her in a deep sorrow. The Windsors sat with Sita and whispered to her comfortingly until she was able to move out of her sadness and accept she had to be the one to lead and guide her family through the next few hours.

"We have brandy," Mrs. Windsor said, her voice a melodic near whisper that matched the diaphanousness of her white linen tracksuit. "That can help sometimes in times like this."

Sita accepted a tumbler gratefully. For the next half hour, she spoke and asked questions about how the treatment would proceed and, in turn, informed the Windsors that employees from an East Hampton funeral home would arrive on the ferry picking all of them up to transport her mother's body to the home, where she would be cremated immediately. Once the doctor had finished her preparations, Sita sailed back and forth between upstairs and downstairs, gathering items she thought her mother would want to have close at hand at the end: framed family photos, her father's monogrammed handkerchief scented with his cologne, the red flannel blanket for extra warmth. She took one last look at the room, in particular the bed with its snowflake-printed comforter and matching pillowcases, all waiting for her mother. Sita took a deep breath, then closed the door behind her.

⌒

Upon returning to the great room, Sita saw that the fireplace was no longer on, and the room was quiet, save for the music, a song she sort of recognized but could not quite place. As she weaved through the furniture and headed toward her husband, she nearly ran into the pool table while checking her watch, surprised to see it was already past 9:30 a.m. The boat was set to arrive at noon, and they only had about thirty minutes left before Dr. Windsor, a grim reaper with a gentle smile and red sneakers, would join them to signal it was time.

"I need a drink," she muttered to Colin as she plopped down beside him on the sofa to the left of where Dava was seated.

"Seems you already had one," he replied, brushing her hair out of her eyes. "I can get you another."

"Sita, you're back?" Dava said, reclining against the sofa with her eyes closed and a damp pink washcloth on her forehead.

"Yes, Amma," she said, glancing worriedly at her husband, then Kali.

"What did we nickname that family from Disney World?" Dava asked.

"Um..." Sita said, mouthing, *What?* at her sister. The question seemed to catch them all off guard, because they had been sitting in a long, uncomfortable silence after Kali confirmed to them Dava had lost her vision and they had murmured their condolences without knowing what else to say. The kids sat cross-legged on the floor, with Klara braiding Priya's hair, while Theo and Enzo crunched on apple slices. They seemed sad and thoughtful, and studiously avoided looking at their grandmother.

"Mom, are you..." Arvie said slowly. He was sitting on the sofa to the right of his mother, with a cushion-wide space between him and Vincent, who was examining his fingernails with exceptional focus. Then Arvie's face glowed, and he leaned forward. "Oh, wait, yeah! She means the time we went the summer before my freshman year. That weirdo family who were in the hotel room next to ours." He looked to Vincent, who met his gaze for the first time that morning. "It was our first Disney vacation with Rev," he added, nodding at his brother.

"I was only four, but even I remember how they played 'It's a Small World' on repeat. But they cranked it, like they were throwing a rave," Rev said, chuckling. "I wanted to go next door because I thought it was like a kiddie party or something."

"That's because they were all on ecstasy," Sita said, still confused but smiling at the randomness of this memory. "I don't think they were a family, were they? But we called them the

Seven Dwarfs. We went out into the hallway so we could see them escorted out by security, and gave them each a nickname as we watched them go. Speedy, Kooky, Hippie, Goofy—"

"Dad was proud of that one," Kali said, running both hands through her long, thick hair, which, for the first time since they arrived at the island, was out of its trademark braid. "What were the others?"

"Giggly was the one with the orange dreadlocks," Arvie said, and his siblings let out a collective "oh yeah" in recognition. "I can't remember the other two, though."

"Spazzy," Dava said, wheezing slightly but determined to speak. "And...Sparklepants."

The Shastri-Perssons burst out laughing, first at the absurdity of hearing their stately mother say such a silly word and then at the reason for that particular nickname; then the laughter continued on because they could not stop. The grandchildren began tittering too, mostly to see Arvie and Sita, normally so serious, now out of control with gales of laughter, their bodies quaking. The great room echoed with their delight, and Kali knew Dava had hoped to elicit this reaction from all of them. Not only so she could provide a moment of levity in a difficult time, but also so she could hear her family join together in merriment and take heart from the sound of their joy. Kali reached over and squeezed her mother's hand and felt a wave of emotion when her mother squeezed back twice.

⌒

Other memories that made them laugh during that final morning on Beatrix Island: Sita and Kali's epic teenage fight over who should get to date a slouchy, unsmiling boy named Benz; Vincent and Arvie's cruise ship wedding portrait photobombed by a humpback whale; the twins learning Enzo's first word was

"Theo" but Theo's first word was "potty"; Rev recalling the photo shoot that led him to quit modeling, which involved lime-green bicycle shorts and a pool filled with eels; infant Klara's inability to say "Grandma," leading her to call Dava "Gamma" instead, and later insisting her sister and cousins do the same. Dava listened to all of the stories, the gentle teasing, and the spirited debate over minutiae ("He asked me out first!"; "The captain said it was the biggest humpback he'd ever seen!") and felt better about leaving them, as she believed these past few days, as difficult and strange as they had been, had deeply bonded the Shastri-Perssons, uniting them in an experience that would hopefully keep them in each other's lives for years to come.

And so Dava let her thoughts focus on the immediate future, to a time when she would slip off her house slippers and allow her daughters to help her into a bed she had never used before. Only her children would be present in the room with her and Dr. Windsor, as she wanted to drift toward the darkness accompanied by their murmuring voices and steady breathing. She hoped that as her life faded, her vision would be restored, and Arvid would be the first thing she would see on the other side.

Her family's amusement was still ringing throughout the great room, fluttering to the top of the cathedral ceiling, when Dr. Windsor entered, striding in slowly in front of the fireplace, her hands clasped behind her back. The doctor looked pained to see how her presence caused the levity to diminish, until the only sound left was the song playing on Enzo's tablet.

"Dava," she said softly.

Dava felt every person in the room turn toward her. With great precision, Dava took the washcloth off of her forehead, folded it neatly and set it aside, then reached her hand toward Kali's lap until her fingers found the bowl of strawberries. She felt around for the largest one, then took a bite before returning it to the bowl. She squeezed her eyes shut and hummed along, smiling to herself, as she listened to "You're All I Need to Get By." As the melody faded into the opening notes of "My Girl," the Motown playlist looping back and starting from the beginning, Dava stood up so swiftly that Kali and Rev did not even have time to try to help her.

"I'm ready."

Flowers Shall Grow

"From my body, flowers shall grow and I am in them and that is eternity." —Edvard Munch

> —*A quote printed inside the program for Dava's memorial service*

SATURDAY, JANUARY 10

Arvie

"My mother was a legend. In her own mind. Ha ha...ha." He hadn't meant to say that last part out loud, and he winced as three hundred faces stared back at him with solemn expressions. Tugging at the striped black-and-green tie he let his daughters choose for him, he continued. "But, um, also a legend in the world too. In what she set out to do and all she accomplished, I mean." He wiped under his nostrils with sweaty fingers. "My mother liked to say charity is a family business—it's what she always wanted for us. She always wanted the best and expected the best. Because...she was the best." He coughed, a phlegmy sound that reverberated noisily into the microphone. "At being herself."

TWO WEEKS AFTER HIS mother's memorial service, Arvie checked into the Kahuna Lua Rehabilitation and Meditation Retreat, as he contemplated a future not created in defiance of what he was born into, but by his own choices. Arvie was not used to speaking about himself on a daily basis, and in opening up in group therapy as part of his forty-five-day stay, he confronted the puzzle pieces that made up his life and how they fit together. He uttered the words "blame," "fault," and "cheating" so many times during the fifth session that the words temporarily lost all meaning and sounded foreign on his tongue.

In therapy, his fellow group members pointed out to him how often he would blame his life and circumstances on external forces rather than look at himself, to the point that even Arnold, a Michelin-starred chef who had entered rehab after burning down his own restaurant in a fit of rage, wondered if Arvie was capable of any culpability for his unhappiness. Arvie squirmed like a fly trapped under a glass when "Arson Arnold" had called him out as the others nodded in agreement, completely exposed in a way he had never been before.

In the aftermath of his humiliation, Arvie began the work of examining himself, the things that drove him, and the decisions he made. As part of that process, he officially tendered his resignation from Helping Perssons as soon as he completed his stay at Kahuna Lua, then legally changed his name to Arvind Persson-Lindqvist, eventually going by his birth name too. He became a full partner in Vincent's restaurant and began taking piano lessons on the cherrywood piano he had shipped to Stockholm, the only possession of his mother's he had claimed.

For years he felt alternately touched and tortured about the last thing Dava had said to him, wanting to believe her and yet also feeling her affair had proved otherwise. Eventually, Arvie would reach a point—a full decade after the events of Beatrix

Island—when he decided it no longer mattered. And he, too, would arrive at a time when he thought of himself as 79 percent happy, but that would take until he was close to seventy-nine himself.

⌒

Rev

"My mother would be so moved to see how many musicians, including Medici Artists, are here today to celebrate her life. Music was her lifeblood—it's what inspired her dreams and brought her and my father together. There have been over three hundred Medici grantees over the past four decades. Wow, right?" He laughed nervously. "If she had done nothing else in her life, the impact she had on these artists alone would be incredible."

His eyes alighted on Sandi, who was beaming at him proudly even as she looked a tad green. She clutched her tiny black purse against her stomach, as if she could use it to stem her nausea. *Shit*, he thought as his watery eyes returned to his handwritten speech. When he couldn't find his place, Sandi's smile flashed in his mind, and he spoke from the heart.

"To the very end of her life, my mother imparted grace. Grace and wisdom. She cemented our family in her love for us. And that," he said, locking eyes with Sandi, "will never change."

He called off their engagement later that night. As they stood in their bedroom closet, hurrying to strip off their funereal clothing, Rev gave Sandi the speech that had been running through his mind from the moment they stepped on the ferry taking them off Beatrix Island—that he was not ready to be married while still unsure of who he was as a person. Once he reached the end of his speech, he rambled on for several more minutes until he ended with a sad, desperate "I'm sorry."

Sandi, standing in only a black slip and fuzzy house slippers, took this all in with a surprising calm. The two stood in silence as she cocked her head to one side and closed her eyes, seeming to turn things over in her mind. After several moments passed, she responded by telling him she did not want to marry someone who felt like he had to be with her because they were about to have a child together.

"I'm fine with co-parenting until you figure out whether you want to be in this relationship. As long as you actually parent, no matter what," Sandi said, briefly placing her hand on his chest, over his panicked heartbeat. "I just can't guarantee I'll be waiting for you when you decide what you want."

Rev would always remember Sandi standing before him, her long brown hair streaming behind her and her hands defiant on her hips, like a superhero right before she put on her costume, and how unbroken she was when she delivered those words to him. And he would feel a small sting of regret when, years later, during the premiere of his short documentary spotlighting Medici grant winners, Sandi gave him a warm hug of congratulations, whispering in his ear, "Your mother would be so proud."

$\sim$

Sita

"You might not know this, but my brothers and sister like to tease me by calling me Dava Junior." She looked into the front row, where her younger siblings grinned at her with amused embarrassment. "When I was younger, this annoyed me. But now, I embrace it. I'm so honored I was able to work by her side to help fulfill her life's mission through her foundation." She choked up but found the words to continue when she saw Colin nod at her encouragingly. "And even though my mother is no longer with us, the Dava Shastri Foundation—and all it stands for—will endure for generations to come."

Prior to her mother's death, Sita had decided to not tell Dava she wouldn't fulfill her final wishes and take over as head of the foundation. And it was a decision Sita never regretted. Nor did she regret that her six-month sabbatical was extended into a year, allowing her family to travel the world, with stops on every continent, even Antarctica. Because the time would come, just after their twenty-fifth wedding anniversary, when Colin would be diagnosed with Parkinson's, and the hard lessons she had learned from watching her father ailing for years, and from her mother's quicker but no less devastating medical journey, equipped her to handle the logistics of her husband's chronic illness. For emotional support, she was grateful for her sons and her sisters, who never wavered in giving her their time and energy through the decades-long ups and downs of navigating Colin's disease.

"Dava Junior to the end," she murmured to herself at her husband's bedside at his hospice, a very long time from now, preparing herself to say goodbye to another loved one and become a widow much sooner than she anticipated.

Kali

"My mother's birth name was Deva, spelled d-e-v-a. The name means 'celestial,' or 'divine, shining one.' It's a beautiful name, with a beautiful meaning. But what my mother accomplished can be found in the name she gave herself. The name Dava is synonymous with altruism, benevolence, self-sacrifice, power." She smiled with tears shining in her eyes, as she recognized a middle-aged woman with curly hair standing in the back of the room. "And love—a mother's incomprehensible love."

Even though Kali invited Chaitanya to the memorial service, she wouldn't give her Dava's letter until three months later. Dava had assured her she could readily tell her the truth without having to be concerned Chaitanya would demand a portion of the Shastri-Persson estate or give a tell-all interview, but Kali wanted to judge for herself. Beyond wanting to vet her sister's character, she simply wanted to get to know what kind of person Chaitanya was—her temperament and opinions— before revealing her true parentage. Not only the identity of her mother, but also of her father, and their entire story. Because this aspect Dava did not want to become public, and Kali wanted to be sure Chaitanya could accede to that wish.

By the time the two met again at Chaitanya's home, where Kali hand delivered their mother's letter, the two had formed a strong bond based not just on their relationship to Dava, but also on how they found themselves making choices with her in mind. Over the course of Kali's lifetime, that meant taking over for Arvie as the head of Helping Perssons for several years, until she ceded the position to Klara; traveling to Ruiz with Rev and Sita to commemorate their parents' forty-fifth wedding anniversary with a sizable contribution to the town's rain forest–

preservation fund; and donating her "hush money" from Dava's will, partly to the charities started in her nieces' and nephews' names that originated from their last conversation with their grandmother, and partly to Oakland Springtime Community Garden.

But the choice that meant the most to Kali was her first: a three-dimensional installation that was a mural-size portrait of the goddess Kali, with the face transforming into different visages including Dava's, and the items the multiarmed goddess held shifting depending on whose face she wore. For her mother, these items included a scale of justice, a sword, aarti fire, a compact disc, a BlackBerry, the *Titan* hardcover, and a mirror, in which one who looked closely enough could see a photo-realistic painting of the entire Shastri-Persson clan in a fit of laughter from when they were gathered together on the last day of her mother's life. And embroidered in gold on the sari's hem were the names of three women from three different generations, two of whom never knew each other, but all of whom were deeply connected.

A note from Kali: My mother penned this letter for you after learning her condition was terminal. She originally had no intention for you to read it, but right before she passed, she told me I could share this with you. Based on what she wrote in this letter (which none of us have read), Amma said you could decide if you forgave her, and if that forgiveness extended toward wanting to be a part of her foundation and becoming acquainted with the rest of her family. We gladly welcome you, but the choice is yours.

December 1, 2044

My dearest Chaitanya,

My biggest regret, and biggest relief, was not holding you after you were born. I knew if I held you, my life would change, and I would not get to accomplish all I was capable of achieving. And each time something important and lovely happened in my life thereafter, I knew it was right not to hold you. Because of that choice, I was able to make so many other choices.

As the years went on, I was able to compartmentalize the fact you existed, make it small and hide it away at the bottom of a drawer, and so when I arrived at major family milestones—the births of my children, their first steps and first words—there was no sadness, no thoughts of you, just pure, unmitigated joy.

Yet when I first met you, I held you for a very long time, surprising even myself. I am not big on hugs, even with my own children and grandchildren. But did you notice that each time we greeted each other or said goodbye, it was with a hug?

All those accumulated seconds when you were in my arms almost made up for when I turned away from you that first time and told the nurse I did not want to hold you.

I am sorry I never told you that you were my daughter. Each time we would meet, I liked to tell myself on a deeper level you already knew. But that does not excuse my actions, including how I am still not telling you now and hoping that by writing down these words I will be able to let go and make peace with all the decisions I have made when it comes to you.

The days we spent together were some of the happiest of my life. Your friendship helped me find a new purpose and contentment I did not think possible after Arvid died. And reflecting on our time together revealed something crucial to me.

I never talked to you about my own mother. Perhaps you asked, and perhaps I deflected. The circumstances of her loss made it an unspeakable grief, all the more unspeakable because you did not know the truth about me.

Yet even with all that remained unsaid, the truth of our connection still emerged: we all chose to dedicate our lives to helping others. Late in life, my mother volunteered at a women's shelter. She was always a generous person, but it was at the shelter I believe she found her calling. And you are so much like her, Chaitanya. You are nearly her mirror image in your kindness and gentle temperament. All I can do is marvel at the strength of our familial bonds, even though you did not know her or truly know me.

Throughout my life, I sought to control as much as I could, especially when it came to the Shastri name. I had disliked the John Lennon lyric about life happening while we make other plans, but now I can see the grace in that too. With no planning or effort, three generations are forever linked in the most profound way. It is a very comforting thing to realize when drawing near one's end.

I am still grappling with how to say goodbye to everyone else. But I already know how to say goodbye to you: by sharing my utmost gratitude. Your existence set me on a path toward an extraordinary life, one that gave me Arvid, my foundation, my family. And our reconnection imbued my twilight years with new meaning and unexpected joy.

So I send all my love to my firstborn, my divine radiance, my Chaitanya. When I take my final breath, my four children will be in the room, and you will be in my heart. And I will be able to depart this world surrounded by love, knowing that love will continue on through each of you. What more could a mother ask for?

Acknowledgments

When I first started writing this novel, I wrote it without thinking about anyone actually reading it. It was more about pouring all my longtime preoccupations into a book, because if I was going to really try to write one for the first time in seven years, I wasn't leaving anything on the table. But after I completed the first draft, I realized how much I didn't want to be the only person to ever read this story, and maybe this could be something.

So I'd like to start by thanking my agent, Andrea Somberg, who, from the first time we spoke, radiated so much warmth, kindness, and enthusiasm for my writing that I immediately knew I wanted to work with her. Andrea's positivity and clear-eyed advice has been my compass through many ups and downs, and I am very grateful.

It's been a true pleasure working with the Grand Central Publishing team. Many thanks to my smart and generous editor Karen Kosztolnyik. Before working with her, I would have never described revisions as fun, but her thoughtful and thought-provoking suggestions made returning to the work an enjoyable experience. My gratitude to Ben Sevier, Brian McLendon, Albert Tang, Luria Rittenberg, Kristin Nappier, Marie Mundaca, Andy

Dodds, Morgan Swift, Ali Cutrone, Karen Torres, and Rachael Kelly, especially for coming up with the title for this novel. And warmest thanks to Sarah Congdon for designing such a brilliant, eye-catching cover. My utmost appreciation to Rich Green at The Gotham Group as well.

Thank you to Suzanne Strempek Shea, someone I'm proud to call a mentor and friend, who is the indefatigable cheerleader that every writer should have in her corner. Carrie Frye was the first person to read this novel, and her empathetic and insightful comments are the only reason this book exists in the world rather than remaining on my hard drive. I was so lucky to have a group of readers who gave me the most incredibly helpful feedback: Mayuri Amuluru Chandra (whose sweet emails were often the highlight of my day), Ella Kay, Barbara Greenbaum, and Sailaja Suresh, whom I've asked to read my writing since we were both in high school, and I'm lucky still makes time to read my work now.

I have always shared a bond with my brother, Pavan Ramisetti, over our mutual love of pop culture, and his CD collection (and listening to KROQ while driving us to school each day) was my entryway into my own love of music. My loving thanks to him for being such a wonderful big brother.

I'm blessed to have four incredible women in my family, each of whom has taught what it is to have a "mother's incomprehensible love": Rekha Kandriga, Anjali Ramisetti, Shuba Ramisetti, and Leela Srinivasan. It's an honor to be their niece, sister, daughter, and granddaughter. Leela Avva is our beloved matriarch, and her inherent goodness and self-sacrifice has shaped generations and will continue to do so. And "parapata" to my niece Leela Anoushka Rush: watching you grow up to be just as kind and loving as your momma has been one of the great joys of my life.

My love and gratitude to my parents, Dr. Dattatreya Kumar

and Shuba Ramisetti, for always encouraging my dream to be a writer. There are not enough words to express how much I owe them, and their belief in me has been such an incredible gift. The earliest lessons they instilled are selflessness and generosity, and we always do our best to live up to their example. Special thanks to my dad for his invaluable suggestions and advice related to Dava's medical condition.

I am beyond blessed to have the love and support of my husband, Corey. Since we met, I haven't gone a day without receiving a kind word, cheesy compliment, and thoughtful gesture, occasionally all within the span of a single minute. I treasure our partnership, and our ability to find humor and joy in difficult times and good ones too. And since I have the last word, I get to tell him this: yes, you are.

Reading Group Guide for

DAVA SHASTRI'S LAST DAY

DISCUSSION QUESTIONS

1. The mission of the Dava Shastri Foundation is to support artists and empower women. If you had the funding and resources to build your own foundation, which cause would you champion?

2. Beatrix Island is named after the beloved children's author Beatrix Potter, who created the iconic character Peter Rabbit. Beatrix Potter is also quoted at the start of chapter 2: "I hold that a strongly marked personality can influence descendants for generations." Why do you think the author chose to call attention to this particular author? In your own life, is there a story you read growing up that continues to resonate with you as an adult?

3. When Dava's children arrive at Beatrix Island, they are instructed to leave their computers and phones in a lockbox. Have you ever gone on a trip without electronic devices or access to the internet? Did you find the experience freeing or confining? Why?

4. Dava's compound, while palatial, is also described as feeling "hollow," and her design specifications as "arbitrary and downright odd." What does the way the house is described tell you about Dava's personality and the values she holds most dear?

5. Dava wanted to make sure that her life—and her death—would have a genuine impact on the world. How important do you believe it is to leave a noticeable mark on the world? Is fame or public recognition something you've ever aspired to achieve?

6. The author takes the time to explore the backstories and viewpoints of each of Dava's children. How did this affect your impressions of—and sympathies toward—the problems and prejudices facing Dava's family?

7. Dava reconnects with Chaitanya when she is an adult but doesn't tell her that she is her biological mother. Dava's decision is a difficult one, but she is resolute in her desire not to let Chaitanya fully know her and her other children. Why do you think Dava did this? And how would you feel if you were in Chaitanya's position, only finding out about Dava's connection to her after her death?

8. In *Dava Shastri's Last Day*, references are made to climate change, technology, and songs that Dava gravitated toward throughout her life. How did these mentions shape your understanding of the novel's time, setting, and place?

9. When Dava starts reading the headlines surrounding her death, she is disappointed to find that journalists are

focusing more on her personal life than her professional achievements. Do you believe the personal and professional should be tied together or evaluated separately? Why?

10. As a woman, Dava is passionate and ambitious and driven and brilliant. She is also, at times, ruthless, selfish, calculating, and secretive. How did the character of Dava make you feel, in all her complexity? Did you like Dava or did you find her deeply flawed? Did her "flaws" endear her toward you even more?

11. Rev tells Sandi that Dava asks a lot of her children, and he says so with exasperation and resentment. Parents often ask a lot of their children—did you think Dava's expectations for Rev, Kali, Arvie, and Sita were reasonable or unreasonable? Why? What did you think of Dava's insistence that each child play a part in her foundation?

12. After Dava receives her diagnosis, she elects to forgo any kind of treatment or procedure that would prolong her life because she believes the *quality* of her life would be greatly diminished. How did this decision make you feel? If you had been in Dava's position, would you have made the same call or would you have made a different one?

13. Arvid and Dava share a beautiful connection through music. What do you think of music's ability to invoke memories or bring people together? What role does music play in your life? Do you share a special song with someone?

14. In chapter 8, Dava tells Kali she needs to break up with her significant others. What did you think of Dava's interference

here? If you knew your child was romantically involved with individuals who could hurt them in some way, would you intercede? Or would you let your child make their own mistakes?

15. Rev and Dava find "free happiness" with one another by singing together. What's something you do for yourself, or with friends and family, that brings you free happiness?

16. Dava asks her personal physician to end her life medically, a practice that is gaining legal traction for patients with terminal illnesses in some parts of the world. What do you think of society's growing acceptance of individuals leaving the world on their own terms? How did this scene affect you emotionally and intellectually?

17. At its core, *Dava Shastri's Last Day* is a book about love and family. What did you think of the author's portrayal of sibling dynamics in the novel? What about the dynamics between Dava and her children? Did the author's descriptions complement or contradict the way you interact with your own family?

18. After Dava's death, we are shown glimpses of her children's lives several years into the future. How do these scenes demonstrate how they were affected by their mother's passing and the events at Beatrix Island?

19. How did you feel when you read Dava's letter to Chaitanya in the final chapter?

AUTHOR'S NOTE

The idea for this book started with a question.

There's no bigger entertainment news than a celebrity's death. During my time as an entertainment reporter, there were occasions when our reportage lasted for days or even weeks, either due to the untimeliness or shocking event surrounding the passing, or if the star was so iconic that reader interest necessitated continuous coverage.

Social media played a major part in our reporting as fans, friends, critics, and colleagues shared their tributes and grief on Twitter, Instagram, and Facebook. This collective outpouring then became a part of the story. On the flip side, past controversies, gossip, or rumors would also be rehashed as part of the real-time reaction to a celeb's death, potentially affecting the notable figure's standing in public opinion in the short term, and their legacy in the long term.

During my stint in the newsroom, when so much of my time would be devoted to finding new angles on a famous person's life and death, I often wondered whether celebrities ever became curious about the reactions their deaths would receive. And my idle speculation one day sparked a strange but intriguing question: would someone ever be so self-obsessed with how they would be remembered that they would actually fake their death to find out?

That is when the first seeds of this book began. But it would take a song and a documentary to galvanize me to explore the idea through fiction.

"Who Lives, Who Dies, Who Tells Your Story," the final song from *Hamilton*, imparts the message that no one can really control how they'll be remembered; instead, their legacy lies in the people they leave behind. And I found this concept incredibly moving, especially seen through Eliza Hamilton's decades-long dedication in keeping her husband's memory alive, despite having been humiliated after he made his infidelity public to save his political career.

Then I watched a documentary that was a dark echo of Eliza's sacrifices in honor of her late husband. In the film about a renowned rock star, his widow admitted that the musician had often cheated on her, and didn't seem to care how his infidelity affected her. Yet like Eliza, she dedicated herself to the preservation of her husband's legacy, to the point that she had no real identity beyond "Mrs. Rock Star." And it rankled me deeply. Because if the roles were reversed, it seemed highly unlikely that the cheating rock star would do the same for his wife. More likely, he would have simply remarried. (She has not, of course. Neither did Eliza.)

As all these disparate ideas took over my thoughts, the premise for a novel started to coalesce. I wanted to meet the person who would do the near unthinkable in order to discover what the world thought about her before she died. Only for that decision to backfire in a way she could not anticipate because of a gossipy news story that comes out as part of the coverage of her death.

But before I determined her name, her level of fame, and what drove her obsession, I had already decided on two things: 1) the character *would* be a her, and 2) she would be Indian-American.

Patriarchs have long been a cornerstone of pop culture: the powerful male figures who command respect in their professional spheres and demand respect from their families. From *King Lear* to *The Godfather* to *Succession*, there are countless examples of these kinds of "great" men in film, TV, and literature, many with long-suffering spouses by their sides.

So when developing my protagonist, I wanted to create a legacy-obsessed female character who detested "The Wife Of" designation, and did everything in her power not to be regulated to the sidelines of history. I wanted to give her a husband who not only supported her, but understood how deeply important this notion was to her.

And I wanted this woman to be the head of a powerful family—and be an Indian woman, at that.

Most people create novels out of a desire to write the book they have always wanted to read. Some of my favorite books have a high-concept premise: *The Westing Game*, *Life After Life*, *A Visit from the Goon Squad*, *Midnight's Children*, *The Immortalists*. And I've longed to see an Indian-American woman at the center of one, where her ethnicity was a vital part of who she is, but not the only thing that makes her interesting.

When I first began drafting this novel, I indulged myself as much as possible by incorporating everything I loved or had long been fascinated by into the manuscript: family, legacy, media, fame, obituaries, gossip. It was akin to ingredients in a stew, and I had to find a way to blend them so they all made sense together.

And so I turned to music.

Books and writing have been a lifelong love—it feels like as long as I've been breathing, I've been reading. As it does for most people, music came a little later, when I was a teenager. My own "light bulb" moment came from listening to R.E.M.'s haunting "Country Feedback." I think it's the first time the marriage of lyrics and music in a song moved me in a way that felt transcendent, and also transformational.

And my love of music fused with my love of writing with my first professionally published piece: "Is the End of the Album Near?" a lament that the album format—a collection of songs listened to from beginning to end—seemed to be falling out of favor due to the rise of iPods and Napster. (It was as screamingly earnest as you can imagine.)

When I say I turned to music to write this book, I did so in two ways. I needed to figure out what kind of person would take such extreme measures to know what her legacy would be, so aligning Dava's life story to music—as a guiding force in her life, and how she'd largely be remembered, though not necessarily on the terms she wanted—became key. But what was also impactful was listening to music as I wrote this novel. And not just music, but albums.

From Kacey Musgraves to Mercury Rev, from Natalie Prass to The Band to H.E.R, a soundtrack of old and new favorites accompanied every single word I wrote, and rewrote, and rewrote again. Albums are what let me dream this book into reality. And it's not something I could have ever predicted when I published my first article nearly twenty years ago.

⌒

As I finish writing this essay, I've just witnessed a Black and South Asian woman sworn in as our nation's vice president. When I was growing up, I would not have even known it was possible for me to dream such a thing. So to have it now as a reality, and have it happen in my grandmother's lifetime, my mother's and sister's and mine, and, most important, my young niece's, is beyond meaningful.

Watching Kamala Harris's swearing-in ceremony reminds me of the advice that her late mother had impressed upon her at a young age, which Kamala has made a core tenet of her career: "You may be the first to do many things, but make sure you are not the last." Shyamala Gopalan Harris unfortunately did not get to see her daughter's extraordinary achievement, but her message shines through Kamala's example, which the vice president, in turn, passes on to each of us watching her ascend to the highest office a woman has ever held in this country. It's remarkable to think how words that were passed from mother to daughter now resonate around the globe, and that people from all walks of life will absorb that message and follow in kind.

I started my book with a question that largely had to do with themes related to celebrity, legacy, and ego. I completed it by receiving answers I did not know I was seeking: about love, empathy, and gratitude; about the ways our families shape us, sometimes in ways we can never fully understand; about how personal narratives can be read very differently, depending on who's turning the page.

And above all, I learned about the value of one life lived, and how those echoes can continue to ripple through decades and generations.

Kirthana Ramisetti
January 20, 2021

ADVIKA AND THE HOLLYWOOD WIVES

When failed screenwriter Advika Srinivasan meets the legendary producer Julian Zelding, she's swept off her feet—and straight to the altar.

But is her Hollywood ending what it seems? Julian's ex-wife just left Advika a message: divorce him for $1,000,000 and a secret reel of film.

Shaken, Advika delves into the lives of her husband's three ex-wives—and soon realizes how little she knows about the man she married.

Please turn the page for an excerpt.

CHAPTER ONE

IT HAPPENED ONE NIGHT

ADVIKA SRINIVASAN COULDN'T TAKE her eyes off the Oscar. It was tottering on the edge of the bar, its golden bald head catching the light in the midst of a swirl of conversations and shouted drink orders. As she nodded at requests of "martini" directed to her face and "Scotch, neat" to her chest, Advika still found her gaze drawn to the gold statuette, disbelieving that something could seem so magnificent and mundane at the same time. Only when she was making a martini for a pink-haired woman wearing a feathery blue dress did she stop to wonder why an Academy Award was perched there for so long. By the time she poured four glasses of champagne and a tray of tequila shots, it was gone.

The awards show had ended an hour ago. Yet new waves of people kept streaming into the Governors Ball from the nearby Dolby Theatre, and as the first official afterparty following the Oscars, the undulating, sparkling mass all seemed intent on getting drunk. Luckily for Advika, her station was out of the way of the main scrum, situated next to the unofficial smoker's patio at the far north edge of the ballroom. She liked that this gave her an outside view of the revelry, which was spotlit in violet by an impressive array of lotus-shaped lights twirling above.

Interspersed amid the tuxedos and haute couture gowns were flashes of gold. That was where most people were clustered, around the people clutching trophies, their faces overtaken by enormous smiles. Advika envied their joy—the kind so pure and overwhelming that it's impossible to hide, so why bother trying. She shook her gaze off the throng, willing herself to focus on her job, so that there would be another job, and another one after that.

The steady stream of patrons to her bar continued for another half hour before finally dissipating. As she contemplated taking her break, someone arrived at the party whose presence electrified the crowd, and they all seemed to surge en masse toward the movie star—because of course it was a movie star.

"What's going on?" said Dean, her co-bartender. He towered a foot above her, which meant his body odor drifted down on her like a treetop shedding leaves.

"Ramsey Howell," Advika said. She briefly spied the actor's blond hair and the Oscar in his hand before he was swarmed by well-wishers. An awed, excited chant of "Ramsey's here" went up and circulated in the air, a low, persistent buzz that kept heads swiveling in his direction.

"Oh!" Dean scratched behind his ear. "Um, be right back, then," he said, bending down to shout in her face. But instead of walking to their break area, he joined the party guests flocking toward the actor.

"Wait! No." But it was too late, Dean's scarecrow height and narrow shoulders quickly disappearing amongst the people crowded into the ballroom.

Dean was a newbie, but she hadn't pegged him as a total amateur. How did he even get this gig? Advika wondered, hopping from one foot to another, her toes numb from having squeezed them into black one-size-too-small loafers she had hurriedly purchased hours earlier from Payless. She gripped the edge of the bar with slippery fingers and debated whether she should take off her shoes, worrying that once she did, her feet would rebel against going back in.

With Dean's desertion, there went Advika's hopes for taking her break. To distract herself from her foot pain, she imagined herself as one of the party guests rather than a mere bartender. If Advika were invited to the Oscars, of course she would be there as a nominee. And as long as she was daydreaming, she might as well make herself a winner too. She didn't know much about designers beyond the big names: Versace and Oscar de la Renta and Ralph Lauren. But for her moment in the spotlight, Advika would choose an up-and-coming Indian designer, and the form-fitting gown would be a brilliant shade of crimson with tasteful gold accents, which she'd wear along with stylish but comfortable shoes—maybe a custom pair from Converse? Her makeup would be simple, just soft, red lips and winged eyeliner. It would be the kind of look—dramatic, elegant, a touch whimsical—that would get her on all the best-dressed lists, despite being a mere screenwriter.

Usually, when Advika let herself daydream about winning an award, it was about the speech she would give: touching yet funny, eliciting laughter from the front row of A-listers, and by the end of it, they'd be wiping away tears as they applauded. The camera would then cut to Advika's handsome partner, who would jump out of his seat and give her a standing ovation, as everyone around him marveled at how supportive he was of her. It was a fantasy she had envisioned for herself since her junior year of high school, and the shape of it had rarely changed over the past ten years. (The one swap she made was having Emma Thompson present her the award instead of Johnny Depp.) But to be at the Governors Ball, in the midst of actual winners high on their own achievements, watching several famous women exchange embraces in between gabfests, gave Advika a new, aching dream. She didn't want to just win; she wanted to be a part of all of this. Not just a tourist, given a day pass into the Hollywood dream, but an esteemed member of this community, ensconced in an inner circle.

More revelers arrived at Advika's station. She forced a smile as she looked past the twentysomethings who seemed to be around her age, standing on her outraged toes and trying and failing to spot Dean. As she busied herself pouring drinks for the impatient guests, who obviously didn't know or care that she had to handle their orders by herself, Advika thought of her draft waiting for her at home. She wanted it to be good enough to get her into this room as a guest, or at least the guest of some-one successful. But even though Advika loved her screenplay and replayed the scenes in her head constantly (while driving to work, at work, in the shower, and making ramen for dinner), it didn't mean that anyone else would too. The screenplay was by far the best thing she had ever written, and as far as Advika knew, she'd be the only one ever to read it.

"Can you, like, do a heavier pour?" A lithe brunette with heavy bronzer and a miniature nose told Advika after she handed her a Fireball shot. "We're not at some cheapo bar."

"Of course. Sorry." When confronted by rude customers, Advika avoided eye contact at all costs. Because if she didn't, she would see the smug expressions on their (almost always white) faces and lose it on them.

"These people, man," her date laughed, scratching his chin with his middle finger.

The group walked away without giving her a tip. Advika stifled a groan, her body tense from the new surge of pain biting her feet. She wiped away a thread of sweat above her upper lip, feeling as if everyone in the ballroom had seen how those guests had made her feel less than. An encounter like that only magnified how small her life had turned out. Especially on a night like this, when there was no way but to be highly attuned to the chasm between the haves and have-nots, the famous and the nobodies, the beautiful people and those who served them.

An Oscar, wearing a cape fashioned out of a black cocktail napkin, popped up inches from Advika's nose.

"Scotch and soda. Por favor."

She jumped back, startled. A silver-haired man with an elegantly undone bow tie grinned at her, and he was still holding his statue up, as if the award were asking for a drink. At the same time, a large group of bearded men, their faces flushed as they hollered and clapped each other on the back, made an unsteady beeline toward her. Judging by their science teacher looks and puffed-up bravado, she surmised they had been favored to win the Academy Award for something technical—special effects, or perhaps sound mixing—but lost in an upset. Advika made a "pfft" sound, annoyed and nervous about the approaching drunken horde. The silver-haired man saw where she was staring, and turned around to speak to them.

"Gentlemen, why don't you..." was all she heard him say. The beards looked at her quizzically but then collectively turned away, leaving her alone with the strange, handsome man. In the ballroom's dim lighting, he sort of looked like a tall, lanky George Clooney from the *Ocean's Eleven* poster, as if he too starred as a charming rogue in a heist film. Even though the man was at minimum twenty years older than her, Advika found herself magnetized by him. He had the cocky yet endearing confidence of a movie star headlining his own hit franchise, training all of his attentions on her as if she were his co-star instead of an extra. *He's very keen on you*, her sister would have told her if she were there, in a dramatic fake British accent punctuated by a giggle.

"I was here earlier, but you didn't notice me," the man said, flashing a dazzling, gap-toothed smile. "So I thought it might help if I dressed him up a bit. It's a little vulgar, isn't it, for him to parade around without a stitch of clothing?"

"I...guess?" Advika poured his Scotch and soda, and as she handed it to him, their fingers briefly touched, giving her a pleasant jolt. "Congratulations, by the way," she said, nodding at his award.

"Oh, this?" He chuckled. "It's always nice to win one. Shows that the folks here still tolerate me well enough." He turned around and briefly surveyed the crowd. Three women in black gowns and sensible pumps stood in a semicircle a few feet away. Advika noted how they took the man in, as if he were a gallon of ice cream on a sweltering day. She briefly made eye contact with the one in the middle, an older blond woman who had been actually biting her lip while staring at him. The woman (a talent manager, likely, or some kind of studio flack) looked away, embarrassed, and Advika returned her attention to this man who apparently made the over-forty ladies salivate.

The man swung back around, and the women huddled together to whisper.

"I like it over here. It's not too crowded, and I don't have to shout to be heard. Maybe I'll hang out here for a while, help fend off other drunken losers. Wait, that's not kind. Nonwinners." He gave her a crooked grin.

"Sure," Advika said, carefully rocking back onto the balls of her feet to give her toes some relief. Where was Dean? Everything below her ankles was about to mutiny.

"You're on the job, maybe we shouldn't bother you." The silver-haired man cocked his head to indicate he was speaking on behalf of himself and his statue. Advika caught a glimpse of the name emblazoned on the bottom, but with the lighting so dim, all she caught was the letter J.

"No, it's fine." As if Advika would tell an Oscar winner to leave so she could take her break already. Not that she exactly wanted him to leave either—even though she had no idea who he was. Advika's pain was clouding her thinking, which was surely why she didn't recognize him. But by the way the industry women, who were inching forward with birdlike steps, were wowed by J, he must have had some power within the industry. He didn't carry himself like a sound mixer or composer or film editor, all of whom Advika had served that night, creating a game for herself by trying to determine their jobs based on their behavior and snippets of conversation. J was a Somebody with a capital S, but he didn't strike Advika as a director. Perhaps he was a producer?

"Excuse me." The blond woman had practically leaped over to J's right, her elbow knocking into his Oscar. "I just wanted to say congratulations. I adored your film."

J turned to face her while smoothly pushing his trophy away from her arm. "Is that so?" He took a sip of his Scotch and then flashed Advika a bemused look, raising his eyebrows and making a "yikes" expression with his lips. She responded by giving him a small smile and a shrug. Their fleeting, wordless exchange was oddly invigorating. Advika was used to being invisible in situations like these, mini-dramas that lasted for the entirety of people waiting for their drinks. But J acted as if this woman had intruded on the two of them.

"Oh yes," the woman persisted. "My name's Lynn, by the way. We met at the SAG after-party last week?" Then Lynn turned to Advika. "Champagne, with a splash of vodka. But it has to be top-shelf." The dismissive tenor of her voice went silken as she returned to J. "So listen. I'm not usually this bold, but my friends"—and here she gestured at the women watching them with rapt attention, their feet both slipped out of their heels—"put me up to this. They know I've had the biggest crush on you since—"

"My dear, I'm not interested. But thank you." J took his Oscar and stepped to the side, where Advika had just poured a dollop of her bar's cheapest vodka into Lynn's champagne flute. Lynn grabbed the glass like a microphone, large drops spilling out as she stomped away. J chuckled under his breath.

"That really doesn't happen to me anymore," he said out loud, more to himself than Advika. "At least not that overt." J shook his head and ran his fingers over the lapel of his tuxedo jacket. "What were we talking about?"

"You said you'd look out for me, help me fend off the sad sacks who didn't win Oscars like you." *Are you flirting?* Anu's voice popped up in Advika's brain.

"Ha," J responded. He raised his finger and mouthed, *One sec*, as he pulled out his phone from his breast pocket. As J turned his back to her again, Advika admired J's silhouette: tall and lean, yet also broad shouldered. He almost looked like an Oscar himself, except the trophy had a round head and J's was more squarish. He had what Advika liked to think of as "Goldilocks height": not too tall, not too short, but just right. If they danced together, she wouldn't have to wear flats or stand on her tiptoes. Instead, Advika's chin would graze J's shoulder, which meant he could press his cheek against hers as they danced. Advika pressed her palm hard against her forehead, as if she could push away the absurd concept of dancing with J out of her mind.

He swung toward her once more, then leaned against the bar and pretended to tip his hat to her. She blushed. Advika waited for him to say something, her gaze going to his bow tie, too nervous to meet his eyes. But J said nothing, only taking another sip from his drink. Surely he couldn't be waiting for her to speak? What could she possibly even say? Advika pulled her foot out of her right shoe and pointed it behind her, as if she were a flamingo. The agony of one foot diminished while that of the other increased. So she was already in a highly agitated state when she realized that J was now peering at her chest with the intensity of someone taking an eye exam trying to read the letters on the last row. Living, and especially working, in LA meant receiving these kinds of glances on a near-daily basis. But to be outright stared at in this audacious manner was so bizarre she wanted to laugh.

"No name tag. So I guess I'll just have to ask you your name," he finally said, looking up at her apologetically, as if it were his fault he didn't know it.

"Advika," she mumbled. She couldn't recall the last time a stranger had asked this of her, and she fumbled the syllables in her mouth, as if her own name were a new language to her.

"I'm sorry, my dear. I didn't catch it."

"Advika," she said, raising her voice to be heard over the brief tidal wave of applause as Ramsey winded through the center of the party.

"Aretha?"

"Sure!" she shouted back. What was the point in correcting him? The silence stretched between them as the noise swelled when the actor crossed just mere feet away from Advika's station. She had been searching the crowd gathered around Ramsey, hoping to catch sight of Dean, when J surprised Advika by circling behind the bar to stand beside her. She quickly returned her right foot back into her shoe and stifled a howl of pain.

"Here comes young Mr. Howell," he said into her ear, pointing his Oscar in the direction of the crowd. "Or not so young anymore, is he?" They both watched as Ramsey and his entourage entered the smoker's patio, seeming to take a quarter of the party with them. "There's always a prince who feels the crown is owed to him," J mused, the violet lights giving a warm tint to his silver hair. "And this one finally got his."

Despite the sensation of her toes being fed into a meat grinder,

Advika tingled with excitement. Unlike seemingly everyone else in the Dolby ballroom, J had not been captivated by the movie star or his Oscar-winning performance. Advika had seen *The Executioner's Final Reply*, and twenty minutes in she knew that the gruesome medieval drama was Ramsey's Hail Mary, a bid to score the best actor prize that had long eluded him.

"But it's such a crock, right?" Advika met the silver-haired man's eyes and felt a frisson of connection between them. "He's the kind of guy who pretends he doesn't want accolades and awards, but he was so thirsty for it."

"Ha, yes. Exactly. So I assume you don't think he's the best actor of your generation?" J took a sip of his drink, his middle finger tapping the glass as he did so.

"He's not from *my* generation, but I think he's very good. I just wouldn't have given him an Oscar because he ate a raw bison heart and screamed at everyone like a belligerent toddler. The CGI dragon was more realistic than his performance, honestly."

The silver-haired man chuckled. "I'm Julian. You're hilarious." He held out his hand, and before shaking it, Advika wiped her damp palm on her pants. He held on to her hand a beat longer than necessary, and she looked away, embarrassed.

"Would you like another drink?" she asked. Julian was still standing next to her, crossing the invisible line separating some-bodies from nobodies. This development was so discomfiting, with a splash of thrilling, that Advika needed to reestablish that boundary by reminding him she was just a service worker.

"Better company back here," Julian said with a wink. She blushed, and the tingling sensation intensified. "Plus, closer access to this," he added, sweeping a bottle of Scotch from behind the bar to refill his glass. "Would you like one too?"

Advika shook her head, feeling her face grow hot. As Julian busied himself making a new drink, Advika pinched the inside of her wrist to remind herself she wasn't dreaming, that this terrifically good-looking man was ignoring Hollywood's biggest party to chat with her. Which again brought her back to wondering who this man was, exactly. And what had he won the Oscar for? Unlike everyone else holding gold, he seemed pretty blasé about his award. She wouldn't have been surprised if he ambled back into the party and forgot to take it with him.

"So," Julian said, "obviously you're a fan of movies. What is it you like so much?"

Advika glanced briefly at him, then at his Oscar, glowing like a small flame on a starless night, somehow managing to still look dignified despite wearing a superhero cape made out of a cocktail napkin. To have it in such proximity made Advika feel as if she were about to speak to the movies itself. Like a worshiper at a temple speaking directly to her deity, Advika answered Julian's question by addressing his award.

"It's the structure. The rising action, the falling action, the resolution—I can follow it like a line on my palm. When nothing else in the world is predictable, you can time when each story beat will happen. Everything else can surprise you—the acting choices, the score, the sound mix, the plot twist even—but not the structure. If you know what kind of movie you're watching, like a rom-com, then you can predict the turning point or the climax. I like that. Nothing else in the world feels more comfortable to me than knowing the rhythms of a movie."

Advika had never articulated that out loud before, because no one had ever asked her. Dazed by her own admission, she was about to look up to see J's response, when there was a sharp rap on her left shoulder: Dean had finally returned. He was breathing heavily, his forehead dotted with sweat, and his smell had gone from trash can to garbage dump.

"You can take five now if you want," he said, bending down

toward her ear. Then Dean looked past her and gushed, "Julian Zelding!" He fiddled with something tucked in the back of his waistband that looked like a rolled-up screenplay.

"Don't," she hissed. Startled by Advika's admonition, Dean seemed at a loss for what to do. Still awed by Julian, he gave him an awkward military salute.

"Stand down, I'm not your captain," Julian told Dean with a bemused smile. He picked his Oscar up off the bar and nodded at Advika, indicating he was about to leave. Advika's jaw tightened. She wanted so badly for him to stay, especially now that she knew his name and that—based upon Dean's response to him—he really was a Somebody. A Somebody whose name seemed so familiar, but she still couldn't place it.

"Excuse me!" And now Lynn was back, her half-empty champagne flute squeezed tight in her fist. "Did I not ask you for top-shelf vodka? This tastes like dog shit."

"Oh. Right." The night was beginning to take on the farcical absurdity of a Marx Brothers film. Who would stop by next— Ramsey Howell? "My mistake. Can I get you another one?"

"Like I'd trust you to tie my shoe, let alone make my drink." Lynn nodded at Dean. "You make it." She set down the champagne flute carelessly, and it toppled on its side, splashing all over. Dean stared dumbly as Advika grabbed it before it could smash to the floor. Advika set it down behind the bar, and as she did so, she registered that Julian, and his Oscar, was gone.

"Taking my break now," she announced, leaving before either Dean or Lynn had a chance to respond. Let stupid, wandering Dean deal with entitled, overserved guests. Advika limped off toward the swinging doors that would take her through the kitchen to the employee bathrooms. How she longed to chuck her loafers in the trash, and the whole night along with it. Advika never, ever drank on the job. But she was seriously considering downing a shot of tequila after she returned from her break. It might be the only way she could stand doing this job for several more hours.

Because to have had Julian's attentions, even for a brief moment, showed her how starved she was to be seen. Even now, walking past party attendees who barely acknowledged her presence, reminded Advika how much her life had shrunken down to basics: work, eat, sleep, survive. And although she had been thrilled at the opportunity to work her first Governors Ball, the whole job had turned into a bright red arrow flashing in her face, a stinging reminder of all the ways she was a failure.

Advika felt fingernails dig into her skin as someone grabbed her forearm. She stumbled back and her foot connected with the square toe of a leather heel.

"You," Lynn said into her face. "You just don't walk away from me like that."

Advika was too in shock to respond. The fingernails went in deeper.

"I'm going to report you to your manager. You have no right to be so rude to me. You practically poisoned my drink!" Lynn swayed slightly, and her grip loosened. With their faces so close together, Advika could now see that this woman, with her unfocused eyes and smeared red lipstick, was full-on drunk, as if she had just downed several tequila shots in succession. "You don't treat people this way. Do you hear me?"

You're going to let her treat you this way? Anu's incredulous voice echoed in her head. *Sure,* Advika thought. *Nothing matters. I don't matter.*

"Ladies," Advika heard Julian interject. Her heartbeat sped up, and she was so jittery with relief she was near tears. "Mind if I join this conversation?"

Lynn finally let go of Advika's arm. "Why, Julian, I thought you had left," she slurred. "Could we chat? I think we got off on the wrong foot. I'm just such a fan, you know." She lifted her left leg as if trying to do a high kick. "I've been told I have foot-in-mouth disease, ha ha."

"Let's go get you a drink. A real one," Julian soothed, placing his hand on the small of Lynn's back. Advika watched them go, tears streaming down her cheeks and bouncing off her chin. *Get the fuck out of here*, Anu's voice admonished. Advika fled the ballroom, through the swinging doors and the kitchen buzzing like a shaken beehive, past red-faced chefs and sous chefs chopping and sweating and shouting at each other, and through another door into a nearly empty hallway. For the first time since early that afternoon, Advika was not surrounded by a sea of other people. It should have been a relief to finally have a moment to herself, but instead, the stillness only magnified her isolation. One of the overhead lights flickered in a menacing way, the dim fluorescent bulb making a "bzzz" sound as if announcing the arrival of a monster creeping toward her with unhurried steps. Advika shivered as she ran her fingers over her forearm, wincing at the three tiny half-moons left in her skin by Lynn's fingernails. From down the hall, Advika heard a door creak open. She was just about to escape to the sanctuary of the women's bathroom when she heard Julian speak.

"There you are." He strode toward her, his Oscar glinting in his hand. "Are you okay?"

Advika found herself unable to immediately respond, so stunned she was to see him heading toward her. She hiccupped, then looked down at her cursed feet through tear-streaked eyelashes.

"Yes," she finally managed to say.

"I worked as a waiter about three lifetimes ago," Julian said with a sigh. "There were so many times I had to bite my tongue, when all I wanted to do instead was throw a punch. And once, I did."

"Really?" Advika said, looking up with surprise. Julian had

the refined, debonair comport of James Bond crossed with a European prince. He did not look like someone who ever had to wipe down sticky tables, plunge toilets, or refill drinks.

"This man decided to express his unhappiness with the temperature of his steak by trying to shove it down my throat. Instead, my fist met his mouth. I lost the job, but not my dignity." He shrugged modestly, a cheeky grin lining his face. "No regrets."

"Wow," Advika said. The lighting in the hallway, which just moments ago had the hallmarks of a horror movie, now cultivated the intimacy of candlelight. Julian's presence had the effect of standing near a fireplace after being rescued from a blizzard, the surging warmth not just restorative but lifesaving.

"Did she hurt you?" Julian's eyebrows creased in concern, and his eyes traveled to Advika's arm, which she was still cradling.

"Oh, it's nothing. I just can't believe she'd grab me that way." A charred, slightly garlicky aroma emanated from the nearby kitchen, and Julian's mouth twisted into a comic grimace.

"It looks like the kitchen staff isn't having a good night either," he said. Advika felt her lips tremble into a nervous smile. "The people in this town can be obscenely awful and selfish, especially to the people who work the hardest and deserve their ire the least." Julian placed a gentle hand on Advika's shoulder. "I am so sorry you had to endure that. And I'm very sorry that I inadvertently brought that woman into your orbit. I had her escorted out of the party."

"You did?" Advika gasped.

The door opened again, accompanied by a strong burnt odor and flurry of tense voices.

"Let's go somewhere where we can have a proper conversation," Julian said, his eyes twinkling. "Without any more interruptions. What do you say?"

About the Author

As a former entertainment reporter for *Newsday* and the *New York Daily News*, Kirthana Ramisetti has written her fair share of stories about the lives (and deaths) of the rich and famous. She has a master's degree in creative writing from Emerson College, and her work has been published in the *New York Times*, the *Wall Street Journal*, *Entertainment Weekly*, *The Atlantic*, and elsewhere. *Dava Shastri's Last Day* is her first novel, and she lives in New York City. Find out more at KirthanaRamisetti.com.